Harriet and the Piper

By Kathleen Thompson Norris

NATAL PUBLISHING LLC
ARS LONGA, VITA BREVIS

CHAPTER I

Richard Carter had called the place "Crownlands," not to please himself, or even his wife. But it was to his mother's newly born family pride that the idea of being the Carters of Crownlands made its appeal. The estate, when he bought it, had belonged to a Carter, and the tradition was that two hundred years before it had been a grant of the first George to the first of the name in America. Madame Carter, as the old lady liked to be called, immediately adopted the unknown owner into a vague cousinship, spoke of him as "a kinsman of ours," and proceeded to tell old friends that Crownlands had always been "in the family."

It was a home hardly deserving of the pretentious name, although it was beautiful enough, and spacious enough, for notice, even among the magnificent neighbours that surrounded it. It was of creamy brick, colonial in design, and set in splendid lawns and great trees on the bank of the blue Hudson. White driveways circled it, great stables and garages across a curve of green meadows had their own invisible domain, and on the shining highway there was a full mile of high brick fence, a marching line of great maples and sycamores, and a demure lodge beside the mighty iron gates.

Much of this was as Richard Carter had found it five years ago, but about the house, inside and out, his wife had made changes, had lent the place something of her own individuality and charm. It was Isabelle Carter who had visualized the window-boxes and the awnings, the walks where emerald grass spouted between the bricks, the terrace with its fat balustrade and shallow marble steps descending to the river. Great stone jars, spilling the brilliant scarlet of geraniums, flanked the steps, and the shadows of the mighty trees fell clear and sharp across the marble. And on a soft June afternoon, sitting in the silence and the fragrance with boats plying up and down the river, and birds twittering and flashing at the brim of the fountain, one might have dreamed one's self in some forgotten Italian garden rather than a short two hours' trip away from the busiest and most congested city of the world.

On one of the wide benches that were placed here and there on the descending terraces, in the late hours of an exquisite summer afternoon, a man and a woman were sitting. They had strolled slowly from the tennis court, where half-a-dozen young persons were violently exercising themselves in the sunshine, with the vague intention of reaching the tea table, on the upper level. But here, in the clear shade, Isabelle Carter had suddenly seated herself, and Anthony Pope, her cavalier, had thrown himself on the steps at her feet.

She was a woman worthy of the exquisite setting, and in her richly coloured gown, against the clear cream of the marble, the new green of the trees and lawns, and the brilliant hues of the flowers, she might well have turned an older head than that of the boy beside her. Brunette, with smooth cheeks deeply touched with rose, black eyes, and a warmly crimson mouth that could be at once provocative and relentless, she glowed like a flower herself in the sweet and enervating heat of the summer's first warm day. She wore a filmy gown of a dull cream colour, with daring great poppies in pink and black and gold embroidered over it; her lacy black hat, shadowing her clear forehead and smoke-black hair, was covered with the soft pink flowers. She was the tiniest of women, and the little foot, that, in its transparent silk stocking and buckled slipper, was close to Anthony's hand, was like a child's.

The man was twice her size, and as dark as she, earnest, eager, and to-day with a troubled expression clouding his face. It was to banish that look, if she might, that Isabelle had deliberately stopped him here.

She had been behaving badly toward him, and in her rather irresponsible and shallow way she was sorry for it. Isabelle was a famous flirt, her husband knew it, everyone knew it. There was always some man paying desperate court to her, and always half-a-dozen other men who were eager to be in his place. Now it was a painter, now a singer, now one of the men of her husband's business world. They sent her orchids and sweets, and odd bits of jewellery, and curious fans and laces, and pictures and brasses, and quaint pieces of china. They sent her tremendously significant letters, just the eloquent word or two, the little oddity of date or signature or paper that was to impress her with an individuality, or with the depth of a passion. Isabelle lived for this, went from one adventure to another with the naive confidence of a woman whose husband smiles upon her playing, and whose position is impregnable.

But this boy, this Anthony, was different. In the first place he was young, he was but twenty-six. In the second place he was, or had been, her own son's closest friend. Ward Carter was twenty-two, and his mother nineteen years older.

Yes, she was forty-one, although neither she nor her mirror admitted it readily. Anthony, she thought, must realize it. He must realize that his feeling for her was unthinkable, not to say absurd. It had taken her by surprise, this last conquest. She had known the boy only a few weeks. Ward had brought him home for a visit, at Easter, but Isabelle, besides admiring his unusual beauty and identifying him with the Pope fortune, had paid him small attention. She had been absorbed then in the wretched conclusion of the Foster affair. Derrick Foster had been distressing and annoying her unmercifully. After the warm and delightful friendship of several months, after luncheons and teas, opera and concerts in the greatest harmony, Derrick Foster had had the daring, the impudence, to imply--to insinuate--

Well, Isabelle had gotten rid of him, although she could not yet think of him without scarlet colour in her cheeks. And it had been on a particularly trying afternoon, when the unshed tears of anger and hurt pride had been making her fine eyes heavier and more mysterious than usual, that this nice boy, this handsome friend of Ward, had gone riding with her, and had shown such charming sympathy for her dark mood. They had had tea at the Country Club, and Tony, as she had begun at once to call him, had been wonderfully amusing and soothing. Isabelle, when they came back to the house, had turned impulsively in the hall, had laid her small hand, in its dashing gauntlet, upon his big shoulder.

"You've carried me over an ugly bog, Little Boy!" she had said. "I like you--such a lot!"

That was six weeks ago, but in those short six weeks the little boy that she had patronized had entirely upset her preconceived ideas of him. He was young, and he was absurd, but he did not know it, and Isabelle began to feel the difficulty of keeping the whole world from discovering it before he did. He made no secret of his passion. He came straight to her in any company; he never looked at anybody else. The young girls to whom she introduced him bored him, he was rude to them. To her own daughter Nina, seventeen years old, his attitude was almost paternal; he ignored Ward as if their friendship had never been. Toward Richard Carter, who was pleasantly hospitable toward the lad, he showed an icy and trembling politeness.

Isabelle saw now that she had made a mistake. She should have killed this affair at the very beginning. Tony was not like the older men, willing to play the game with just a little scorching of fingers. Appearances meant nothing to Tony, and she had let the play go too far now to convince him that she did not return something of his feeling.

Indeed, to her own amazement, his fire kindled fire in return. When he was not at Crownlands she could laugh at him, even though her thoughts were full of him. But when he was there, life to her was more radiant, more full, more glowing with colour and fragrance. The books he touched, the chair he had at breakfast, his young, lithe body in its golfing knickerbockers, or his sleek black head above the dull black of evening wear, haunted her oddly. He troubled her, but she had neither quite the power nor quite the desire to banish him.

She looked down at him now, content to be alone with her and at her feet, and a hundred mixed emotions stirred her. His feeling for her was not only pitiable and absurd in him, but it was rapidly reaching the point when it would make her absurd and pitiable, too. Nina, instinctively scenting the affair, had already expressed herself as "hating that idiot"; Ward had scowled, of late, at the mere mention of Tony's name. Even her husband, the patient Richard, seeing the youth ensconce himself firmly beside her in the limousine, had had aside his mild comment: "Is this young man a fixture in our family, dear?"

"You should be playing tennis, Tony," said Isabelle.

"Tennis!" He laughed; there was a slight movement of his broad shoulders.

"I think Miss Betty Allen was a little disappointed," the woman pursued. A look of distaste crossed Anthony's face.

"Please--CHERIE!" he begged.

There was a silence brimming with sweetness and colour. Tony laid his hand against her knee, groped until her own warm, smooth fingers were in his own.

"Does Mr. Carter play golf to-morrow?" he asked, presently.

"I suppose so!"

"And you--what do you do?"

"Oh, I have a full day! People to lunch, friends of Madame Carter-"

The boy laughed triumphantly.

"I knew you'd say that!" he said. "Now, I'll tell YOU about to-morrow. You and I are going to slip away, at about one o'clock, and go off in the gray car. We'll go up to--well, somewhere, and we'll have our lunch under the trees. I'll have Hansen pack us something at the club. We'll be back at about four, for the tea callers, and they may have you until I come back for dinner. After dinner we'll walk on the terrace--as we did two wonderful, wonderful nights ago, and perhaps--" His voice had fallen to a rich and tender note, his eyes were rapt. "Perhaps," he said, "just before we go in, at the end of the terrace, you'll look up at the stars again--"

"Tony!" Isabelle interrupted, her face brilliant with colour. "My dear boy--my dear boy, listen to me--"

"Well?" he asked, looking up, as she paused.

"My dear," she said, with difficulty, "think where this is going to end."
He jerked his head impatiently.

"Oh, if you are going to begin THAT again!"

"My dear, I have to begin that again! In all reason--in all REASON----
"

"Isabelle, what in God's name has reason to do with it!" He knelt before her, and caught her hands, and Isabelle had a terrified fear that Ward, or Nina, or any one else, might start up or down the terrace steps and see him. "The instant you realize what you and I are to each other, my darling," he said, "you begin to talk of reason. Love isn't reason, Cherie. It's the divinest unreason in the world! Cherie, there's never been another woman for me; there never will be! It's nothing to me that there are obstacles--I love them--I glory in them! I can't live without you; I don't want to! You're frightened now, you don't know how we can manage it. But I'll find the way. The only thing that matters is that you must belong to me--you SHALL belong to me--as I to you in every fibre of my being--"

"Tony--for Heaven's sake--!" Isabelle was in an agony. Somebody was approaching. He had gotten to his feet, and was gloomily staring at the river, when Nina Carter, followed by a great white Russian hound, came flying down the steps.

"Mother--" Nina, a tall, overgrown girl, with spectacles on her straight nose, and straight, light-brown hair in thick braids, stopped short and gave her mother's companion a look of withering distaste. "Mother," she began again, "aren't you coming up for tea? Granny's there, and the others, from tennis, and Mrs. Bellamy telephoned that she's bringing some people over, and there's nobody there but Granny and me!"

Nina was like her New England father, conscientious, serious, gravely condemnatory of the lax and the unconventional.

"Ask Betty Allen to pour," said Mrs. Carter, regaining her composure rapidly, and assuming the air of hostess at once.

"Betty went home for a tub," Nina explained. "She's coming back. But, Mother," she added, with a faintly reproachful and whining intonation, "really, you ought to be there--"

Mrs. Carter knew this as well as Nina. But she found the child extremely trying in this puritanical mood. Granting that this affair with Tony did her, Isabelle, small credit, at least it was not for Nina to sit in judgment. Rebellious, Isabelle fondled the loving nose of the hound with a small, brown, jewelled hand, and glanced dubiously at Tony's uncompromising back.

"Trot back, Nina love," said she to her daughter, cheerfully, "and ask Miss Harriet to come out and pour. I'll be there directly. We'll come right up. Run along!"

To Nina, in this ignominious dismissal, there was sweet. She adored "Miss Harriet," the Miss Field who had been her governess and her mother's secretary for the three happiest years of Nina's somewhat sealed young life. It would be "fun" to have Miss Field pour. Nina leaped obediently up the steps, with a flopping of thick braids and the scrape of sturdy shoes, and the sweet summer world was in silence again.

Isabelle sat on, stroking the hound, her soul filled with perplexity. The shadows were lengthening, the shafts of sunlight more bold and clear. The hound, surprised at the silence, whined faintly.

"I wish it might have been Nina!" Isabelle said. Anthony's eloquent back gave her sudden understanding of his fury. She got up, and went noiselessly toward him, and she felt a shudder shake him as she slipped her hand into his arm. "Ah, please, Tony," she pleaded, "what can I do?"

"Nothing!" he answered, suddenly pliant. "Nothing, of course." And he turned to her a boyish face stern with pain. "Of course you can do nothing, Cherie. I'm not such a--such a FOOL--" his voice broke angrily--"that I can't see that! Come on, we'll go up and have tea--with the Bellamys. And I--I'll be going to-night. I'll say good-bye to you now--and perhaps you'll be good enough to make my good-byes to the others--"

The youthfulness of it did not rob it of real dignity. Isabelle, wretchedly mounting the steps beside him, felt her heart contract with real pain. He would go away--it would all be over and forgotten in a few weeks--and yet, how she longed to comfort him, to make him happy again!

She looked obliquely at his set face, and what she saw there made her feel ashamed.

On the bright level of the upper terrace tea was merrily in progress. In the streaming afternoon light the scene was strikingly cheerful and pretty: the wide wicker chairs with their gay cretonne cushions, the over-shadowing green trees in heavy leaf, the women's many-coloured gowns and the men's cool whites and grays. On the broad white balustrade Isabelle's great peacock was standing, with his tail fanned to its amazing breadth; two maids, in their crisp black and white, were coming and going with silver and china on their trays.

Miss Field had duly come down to preside, and all was well. Isabelle, as she dropped into a chair, gave a sigh of relief; everyone was amused and absorbed and happy. Everyone, that is, except the magnificent and sharp-eyed old lady who sat, regally throned, near her, and favoured her immediately with a dissatisfied look. Old Madame Carter had her own good reasons for being angry, and she never spared any one available from a participation in her mood.

She was remarkably handsome, even at seventy-five; with a crown of puffed white hair, gold-rimmed eyeglasses, and an erect and finely preserved figure. Her silk gown flowed over her knees, and formed a rich fold about her shining slippers; a wide lace scarf was about her shoulders, and she wore an old-fashioned watchchain of heavy braided gold, and a great many handsome pins and rings. Her voice was theatrically deep and clear, and her manner vigorous and impressive.

"Well, my dear, your friends were naturally wondering what important matter kept their hostess away from her guests," she began. Isabelle had not been her daughter-in-law for more than twenty years for nothing. She shrugged and smiled carelessly, with an indifferent glance at the group. Ward's friends, the tennis-players, and old Doctor and Mrs. Potter and their niece, from next door. Nobody here of any especial importance!

"Harriet is managing very nicely," Isabelle said, contentedly, as Tony, with a sombre face and averted eyes, brought her her tea.

"So Ward seems to think," observed Ward's grandmother with acidity. Isabelle laughed indifferently. Her son, slender and tall, and with something of her own eagerness and fire in his sunburned young face, was beside Miss Field, who talked to him in a quiet aside while she busied herself with cups and spoons.

"Perfectly safe there!" Isabelle said.

"I should hope so!" old Madame Carter remarked, pointedly. "At least if there's any of OUR blood in his veins--but of course he's all Slocum. They used to say of my Aunt Georgina that she never married because the only man she ever loved was beneath her socially--"

Isabelle knew all about Aunt Georgina, and she looked wearily away. Tony, sighing elaborately, drew upon himself the old lady's fire.

"Why don't you go over and join the young people, Mr. Pope?" she asked, pleasantly. "Isabelle and I can manage very well without a cavalier. You're tired, Isabelle--I can always tell it. Be glad that you're too young to know what that means, Mr. Pope. Go over there--there's a chair next to Nina. What shall we suspect him of, Isabelle--a quarrel with pretty Miss Allen?--if he avoids the young people, and looks like such a thunder-cloud."

Isabelle sighed patiently.

"The Bellamys are coming in for awhile," she observed, with deliberate irrelevance, "and I hope they'll bring their Swami--or whatever he is, with them. He must be a queer creature."

"He's not a Swami, he's an artist," Tony said, drawn into a casual conversation much against his will. "Blondin--I've met him. He has a studio up on Fifty-ninth Street--goes in for poetry and musical interpretations and I don't know what else. Now I believe it's Indian philosophies--I can't bear him, he makes me sick!"

He relapsed into gloomy silence, and Isabelle put into her laugh something affectionate and soothing.

"He evidently lives by his wits," she suggested, "which is something you have never had to do!"

Tony scowled again. It was part of his charm for her that he was the spoiled darling of fortune. Handsome and young, and with no family ties to restrain him, he had recently come into his own enormous fortune. Isabelle knew that his New York apartment was fit for a prince, that his man servant was perfection, that he had his own pet affectations in the matter of monogrammed linen, Italian stationery, and specially designed speed cars. His manner with servants, his ready check book, his easy French, and his unruffled self-confidence in any imaginable contingency, coupled with his youth, had strong attraction for a woman conscious of the financial restrictions of her own early years and the limitations of her public school education.

"Why don't you go to the club and dress now, and come back and dine with us?" she said, in an undertone.

"Do you want me?" he asked, sulkily.

"I'm ASKING you!"

For answer he stood up, and smiled wistfully down upon her, with a hesitancy she knew well how to interpret in his eyes. She should not have asked him to dinner; he should not accept her invitation. Yet he had been longing so thirstily for just that permission, and she had been yearning so to give it! Happiness came back into both their hearts as he turned to go, and she gave him just a quick touch of a warm little hand in farewell. At such a moment, when her mood of heroism gave way to melting, Isabelle had a desperate sort of hope that one more concession would not alter the inevitable parting, whenever it came. This time--and this time--and this time--must positively be the last.

Other guests had come in, and Miss Field was extremely busy, and Ward, helping her officially, was busy, too. She had indeed offered her place to Isabelle, but Isabelle, spurred by her mother-in-law's criticism, would not have disturbed her secretary for any consideration now.

"No, no--stay where you are, my dear!" she had said. And Miss Field remained.

"Fun to have you down here!" said Ward, in her ear.

Harriet Field had an aside with a maid regarding hot water. Then she gave Ward an indulgent, an older-sisterly glance. He was in years almost twenty-two, but at twenty-seven the young woman felt him ages her junior. Ward was broad and fair, his light brown hair was somewhat tumbled about from the tennis; his fine, strong young throat showed brown where the loose collar turned back. Even in his flat tennis shoes he stood a clear two inches above Miss Field, although she was not a small woman by any means. He was a joyous, irresponsible boy, and he and his mother's secretary had always been good friends since the day, four years ago now, when the silent, somewhat grave Harriet Field had first made her appearance in the family. Ward was so much a child in those days that Harriet used to go with him to pick out suits and shirts, and to buy matinee seats for him and his school friends, and they laughed now to remember his favourite and invariable luncheon order of potato salad and French pastries. Nina had had a nurse then, and Harriet practised French with both the boy and girl, but now the nurse was gone, and Ward could buy his own clothes, and Nina went to a finishing school. So Miss Field had made herself useful in new ways; she was quite indispensable now. The young people loved her; Richard Carter occasionally said to his wife, "Very clever--very pretty girl!" which was perhaps as close as he ever got to any domestic matter, and Isabelle confided to her almost all her duties and cares. She patronized Harriet prettily, and told her that she was too pretty to be getting up to the thirties without a fiance, but Harriet only smiled her inscrutable smile, and made no confidences on the subject of admirers. Nina, insatiably curious, had gathered no more than that Miss Harriet's father had been a college professor of languages, and that her only relative was a married sister, much older, who had four children, and lived in New Jersey.

She was a master of the art of keeping silent, this young woman, and but for her beauty she might have been as inconspicuous as she sincerely tried to be. But her simple gowns and her plainly massed hair only served to emphasize the extraordinary distinction of her appearance, and her utmost effort to obliterate herself could not quite keep her from notice. Men raised their eyebrows, with a significant puckering of the lips, when she slipped quietly through the halls; and women narrowed their eyes, and looked questioningly at one another. Isabelle, who was far too securely throned to be jealous of any one, sometimes told her that she would make a fortune on the stage, but old Mrs. Carter, who for reasons perfectly comprehensible in an old lady who had once been handsome herself, detested Harriet, and said to her daughter-in-law that in her opinion there was something queer about the girl.

There was nothing queer in her aspect to-day, at all events, as she demurely performed her duties at the tea table. To the occasional pleasant and surprised "Hello, Miss Field!" she returned a composed and unsmiling nod of greeting; for the rest, she poured and sweetened, and conferred with the maids, in a manner entirely businesslike.

She was of that always-arresting type that combines a warm dusky skin with blue eyes and fair hair. The eyes, in her case, were a soft smoky blue, set in thick and inky black lashes, and the hair was brassy gold, banded carelessly but trimly about her rather broad forehead. Her mouth was wide, deep crimson, thin-lipped; it had humorous possibilities all its own, and Nina and Ward thought her never so fascinating as when she developed them; it was a mouth of secrets and of mystery, of character, a mouth that had known the trembling of pain and grief, perhaps, but a firm mouth now, and a beautiful one.

And in the broad forehead and the cheek-bones, just a shade high, and the clearly pencilled brows and the clean modelling of the straight young chin, there was a certain openness and firmness, a fortuitous blending of form and proportion that would have made the head a perfect model for a coin, a wonderful study in pastels. Looking at her, an artist would have fancied her a bold and charming and boyish-looking little girl, fifteen years ago, with that Greek chin and that tawny mane; would have seen her sexless and splendid in her early teens, with a flat breast and an untamed eye. And a romancer might have wondered what paths had led her, in the superb realization of her beautiful womanhood, at twenty-seven, to this subordinate position in the home of a self-made rich man, and this conventional tea table on a terrace over the Hudson. The smoky blue eyes to-day were full of an idle content; the rounded breast rose and fell quietly under the plain checked gown with its transparent frills at wrists and throat. Harriet may have had her moments of rebellion, but this was not one of them. She had been here for four years; she had held more difficult and less well-paid positions for the four years before that; she had known fatigue and ingratitude, and snubs and injustices, as every business woman, especially in secretarial work, must know them, and she had no quarrel with this particular occasion. Indeed, Nina's open adoration, Ward's pointed attentions, and Isabelle's graciousness were making her feel particularly cheerful, and more than offset the old lady's disapproval, which was always more stimulating than otherwise to Harriet.

"Nearly half-past five, Nina," she said, presently. "Go and change and brush, that's a darling! You look rather tumbled."

Nina, reaching for a marron, obediently wandered away, and immediately the empty chair beside Harriet was taken by a newcomer, Richard Carter himself, the owner of all this smiling estate, who had come up from the little launch at the landing, had changed hastily into white flannels, Harriet saw at a glance, and had unexpectedly joined them for tea. His usual programme was to go off immediately for golf, and to make his first appearance in the family at dinner-time, but perhaps it had been unusually tiring in the city to-day--he looked pale and tired, and as if some of the grime of the sun-baked streets clung about him still.

"Tea, Mr. Carter?" Harriet ventured.

He was watching his wife with a sort of idle interest. She had to repeat her invitation.

"If you please, Miss Field! Tea sounded right, somehow, to me to-day. It's been a terrible day!"

"I can imagine it!" Harriet's voice was pleasantly commonplace. But the moment had its thrill for her. This lean, tall, tired man, with his abstract manner, his perfunctory courtesies, his nervous, clever hands, loomed in oddly heroic proportions in Harriet's life. His face was keen and somewhat lined under a smooth crest of slightly graying hair; he smiled very rarely, but there was a certain kindliness in his gray eyes, when Nina or Ward or his wife turned to him, that Harriet liked. He came and went quietly, absorbed in his business, getting in and out of his cars with a murmur to his chauffeur, disappearing with his golf sticks, presiding almost silently over his own animated dinner table. He was always well groomed, well dressed without being in the least conspicuous; always more or less tired when she saw him. In the evenings he smoked, listened to music, went early to bed. But he never failed to visit his mother, or pay her some little definite attention when she was with them; and when Madame Carter was in her New York apartment he called on her nearly every day.

For Harriet he had hardly a dozen words a year. He merely smiled kindly when she thanked him for the Christmas gift that bore his untouched card; if she went to her sister for a day or two, he gave her only a nod of greeting when she came back. Sometimes he thanked her for a small favour, briefly and indifferently; now and then asked with sharp interest about Nina's teeth or his mother's headache.

But Harriet had known other types of men, and for his very silences, for his indifference, for his loyalty to his own women, she had begun to admire him long ago. She had not been born in this atmosphere of pleasure and ease and riches; she was not entirely unfitted to judge a man. There was not much to awaken respect in the men she met at Crownlands, still less in the women. She liked Ward for his artless boyishness; forgave Anthony Pope much because he was straight and clean and self-respecting; but there were plenty of other men, spoiled and selfish, weak and stupid; men who amused and flattered Isabelle Carter perhaps, but among whom her husband loomed a very giant. Harriet had watched Richard Carter with a keenness of which she was hardly conscious herself, ready to detect the flaw, the weakness in his character, but she never found it, and after awhile she became his silent champion, his secret ally in all domestic matters, quick to see that his mail and his telephone messages were sacred, that his meals never were late, and that any small request, such as the use of the study for some unexpected conference, or the speedy sending of a telegram, was promptly granted.

Isabelle was always breezily civil to her husband; he had long ago vanished as completely from among the vital elements of her life as if he were dead, perhaps more than if he were dead. She thought--if she thought about him at all--that he never saw her little affairs; she supposed him perfectly satisfied with his home and children and club and business, and incidentally with his beautiful figurehead of a wife. They had quarrelled distressingly, several years ago, when he had bored her with references to her "duty," and her influence over Nina, and her obligations to her true self. But that had all stopped long since, and now Isabelle was free to sleep late, to dress at leisure, to make what engagements she pleased, to see the persons who interested her. Richard never interfered; never was there a more perfectly discreet and generous husband. Half the women Isabelle knew were attempting to live exactly as she did, to cultivate "suitors," and drift about in an atmosphere of new gowns and adulation and orchids and softly lighted drawing rooms, and incessant playing with fire; it was the accepted thing, in Isabelle's circle, and that she was more successful in it than other women was not at all to her discredit.

Even Harriet, who was in her secrets, who saw maid and masseuse and hair-dresser in desperate defence of Isabelle's beauty every morning, who knew just what scenes there were over gowns and cosmetics, and the tilt of hats--even Harriet admired her.

"Why not?" said Harriet sometimes to her sister, when she went to visit Linda, and the subject of the beautiful Mrs. Carter was under discussion. "She has a boy and a girl, her house runs perfectly, her husband adores her--"

"Oh, he CAN'T adore her, Harriet!" Linda would protest. "No man could adore that sort of--of shallowness, and selfishness, and vanity--"

"Well, I assure you he does! I think that sort of thing keeps a man admiring a woman," the younger sister would maintain, airily. "He sees her looking like a picture all the time, he sees other men crazy about her--"

"Too much money!" Linda usually summarized, disapprovingly. But this was always fuel to Harriet's flame.

"Too much money? You CAN'T have too much money! I've seen both sides-don't ever say that to me! There's nothing in this WORLD but money, right down at the bottom. If you haven't any, you can't live, and the more you have the more decently and prettily--yes, and generously, too--you can live! Look at Madame Carter, she was doing her own work when she was my age--not that she ever mentions that, now! Can you tell me that she isn't a thousand times happier now, with her maids and her car and her dresses? And money did it--and if you and Fred had two thousand, or twenty thousand, a month, instead of two hundred, do you mean to tell me your lives wouldn't be fuller, and richer, and happier? You shake your head, Linda, but that's just to make me furious, for you know it's true! I admire Mrs. Carter, and I assure you that if ever I do marry--which as you know I won't--you may be very sure that money is the first thing I shall think about!"

It was their only ground for real dissension. Harriet usually was ready to laugh and forget it almost instantly; but Linda, who was deeply spiritual, never ceased to pray that all the dangers of life at Crownlands would pass safely over the little sister's beloved head, and that some real man, "like Fred," would win Harriet's turbulent and restless heart, after all.

CHAPTER II

Madame Carter, gathering her draperies about her, was one of the first to leave the terrace. Dressing for dinner was a slow and serious business for her. She gave Harriet a cold, appraising glance as she passed her; Richard Carter had risen to escort his mother, but she delayed him for a moment.

"Miss Nina gone in, Miss Field?"

Harriet, whose manner with all old persons was the essence of scrupulous formality, rose at once to her feet.

"Nina has gone to change her dress, Madame Carter."

"She took it upon herself to ask you to help us out this afternoon?" the old lady added, with the sort of gracious cruelty of which she was mistress. Richard Carter gave his daughter's companion a look that asked indulgence. Harriet coloured brightly, fixing her eyes upon his mother.

"Nina brought me a message from her mother, Madame Carter."

"Miss Nina did?" Madame Carter amended the title as if absently. "Mrs. Carter," she added, with a glance toward the near-by group in whose centre they could see the cream-coloured gown with its pink poppies, "told me that she was surprised to see that you had--had stepped into the breach so nicely--" Her son's reproachful glance had the effect of interrupting her, and she turned to him. "Well, I am saying that it was very nice of Miss Field, Richard," she protested. "I am sure there is no harm in my saying that, my dear!"

Harriet said nothing, and resumed her seat as the old lady rustled slowly away. Her heart was hot with fury, and she was only partly soothed by hearing Richard Carter's murmur of reproach: "How can you be so perverse, Mother--"

"Of all the detestable, horrible, maddening--" Harriet thought, splashing hot water and clattering tea-cups. "Who's coming?" she added aloud in an undertone to Ward, as one more motor swept about the carriage drive.

"What is it, Beautiful?" Ward laughed. Harriet's glorious eyes widened into smiling warning. His open and boyish admiration was a sort of joke between them. Yet in this second, as he craned his neck to get a glimpse of the approaching guests, a sudden thought was born in her. Honour had compelled her to a generous policy with Ward. She had held his admiration firmly in check, she had maintained a big-sister attitude that was as wholesome for herself as for him.

But here, she thought with sudden satisfaction, might be her answer to his grandmother's snubs, might be the realization of her own ambition, after all. Ward was but four years her junior, and Ward would be Richard Carter's heir.

No, that was nonsense, of course. And yet she played with the thought amusedly, enjoying the vision of the old lady's anger and confusion, and of the world's amazement at the masterly move of the quiet secretary. Richard would be generous, thought Harriet idly, Isabelle philosophical and indifferent, but how old Madame Carter would writhe!

"It's the Bellamys and their crowd," said Ward, watching the approach of newcomers. "Look at that man with them, that fellow with the hair-- that's Blondin! That's the man I was telling you about the other night, the man whose name I couldn't remember!"

"WHO?"

Harriet did not know whether she said it or screamed it. She lost all consciousness of her surroundings and her neighbours for a few terrible seconds; her mouth was dry, her throat constricted, and a hideous weakness ran like nausea through her entire body. The brilliant terrace swam in a mass of mingled colours before her eyes; the casual, happy chatter about her was brassy and unintelligible. The hand with which she touched the sugar tongs was icy cold, a pain split her forehead, and she felt suddenly tired and broken. She sat perfectly still, like a trembling little mouse in a trap, the colour drained from her face, her breast rising and falling as if she had been running.

Ward had gone across to greet the Bellamys; Harriet fixed her eyes with a sort of fascination upon the man to whom she presently saw him talking. Almost everyone else in the group was looking at him, too; Royal Blondin was used to it; one of his favourite affectations was an apparent unconsciousness of being observed.

He talked to everyone, to children, to great persons and small, with the same air of intense concentration with which he was now honouring Ward. Well over six feet in height, he had dropped his leonine head, with its thick locks of dark hair, a little on one side; his mobile, thin lips were set, and his piercing eyes searched the boy's face with a sort of passionate attention.

His figure was one to challenge attention anywhere. He wore a loosely cut suit of pongee silk, the collar of the shirt flowing open, and a blue scarf knotted at the throat. On one of his long dark hands there was a blazing sapphire ring, and about his wide-brimmed Panama hat the folded silk was of the same colour. Harriet could catch the intonations of his voice, a deep and musical voice, which turned the trifles they were discussing into matters of sudden import and beauty.

Introductions were in order, everyone wanted to meet the Bellamys' friend, and Harriet saw that it pleased him, for some inscrutable reason, to continue his ridiculous conversation with the flattered Ward, and to accept names and greetings absently, in an aside, as it were, smiling perfunctorily and briefly at the eager girls and women, and returning immediately to his concerned and passionate undertones with the boy.

Isabelle fluttered forward, to fare a little more fortunately. Ward dropped into the background now, and his beautiful little mother stood in a full sunset flood of light, with her small hand in that of the lion, and the cream and black hat, with its pink roses, close to the drooping, reverential head.

It was Isabelle who brought him to the tea table. Harriet had felt, with a sure premonition of disaster, that it must be. She might not escape, there was nothing for it but courage, now. Her breath was behaving badly, and the muscles contracted in her throat, but she managed a smile.

"And this is Miss Field, Mr. Blondin," said Isabella. "She will give you some tea!"

"Miss Field," said Royal Blondin, and his dark hand came across the tea-cups. Harriet, as his thin mouth twitched with just the hint of a smile, looked straight into his eyes, and she knew he was as frightened as she. But from neither was there a visible sign of consternation. "No tea," the man said, making of the decision a splendid and significant renunciation. "Nothing--nothing!"

"He only eats about once a month, and then it's dates and hay and camel's milk and carrots!" Ward was beginning. Royal Blondin gave him a look, deeply amused and affectionate.

"Not quite so bad, Laddie!" he protested, mildly.

"We might manage the dates," Isabelle smiled. Harriet had not spoken because she was quite unable to command her voice. But she gained it now to say in an undertone:

"I think I shall have to go in, Mrs. Carter. I promised Nina some help with her Spanish. I wonder--"

"You speak Spanish, Miss Field?" said Royal Blondin, in Spanish.

This was an invitation to Ward to burst into involved sentences in the tongue; Royal Blondin turned to him seriously. The rest of the company might be bored or not, as they pleased, but he was only interested in testing the boy's accent and vocabulary. As a matter of fact, everyone laughed and listened, perfectly appreciating Ward's mad ventures and the other man's liquid and easy assistance. A few seconds later Harriet Field slipped from her place, crossed the terrace with her heart beating sick and fast with fright, and made her escape.

She ran up the awninged steps that led to the square great hall, and ascertained with relief that it was empty. On all sides wide doorways gave her perspectives: the drawing rooms, in their brilliant summer covers; the porches, with wicker tables and chairs; the music room; the breakfast room all cheerful green and white; the library, in cool north shadow; and the dining room, long and dark and dignified, where maids were already moving noiselessly about the business of dinner. Here in the hall was the pleasant shade and coolness, the subtle drifting scent of early summer flowers, space, and the simplicity of dark polished floors and sombre rugs. The whole house seemed empty, lovely, silent, after the confusion of the terrace and the heat of the summer day.

Harriet mounted the stairs, threaded the familiar, pleasant hallways above. She and Nina had a luxurious suite on the second floor, shut off from the rest of the house by a single door, and rather remotely placed in a wing that commanded a superb view of the river. There were guest rooms on this floor, Richard Carter's room and his wife's beautiful rooms, and there was an upstairs sitting room. But Madame Carter and her grandson and his friends had their rooms on the third floor, the old lady demanding a quiet and isolation that her daughter-in-law's proximity did not favour.

Nina, half-dressed, was sprawling luxuriously on her bed when Harriet came in. The three rooms of their suite were joined by doors almost always open; they were small rooms, but to both the young women they had always seemed entirely satisfactory. Just now they were in shade, but outside the windows the blue river glittered, and the fresh, heavy foliage of the trees moved softly, and inside was every charm of furnishing, of brilliant flowered draperies, and of exquisite order. There was a business-like heap of mail on Harriet's big desk; there were flowers everywhere; fan-tailed Japanese gold fish moved languidly about in a tall bowl of clear glass, and Nina's emerald-green parrot walked upon his gaily painted perch, and muttered in a significant and chuckling undertone. Glass doors were open upon a square porch, and the sweet afternoon air stirred the crisp, transparent curtains.

Harriet shut the door, and leaned against it, and the world spun about her. What now? What now? What now? hammered her heart. Nina tossed aside her magazine, and regarded her with affectionate reproach.

"You ran upstairs!" she said. "I'm lying on your bed because Maude had the laundry all over mine. Are you going to lie down?"

"No, my dear!" said Harriet, in an odd, breathy whisper.

"You DID run upstairs!" murmured Nina. She sat up, and put her bare feet on the floor, groping for slippers, and yawned, with a red face. "What time is it?"

"It's--" Harriet shook back the ruffle at her wrist, twisted her arm slightly, and looked blindly down.

"Well?" said Nina, when she dropped her hand. But Harriet, smiling at her blankly, had to look again.

"Six, dear--almost. Brush your hair, and get into something, and we'll have half an hour before dinner comes up. I must be downstairs for awhile to-night, I want to see just how the new cook sends dinner in Your mother wasn't at all satisfied with luncheon yesterday. I don't know why this comes to me," she added, busy with her mail in the little sitting room. "Something your father ordered through the club. I'll send that to Mr. Fox. Here's the bill for your two hats--Miss Nina Carter, by Miss Field."

"What was the blue one?" asked Nina in the doorway, from a cloud of hair.

"The-blue-one," Harriet said, absently, "was forty-five dollars. Not bad for a smart little English hat with a little curled cock feather on it, was it? It's quite the nicest you've ever had, I think." What now?--What now? hammered her heart.

"Granny paid three times that for that brown hat last winter," observed Nina.

"I know she did, and it was absolutely an unsuitable hat, and your mother wouldn't let you wear it," Harriet said, mildly. "You are a type, my dear. You must dress for that type."

Nina looked pleased. She was at an age when all girls are vain. Few people noticed the appearance of the young heiress of Richard Carter, except perhaps with kindly pity, but it was part of Miss Field's duty to make the best of it, and Nina was grateful.

"I'll wear it to Francesca's tea!" she said, of the blue hat. The social bow of a young neighbour, a little older than Nina, was to be made in a few days' time, at a garden party, and Nina was absorbed in the exciting prospect of assisting formally.

"No, it's not full dress," Harriet told her. "You'll have to wear the white mull, and the white hat, and look very girly-girly."

"My eye-glasses make me look like a school-teacher playing baby," Nina said, gloomily. Harriet laughed, dazed, but not ungrateful to find that she could laugh and speak at all.

"He's come back!" she said in her heart. "My darling child, you aren't going to wear your glasses!" she assured Nina, aloud. "Not if you have to have a dog and a cane! Not if you fall into the fountain!"

"I shall be scared stiff!" Nina grumbled, coming out with her Spanish books. Harriet, distracted for a moment, came to lean over her shoulder, and the terror of half an hour ago began to flood her soul and mind again. She went out to the porch, and looked down into the clear shade of the early twilight, under the trees. The terrace was deserted; every sign of the tea-party had vanished, not a crumb marred the order of the grass-grown bricks. The chairs held formal attitudes, the table was empty. All the motor-cars were gone from the drive. She turned back into the room, breathing more easily.

At half-past seven she came up from a little diplomatic adjusting in the service end of the house, to peep at Nina, who was reading in bed, and to go on to Isabelle's room. If Mrs. Carter was alone, she liked to see Harriet then, to be sure of any last message, or to discuss any domestic plan.

Harriet found her, exquisite in twinkling black spangles, before her mirror. Isabelle's hair was dressed in dark and shining waves and scallops, netted invisibly, set with brilliant pins. There was not an inch of her whole beautiful little person that would not have survived a critical inspection. Her skin, her white throat, her arms and hands and fingernails, her waist and ankles and her pretty feet, were all absolute perfection. The illusion that veiled her slender arms stood at crisp angles; the silk stockings showed a warm skin tint through their thinness; her lower eyelids had been skillfully darkened, her cheeks delicately rouged, and her lips touched with carmine; her brows had been clipped and trained and pencilled, her lashes brushed with liquid dye, and what fragrant powders and perfumes could add, had been added in generous measure. She wore diamonds on her fingers, in her ears, and about her throat, and her gown was held at her full smooth breast by a platinum bar that bore a double line of magnificent stones. Harriet always thought her handsome; to-night she had to admit that her employer was truly beautiful.

Mrs. Carter was in a pleasant mood; she had a good disposition, and there was nothing in her life now to ruffle it. She liked her bright, luxurious dressing room, and the progress of her toilette was soothing and restful. Her maid had been busy with her for nearly two hours. The air was warm and fragrant, the prospect of dinner, with its eagerly attendant Tony, rather stirred her, and the mirror had everything delightful to say. Like all women of forty, Isabelle liked the night, tempered lights and becoming settings, and the dignity of formal entertaining. Last but not least, she had a new toy to-night, a great black fan of uncurled wild ostrich plumes whose tumbled beauty she waved about her slowly as Harriet came in, watching the effect in the mirror with intense satisfaction.

"Oh, pretty--pretty!" Harriet said, seeing it.

"Isn't it ducky? Anthony Pope just sent it to me--the dear boy. I don't know where he picks things up, or how he knows what's right." Mrs. Carter half-closed the fan, and laid it against her bare shoulder, and looked at it with tipped head and half-closed eyes.

"Did you see What's-His-Name?" she asked.

Harriet understood the allusion to the new chef.

"I've just been down there," she said. "Everything seems to be all right, and looks delicious!"

"That's nice of you, Harriet," Isabelle said. The kitchen was not strictly Harriet's responsibility, but Mrs. Carter had been making changes there of late, and the girl's interest and interference were invaluable. She laid down the fan, and pushed a silver case toward her secretary, at the same time helping herself to a cigarette. But Harriet shook her head.

"You're very clever, you know," Isabelle smiled, through a cloud of pale smoke. "You're always in character, Harriet!"

Harriet smiled her inscrutable smile; there was just the suggestion of a shrug. She had her own cigarette-case, and not infrequently used it in Isabelle's presence. But at this hour, when Richard or Ward or Nina, or even Madame Carter, might come in, she felt any familiarity unsuitable. Isabelle, the least affected of women, for all her spoiling and vanity, perfectly appreciated this, and liked Harriet for it.

"You amuse me," said Isabelle, making a long arm to brush away the ash from her cigarette, "playing your part so discreetly. Your neat little old-maidy silks--"

"Is it old-maidy?" Harriet asked, mildly, glancing down at the severe blue cross-barred gown she wore, and straightening a transparent cuff.

"Not on you!" Isabella assured her. But her thoughts never left herself long, and presently she discontentedly introduced her favourite topic: "I could have been a business woman," she announced, thoughtfully, "my father wouldn't hear of it, of course. We had no money!"

"We had no money, and no father," Harriet observed. "So I had no choice. At eighteen I had to make my own way."

"At eighteen I jumped into marriage," the older woman said, still with a reminiscent resentment in her tone. "Mr. Carter had his mother to support, of course. We thought we were pretty reckless to pay sixty dollars rent. He was only twenty, he was getting what was supposed to be an enormous salary then. Heavens--it seems thousands of years ago!"

Harriet, who had imagination, could see it. The little brilliant wife, insisting upon the fashionable apartment, worrying over the extravagances of the one maid. The man eager only to push on, to more money, more responsibility, wider fields, to make to-day's extravagance to-morrow's reasonable expenditure.

Isabelle picked up the fan again, and gave her brilliant presentment in the mirror a complacent glance.

"Is Mr. Pope's apartment attractive?" Harriet, who knew where her thoughts were, asked idly. The older woman heard her perfectly, but she affected indifference.

"Is--I didn't hear you. Oh--Mr. Pope's apartment. My dear, it is perfection--absolutely. I have never seen anything so beautiful, and so beautifully managed. And all by that boy. He has two coloured women and the man--just a perfect menage. And they adore him. Absolutely!" She mused happily, her lips twitching with some amusing memory. Then she became businesslike. "Harriet, do you go to the city this week?"

"Nina and the girls are to see Ruth St. Denis on Friday," Harriet said. "I thought Madame Carter would take them, but now she says no. But if Nina stays with her grandmother overnight, I thought I would like to see my sister; she hasn't been very well. That can wait, of course. Miss Jay's tea-party is to-morrow; that's Thursday--"

"And that reminds me that Louise Jay telephoned to-day, and asked me if you would take charge of the tea table," Isabelle said, with a shrewd glance.

"At Mrs. Jay's house?" Harriet asked, after a second.

"Yes, at Francesca's tea-party!"

Harriet hesitated, and the colour crept into her smooth cheeks.

"I wonder why she asked that?"

"Because, in the first place, no one will drink tea," Isabelle who was watching her intently said promptly. "In the second, Morgan won't be there, because she says it's a kiddies' tea. I can't be there, and presumably Mrs. Jay wants to depend on someone."

"One wonders," mused Harriet, in a most unpromising tone, "whether one is asked as a maid, or a guest?"

"In this case, as a mother," Isabelle was inspired to answer. "Personally, I should very much like it for Nina's sake. But you suit yourself!"

The tone denied the words; Harriet knew what she was expected to do. She knew that Isabelle would tell Mrs. Jay, in a day or two, that she had simply mentioned it to Miss Field, and Miss Field had been free to act exactly as she pleased. She knew that faintly annoyed expression on Isabelle's face.

"I'll be delighted to help!" she said, lifelessly. "A lot of women and children," she reflected, "and nobody drinking tea anyway, this weather!"

"I say, Mater," Ward said from the doorway, with what he fondly believed to be an English accent, "I'm no end peckish, what what? Say, Mother," he added, becoming suddenly serious, "what do you think of Blondin? Isn't he a corker? Say, listen, are you going to ask him to dinner? Do we have to have the whole Bellamy tribe if we ask him, Miss Harriet?"

"DON'T spill things and fuss with things, Ward," his mother protested plaintively, protecting her bottles and jars from his big hands as he sat down. "Yes, dear, we'll have him. I like him because he was so enthusiastic about you. He's really quite a person."

"Person--you bet he is!" Ward said. "Gosh, he knows everything. You ought to get him started about--oh, I don't know, philosophy, and the way we all are forever getting things we don't want, and music--he can beat the box, believe me! He gave talks at the Pomeroys' last year--"

Nina, trailing in in a blue wrapper, sat herself upon a chair, wrapped her garments about her, and entered interestedly into the conversation.

"'The Ethics of the Everyday'," she contributed. "I remember it because Adelaide Pomeroy and I used to be in the pantry, eating the tea things. And he talked at our school about Tagore."

"I remember those talks at Lizzie Pomeroy's," Isabelle said, thoughtfully. "I wish I had gone! I suppose he's got a book out. Will you see if you can get me anything he's written when you're in town, Harriet? If we're going to have him here--"

She glanced at herself in the glass, where a more primitive woman, in a jungle, would have commenced a slow, solitary dance and song. If the hint of a scornful smile touched the secretary's beautiful mouth, she suppressed it. She had a little notebook in her pocket, and in it she duly entered the name of Royal Blondin.

"Too much rouge on this side, Mother," said Ward. Mrs. Carter picked up a hand-mirror, and studied herself carefully. When she had powdered and rubbed one cheek, she thoughtfully rouged her lips again, pouting them artfully, while Harriet and the children chattered. Nina was full of excited anticipation. Francesca's tea to-morrow, and the box-party on Friday, and a new gown for each-Nina fancied herself already a popular and lovely debutante. Harriet imagined that she saw something of a brother's pity in Ward's eyes as he watched her. Ward himself looked his best in his evening black, and several years older than he really was.

"We're a handsome couple, Miss Harriet," said Ward, with a glance toward the door of solid mirror that chanced to reflect them both. "Aren't we, Mother?"

"You're an idiot!" said Nina, scornfully. Harriet laughed maternally, but in spite of herself her idle dream of the afternoon returned for a second, and she wondered just how that faintly supercilious smile of Isabelle's would be affected if she had her own right, here in this family group, a Carter of the Carters, daughter of the house. And thinking this, her smoky blue eyes met Ward's, and perhaps there was something in them that he had not seen there before. At all events, she was ashamed to see him colour suddenly, and become a little incoherent, and to have him turn to her his full attention, with a sort of boyish clumsiness that was touching in its way. Imaginary or not, the trifling episode troubled her, and as Madame Carter came majestically in and the little clock on the dresser pointed to the hour, she said her good-nights, and carried Nina off again.

Richard Carter's wife and mother differed in no particular more strikingly than in their attitude toward the toilet artifices they both employed so lavishly. The old lady's beauty was even more than Isabelle's assisted by art, for her snowy-white hair was a wig, her teeth not her own, and her eyebrows quite openly manufactured without one single natural hair to build upon. But it pleased her generation to regard these facts as sacred, and to assume that the secrets of the boudoir were unsuspected. Even Nina never saw so much as a powder puff in her grandmother's dressing room, and any compliment upon her hair or complexion Madame Carter received with gracious dignity.

She looked at Ward's departing back, now, and remarked with pointed reproof:

"My son has never seen his mother even in the act of brushing her hair! There are reserves--there are niceties--"

"Where did you have it brushed--down at the shop?" Isabelle asked, laughing. Madame Carter never failed to be staggered by her daughter-in-law's irreverence, yet she never could quite resist the criticisms that courted it.

"For the last few years, I admit," she conceded with a somewhat shaken dignity, "I admit that I have had recourse to what they call 'puffs'--you know what I mean? Made of my own hair, of course--"

"Made of your own imagination!" Isabelle amended, in her own heart. But she only gave the old lady a somewhat disquieting smile as she picked up the tumbled black fan and led the way down to dinner.

Harriet and the Piper

CHAPTER III

Nina was duly dressed for the tea-party the next day, and went to show herself to her mother while Harriet dressed. The young girl really did look her best in the filmy white with its severely plain ruffles, and with a wide white hat on her thick, smoothly dressed hair. Miss Field, too, although she was very pale to-day, looked "simply gorgeous," as Isabelle expressed it, when she saw them off in the car, although Harriet's gown was not new, and the little flowered hat she had crushed down upon her splendid hair had been Isabelle's own a season ago. Harriet was in no holiday mood; she felt herself in a false position; this was to be one of the times when she paid high for all the beauty and luxury of her life.

"... so then when she came to me," Nina was recounting the reception of some celebrity at school, "of course I was awfully shy; you know me!" She was suddenly diverted. "But I'm not as shy as I used to be, am I, Miss Harriet?" she asked, confidingly.

"Not nearly!" Harriet made herself say, encouragingly.

"Well, then," Nina resumed, "when she came to me I don't know what I said--I just said something or other--I can't for the life of me remember what it was! Probably I just said that I had seen her in her last three plays or something like that, anyway--anyway, she said to Miss King that she had noticed me, and she said, 'It's an aristocratic face!' Amy Hawkes told me, for a trade last. The girls were wild--they were all so crazy to have her notice them, you know, and I thought--I thought of course she'd speak of Lucia or Ethel Benedict or one of those prettier girls; although," said Nina, with her little air of conscientiousness, "Ethel didn't look a bit pretty that day. Sometimes she does; sometimes she looks perfectly lovely! But that day she looked sort of colourless. 'Aristocratic'!" Nina laughed softly. "Well, I'd rather look aristocratic than be the prettiest girl in the world, wouldn't you?"

Harriet glanced at her with something like pity. This was Nina in her before-the-party mood. Her confidence and complacency would all begin to ooze away from her, presently, and the words that came so readily to Harriet would refuse to flow at all to any one else. She would come home saying that she hated parties because people were all so shallow and uninteresting, and that she couldn't help what her friends said of her, she just wouldn't descend to that sort of nonsense.

"Here we are!" Harriet rather drily interrupted the flood. Nina gave a startled glance at the lawns and gardens of the Jay mansion already dotted with awnings and chairs, and sprinkled with the bright gowns of the first arrivals. They were early, and their hostess, a handsome, heavily built woman with corsets like armourplate under her exquisite gown, and a blonde bang covering her forehead, came forward with her daughter to meet them. Francesca was as slight as a willow, with a demurely drooped little head and a honeyed little self-possessed manner.

"Very decent of you, Miss Field!" breathed Mrs. Jay, in a voice like that of a horn. "You girls run along now--people will be comin' at any minute. I'm going to take Miss Field to the table. Three hundred people comin'," she confided as Harriet followed her across the lawn, and to the rather quiet corner of the awninged porch where the tea table stood, "and Mist' Jay just sent me a message that he won't be here until six. My older daughter, Morgan, is stayin' with the Tom Underbills--you know their place--lovely people--Well, now, I'll leave you here, and you just ask for anything you need--"

The matron melted away; Harriet looked after her broad, retreating back indifferently. Everyone knew Mrs. Jay, a harmless, generous, good-natured and hospitable target for much secret criticism and laughter. The odd thing was, old Mrs. Carter had sometimes pointed out to the dutifully listening Harriet, that the woman really came of an excellent family, so that her little affectations, her fondness for the phrases "my older daughter, Morgan," and "lovely people, loads of money, you know them?" were honest enough, in their way. She would have loaned Harriet any amount of money, the girl reflected, smouldering, she would have shown her genuine friendship and generosity in a crisis. But she would not introduce people to Harriet this afternoon, and in a day or two she would send Harriet a bit of lace, or a dainty waist, as a delicate reminder that the courtesy had been a business one, after all.

The afternoon was the perfection of summer beauty, and after a few moments' solitude Harriet began to feel its spell. She put her cups and spoons in order, and chatted with a hovering maid. Some elderly persons came out and sat near, and were grateful for the quiet and the tea. From the reception line, on the lawn, came such a brainless confusion of jabbering and chattering as might well appall the old and nervous.

And presently the sun came out for Harriet in the arrival of a tall, swiftly moving, dark-eyed woman some ten years older than she was herself: Mary Putnam, one of the real friends the girl had gained in the last four years. Young Mrs. Putnam, Harriet used to think, with a little natural jealousy under her admiration, had everything. She was not pretty, but hers was a distinguished appearance and a lovely face; she had the self-possessed manner of a woman whose whole life has been given to the social arts; she had a clever, kindly, silent husband who adored her; her home, her garden, her clubs and her charities, and finally she had her nursery, where Billy and Betty were rioting through an ideal childhood.

"Harriet--you dear child!" said the rich and pleased voice, as Mary's fine hand crossed the tea table for a welcoming touch. "But how nice to find you here! I'm trying to get some tea for Mr. Putnam's aunt and mother, but, my dear--it's getting very thick out there!"

"I can imagine it!" Harriet glanced toward the lawn.

"I've been wanting to see you," Mrs. Putnam said in an undertone. "But suppose I carry them a tray first? Harriet, you are prettier than ever. I love the green stripes! I've just been trying to think how long it is since I've seen you."

"Not since the day you lunched with Mrs. Carter, and that was almost two weeks ago!" Harriet's hands were busy with cups and plates; now she nodded to a maid. "Mayn't Inga carry this to your mother, Mrs. Putnam?" she asked. "And couldn't you stay here and have some tea yourself?"

Mrs. Putnam immediately settled herself in the neighbouring chair.

"I'm chaperoning little Lettice Graham for a week," she began, in the delightful voice upon which Harriet had modelled her own. "But Lettice is trying her little arts upon Ward Carter. Dear boy, that!"

"Ward? He IS a dear!" Harriet said, innocently.

"No blushing?" Mary Putnam asked, with a smiling look. The colour came into Harriet's lovely face, and the smoky blue eyes widened innocently.

"Blushing--for WARD?" she asked.

Mrs. Putnam stirred her tea thoughtfully.

"I didn't know," she said. "You're young, and you know him well, and you're--well, you have appearance, as it were!"

Harriet laughed.

"Ward is twenty-two," she observed.

"And you're--?"

"I shall be twenty-seven in August."

"Well, that's not serious," the older woman decided, mildly. "The point is, he's a man. Ward has fine stuff in him," she added, "and also, I think, he is beginning to care. It would be an engagement that would please the Carters, I imagine."

The word engagement brought a filmy vision before Harriet's eyes, born of the fragrance and sunshine of the summer. She saw a ring, laughter and congratulations, dinner parties and receptions, shopping in glittering Fifth Avenue.

"Perhaps it would," she said, with a hint of surprise in her tone. "They are really very simple, and always good to me! But old Madame Carter," she laughed, "would go out of her mind!"

"A boy in Ward's position may do much worse than marry a lovely and sensible woman," Mrs. Putnam said. "Well, it just occurred to me. It is your affair, of course. But looking back one sees how much just the--well, the lack of a tiny push has meant in one's life!"

"And this is the push?" Harriet said, her heart full of the confusion and happiness that this unusual mood of confidence and affection on Mary Putnam's part had brought her.

"Perhaps!" The smooth, cool hand touched hers for a second before Mrs. Putnam went upon her gracious way. Harriet hardly heard the bustle and confusion about her for a few minutes. She sat musing, with her splendid eyes fixed upon some point invisible to the joyous group about her.

To Nina, meanwhile, had come the most extraordinary hour of her life. It had begun with the familiar and puzzling humiliations, but where it was to end the fluttered heart of the seventeen-year-old hardly dared to think.

She had sauntered to a green bench, under great maples, with Lettice Graham and Harry Troutt and Anna Poett. And Joshua Brevoort had come for Anna, and they had sauntered away, with that mysterious ease with which other girls seemed to manage young men. And then Harry and Lettice had in some manner communicated with each other, for Lettice had jumped up suddenly, saying, "Nina, will you excuse us? We'll be back directly," and they had wandered off in the direction of the river, giggling as they went. Nina had smiled gallantly in farewell, but her feelings were deeply hurt. She hated to sit on here, visibly alone, and yet there was small object in going back to the absorbed groups nearer the house.

Then came the miracle. For as she uncomfortably waited, Ward's friend, the queer man with the black eyes and thick hair, suddenly took the seat beside her. Nina's heart gave a plunge, for if she was ill at ease with "kids" like Harry and Joshua, how much less could she manage a conversation with the lion of the hour! But Royal Blondin needed no help from Nina.

"You're little Miss Carter, aren't you?" he said. "We were introduced, back there, but there were too many young men around you then for me to get a word in! However, I was watching you--I wonder if you know why I've been watching you all afternoon?"

Nina cleared her throat, and gave one fleeting upward glance at the dark and earnest eyes.

"I'm sure I don't know why any one should watch me!" she tried to say. But everything after the first three words was lost in the ruffles of the white gown.

"I'll tell you why. I watched you because, from the moment I saw you, I said to myself, 'if that little girl isn't utterly wretched and out of her element, among all these shallow chatterers and gigglers, I'm mistaken!' I saw the lads gather about you, and I had my little laugh--you must forgive me!--at the quiet little way you evaded them all. Nice boys, all of them! But not worth YOUR while!"

Nina murmured a confidence.

"What did you say?" Blondin said. "But come," he added, frankly, "you're not afraid of me, are you? My dear little girl, I'm old enough to be your father! Look up--I want to see those eyes. That's better. Now, that's more friendly. Tell me what you said?"

"I said--that Mother expected me to--to like them."

"To--? Oh, to like the boys. Mother expects it? Of course she does! And some day she'll expect to dress you in white, and bid us all to come and dance at the wedding! But in the meantime, Mother mustn't blame someone who has just a LITTLE more discernment than--well, young Brevoort, for example, for seeing that her tame dove is really a wild little sea-gull starving for the sea. Now, look here, Miss Nina, you hate all this society nonsense, don't you?"

"Loathe it!" Nina stammered, with a little excited laugh.

"Loathe it? Of course you do! Of course you do! And you don't want to fall in love with one of these lads for a year or two, anyway?"

"Oh, my, no!" Nina felt the expression inadequate, but her breath had been taken away. The man had turned about a little, his eyes were all for her, and his arm, laid carelessly along the back of the green bench, almost touched the white ruffles. They were in full sight of the house, too, and if Lettice or Anna came back, they would see Nina in deep and lasting conversation with the man that all the older women were so mad about--

"You don't. But--what?" He bent his dark head.

"I said, 'But I don't know how you knew it'!" Nina repeated, looking down in her overwhelming self-consciousness, but with a smile of utter happiness and excitement.

A second later she looked up in some alarm. He was silent--she had somehow said the awkward thing again I Nina's heart fluttered nervously.

But what she saw reassured her. Royal Blondin had squared himself about, and had folded his arms, and was staring darkly into space.

"How I knew it!" he said in a half-whisper, as if to himself, after a full half-minute of silence that thrilled Nina to the soul. "Child, I don't know! Some day you and I will read books together--wonderful books! And then perhaps we will begin to understand the cosmic secret--why your soul reaches out to mine--why I not only want to know you better, but why it is my solemn obligation to take the exquisite thing your coming into my life may mean to us both! You're only a child," he went on, in a lighter tone, "and I can read those big eyes of yours, and can see that I'm frightening you! Well, this much remains. You and I have somehow found each other in all this wilderness of lies and affectations, and we're going to be friends, aren't we?"

"I--hope we are!" Nina said, clearing her throat, with a bashful laugh.

"You know we are!" Royal Blondin amended. And in a musing tone he added: "I'm afraid I was a little bitter a few hours ago. And then I saw you, just an honest, brave, bewildered little girl, wondering why the deuce they all make such a fuss about nothing--clothes and bridge parties and dinners--"

"They never SAY anything worth while!" Nina said, with daring. There was exquisite homage in the dropped, listening head, the eyes that smiled so close to her own. "But if I tell Mother that, she thinks I'm crazy!" she added, lapsing into the school vernacular against a desperate effort to sustain the conversation at his level.

"Because you're a little natural rebel," interpreted the man, smilingly. "And that's the price we pay for it!"

"I'm afraid I've always been a rebel, then!" confessed Nina.

"Yes, those eyes of yours say that," Blondin conceded, sadly. "And it doesn't make for happiness, Little Girl!" he warned her.

Nina narrowed her eyes, and stared into the green garden. She was not wearing her glasses to-day, and hers were fine eyes, albeit a trifle prominent, and with a somewhat strained expression.

"Oh, I know that!" she said. "Mother and Father," she confided, with the merciless calm of seventeen, "they'd like me to be exactly like all the other girls, flirting and dressing, and rushing about all day and all night! But oh--how I hate it! Oh, I like the girls and boys--truly I do, and I am popular with them all, I know that! But 'CASES'!" said Nina with scorn.

"Dear Heaven!" Royal said, under his breath. "No--no--no--that's not for you!" he murmured. "And yet--" and he turned upon her a look that Nina was to remember with a thrill in the waking hours of the summer night--"and yet, is it kindness to wake you up, child?" he mused. "Is it right to show you the full beauty of that questing soul of yours?"

It was said as if to himself, as if he thought aloud. But Nina answered it.

"I often think," she said, mirthfully, "that if people knew what I was thinking, they'd go crazy! 'Oh, isn't the floor lovely--isn't the music divine! Are you going to the club to-morrow? What are you going to wear?'"

It was not a very brilliant imitation of a society girl's tone and manner, but Royal Blondin seemed deeply impressed by it.

"Look here!" he said. "You're a little actress!"

"No. I'm not!" Nina laughed. "But I can always imitate anything or anybody," she admitted. "It makes the girls perfectly wild sometimes! But Ward's different," she resumed, going back to the more serious topic. "I envy Ward! He is just as different from me as black and white. Now Ward likes everyone--and everyone likes him. He just drifts along, perfectly content to be popular, and to have a good time, and to do the regular thing, and of course he knows NOTHING of moods--!"

"Bless the lad!" Blondin said, paternally.

"Oh, I manage to keep the appearance of doing exactly what the others do," Nina hastened to say, "and I laugh and flirt just as if that was the only thing in life! If people want to think I am a butterfly, why, let them think so! My friend Miss Hawkes says that I have two natures--but I don't know about that!"

She looked up at him to find his eyes fixed steadily upon her, and flushed happily, with a fast-beating heart.

"With one of those natures I have nothing to do," Royal said. "But the other I claim as my friend. Come, how about it? Are we going to be friends? I am old enough to be your father, you know; you may tell Mother that it is perfectly safe. When the right young man comes to claim you, why, I'll resign my little friend with all the good will in the world. But meanwhile, am I going to pick you out some books, am I going to have some talks as wonderful as this one now and then? No--not as wonderful, for of course this sort of thing doesn't come twice in a lifetime! Will you give me your hand on it--and your eyes? Good girl! And now I'll take you back to be scolded for running away from your own friends for so long. I'm dining with Mother to-morrow. Shall I see you?"

"Oh, yes--if Mother lets me come down!" fluttered Nina. "But, no-- we're to be at Granny's!" she remembered.

"Soon, then!" He left her in the circling group, but all the world saw him kiss her hand. Nina wandered about in a daze of pleasure and satisfaction for another half-hour, paying attentions to Mother's poky friends with a sparkle and charm that amazed them. Presently Ward and the demure Amy Hawkes found her; the car was waiting. Miss Field, Ward said, was no longer at the tea table; she had left a message to the effect that she was walking home and would be there as soon as they were.

He asked Amy and Nina, whose irrepressible gossip and giggling met with only silence and scowls from his superior altitude, if they knew why Miss Harriet had decided to walk. They stared at each other innocently, on the brink of fresh laughter. No; they hadn't the least idea.

CHAPTER IV

Royal Blondin went straight from Nina to the tea table, which was almost deserted now. Harriet saw him coming, and she knew what hour had come. She stood up as he reached her, and they measured each other narrowly, with unsmiling eyes.

There was reason for her paleness to-day, and for the faint violet shadows about her beautiful eyes. Harriet had lain awake deep into the night, tossing and feverish. She had gotten up more than once, for a drink of water, for a look from her balcony at the solemn summer stars. And among all the troubled images and memories that had trooped and circled in sick confusion through her brain, the figure of this smiling, handsome man had predominated.

She had always thought that he must come back; for years the fear had haunted her at every street crossing, at every ring of Linda's doorbell. At first it had been but a shivering apprehension of his claims, an anticipation of what he might expect or want from her. Then came a saner time, when she told herself that she was an independent human being as well as he, that she might meet his argument with argument, and his threat with threat.

But for the past year or two her lessening thoughts of him had taken new form. Harriet had hoped that when they met again she might be in a position to punish Royal Blondin, to look down at him from heights that even his audacity might not scale.

That time, she told herself in the fever of the night, had not yet come. Her pitiful achievements, her beauty, her French and Spanish, her sober book reading, and her little affectations of fine linen and careful speech, all seemed to crumple to nothing. She seemed again to be the furious, helpless, seventeen-year-old Harriet of the Watertown days, her armour ineffectual against that suave and self-confident presence.

"Oh, how I hate him!" whispered the dry lips in the silence of the night. And looking up at the wheeling grave procession of powdery jewels against the velvet of the sky, Harriet had mused on escape, on a disappearance as complete as her flight years ago had proved to be.

She had forced herself to unbind the wrappings, to look at the old wound. She had gone in spirit to that old, shabby parlour to which Linda and Fred had carried Josephine's crib late every night, and where sheet music had cascaded from the upright piano. She saw, with the young husband and wife, a fiery, tumblehead girl of fifteen or sixteen, who helped with her sister's cooking and housework, who adored the baby, who planned a future on the stage, or as a great painter, or as a great writer--the means mattered not so that the end was fame and wealth and happiness for Harriet.

Fred had brought Royal Blondin in to supper one night, and Royal had laughed with the others at the spirited little waitress who delivered herself of tremendous decisions while she came and went with plates, and forgot to take off her checked blue apron when she finally slipped into her place.

The man had been a derelict then, as now. But he was nine years older than Harriet Field. He had had the same delightful voice, the same penetrating eyes. He had brought poetry, music, art, into the sordid little parlour of the Watertown apartment; he had helped Harriet to tame and house those soaring ambitions. Seated on Linda's stiff little fringed sofa, they had drunk deep of Keats and Shelley and Browning, and Harriet's eyes had widened at what Royal called "world ethics." To live--that was the gift of the gods! Not to be afraid--not to be bound!

Reaching this point in her recollections, the girl recalled herself with a start. She was safe in luxurious Crownlands, it had all been years ago. But again the abyss seemed to yawn at her feet. She felt again those kisses that had waked the little-girl heart into passionate womanhood; she shut her eyes and pressed her hand tight against them. So young--so happy--so confident!--plunging headlong into that searing blackness.

And now Royal Blondin was back again, and she was not ready for him. She could not score now. But he could hurt her irreparably if he would. Isabelle was an indifferent mother, and an incorrigible flirt, but at the first word, at the first hint--ah, there would be no arguing, no weighing of the old blame and responsibility! If there was the faintest cloud of doubt, that would be enough! Better the driest and fussiest old Frenchwoman for Nina, the dullest and least responsive of Englishwomen. But by all means settle accounts at once with Miss Field, and pay her railway fare, and wish her well.

Harriet had shaken back her mane of hair, had hammered furious fists together up on the dark balcony. It wasn't fair--it wasn't fair--just now, when she was so secure and happy! She had flung her arms across the railing, and buried her hot face on them, and had wept desperate and angry tears into the silken and golden tangle that shone dully in the starlight.

The stars were paling, and the garden stirred with the first languid breath of the hot day to come, when she suddenly rose and bound up the loosened hair, and went in. Harriet was not yet twenty-seven, and every fibre of her being cried out for sleep. Cold water on the tear-stained face, and the childish prayer she never forgot, and she had crept gratefully into the soft covers, and had had perhaps four hours of such rest as only comes to youth.

So that the morning brought courage. Her heart was heavy and fearful, but she knew that Royal would seek her, and she hoped much for the talk that they were to have now. She did not refuse him her hand when he came to the tea table, or her eyes, and there was friendliness, or the semblance of it, in the voice with which she said his name. That he was waiting, perhaps as fearfully as she, for his cue, was evidenced by the quick relief with which he echoed the old familiarity.

"Harriet! I find you again. I've been waiting all this time to find you! I'd heard Ward speak of 'Miss Field', of course! But it never meant you, to me. I've been thinking of you all night."

"I've been thinking, too," she said, simply.

"It's after six," Blondin said with a glance about. "We can't talk here. Can you get away? Can we go somewhere?"

Without another word she deserted her seat, pinned on her hat, and picked up her gloves.

"There's a very quiet back road straight to Crownlands," she said, considering. "We might walk."

"Anything!" he assented, briefly.

Guided by Harriet, who was familiar with the place, they slipped through the hallway, and out a side door, crossing the lane that led down to the garage, and striking into a splendid old quiet roadway barred now by the shadows of elms and sycamores and maples, and filled with soft green lights from the thick arch of new leaves. They had no sooner gained the silence and solitude it afforded them than the man began deliberately:

"Harriet, I've not thought of anything else since I came upon you yesterday, after all these years. I want you to tell me that you--you aren't angry with me."

There was a moment of silence. Then the girl said, quietly:

"No. I'm not angry, Roy."

"You knew--you knew how desperately I tried to find you, Harriet? What a hell I went through?"

If she had steeled herself against the possibility of his shaking her, she failed herself now. It was with an involuntary and bitter little laugh that she said:

"You had no monopoly of that, Roy."

"But you ran away from me!" he accused her. "When I went to find you, they told me the Davenports had moved away. Won't you believe that I felt TERRIBLY--that I walked the streets, Harriet, praying--PRAYING!--that I might catch a glimpse of you. It was the uppermost thought for years--how many years? Seven?"

"More than eight," she corrected, in a somewhat lifeless voice. "I was eighteen. My one thought, my one hope, when I last saw you, in Linda's house," she went on, with sudden passion, "was that I would never see you again! But I'm glad to hear you say this, Roy," she added, in a gentler tone. "I'm glad you--felt sorry. Our going away was a mere chance. Fred Davenport was offered a position on a Brooklyn paper, and we all moved from Watertown to Brooklyn. I was grateful for it; I only wanted to disappear! Linda stood by me, her children saved my life. I was a nursery-maid for a year or two--I never saw anybody, or went anywhere! I think Linda's friends thought her sister was queer, melancholy, or weakminded--God knows I was, too! I look back," Harriet said, talking more to herself than to him, and walking swiftly along in the golden sunset light that streamed across the old back road, "and I wonder I didn't go stark, staring mad! Strange streets, strange houses, and myself wheeling Pip Davenport about the curbs and past the little shops!"

"Don't think about it," he urged, with concern.

"No; I'll not think about it. Royal, don't think that all my feeling was for myself. I thought of you, too. I missed you. Truly, I missed what you had given my life!"

A dark flush came to the man's face, and when he spoke it was with an honest shame and gratitude in his voice that would have surprised the women who had only known him in his later years.

"You are generous, Harriet," he said. "You were always the most generous girl in the world!"

More stirred than she wished to show herself, Harriet walked on, and there was a silence.

"I hunted for you," Royal said presently. "For months it seemed to me that we must meet, that we must talk! I came back from Canada in August, I went to the house; it was taken by strangers. I went to Fred's paper; he had been gone for months!"

"I know!" Harriet nodded. The wonderful smoky blue eyes met his for a second, and there was something of sympathy now in their look. "I know, Roy! It was," she shuddered, "it was a wretched business, all round!"

"Linda and Fred made it hard for you?" he asked.

"Oh, no! They were angels. But of course in their eyes, and mine, too--I was marked."

Silence. Royal Blondin gave her a glance full of distress and compunction. But he did not speak, and it was Harriet who ended the pause.

"Well, that's what a little girl of eighteen may do with her life!" she said. "I have been a fool--I have made a wreck of mine! Ambition and youth went out of me then. It wasn't anything actual, Roy. But I have known a hundred times why when I should have courage I had nothing but fear, when I should have self-confidence I failed myself. Something in my soul got broken!"

"You are the most beautiful woman in the world," Royal Blondin said, steadily, "you are established here, they all adore you! Why do you say that your life is a wreck?"

"I am the daughter of Professor Field," said Harriet, "and at twenty-seven I am the paid companion of Mrs. Richard Carter's daughter! Oh, well--I was happy enough to have the opportunity. I had studied French, you know; and Mrs. Rogers took me abroad with her. She was an outrageous old lady, but not curious! No reasonable woman could live with her--I made myself endure it. Then I went to her daughter, Mrs. Igleheart, the famous suffragette, for two years. And the Carters took me from her." She shrugged indifferently. "What of yourself? Where have you been?"

But he was not quite ready to drop the personal note.

"Harriet, now that we have met, we'll be friends? My life now is among these people; you'll not be sorry if we occasionally meet?"

"In this casual way--no, we can stand that!" she agreed. The fears of the night rose like mist, melted away. It was bad enough, but it was not what her inflamed and fantastic apprehension had made it. He was no revengeful villain, after all. He did not mean to harm her.

"I've been everywhere," he said, answering her question. "I made two trips to China from San Francisco. I was interested in Chinese antiques. Then I went into a Persian rug thing, with a dealer. We handled rugs; I went all over the Union. After that, four years ago, I went to Persia and into India, and met some English people, and went with them to London. Then I came back here, as a sort of press agent to a Swami who wanted to be introduced in America, and after he left I rather took up his work, Yogi and interpretive reading, 'Chitra' and 'Shojo'--you don't know them?"

She shook her head, sufficiently at ease now even to smile in faint derision.

"They eat it up, I assure you!" Royal Blondin said, in self-defence.

"Oh, I know they do!" Harriet agreed. "I've been hearing a great deal about you lately! You have a studio?"

"I have--really!--the prettiest studio in New York. I rented my London rooms, with my furniture in them, and I have a little apartment in Paris, too, that I rent."

"And what's the future in it, Roy?" Now that the black dread was laid, she could almost like him.

"The present is extremely profitable," he said, drily, "and I suppose there might be--well, say a marriage in it, some day--"

"A rich widow?" Harriet suggested, simply.

"Or a little girl with a fortune, like this little Carter girl," he added, lightly.

Harriet gave him a swift look.

"Don't talk nonsense! Nina's only a child!"

"She's almost eighteen, isn't she?"

The girl walked swiftly on for a full minute.

"How do you happen to know that?"

"Is it a secret?"

The possibility he hinted, however remote, was enough to stop her short, actually and mentally. Considering, she stood still, with a face of distaste. The hush before sunset flooded the quiet road. A bird called plaintively from some low bush, was still, and called again. From the river came the muffled, mellow note of a boat horn. Two ponies looked over the brick wall, shook their tawny heads, and galloped to the field with a joyous affectation of terror. Nina! By what fantastic turn of the cards was Royal Blondin to be connected in her thoughts, after all these years, with Nina?

She looked at Blondin, who was watching her with a half-sulky, half-ingratiating air.

"My dear girl, that was merely an idle remark!" he said.

"Well, I hope so," Harriet said, going on, "anyway, she's a child!"

"You weren't--quite--a child, at eighteen," he reminded her.

The colour flooded her transparent dusky skin.

"That's--exactly--what I was!" she said, drily. "But talk to Nina, if you don't believe me! Everything that is school-girly and romantic and undeveloped, is Nina. If you held her coat for her, she would embroider the circumstance into something significant and flattering! She is absolutely inexperienced; she's what I called her, a child!"

"I've been talking to her," Blondin said. His companion looked at him sharply, and after a second he laughed. "There is just one chance in the world that I might make that little girl extremely happy!" he said.

"Don't talk nonsense!" Harriet said again, impatiently.

"Is it nonsense?" he asked, smiling.

"It's--preposterous!"

"I suppose," the man drawled, "that that is a question for the young lady, and her parents, and myself, to decide."

"You suppose nothing of the sort!" Harriet said, sensibly, without wasting a glance upon him. And she added in scorn, "I doubt very much if it's possible!"

"Very probably it isn't," he conceded, amiably. "I seem middle-aged to her. I--"

"You ARE thirty-eight," Harriet said.

"Exactly! But--don't forget!--I shall have the field to myself. The mother won't interfere. Of the grandmother I have my doubts, but if the father is like the usual American male parent, he will give the girl her head!"

Harriet bit her lip. This was utterly unexpected. Into her calculations, up to this point, she had taken only Royal Blondin and herself. If this casual hint covered any truth, then the matter did not stop there. Nina was involved, and with Nina, Ward and Nina's father and Isabelle--

The complications were endless; her heart sickened before them. For she read Nina's susceptible vanity as truly as he, and she knew besides, what he did not know, that the formidable-appearing grandmother was secretly a little piqued at Nina's lack of masculine attention, and would probably further any romantic absurdity on the girl's part with all her determined old soul. Nina adored at eighteen by the much-talked-of poet; Nina, young and gauche perhaps, but married, and entertaining guests in her husband's studio, would be a Nina far more satisfying to her grandmother than the bread-and-butter Nina of to-day.

And yet, the conviction that Royal dared not betray her had been flooding Harriet's heart with exquisite reassurance during this past half hour. She was safe; her life at Crownlands took on a new and wonderful beauty with that knowledge. And if she was fit to continue there, Nina's companion, Isabelle's confidante, guide and judge for the whole household, could she with any logic warn them against this man?

He had her trapped, and she saw it. If she was to have her safety, as all this talk implied, then she must give him the same tacit assurance. To threaten his standing was to wreck her own.

"Don't make a tragedy of it," Royal, watching her narrowly, interrupted her thoughts to say lightly. "The girl will marry where she pleases. She makes her own choice. If I can make the right impression on her and convince her father and mother that I am fit for her, why, it isn't your affair!"

"Isn't it?" Harriet whispered the question, as if to herself. Her eyes looked beyond him darkly; the girl was young and innocent, greedy for flattery, eager to live. What chance had little Nina Carter against charm like his--experience like his? Harriet wondered if she could look dispassionately on while Nina dimpled and flushed over her love affair, while gowns were made and presents unpacked. Could she help to pin a veil over that stupid little head; could she wave good-bye to Royal Blondin and his girl wife; could she picture the room where Nina's ignorance that night must face his sophistication, his passion, his coarseness?

They had come to the particular lane that led to Crownlands now, and she stood still by the ivy-covered brick wall, her face dark and sober with thought in the soft, clear twilight.

"There won't be any kidnapping or chloroform about it!" Royal reminded her.

"No--I know!" she answered, with a swift glance of pain. "But--"

But what? The alternative was Linda's house, at twenty-seven instead of seventeen, and with the vague cloud over her even more definite than before. Harriet winced. Nina, whispered her mind, was far less ignorant than Harriet had been at her age.

"Life--the truths of life," Royal said, as if he read her thought, "may not be to everyone what they--might be--might have been--to you!" The colour rushed to her face.

"PLEASE, Roy--!" she said, suffocated.

"I may never be asked to the house after to-morrow night," said Blondin, after a pause, realizing that he was gaining ground. "She won't be here to-morrow night. This may be the beginning and end of it. All I ask is that if I am made welcome here, on my own merits, you won't interfere! The mere fact that you're living here doesn't mean that you have the moral responsibility of the family on your shoulders, does it? Does it?"

"No-o," Harriet admitted, in a troubled tone.

"Of course not! You live your life, and I mine. Is there anything wrong about that?"

He looked down with quiet triumph at the exquisite face, never more beautiful than in this soft light, against the setting of maples and brick wall.

"You know you would never look at that girl except for her money, Roy!" she burst out.

"Nor would any one else!" he amended, suavely.

Harriet gave a distressed laugh.

"Come! You and I never saw each other until this week," Blondin urged. "That's the whole story."

Before she answered, the girl looked beyond him at the splendid stables and lawns of Crownlands. One of the great cars was in the garage doorway, its lamps winking like eyes in the dusk. An old gardener was utilizing the last of the daylight, his back bent over a green box border. Beyond, lights showed in the side windows of the great house. Harriet could see pinkish colour up at her own porch; Nina was at home, or Rosa was turning down the beds and making everything orderly for the night. She had a swift vision of the great hallways, the flowers, the silent, unobtrusive service; of Ward and his friends racketing upstairs; the old lady majestically descending; of Isabelle at her mirror. Richard Carter would come quietly down, groomed and keen-eyed; he would glance at his mail, perhaps saunter out to the wide porch for a chat with his mother before dinner was announced.

It had never lost its charm for her, her castle of dreams; she had longed to be part of just such a household all her life! Now she actually was part of it, and--if what Mary Putnam had hinted was true, if her own fleeting suspicion only a few evenings ago was true; then she might some day really belong to Crownlands, in good earnest!

After all, Nina was bound for some sort of indiscretion; nobody could save her that! Even if there was any probability that Royal could carry out his plan.

Harriet made her choice.

"Very well," she said, briefly. "I understand you. I turn in here. Good-night!"

"Just a second!" he said, detaining her. "You won't hurt me with any of them, Ward or the girl, or the father?"

The girl's lips curled with distaste.

"No," she said, tonelessly.

"The look implies that you despise me!" Royal said, smiling.

"Oh, not YOU!" she said, in a tone of self-contempt. And in another second she was gone. He saw the slender figure, in its green gown, disappear at a turning of the ivied wall. She paused for no backward glance of farewell. But Royal Blondin was satisfied.

CHAPTER V

Again Harriet fled through the quiet house as if pursued by furies, and again reached her room with white cheeks and a fast-beating heart. Nina was not there. She crossed to the window, and stood there with her hands clasped on her chest, and her breath coming and going stormily.

"Oh, he's clever!" she whispered, half aloud. "He's clever! He never made a threat. He never made a threat of any kind! He knew that he had me--he knew that he had me just where he wanted me!" And looking down toward the lane, invisible now behind the trees and stables, in the gathering dusk, she added scornfully, "You're clever, Roy. I wonder if there's anything you wouldn't do, if it made for your own comfort or brought you in money!

"But, at all events," summarized Harriet, quieting a little under the soothing influence of solitude and safety, "I'm out of it! He won't touch ME. And what he does here, in making his way with this family, doesn't concern me! Nina is old enough to decide for herself--I had my own living to make at her age, and no father to write me checks for my birthdays, and no Uncle Edward to die and leave me a hundred and fifty thousand dollars!"

She mused about the little fortune, left most unexpectedly five years before to Nina and Ward by an uncle of their mother. Edward Potter had been a bachelor, had been young when an accident flung him out of life, and made his niece's children, the twelve-year-old Nina, and Ward at sixteen, his heirs. The expectation had been that he would marry, that sons and daughters of his own would disinherit the young Carters. But his affianced wife had married someone else, after awhile, and the fortune had gone on accumulating for Ward and for the girl whose eighteenth birthday was only a few months off now. Harriet wondered if Royal Blondin knew about it. Of course he knew about it! Harriet had seen a check for one million dollars exhibited, under glass, among the wedding gifts of one twenty-year-old girl a few months ago. She did not suppose that Richard Carter would do that for his daughter, even if he could. But he would probably double Uncle Edward's legacy, and the bride would begin her new life with a fortune that was no contemptible fraction of a million.

"And I am worrying about my responsibility to poor, dear little Nina!" the girl said to herself, with a rather mirthless laugh, as Nina herself came into the room.

Nina had been experiencing what were among the pleasantest hours of her life. A school friend, Amy Hawkes, had come back with her from Francesca Jay's tea, and the two had been prettily invited by Isabelle to join the family downstairs at dinner. Coming at this particular moment, it had seemed to Nina that she was emerging from the chrysalis indeed.

But more than that. Amy, who was romance personified, under a plain and demure exterior, had observed Nina's long conversation with Royal Blondin, and had found an arch allusion to it so well received by Nina that she had followed up that line of conversation, almost without variation, ever since. By this time the girls had confided to each other, over a box of chocolates in the deep chairs of the morning room, everything of a sentimental nature that had ever happened to them in their lives, and much that had not. Amy was convinced that Mr. Blondin was just desperately in earnest, and that, for the sake of other aspirants, Nina ought not to trifle with him, and Nina, with blazing cheeks and tumbled hair, was assuming rapidly the airs of a sad coquette.

Amy was to sleep with Nina, and Harriet realized, as she superintended their fluttered dressing, that she, Harriet, would be obliged to go to their door five times, between eleven and one o'clock that night, and tell them that they must stop talking. With the grave manner that always impressed young girls, and with a somewhat serious face, she was busying herself with their frills and ribbons, when from the bathroom, where Amy was drawing on silk stockings, and Nina had her toothbrush in her mouth, she was electrified by a chance scrap of their conversation.

"If I do mention it to Mother," said Nina, rather thickly, "she will only scold me! A man of his age--she'd be furious!"

"And don't you think you deserve to be scolded?" said Amy, in a delightfully rebuking undertone. "My dear--he must be in the thirties!"

"No, I don't, Amy!" Nina protested, in a tone of great honesty and innocence. "I can't help being like that. If I don't like a man, why, I have nothing to say to him! If I do, why--his age--NOTHING--matters!"

She hesitated, and laughed a little laugh of pure pleasure.

"You flirt!" Amy said.

"Truly, honestly--" Nina was beginning, when both girls were smitten into panicky silence by the sound of the slipper Harriet deliberately dropped on the floor. Nina noiselessly bent her stocky young body far forward, to look through the crack of the bathroom door. Harriet went on quietly spreading the youthful dinner dresses on Nina's bed, snapped up a dressing-table light, went on into her own room. But she had been taken far more by surprise herself, if they had only known it, than had Amy and Nina. Could Royal possibly have been the subject of their confidences? Could he have made such progress in a single afternoon? Knowing Royal, and knowing Nina, she was obliged to confess it possible.

While she stood pondering, in her own beautiful room, there was a modest knock at the door, and Rosa came in with a box. She smiled, and put it on Harriet's desk.

"For me?" the girl said, smiling in answer, and with some surprise. Rosa nodded, and went her way, and Harriet went to the box. It was not large, a florist's box of dark green cardboard; Harriet untied the raffia string, and investigated the mass of silky tissue paper. Inside was an orchid.

She took it out, a delicate cluster of flaky blossoms, poised carelessly, like little white hearts, on the limp stem. She opened the accompanying envelope, and found Ward's card. On the back he had written,

"Just a little worried because he's afraid you're cross at him!"

Harriet stood perfectly still, the orchid in one hand, the card crushed in the other. Ward Carter had sent orchids, no doubt, to other girls. But Harriet Field had never had an orchid before from a man.

She put the card into her little desk, and the orchid into a slender crystal vase. Then she went back to advise Amy and Nina as to gold beads and the arrangement of hair. But a little later, when she was in the big housekeeper's pantry, where several maids were busy with last-minute manipulations of olives and ice and grapefruit, Ward came out and found her, soberly busy in her old checked silk.

"Why didn't you wear it?"

"Wear it--you bad, extravagant child! I'll wear it to town to-morrow."

"No; but--" he sank his tone to one of enjoyable confidences--"but WERE you mad at me?"

"Mad at you? But why should I have been?" Harriet demanded.

"Oh, I don't know! You looked so glum at breakfast."

"Well, you had nothing to do with it!" she assured him, in her big-sisterly voice. "And it was the first orchid I ever had, and I loved you for it!"

It was said in just the comradely, half-amused voice with which she had addressed Ward a hundred times in the past year, but perhaps the boy had changed. At all events, it was with something like pain and impatience in his tone that he said gruffly:

"Yes, you do! You like me about as much as you like Nina, or Granny!"

"I like you--sh! just a LITTLE better than I do Granny!" Harriet confided. "Don't spoil your dinner with olives, Ward! Don't muss that--there's a dear! Dinner's announced, by the way. It's quarter past eight."

"I'm going!" he grumbled, discontentedly.

"At any rate, I LOVE the orchid!" Harriet said, soothingly. He was laughing too, as he disappeared, but something in his face was vaguely troubling to her none-the-less, and she remembered it now and then with a little compunction during her quiet evening of reading. She was tired to-night, excited from the talk with Blondin that afternoon, and by the general confusion and noise of the household. Ward--Nina--Royal--their names flitted through her thoughts even when she tried to read; at such a time as this she felt as if the life at Crownlands was like the current of a river that moved too swiftly, or more appropriately perhaps, like some powerful motor-car whose smooth, swift passage gave its occupants small chance to investigate the country through which they fled. Well, she would see Linda on Saturday, and have Sunday with her and the children, and that meant always a complete change and a shifted viewpoint, even when, as frequently happened, Linda took the older-sisterly privilege of scolding.

CHAPTER VI

Linda, who had been Mrs. Frederick Davenport for some seventeen years, had lived for the last ten in a quiet New Jersey village. The house for which she and her husband paid the staggering rent of forty dollars a month had proved to be in a region toward which the expected tide of fashion did not turn, but it remained a quiet and eminently respectable neighbourhood, remained almost unchanged, in fact, and Linda was satisfied.

When Harriet had chaperoned Nina and Amy to the Friday afternoon matinee, and had duly deposited Amy afterward in the Hawkes mansion, and had escorted Nina to her grandmother's apartment, she was free to direct Hansen to drive her to the Jersey tube, and to spend a hot, uncomfortable hour in a stream of homegoing commuters, on the way to Linda's house. She was unexpected, but that made no difference; the Davenports had little company, and they were always ready to welcome the beloved sister and aunt.

Linda's home was a shingled brown eight-room house, built in the first years of the century, and consequently showing the simplicity and spaciousness that were unknown in the architecture of the eighties. It was exactly like a thousand other houses here in the Oranges, and like a million in the Union. There was a porch, with a half-glass door covered by a wire netting door, and a rusty mail box; there was a square entrance hall with a side window and an angled stairway; there was a kitchen back of the hall, and a square parlour with a green-tiled mantel to the left; a square dining room back of the parlour, with a window at the back and another at the side. The side window gave upon the neighbouring house, a duplicate of this house, forty feet away, and the back window commanded an oblong backyard in which clotheslines and bean poles and a dog house, and a small vegetable garden protected by collapsing chicken wire, and various pails and buckets appertaining to the kitchen, all had place.

But up the slope of meadow beyond this yard were the woods, and the Davenport children had always considered these woods as a part of their legitimate domain, combining thus, as their mother said, "the advantages of the country with all the conveniences of the city." What the conveniences of the city were Harriet was unable to decide, but to Linda's practical mind electric light, adequate plumbing, and a gas stove were all extremely important.

A chipped cement path led to Linda's steps; there was no front fence. It was considered vaguely elegant, in the neighbourhood, to let the fifty-foot plots run together, as boundless estates might unite. So that the old prim charm of pickets and protected gardens, and protected babies playing in them, had long ago vanished from country homes, and although the lawns here were all well tended, there was a certain bareness and indefiniteness about the aspect that partly accounted for the little curl of distaste that touched Harriet's mouth when she thought of Linda's home.

She mounted the three cement steps from the sidewalk level, and the four shabby and peeling wooden ones that rose to the porch. On this hot summer afternoon the front door was open, and Harriet stepped into the odorous gloom of the hall, and let the screen door bang lightly behind her. There was a confused murmur of voices and the clinking of plates in the dining room, but these ceased instantly, and a hush ensued.

Immediately, in the open archway into the parlour, a girl of fifteen appeared, a pretty girl with blue eyes and brown hair, a shabby but fresh little shirtwaist belted by a shabby but clean white skirt, and a napkin dangling from her hand.

She made a round O of her mouth, and then gave a shout of pleasure.

"Oh, Mother--it's Aunt Harriet! Oh, you darling--!"

Harriet, laughing as she put down her bag and divested herself of her hat and wraps, went from the child's wild embrace into the arms of Linda herself, a tall, broadly built, pleasant-faced woman with none of Harriet's own unusual beauty, but with a family resemblance to her younger sister nevertheless.

"Well, you sweet good child!" she said, warmly. "Fred--here's Harriet! Well, my dear, isn't it fortunate that we were late! We'd hardly commenced!"

The remaining members of the family now streamed forth: Fred Davenport, a thin, rather gray man of fifty, with an intelligent face, a worried forehead, and kindly eyes; Julia, a blonde beauty of twelve; Nammy, a fat, sweet boy of five, with a bib on; and Pip, a serious ten-year-old, with black hair and faded blue overalls, and strong little brown hands scrupulously scrubbed to the wrist-bones, where dirt and grime commenced again unabated. Josephine, the oldest child, continued to dance about the visitor delightedly, but the little thoughtful Julia disappeared, and when presently they all went out to resume the interrupted meal, a place had been set freshly for Harriet, and a clean plate was waiting for her.

"Now, I don't know whether to take this out and heat it up for you, or whether it's still hot," said Linda, beaming from her place at the head of the table.

"I'll do it!" said Julia, half launched from her chair.

"Oh, Mother, it's plenty hot enough!" Josephine contended, good naturedly. Harriet protested against the reheating plan. It seemed to her the middle of the afternoon, with the blazing, merciless sunlight streaming across the backyards. She had forgotten that Linda had dinner at half-past six.

"Iced tea! Oh, don't you love it? I could die drinking it!" Julia said, drawing the beverage from off the ice in her glass with Epicurean delight.

"You very probably will!" her father said. The children laughed hilariously. Linda put Harriet's plate before her, and Harriet attacked codfish cakes and boiled potatoes and stewed tomatoes with pieces of pulpy bread in them, with what appetite she could command. The stewed blueberries that followed were ice-cold, and she enjoyed them as much as the others did.

The talk ranged wholesomely from family to national affairs. Fred was a newspaper man, one of the submerged many, underpaid, overworked, unheard, yet vaguely gratified through all the long years by the feeling that his groove was not quite the groove of the office, the teller's desk, or the travelling salesman's "beat." Here in the little suburban town his opinion gained some little weight from the fact that he had been ten years with a New York evening paper. Fred held vaguely with labour parties, with socialists and single-taxers; his sister-in-law had a somewhat caustic feeling that if Fred had ever given Linda a really capable maid, his opinions might have been more endurable, to her, Harriet, at least. Linda had had maids, Polack and Swedish girls, and Irish country girls hardly intelligible in speech. But now she had no maid, she preferred the economy and independence of doing her own housework.

They sat on into absolute darkness, finishing the last teaspoonful of blueberry preserve, and the last crumby cooky. Mrs. Davenport was interested in everything her sister had to say; knew the Carters, and even some of their closest friends, by name, and asked all sorts of questions about them. Josephine, after a half-hearted offer to help with the dishes, departed for a rehearsal of "Robin Hood," which was to be given by the women of the church as their annual entertainment. While she was upstairs, little Nammy was sent up to bed, but when it was absolutely necessary to have lights, and the group at the table naturally adjourned, little Julia and Pip gallantly did their share of the work.

Harriet knew that work by heart; no amount of absence could ever make her unfamiliar with any detail of it. The clearing of the table, the shaking of the crumpled tablecloth, the setting of the breakfast table, the hot glare of electric light in the cluttered and odorous kitchen, the scraping of congealed plates, the spreading of her damp tea towel on the rack by the sink, the selection of a dry towel.

Linda, she reflected, had had seventeen years--had had something nearer twenty-five years of it. For Linda had been only Josephine's age when their mother died, and Professor Field's daughters had assumed the management of his little home. Linda might have been anything, thought her sister, as the older woman rinsed and soaped cheerfully, in the insufferable heat of the kitchen, but she had always had cooking and dishes to do. She said that she liked them.

Julia was Harriet's favourite among the children. Pip had been a baby, entirely absorbing his mother, in those terrible days nine years ago, but Julia had been a delicious, confidential two-year-old, with a warm soft hand, and a flushed little friendly face under tumbling curls. Harriet had bathed her, dressed her, fed her, and taken her for silent walks. And on many a moonlit night the unconscious little body had been held tight in Harriet's arms, and the unconscious little face wet with passionate tears.

Julia had never known this, but Harriet never forgot it, and she looked at Julia lovingly, as the small, sturdy girl in her shabby little school-frock went to and fro busily.

"And now we can talk!" Linda said at last, when the kitchen was dark and hot and orderly, and the children gone upstairs to bed in hot darkness, and she and Harriet had taken the seats on the small, hot porch. "This is a terrible night--nine o'clock--and they are hardly settled off yet!"

Nine o'clock. They would still be at dinner at Crownlands, and the river breeze would be blowing the thin curtains of Harriet's French windows straight into the cool, fresh room. She would be out on the porch, now, looking at the river lights, her book forgotten in her lap. At the head of the table Richard Carter would be sitting, in his cool and immaculate white, and at the foot, sparkling and beautiful, with her fresh bare arms and her firm bare shoulders, her exquisitely modelled hair and her bright eyes, Isabelle. And beside her, to-night, Royal Blondin, musical, poetical, playing the game with all his consummate art, scoring with every glance and word--

Fred was at the piano. It was a poor piano, and he was a poor player who smoked his old pipe while he painstakingly fingered Mendelssohn's "Songs Without Words" or the score of "The Geisha." But Linda loved him.

"He will putter away there, perfectly content, for an hour," she told Harriet. "And at ten you'll see him starting to get Josephine. They're great chums--she thinks there's no one in the world like Daddy!"

"How are things at the office?" Harriet asked.

"Oh, just about the same! Old Frank Judson died, you know, and of course Fred expected the A. P. desk. But Allen had a nephew, just out of Yale, it seems, and you can imagine how poor old Fred felt when they put him in. However, I said he wouldn't last, and he didn't last! So Fred has that desk now, and of course he is tremendously pleased."

"More money in it?" Harriet asked, practically.

"Well, there will be. Allen hasn't said anything about it, but Fred is sure he will. But since Fred's mother died, we've felt very much easier. It was an expense, and it was a responsibility, too," said Linda, with her plain, fine, unselfish face only vaguely visible to Harriet in the starlight. "And we were about six months clearing up the final expenses. But now, with only ourselves and the children, it makes me feel positively selfish! I did tell Mrs. Underhill that I would try to sew regularly for the Belgians, and there's the Red Cross, I always manage that. But--I know you'll be as glad as I am, Harriet, we are really saving, at last."

"Well, you told me so last Christmas," Harriet said, sympathetically, "when you and Fred took the Liberty Bonds--"

"Yes, that. But I mean really, for our home, now. And--but don't mention this, Harriet, for we are in perfect DREAD that someone else will have the same idea--you know that old place we've been watching for years? Well, Mr. Adams told David Davenport that he believed that it could be had for seven or eight thousand dollars, and perhaps only one thousand or fifteen hundred paid down."

Harriet remembered the place perfectly, a shabby, fine old house on a corner, with trees and an old stable, a plot perhaps one hundred feet wide, a street flanked by new wooden houses and young trees. Linda and Fred had wanted this house since the Sunday walk, wheeling Pip in the perambulator, when they had first seen it.

"We could do wonders with that house!" said Linda, enthusiastically. "Not all at once. But it has electric light in, that we know, and one bath--"

Harriet's thoughts had wandered.

"How's David?"

"Lovely. He always comes to us for Sunday dinner," Linda said. "And he always asks for you!" she added, with some significance. David Davenport, Fred's somewhat heavy and plodding brother, a successful Brooklyn dentist, had never made any secret of his feeling for the beautiful Harriet. "David is a dear," his sister-in-law said, "the most comfortable person to have about! And he is doing remarkably well. He is going to make some woman very happy, Harriet. He and Fred both have that--well, that domestic quality that wears pretty well! We've promised to give the children a picnic on the ocean a week from Sunday, and you'd be perfectly touched to see how David is planning for it. We're to spend Saturday night with him--"

"I like David!" Harriet said, in answer to some faint indication of reproach in her sister's tone. But immediately afterward she added, in a lower voice: "Ward Carter has had Royal Blondin at the house this week!"

Linda's rocker stopped as if by shock. There was an electric silence. When she spoke again it was with awe and incredulity and something like terror in her tone.

"Royal Blondin! He's in England!"

"He was," Harriet said, drily. "He's been in New York for two years now."

"Harriet! Why didn't you tell me?"

"I didn't know, Sis. He came to tea last week--stepped up and held out his hand--I hadn't even seen him since that night in your Watertown house--"

Linda shuddered.

"I know--I remember!" she said in a whisper. And she added fervently, "I hoped he was dead!"

"So did I!" Harriet said, simply.

There was another moment of silence. Then Linda said:

"Well, what about it? What did he say--what did you say?"

"Nothing very significant; what was there to say?" Harriet answered. "Our meeting was entirely accidental. He had no idea of finding me; was as surprised as I was." She stopped abruptly, musing on some unpalatable thought. "You wouldn't know him, Linda. He is a perfect freak," she said, presently, "talks about Karma and Nirvana and I don't know what all! Whether he's a Theosophist or a Brahmin I don't know--"

"For Heaven's sake!" Mrs. Davenport commented, in healthy surprise and contempt.

"New thought, and poetry, and the occult, and Tagore and the Russian novelists, and the Russian music," Harriet said, "he lectures about them and he has been extremely successful! He wears pongee coats and red ties, and has his hair long, and--well, you never saw women act so about anything or anybody!"

"Royal Blondin!" Linda exclaimed, aghast. "Perhaps their making fools of themselves will make it not worth his while to bother you," she speculated, hopefully.

"He's having dinner with the Carters to-night," Harriet said. To this Linda could only ejaculate again an amazed:

"Royal Blondin!" And as Harriet merely nodded, in the gloom, she added, vigorously, "Why, he hadn't a PENNY! He was always an idiot--he didn't have enough to EAT ten years ago!"

"Well, he has enough to eat now! Ward told me that he gets three hundred dollars for his drawing-room talks--his 'interpretive musings', he called them. And he has a book of poetry out, and he reviews poetry for some magazine--"

"Well, THAT--" Mrs. Davenport was still dazed with astonishment and indignation. "That REALLY--" she began, and stopped, shaking her head. "Tell me EVERYTHING you said!" she commanded.

"I will!" Harriet's voice fell flatly. "I came home to talk it over with you." But it was fully five minutes later that she began the inevitable confidences. "We talked--Roy and I--" she said, briefly. "He doesn't belong in my life, now, any more than I do in his! We simply agreed to a sort of mutual minding of our own business--"

"Thank God!" Mrs. Davenport said, fervently. "He--he doesn't want to--he doesn't still feel--he won't worry you, then?" she asked somewhat diffidently. Harriet's laugh had an unpleasant edge.

"He is after bigger game than I am, now!" she said.

"The brute!" her sister commented in a whisper. "It--it is all right, then?" she asked, a little timidly.

"All right!" Harriet echoed, bitterly. "I haven't drawn a happy breath since I saw him! All that time came up again, as fresh as if it were yesterday--except that I HAVE climbed a little way, Linda; I was happy--I was busy and useful--and I had--I had my self-respect!"

And suddenly the bright head was in Linda's lap, and she was sobbing bitterly. Linda, with a great ache in her heart, circled her arms, mother-fashion, as she had circled them a hundred times, about her little sister.

CHAPTER VII

Harriet slept in the room with Julia and Josephine that night, or rather tossed and lay wakeful there. The light of a street lamp came squarely in on the white ceiling, and although the hall door was open, there was no breath of air moving anywhere. The children slept in attitudes of youthful abandonment; Harriet heard Fred and Linda murmuring steadily, and could imagine of what they spoke; little Nammy awakened, and there was an interval of maternal comforting, and then silence.

At about two o'clock the wind streamed mercifully in, hot and thick, but prophetic of rain, and Harriet, wandering about to make windows fast, encountered Linda, on the same errand. When the worst of the crackling and flashing was over, the girl glanced at her watch again. Three o'clock, but she could sleep now. She sank deeply into dreams, not to stir until Linda's alarm clock, hastily smothered, thrilled at seven, and the small girls rose with cheerful noise, to let streams of hot sunshine upon her face.

Her head ached; she brushed Julia's hair as a sort of bribe for turning the small girl out of the bathroom, and was in the tub when Pip hammered on the door for his turn. Linda was in a whirl of blue smoke in the kitchen; Fred shouted a request for a little more hot water; Josephine set the table with languid grace, entertaining her aunt with a description of "Robin Hood."

Her face beaming with satisfaction, Linda assembled her brood. There were cocoa and coffee and muffins and omelette and Fred's little bottle of cream, and his paper, and there was, as always, Linda's spontaneous grace before meat: "I wonder if we're thankful enough, when we think of those poor people in Poland and Belgium!"

Immediately after breakfast the two small girls attacked their Saturday morning's work with a philosophic vigour that rather touched their aunt. This morning Linda would leave the whole lower floor to their ministrations while she thoroughly cleaned the floor above. Josephine must bake cake or cookies, all the dishwashing and dusting and sweeping must be done before Mother came down at twelve to put finishing touches on the lunch. Fred had hurried away after his hasty meal; the boys were turned out into the backyard, which Pip was expected to rake while he watched his small brother.

Harriet's heart ached deeply for them all as she watched the Jersey marshes from the car window a few hours later. The poor little pretty girls, gallantly soaking their small hands in dishwater and lye, eager over the church production of "Robin Hood" and a picnic with Uncle David at Asbury! Josephine was to be a stenographer when she finished High School, and little Julia had expressed an angelic ambition to teach a kindergarten class some day. Nina, at their ages, had had her pony, her finishing school, her little silk stockings, and her monogrammed ivory toilet set, her trip to England and France and Italy with her mother and brother and grandmother.

Suppose that she, Harriet, was right in suspecting that Ward's feeling was more than the passing gallantry of a light-hearted boy? She bit her lip, narrowed her idle gaze on the meadows that flew by the car window. It would be a nine-days' wonder, his marriage at twenty-two with his mother's secretary, more than four years his senior. But after that? After that there would be nothing to say or do. Young Mr. and Mrs. Ward Carter would establish themselves comfortably, and the elder Carters would visit them; Isabelle absorbed as usual in her own mysterious thoughts, and Richard Carter--

Harriet's thoughts, none too comfortable up to this point, stopped here, and she flushed. It was impossible to see Richard Carter, as she saw him every day, in the role of husband, father, son, and employer, without holding him in hearty respect. She liked him thoroughly; she knew him to be the simplest, the most genuine and honest, of them all. He had none of his wife's airy selfishness, none of his mother's cold pride. Nina was far more of a snob than her father, and Ward--well, Ward was only a sweet, spoiled, generous boy, at twenty-two. But Harriet always saw behind Richard Carter, the years that had made him, the patient, straightforward, hard-working clerk who had been sober, and true, and intelligent enough to lift himself out of the common rut long before the golden secret that lay at the heart of the Carter Asbestos Company had flashed upon him. Money had not spoiled Richard; he still held wealth in respect, while Ward ordered his racing car, and Nina yawned over twelve-dollar school shoes.

No; she would not enjoy telling Richard that she was to marry his son. Those keen eyes would read her through and through, and while her father-in-law might love her, and see her beauty and charm with all the rest of the world, Harriet knew that she must begin an actual campaign for his esteem on her wedding day. The prospect had an unexpected piquancy. She had little fear of its outcome. She would make Ward Carter a wife for whom his father must come to feel genuine gratitude and devotion. Every fibre of her being would be strained to make the Carter marriage a success. She knew what persons to cultivate, and what elements to weed out of their lives. There would be children, there would be hospitality and music and a garden. And Ward should seriously settle down to his business, whatever it might be, and show himself a worthy son of his clever father.

Isabelle, simply because of her supreme indifference to whatever did not affect her own personal affairs, would be easy to handle. Her son's marriage might pique her, momentarily, but less, on the whole, than the discovery that she had gained eight pounds, or that new wrinkles had appeared about her eyes. She would very probably choose the position of championing Harriet, if only to infuriate the old lady. Madame Carter would of course be frantic, but Ward's wife need have no fear of her. And Nina--

"I would very soon put a stop to that Blondin affair!" thought Harriet at this point. But a sharp little wedge of fear entered her heart at the same second. It would not do to anger Royal, that end of the tangle must be handled very carefully. Whatever influence she might have with Nina must be used with discretion.

"After all, Nina must live her own life, as I have to live mine!" she thought. And her mind drifted to the happier thought of what a brilliant marriage on her part would mean to the little girls who were so busily cleaning an eight-room house in a little Jersey suburb. Josephine and Julia should come to visit her, they should have little frocks that would befit the pretty nieces of Mrs. Ward Carter; they should have a taste of polo games and country clubs, and in a winter or two Josephine's first formal dance should be given in Aunt Harriet's house.

"Why not--why not?" Harriet asked herself, as she reached Madame Carter's pretentious apartment house, and was whisked upstairs. She was to meet Nina here, and she glanced about for the big limousine at the curb, as an indication that the old lady might be ready to accompany them back to Crownlands. But there was no car in sight. The maid's first statement was that Miss Carter had gone home with her brother, and when Madame Carter came magnificently into the room, Harriet could see from the nature of her head-dress that she did not intend to assume a hat for some hours. When Mrs. Carter meant to go out, her maid pinned and pressed and veiled her hat immovably, while dressing her, as a fixture, with the puffs and braids and curls of white hair.

"Well, our bird has flown!" said the old lady. Harriet could see that she was pleased about something.

"Gone home with Ward?" Harriet asked. Madame Carter never shook hands with her; there was conscious superiority in the little omission. She sank into a chair, and Harriet sat down.

"Ward and his friend, this Mr. Blondin," Madame Carter said. "A very interesting--a most unusual man. A very good family, too--excellent old family. Yes. Nina assured us that she had to wait and go home with her Daddy, but that--" Madame Carter gave Harriet a deeply significant smile--"but that didn't seem to please Somebody very much!" she added. "So I told Nina I thought Granny would be able to make it all right with Daddy, and off the young people went."

She rocked, with a benignly triumphant expression, and a complacent rustle of silken skirts. Harriet, beneath an automatic smile, hid a troubled heart. Royal was losing no time, Ward his innocent instrument, and this fatuous old lady of course playing his game for him! Madame Carter had always spoiled Nina in something a trifle more defined and malicious than the usual grandmotherly fashion. She had indulged the child in chocolates when the doctor's prohibition of sweets was being scrupulously enforced by Isabelle and Harriet; she had permitted late hours and unsuitable plays when Nina visited her; she had encouraged her granddaughter in a thousand little snobberies and affectations. And she had taken a mischievous pleasure in thwarting Harriet whenever possible, emphasizing the difference in her position and Nina's, humiliating the companion whenever it was possible, in ways that were far less subtle than Madame Carter imagined them to be.

Harriet saw now that she was pleased and flattered by an older man's apparent admiration of Nina; and that she would further the girl's first definite affair in every way that lay in her power. It was maddening; it was exasperating beyond words. An honest warning would have merely flattered her with its implication of her importance; ah, no, Isabelle and Harriet might try to hold the child back--but Granny knew girl nature better than either of them!

"Well, then, I must follow them home," Harriet said, pleasantly. "You don't come back to-night?"

To this Madame Carter very pointedly made no answer; her plans were not Miss Field's business. She rocked on placidly, in her ornate, pleasant room, at whose curtained and undercurtained and overdraped windows the summer sunshine was battling to enter. It was a large room, but seemed small because the rugs were two and three deep on the floor, and there was so much rich, dark furniture, so many lamps and jars and pictures and boxes and frames, handsome but heterogeneous treasures that must always remain in exactly the same positions. The several tables were angled carefully, their draperies lay precisely placed, year after year; Harriet knew that all the ten rooms were just the same, and that the old lady liked to walk slowly through them, and note the lace over satin, the glint of ranked wineglasses, the gleam of polished silver, the clocks and candlesticks. There were certain ornate ashtrays for Richard and Ward, there was a magnificent piano player, for which his grandmother bought the boy a dozen rolls a month, selecting them with splendid indifference on one of her regal expeditions downtown, and there was a massive Victrola, which had once delighted Nina for hours at a time.

"The child is growing up!" the old lady said, smiling at some thought. "Well, we must look for love affairs now!"

Harriet felt that there was small profit in following this line of conversation. She glanced at her twisted wrist.

"I think I will make that two o'clock train, Madame Carter, unless there is some errand I might do for you?" she said respectfully.

This courtesy, from a beautiful young woman to an old one, always antagonized Madame Carter. Harriet knew that she was casting about for some honeyed and venomous farewell, when the muffled thrill of the bell came to them, and the footsteps of Ella were heard. Immediately afterward Richard Carter came quickly in.

He met Harriet at the door.

"How are you, Miss Field? Tell Nina to hurry; I've got about five minutes!" he said, pleasantly.

"Don't keep Miss Field; she is making her train!" said his mother, coming forward under full sail, and laying both hands about his. "I'll explain about Nina. Come here--you have time to sit down with your mother, I hope!"

Richard Carter gave his mother the peculiarly warm smile that was especially her own.

"Went on with Ward, eh?" he said, in his hearty voice. "That's all right, then. Oh, Miss Field!" he called, after Harriet's discreetly retreating back, "the car's downstairs. Wait for me there; I'll run you home in half the time the train takes. I'm playing in the tennis finals, Mother--"

Harriet, turning for just a nod and smile, heard no more. His voice dropped to a filial undertone, and he sank into a low chair, with his hands still clasping the old lady's hand. But as she entered the lift, the girl said to herself, with a passionate sort of gratitude: "Oh, I like you! You're the only genuine and unselfish and kind-hearted one in the whole crowd!"

She went down to the street, and saw the small car waiting. He was driving himself to-day. With a great sense of comfort and relaxation Harriet got into it, and was comfortably established, and tucked in snugly, when Richard came down. He smiled at seeing her, got into his own seat; the machine slipped smoothly into motion, the hot and sordid streets began to glide by.

"Ever think how illuminating it would be, Miss Field, if we kept a list of the things that are worrying us sick, and read 'em over a few weeks later?"

"I suppose so!" the girl said, a little surprised, and yet with fervour. "We'd have a fresh bunch then, and be worrying away just as hard!"

The spontaneous response in her tone made Richard Carter laugh.

"I've had something on my mind for two months," he said, "to-day I ran into the fellow I thought was going to make the trouble--we had lunch together, and everything was settled up as calm as a June day! I feel ten years younger than I did at this time yesterday! What made me think of it was that I had it on my mind that you and Nina and the bags would be a crowd in this car when I came out to my mother's a few minutes ago. I was figuring on sending the bags on to-morrow, and so on and so on--"

"It's often that way," Harriet smiled. "Only money trouble really seems to have a solid, tangible form," she added, thoughtfully.

"Combined with some other," he surprised her by answering quickly, as if he were quite at home with his subject. "If there isn't sickness--or drink--"

"Oh, you can't say that, Mr. Carter!" Harriet was at home here, too. "Everybody who is respectable and hard working and sober doesn't get rich---"

"No, not rich!" He was really interested. "But our contention isn't that riches are the only happiness, is it?" he countered.

"No, but I say that money trouble is a very real thing," she answered, quickly.

"There is a golden mean, Miss Field, between being rich and being poor!" he reminded her.

"I suppose I am rather bitter," Harriet said, enjoying this confidence more than she could stop to realize, "because I have just been to see my sister in New Jersey. She has four children, pretty well grown now, and her husband is really a good man, and a steady man, too--he is a sort of Jack-of-all-trades on a Brooklyn newspaper. I suppose Fred is paid sixty dollars a week, and they save on that! But--"

"She's unhappy, eh?" asked the man, with a sidewise glance.

"Linda?" Harriet laughed ruefully. "No, she's not! She's too happy," she said, with a little laugh that apologized for the sentiment. "She washes and cooks and plans all day and all night! I'm the one who worries. It makes me sad to have her work so hard for so little--"

She sensed his lack of sympathy, and stopped short, in a little vague surprise. There was a brief silence while he took the car skillfully through a somewhat congested side street, then they were leaving the hot city behind, and the fresh breath of the river was in their faces. Harriet, in self-defence, sketched the Davenport home for him in a dozen sentences.

"You might tell your brother-in-law, from me," Richard Carter said, presently, "that there isn't much that money will buy HIM!"

Harriet flushed. She had had perhaps a dozen brief conversations with Richard Carter before to-day, but they had never touched so personal a note before.

"I sounded mercenary!" she said, a little uncomfortably. "But I didn't mean to be. I suppose it is because I see so many things that money would do for my sister; I'd love so to have the children beautifully dressed and well educated. Little Pip, raking the yard to-day!--when he ought to be in some wonderful Montessori school!"

"Oh, nonsense!" the man said, heartily. "Lord--Lord, I remember Saturday morning, in a little Ohio town, and raking up the leaves, too! That won't hurt them. I wish--I've often wished, that Nina's life ran a little more in that direction," said her father, frankly. "It's hard not to spoil 'em when you have the chance! Girls--well, perhaps it isn't so bad for girls. But I look at Ward, now, and I wonder what on earth is going to keep that boy straight. This Tony Pope, for instance--it's too much, you know! They don't know the value of money, and they don't know the value of life!"

"Ward is too sweet to be spoiled," Harriet ventured, somewhat timidly.

"You like the boy?" his father asked.

"I? Ward?" She was taken unawares, and flushed brightly. "Indeed I do!"

"I'm glad you do," Richard Carter said, in quiet satisfaction. "I've imagined sometimes that you have a good influence on him--he's impressionable." He fell into silence, and for some time there was no further speech between them. Harriet was content to enjoy this restful interval between the hurry and crowding of Linda's house and the currents and cross-currents that she must encounter at Crownlands. She watched the green country go by, the trees silent and heavy with their rich foliage, the villages blazing with the last June roses. It was oppressively hot, yesterday's storm had not much relieved the air, but Harriet was conscious of a lazy feeling that it did not so much matter now, the weather was no longer of importance. A mere accident had made it natural for Richard Carter to drive her home, and yet she was pleasantly thrilled by the circumstance.

They flew by the great gates of the country club, and turned in past Crownlands lodge, and Harriet got out, at the steps, and turned her happy, flushed face toward the man to thank him. A little spraying film of golden hair had loosened under her hat; her cheeks had a summer burn over their warm olive; her eyes shone very blue. Whatever she saw in his face as he smiled and nodded at her pleased her, for she went upstairs saying again to herself, "Oh, you're real----you're honest--I LIKE you!"

It was delightful to get back into the familiar atmosphere, to catch the fragrance of flowers in the orderly gloom downstairs, to take off her hat and her hot, dusty clothing, and have a leisurely hot bath; to put on fresh and fragrant summer wear, and to go down-stairs presently, rejoicing in being young and comfortable, and tremendously interested in life. A maid stopped to question her; there were letters to open; she felt herself instantly a part of the establishment again, and at home here. The significance of Richard Carter's parting look, its honest admiration and friendliness, augmented by her own glance at a chance mirror on her way upstairs, stayed with her pleasantly.

At one end of the terrace there was an awning whose shade fell upon the brick flooring and the jars of bloom; and this afternoon it also shaded Isabelle, in a basket chair, and the big hound, and Tony Pope. Harriet cast them a passing glance, and wondered a little in her heart. The boy was handsome, and fascinating, and rich, but it was just a little unusual to have Isabelle so openly interested in any one. There were no other callers this afternoon; Nina had driven to the golf club with her father, and might be expected to remain there for tea, if any entertainment offered, or to return home when Hansen brought the car back.

The thought of Nina brought Royal Blondin again to Harriet's mind, and she was conscious of a little internal wincing. But that risk must be faced simply, as one of the unpalatable possibilities of life. That Royal would take some step against which she must, in honour bound, protest; that Nina should engage herself to him, and Nina's parents consent; that no fortuitous circumstance should play into Harriet's hands, and that she should be obliged to antagonize him openly was unthinkable on this peaceful, golden afternoon. The canvas was too big, the cast of characters too large, there must be some shifting of scene, some change in plot, before anything so momentous occurred.

Yet the danger, faint though it might be, was already influencing her. She was committed to a certain amount of diplomatic silence now; her position here had subtly changed since the hour that brought Royal Blondin back into her life a few days ago. Linda's concern, and her own agony of apprehension when she first saw him, had shown her just how frail was her hold upon this pleasant and smooth existence, and in self-defence she had begun for the first time to think of making it more definite. If she was to have all the terrors of maintaining a dangerous position, at least she might be sure of its sweets.

Undefined and vague, all this was still somewhere in the background of her thoughts as she returned to Crownlands, and when she met Ward Carter, wrestling with the engine of his own rather disreputable racing car, out in one of the clean, gravelled spaces near the garage. His coat was off, his fresh, pleasant face streaked with oil and earth, his sleeves rolled up to the elbow.

Harriet, who had wandered out idly, felt a little quickening of her pulses as she saw him. There was no mistaking the pleasure in his eyes as she came close.

"Spark plugs?" she asked, with the sympathy of one to whom the peculiarities of the car were familiar.

"She's fixed now; I've just cleaned 'em," Ward announced, flinging away his cigarette, and straightening his back. "She'll go like a bird, now. When did you get back?"

"Your father drove me home, like the angel he is. You came with Nina?"

"Nina and Blondin. Then I drove him on to the Evans's. But she began to act queer on the way home," said Ward, fondly, of the car. "Say--get in and try her, will you?" he asked, eagerly.

"If you could wipe your face---" Harriet murmured, offering a handkerchief. He declined it, but snatched out his own, and distributed the dirt on his face somewhat more evenly. "Come on--come on, be a sport!" he said. But perhaps he was as much surprised as delighted when she very simply stepped into the low front seat. There was a friendly nearness of her fresh white ruffles, and a thrilling fragrance and sweetness and youngness about her this afternoon that was new. Miss Field always, in Ward's simple vocabulary, had been a "corker." But now he gave her more than one sidewise glance as they went dipping smoothly up and down through the green lanes, and said to himself, "Gosh--when she crinkles those blue eyes of hers, and her mouth sort of twitches as if she wanted to laugh, she is a beauty--that's what SHE is!"

And dressing for dinner, some time later, he found himself stopping short, once or twice, with his tie dangling in his hand, or his brushes aimlessly suspended, while he calculated the chances of encountering her again--in the pantry, in one of the hallways, in the side garden, where she often went, at about twilight, with a book.

About a week later they met for a few moments in this very side garden. It was early evening, and twilight and moonlight were mingled over the silent roses, and the trimmed turf, and the low brick walls. The birds had long gone to bed, and the first dews were bringing out a thousand delicious odours of summer-time. Harriet's white gown and white shoes made her a soft glimmering in the tender darkness; Ward was in informal dinner clothes, with the shine of dampness still on his sleek hair, and the pleasant freshness of his scarcely finished toilet still about him.

They came straight toward each other, and stood very close together, and he took both of Harriet's hands.

"Now, what is it--what is it?" the man said, quickly. "I've been waiting long enough. I can't stand it any longer! I can't go away to-morrow, perhaps for two weeks, and not know!" "Ward," the girl faltered, lifting an exquisite face that wore, even in the faint moonshine, a troubled and intense expression, "can't we let it all wait until you get back?"

"I'll keep my mouth shut, nobody suspects us, if that's what you mean!" he answered, impatiently. "But--why, Harriet," and his arm went about her shoulders, and he bent his face over hers, "Harriet, why not let me go happy?" he pleaded.

"You'll see a dozen younger girls at the Bellamys' camp," Harriet reasoned, "girls with whom it would be infinitely more suitable--"

"PLEASE!" he interrupted, patiently. And almost touching her warm, smooth cheek with his own, and coming so close that to raise her beautiful eyes was to find his only a few inches away, he added, fervently, "You love me and I love you--isn't that all that matters?"

Did she love him? Harriet hoped, when she reviewed it all in the restless, tossing hours of the night, that she had thought, in that moment, that she did. It was wonderful to feel that strong eager arm about her, there was a sweet and heady intoxication in his passion, even if it did not awaken an answering passion in return. Under all her reasoning and counter-reasoning in the night there crept the knowledge that she had known that this was coming, had known that only a few days of encouraging friendliness, only a few appealing glances from uplifted blue eyes, and a few casual touches of a smooth brown hand must bring this hour upon her. And back of this hour, and of a man's joy in winning the woman he loved, she had seen the hazy future of prosperity and beauty and ease, the gowns and cars and homes, the position of young Mrs. Ward Carter.

But she told herself that all that was forgotten in that magic five minutes of moonlight and fragrance and beauty in the rose garden; she told herself that she really did love him--who could help loving Ward?--and that she would save him far better than he could save himself, from everything that was not loving and helpful and good, in the years to come.

She had let him turn her face up, in the strengthening moonlight, and kiss her hungrily upon the lips, and she had sent him in to his dinner half-wild with the joy of knowing himself beloved. Harriet had gone in, too, shaken and half-frightened, and with his last whispered prophecy ringing in her ears:

"Wait a year--rot! I'll go to the Bellamys', because I promised to, but the day I come back, and that's two weeks from to-day, we'll tell everyone, and this time next year you will have been my wife for six months!"

CHAPTER VIII

A most opportune lull followed, when Harriet Field had time to collect her thoughts, and get a true perspective upon the events of the past week. On the morning after Ward's departure for the Bellamys' camp she had come downstairs feeling that guilt was written in her face, and that the whole household must suspect her engagement to the son and heir.

But on the contrary, nobody had time to pay her the least attention. Nina was leaving for a visit to Amy Hawkes, at the extremely dull and entirely safe Hawkes mansion, where four unmarried daughters constituted a chaperonage beyond all criticism. Isabelle Carter was giving and attending the usual luncheons and dinners, her husband absorbed in an especially important business deal that kept him alternate nights in the city. The house was quiet, the domestic machinery running smoothly, the weather hot, sulphurous, and enervating.

A letter from Ward brought Harriet's colour suddenly to her cheeks, on the third morning, but there was no one but Rosa to notice her confusion. Ward wrote with characteristic boyishness. They were having a corking time, there was nobody there as sweet as his girl was, and he hoped that she missed him a little bit. He was thinking about her every minute, and how beautiful she was that last night on the terrace, and he couldn't believe his luck, or understand what she saw in him.

There were seven sheets to the letter; each one heavily engraved with the name of the camp, "Sans Souci," and the telephone, post-office, telegraph, and rail directions charmingly represented by tiny emblems at the top of the letter-head. Harriet smiled over the dashing sentences; it was an honest letter. She felt a thrill of genuine affection for the writer; he would never grow up to her, but she would make him an ideal wife none-the-less. She went about his father's home, in these days, with a secret happiness swelling in her heart. It would not be long now before the secretary and companion must take a changed position here. It was not the least of her satisfactions that Ward wrote her that Royal was at the camp, planning a trip to the Orient. But before he went he talked of giving a studio tea for Nina. "I think he is slightly mashed on the kid," wrote Ward, simply.

With Royal in China, Nina safely recovering from her June fever, and Harriet affianced to Ward, the summer promised serenely enough. Harriet answered the letter in her happiest vein. Her reply was but two conservative pages; but she said more in the double sheet of fine English handwriting than Ward had said in three times as much space. A charming letter is one of the fruits of loneliness and reading; Harriet was sure of her touch. His father, his mother, and Nina each had an epigrammatic line or two, and for his grandmother Harriet dared a little wit, and smiled to imagine his shout of appreciative laughter.

She dined as usual alone, that evening, and was surprised, at about eight o'clock, to receive the demure notification from Rosa that Mrs. Carter would like to see her. Harriet glanced at a mirror; her brassy hair was as smoothly moulded as its tendency to curve and ring ever permitted, and she wore a thin old transparent white gown that looked at least comparatively cool on this insufferably hot evening. With hardly an instant's delay she went downstairs.

On the terrace outside the drawing-room windows they were at a card table: Richard, looking tired and hot in rumpled white, Isabelle exquisite in silver lace, and young Anthony Pope. Near by, Madame Carter majestically fingered some illustrated magazines.

It appeared that they wanted bridge; it was too hot to eat, too hot to dance at the club, too hot--said Isabelle pathetically--to live! Harriet had supposed her dining alone with her infatuated admirer, but it appeared that Richard had driven his mother out from the city in time to join them for salad and coffee, and that this angle of the terrace, where the river breeze occasionally stirred, was the only spot in the world that was approximately comfortable.

Obligingly, Harriet took her place, cut for the deal. But her eyes had not fallen upon the group before she sensed that something was wrong, and she had a moment's flutter of the heart for fear that someone suspected her, that she was under surveillance. Had Royal--had Ward--

She turned a card, took the deal, found Anthony Pope her partner, and entered into the game with spirit. Richard's first words to her were reassuring; if there was constraint here, she was not involved in it.

"No trump--says little Miss Field. Well, that doesn't seem to frighten me. Two spades."

"I think we might try three diamonds, Miss Field," Anthony said, gravely and pleasantly, and Harriet felt herself acquitted of any apprehension in that direction as well. It only remained for Isabelle to show friendliness.

"Du hast diamonten and perlen, you two. I can see that! You're down, Harriet!" Mrs. Carter said, thoughtfully. Harriet began thoroughly to enjoy herself! If they were all furious, at least it was not with her. She speculated, as she gathered in her tricks. Was it conceivable that Richard did not enjoy the discovery of the tete-a-tete dinner? But Isabelle had often been equally indiscreet, and he had never seemed to resent it before. Harriet knew that Isabelle was ill at ease; she suspected that Tony was furious. The old lady was obviously quivering with baffled interest and curiosity.

In the little pool of light over the card table the air seemed to grow hotter and hotter; there was suffocation in the velvet darkness. A distant rumble of thunder broke heavily on the silence, the sky glimmered with shaking light, and the great leaves of the sycamores turned languidly in a hot breeze. Harriet, the only interested player, was unfortunate with Tony, unfortunate with Isabelle. After three rubbers the game ended suddenly; Richard said he had some letters to write, and was keeping Fox waiting in the library; Anthony scribbled a check, said brief and unfriendly good-nights; Isabelle merely raised passionate dark eyes to his. She was languidly gathering in her spoils when the lights of his car flashed yellow on the drive and he was gone. Harriet, who had lost more than twenty dollars, gave a rueful laugh. The old lady watched everyone in expectant silence.

But when Richard spoke it was only to Harriet, and then in an undertone almost fatherly:

"You lose no money when we ask you to oblige us by playing, my dear. I won't permit that! Twenty dollars and forty cents, was it? Consider it paid."

"Oh, but truly--" she was beginning to protest. The grave look in his eyes, the authoritative nod, interrupted her, and with a pleasant little sensation of protection and of friendliness she had to concede the point. Immediately afterward he said good-night to his mother and wife, and went in to his study. Madame Carter followed him in, and went upstairs, but Isabelle sat on moodily shuffling and reshuffling the cards, in the bright soft light of the terrace lamps.

"Wait a minute, Harriet," she said, briefly, and Harriet obediently loitered. But Isabelle seemed to have nothing to say. Her eyes were on the cards, her beautiful breast, exposed in the low-cut silver gown, rose and fell stormily, and Harriet saw that she was biting her full under lip, as if anger seethed strong within her. In the gleam of the lamps her dark hair took the shine of lacquer; there were jewelled combs in it to-night, and the jewels winked lazily.

Bottomley, the butler, came out, and began discreetly to adjust chairs and to supervise the carrying away of ashtrays and coffee-cups.

"Come upstairs to my room; I want to speak to you!" Isabelle said, suddenly. Harriet followed her upstairs, and they entered the beautiful boudoir together. Here Isabelle dropped into a chair, sitting sidewise, with one bare arm locked across its rococo back, and stared dully ahead of her, a queen of tragedy. Her silver scarf fluttered free, and the toe of a spangled slipper beat with an angry, steady throb on the floor.

Germaine came forward, evidently more accustomed to this mood than Harriet was. Like a flash the high-heeled shoes, the silver gown, and the brocaded stays were whisked away, and a cool, loose silk robe enveloped Isabelle, and she took a deep, cretonned chair by the window. The lights were lowered, Isabelle nodded Harriet to the opposite chair. Then at last she spoke.

"Can that creature hear?"

Harriet, thrilled, glanced toward the dressing room, and shook her head.

"I ask you," said Isabelle, with a great breath of anger restrained, "I ask you if any woman in the world could stand it!"

"I knew something was wrong," Harriet murmured, as the other made a dramatic pause.

"Wrong!" Isabelle echoed, scornfully. "You saw the way Mr. Carter acted. You saw him make me ridiculous--make a fool of me! The boy will never come to the house again."

"Oh, I don't think that!" Harriet said, in honesty.

"Mr. Carter stalked in upon us, at dinner--" his wife said, broodingly. She fell into thought, and suddenly burst out, "Harriet, my heart aches for that boy! My God--my God--what have I done to him!"

She rested her white full arms on the dressing table, and covered her face with her hands. Harriet saw the frail silk of the dressing gown stir with her sudden dry sobbing.

"My God--if I could cry!" Isabelle said, turning. And Harriet realized, with a shock, that she was not acting. "Mr. Carter only sees what I see," she added, "that it must stop. But I am afraid it will kill him. He isn't like other men. He--" She opened a drawer, fumbled therein. "Read that!" she said.

Harriet took the sheet of paper, pressed it open.

"'My heart,'" she read, in Tony Pope's handwriting. "'I will go away from you if I must. But it will be further than India, Isabelle, further than Rio or Alaska. While we two live, I must see you sometimes. Perhaps outside the world there is a place big enough for me to forget you!'"

"Now--!" said Isabelle, rising and beginning restlessly to walk the floor. "Now, what shall I do? Send him away to his death, or risk Mr. Carter's insulting him again, as he did to-night! Anthony Pope means it, Harriet--I know him well enough for that. His whole life is one thought of me. The flowers, the books, the notes--he only wakes in the morning to hope for, to plan, a meeting, and the days when we don't meet are lost days. You don't know how I've been worrying about it," said Isabelle, passionately, "I'm sick with worry!"

She fell silent. Germaine appeared with a tray, and began to loosen and brush the dark hair, and Isabelle went automatically to the business of creaming and rubbing, still shaken, but every minute more mistress of herself. With the thick, dark switch gone, Harriet was almost shocked by the change in the severely exposed forehead and face. Isabelle looked fully her age now, more than her age. But the younger woman knew that however honest her desire to disenchant her young lover, no woman ever risks his seeing her thus. Isabelle might weep, and pray, and suggest supreme sacrifice, but it would be the corseted and perfumed and beautiful Isabelle from whom Tony parted, whom Tony must renounce.

"Well!" said the mistress, sombre-eyed still, and with a still heaving breast. "There was something else, Harriet--Gently, please, Germaine, my head aches frightfully. Oh, Harriet, will you see what this Blondin man wants with Nina? She tells me he suggested some sort of summer party in his roof garden; I don't know quite what it is. But her heart is set on it. They seem to understand each other--I always felt that when Nina's affairs did begin, she would pick out freaks like this! But," Nina's mother sighed, resignedly, "that's all right. He's interesting, and everyone's after him, and if it pleases her--! And will you go to the Hawkes' for her in the morning? Hansen is going at--I don't know what time, in the big car. Don't--" Germaine had gone to the bathroom for a hot towel, and Isabelle dropped her voice, almost affectionately--"don't worry about this little scene, Harriet. It will be quite all right!"

"Oh, surely!" The companion's voice was light and cheerful; she went upstairs only pleasantly excited and thrilled. And at the breakfast table next morning Harriet could show the head of the house the same bright assurance. She was young. Life was like a fascinating play. Richard had come downstairs early, and they had their coffee alone.

"Nina?" asked her father.

"She comes back to-day," Harriet said. "Mrs. Carter is going to have her masseuse, so she won't be down. She asked you to remember that you are dining at the Jays' to-morrow. There's to be tennis at about four."

"Finals," he said, nodding. "Jim Kelsoe and one of the Irvins--"

"Judson Irwin," the girl supplied.

"Was it?" Richard Carter went out to his car apparently well pleased with himself and his life. Harriet started for the Hawkes' with a philosophic reflection or two as to the ephemeral quality of married quarrels.

She brought Nina back at noon, a garrulous and complacent Nina, who could pity the elder Hawkes as girls who "never had admirers." When they reached the driveway of Crownlands, Harriet recognized the car that was already there, and said to herself that Anthony Pope would join them for luncheon. But just as she and Nina were about to enter the cool, wide, dark doorway, Anthony himself passed them. He was almost running, and apparently did not see them. He ran down the shallow steps and sprang into his car, which scattered a spray of gravel as he jerked it madly about, and was gone before she and Nina had ended their look of surprise. Harriet detected a magnificent astonishment in Bottomley's mild elderly glance as well; she went slowly upstairs, with a dim foreboding far back in her heart.

In Nina's room were three flowers from Royal Blondin. Nina said hastily, and in rapture: "Water lilies!" but a ten-year-old memory told Harriet that they were lotus blooms. Another girl had had lotus blooms years ago; Harriet wondered if Royal always sent them to the women he admired, or rather, to the one whose favour was, for the moment, to his advantage.

Nina had no such thoughts. Radiantly and amazedly she turned to Harriet.

"Oh, Miss Harriet, look! They're from Mr. Blondin! Oh, I do think that is terribly nice of him. The idea! The IDEA! We were speaking of a poem called 'The Lotus Flower'. Did you ever? I think that is terribly decent of him, don't you? Shan't I write him? Would you? Hadn't I better write him right now? Will you help me? I do think that is terribly decent of him, don't you?"

And so on indefinitely. Harriet felt rather sorry for the gauche little creature who flung aside her hat and wrap, and sat biting her gold pen-handle, and spoiling sheet after sheet of paper. But there was protection in Nina's absorption, too; she was far too happy to know or care that Harriet felt somewhat worried, or to make any comment when they went down to lunch to find that Isabelle begged to be excused. They lunched alone with the old lady.

At about three, when the important note was written, and Harriet and Nina were idling on the shady terrace, with the hound, the new magazines, and their books, Hansen brought one of the small closed cars to the side door. Five minutes later Isabelle, in a thin white coat, a veiled white hat, and with a gorgeous white-furred wrap over her arm, came out. Germaine was with her, carrying two shiny black suitcases. Isabelle, Harriet thought, looked superbly handsome, but Germaine had evidently been scolded, and had red eyes.

Isabelle came over to give her daughter a farewell kiss.

"Mrs. Webb has telephoned for me, ducky. Your father isn't coming home to-night, but have a happy time with Miss Harriet, and I'll be back in a day or two."

"I thought that you were dining to-morrow at the Jays'!" Harriet said. That she had not been mistaken did not occur to her until she saw the colour flood Isabelle's face.

"I forgot it. But I wonder if you will be sweet enough to telephone to-morrow morning, and say that I am obliging an old friend?" Isabelle said, smoothly. "I shall be with Mrs. Webb in Great Barrington, Harriet. She made it a personal favour, and I couldn't refuse! Good-bye, both of you. All right, Hansen!"

They swept away, leaving Harriet with a strange sense of nervousness and suspense. The summer air seemed charged with menace, and the silence that followed the noise of the car oddly ominous. She looked about nervously; Nina was drifting through Vanity Fair, the sun was warm, and the air sweet and still. But still her heart was beating madly, and she felt frightened and ill at ease.

Madame Carter was on the terrace when they came back at five from an idle trip to the club, reporting that her son had just returned unexpectedly from the city, and had gone in to change for golf.

Nothing alarming here, yet Harriet experienced a sick thrill of apprehension. Something abnormal seemed to be the matter with them all this afternoon!

"Did you call me, Mr. Carter?" She hardly knew her own voice, as he came down the three broad steps from the house. Her hands felt cold, and she was trembling.

"Do you happen to know where Hansen is, Miss Field?"

"Driving Mrs. Carter to the Webbs' at Great Barrington," the girl answered, readily. "Will young Burke do? Mrs. Webb telephoned, and Mrs. Carter left in a hurry. She did not expect you to-night. Hansen ought to be back at about seven, I should think--"

He was not listening to her; abruptly left her. When Harriet went into the house she saw nothing of him. But she knew he had not gone away for the usual golf, and was conscious still of that odd fluttering of mind and soul, that presage of ill. She made her usual little round, spoke briefly to a maid about some fallen daisy petals, consulted with the housekeeper as to the new cretonne covers. A man was to come and measure those covers this very afternoon--perhaps this was he, modestly waiting at the side door.

But no, this man briefly and simply asked to be shown to Mr. Carter, remarking that he was expected. He disappeared into the library; Harriet saw no more of him for an hour, when he silently appeared beside her, and asked to see the chauffeur Hansen as soon as he came.

Richard brought the strange man to the dinner table; but there was nothing in that to make the dinner so unnatural. To be sure Richard ate little, and spoke hardly at all; but this Mr. Williams was quite entertaining, and the old lady in good spirits. Nina, pleased at being downstairs, as she and Harriet usually were when her father and mother were not at home, or when there was no company, also contributed some shy remarks. But Harriet was beset with sudden fits of nervousness, and oppressed by a heavy sense of impending disaster. She said to herself that she wished heartily the weather would break and clear, she felt like "a witch."

At eight Hansen was back, presenting himself in his dusty road-coat; Mr. Carter immediately drew him with Williams into the library. Nina loitered up to bed, but the old lady and Harriet remained downstairs. They did not like, but they sometimes amused, each other. Suddenly came the summons: would Miss Field please step into the library?

Hansen was going out as she came in; Richard was at the big flat-topped desk, the man Williams standing somewhat in shadow. Harriet's heart leaped; they were going to ask her about Royal.

"Just a moment, Miss Field," Richard said. "Will you sit down?" And as Harriet, looking at him in frightened curiosity, did so, he began quietly: "We are in some trouble here, Miss Field. I hardly know how to tell you what we fear. Did you notice anything strange about--Mrs. Carter's--manner to-day?"

"I thought I did," Harriet admitted.

"Did you think of any reason for it?"

Harriet gave the stranger a glance that made him an eavesdropper.

"I fancied that it was connected with--with what distressed her last night, Mr. Carter."

"You may speak before Mr. Williams," Richard said. He looked down; was silent. "I asked him to help me," he added, slowly. "Was young Mr. Pope here to-day?"

"This morning, I don't know how long," Harriet said, with a great light, or darkness, breaking in upon her mind, "he was leaving when Nina and I came home."

Richard gravely considered this, and nodded his head.

"And immediately afterward Mrs. Carter went away?"

"Not immediately. Not until three."

"Do you know who took the telephone call from Mrs. Webb?" Richard said.

"No, because nobody did. No person named Webb called from Great Barrington, or anywhere else, to-day," said Williams, breaking in decidedly, his voice a contrast to Richard's hesitating tones. "As a matter of fact, Hansen didn't drive to Great Barrington. Two miles from your gate here, Mrs. Carter gave him other directions."

"What directions?" Harriet asked, antagonized by his manner, and feeling her cheeks get red. The man evidently had small respect for womanhood.

"He drove to New London," Richard supplied. "Pope's yacht is there."

His manner was very quiet, he spoke almost wearily, but Harriet felt as if a cannon had exploded in the study. She turned white, looked toward Williams, whose mouth was pursed in a silent whistle, looked back at Richard, who was making idle pencil marks on a tablet of paper.

"I've had New London on the wire," said Mr. Williams. "Mr. Pope had been getting ready for a cruise. The chances are that they have already weighed anchor."

"On the other hand," Richard said, glancing at his watch, "we have an excellent prospect of finding them there. I was not supposed to come home until to-morrow night. I found Mrs. Carter's message at five, twenty-four hours earlier than she expected me to. Williams may be mistaken, of course," he finished, with a glance at the detective.

"Not likely!" said Williams, with a modest shrug.

"However, even if he is right," Richard resumed, "the chances are that they are still there, and if they are, I will bring--my wife back with me to-night. Meanwhile, I leave the house in your care, Miss Field. I needn't tell you that my mother and Nina must be kept absolutely ignorant of what we suspect. You'll know what to tell them, in case I should be longer away. If our calculations are wrong, there's no telling where I may follow Mrs. Carter. I leave this end of things to you!"

The trust he placed in her, and something tired and patient in his tone, brought the tears to Harriet's eyes.

"I'm sorrier than I can say," she said, huskily.

"I know you are! It's--" Richard passed his hand over his forehead--"it's utter madness, of course. But, please God, we can keep it all hushed up. She has Germaine with her; Hansen I can trust. We're off now, Miss Field. I'll keep you informed if I can."

Harriet went back to the drawing room with her heart big with pride. He had mentioned Hansen and Germaine, but he KNEW that he could trust her! The event was sensational enough, was horrifying enough. But back of the excitement lay the joy of being needed and being trusted.

"Mr. Carter going away again?" said Madame Carter.

"Mr. Williams came up from the city to consult him about something," Harriet explained, smoothly. "They may have to go back."

"To-night!" ejaculated the old lady. And immediately she added, suspiciously, "What'd he want Hansen for?"

"Doctor and Mrs. Houghton," Bottomley announced, in his soothing undertone. Harriet could have embraced the uninteresting elderly couple who entered smilingly. They beamed that it was so hot--they were going up to the club; couldn't the Carters join them?

"Mrs. Carter went to visit a friend in Great Barrington," Madame Carter explained, "and my son has one of his clerks here, and may have to return to the office to-night. Too bad!"

"But how about another lesson in bridge, Doctor Houghton?" Harriet ventured. The old wife was instantly enthusiastic.

"Yes, now, Doctor! This is a splendid chance, for I know Madame Carter isn't too good a player to be patient."

"I don't want to bore this pretty girl to death!" protested the old man, gallantly. But Harriet had already signalled the attentive Bottomley, and when Richard Carter came to say good-night a few minutes later they were on the terrace, and hilarious over the beginner's mistakes. Even Madame Carter enjoyed this; she was a poor player, but she shone beside the Houghtons, and Harriet took care to consult her respectfully, and agree seriously as to bids and leads.

"Good-night, Mother!" said Richard, touching with his lips the cool old forehead, next to the white hair. "Wish I could play with you fellers and girls!"

"You!" said old Mrs. Houghton, archly. "You'd scare us to death!"

Richard went smiling to the car, hearing Harriet murmur as he went: "I think he has a two heart bid, don't you Madame Carter? You bid two hearts, Doctor ..."

CHAPTER IX

That Isabelle's madness would run its full gamut did not occur to Harriet until the next day. Then, as the serene hours moved by, and there was no word and no sign from Richard, the possibilities began to suggest themselves. It seemed to her incredible that any woman would risk all that Isabelle had, for the sake of a fiery boy's first love, and yet, on the other hand, there was the memory of Isabelle's suffering two nights ago, and here were the amazing facts to prove it.

The girl went about in a dream, sometimes imagining the meeting of husband and wife, sometimes trying to fancy Isabelle with her lover. As was inevitable, the older woman seemed to lose something charming and intangible in this confession of definite weakness. To be adored by any man merely adds to her glory, but the instant she concedes him an inch, the Beauty throws down her halo, the whole affair becomes mundane and vulnerable. Harriet might have envied Isabelle once, now she saw her frail, forty, her woman's pride weakened by admitted passion, and was sorry for her. She had had all men at her feet, now she must feel herself fortunate if she could hold one.

And with Isabelle's shame came a wholesome sting of shame to Isabelle's companion. Harriet had seen nothing harmful in this affair a few days ago; it was the way of this world of theirs. But she felt within her now the awakening of something clean and stern; she found in her mind odd phrases and terms--"a married woman's duty," "her sense of honour," "owing it to her husband and children."

It was for few women to enjoy the popularity that Isabelle had known. But any woman might run away with a rich admirer. Harriet's admiration for the cleverness with which Isabelle conducted this pretty playing with fire disappeared, and in its place came the sharp conviction that old-fashioned women like Linda had some justification, after all; it was "dangerous," it did "lead to sin," it could indeed "happen once too often."

Harriet felt her own lapsing morality regaining its standard. Just now, when Nina most needed her mother, when Richard was struggling with difficult business conditions, when Ward was engaged--

She interrupted her thoughts here, and tried to make herself feel like a woman engaged to be married. Somehow the fact persisted in baffling her. There was an unreality about it that prevented her from tasting the full sweet. Engaged--to a rich man, and a rich man's son. Well, perhaps when Ward came back, it would seem more believable.

But Ward might come back to a changed home. Harriet fancied a quiet wedding, herself afterward as the true head of the disorganized family. She would be Nina's natural chaperon, then, her father-in-law's--for Richard would be that!--natural confidante. The prospect, and every hour of this warm and silent day seemed to make it more definite, brought the wild-rose colour to her face, and made her heart beat faster. It was certainly a life full and gratifying beyond her dreaming, and it was almost settled now! If Ward did not figure very prominently in this bright dream, she told herself that Ward should have no cause for grievance. He should always be first in everything; but if his wife enjoyed her position, her connections, her place in the family, surely there was no harm in that! There was but one stumbling block: Royal Blondin. Her heart stopped at him.

She had been standing at one of the hall windows, a window deep set in the brick wall, and commanding through elms and beeches the path to the tennis court. Down this path Nina and Francesca Jay had recently disappeared, with their rackets, for some practice. The sun was high, and the sky cloudless; under the trees there was a softly mottled pattern of light and shade. Outside the window the hound was lying, his nose on his paws, his eyes shut. Harriet remembered walking in such a summer wood, years and years ago, a little girl with yellow braids, holding tight to her mother's hand. They had sat down on the ground, and her mother and father had talked, and the little girl had lain on her back for what seemed hours, looking at the sky.

There seemed to be no time for idle walks and dreaming in the woods nowadays. Harriet had been four years at Crownlands, and had looked out at this wood a thousand times, but she had never lost herself in it, or lain staring up through branches there. She was always too busy: the business of eating, and of amusing the others, and of keeping the machinery moving, had always absorbed her. Personalities, microscopic buzzing of midges, had blotted out the beautiful arches and aisles; and if ever Harriet walked through the wood now, she was with chattering women; she was wondering if this one, or that one, or the other one, was hurt, or neglected, or piqued, was paired with the wrong person, or had really intended the meaning that might be read into a look or tone.

--Hands pressed her eyes tight, and she came back to the present moment with a start. Ward Carter was behind her. He laughed at her confusion, and they sat down on the window seat together. Yes, he was going back to the Bellamys', and so was Blondin, but they had both come in just for lunch and the drive. They had driven a hundred and twenty miles that morning, what? And they were going to drive back that afternoon, what-what? And how about eats, old dear?

Instantly he brought reassurance to her. Ward was such a dear! Of course she loved him.

"But you weren't a very good boy last night!" she said. Their hands were locked; but she had shaken a negative when he would have kissed her. Bottomley was everywhere at once.

"Rotten!" he confessed, easily. "I played poker, too. No man ought to do that when he's edged. Sorry--sorry--sorry. Bad, bad, bad little Edward! I lost two hundred to Bates, a curse upon him. But that was nothing; once, there, I was over twelve hundred in. Listen. When we're married it's all off. No smoking, drinking, gambling, wine, women, or song, what?"

"You may not know it, but you never spoke a truer word!" the girl said. His shout of laughter was pleasant to hear.

"Listen. Does the Mater know it? About us, I mean?"

"Oh, Ward--nobody knows it! Hush!" His mention of his mother brought back realization with a rush, and she added uncomfortably, "She's at Great Barrington."

"Oh, darn! I wanted to see her! She wrote me, and told me she loved me, and that she didn't think she had been a very good mother to me!" He laughed, youthfully, with a bewildered widening of his eyes. "I thought she was sick. Well, maybe we can stop there going back."

"Where did you leave Mr. Blondin?"

"He beat it down to the tennis court. Say, listen, is there a chance that he's stuck on Nina? It looks to me like what the watch comes in!"

Harriet glanced at her wrist before she answered him. Her heart was sick within her. Close upon her radiant dream had come this shadow, far more a shadow now, when her responsibility had infinitely increased, and when she had had proof of the love and respect in which they held her here.

"I don't think so!" she said, briefly. "I'll find Bottomley, and have lunch put ahead."

"You don't like him!" Ward said, watching her closely.

"I don't like him for Nina!" she amended.

The boy followed her while she gave her order. Then they went out into the blazing day together.

"Nina isn't going to have more than a scalp a day," said her brother, fraternally.

"Nina has a fortune!" the girl remarked, drily, opening her wide white parasol.

But Ward was rapidly squandering an equal amount, and it was not impressive to him.

"Lord, he could marry a girl with ten times that! Look here, you don't think a man like Blondin would consider that!" he protested.

"I would rather see Nina dead and buried!" The words burst from Harriet against her will, against her promise to Royal. There was no help for it, her essential honesty would have its way. "I make a splendid conspirator!" she said to herself, in grim self-contempt.

"Talk to him!" Ward, fortunately, was not inclined to take her too seriously. "You'll like him! Gosh, he certainly has a good effect on me," added the youth, modestly. "He doesn't drink, and he talks to me--you ought to hear him!--about character being fate, and all that! Say, listen, before we get out of the woods--?"

His sudden sense of her nearness and beauty belied the careless words. Harriet found his arms tight about her, her face tipped up to the young, handsome face that was stirred now with trembling excitement. The quick movement of his breast she could feel against her own, and the passion of his kisses almost frightened her; she was held, bound, half-lifted off her feet.

"Ward!" she gasped, freed at last, and with one hand to her disordered hair, while the other held him at arm's-length. "Dear! PLEASE!"

It was no use. Soul and senses were enveloped again, and close to her ear she heard his whisper: "I'm mad about you! Do you know that! I'm mad about you!"

"I think you are!" she stammered, breathless and laughing. "You mustn't do that! You mustn't do that! Why, we might be seen!"

Breathless, too, he flung back his hair, and stooped to pick up her parasol.

"Do you think I care!" he panted, indifferently. "I wouldn't care if the whole world saw!"

"Sh--sh!" By the magic only known to youth and womanhood Harriet had gathered herself into trimness and calm again. She took her parasol composedly. Her eyes told him the whole story. Nina and Royal Blondin were two hundred feet away, coming up from the tennis court.

The four met cheerfully; apparently all at ease. Nina was stammering and blushing a trifle more than usual, but Royal's presence would account for that. Ward burst into a stream of idiotic conversation; Harriet found herself sauntering ahead of the young Carters, discussing Sheringham fans with the dilletant.

"You fool--fool--fool!" she said to herself. What had they seen? What new twist to the situation would Nina's suspicions afford? Richard Carter trusted her; this was no time to tell him that she loved his son. Did she love Ward?--or with his keen and kindly eyes would Ward's father see exactly what she saw in the marriage? Caught kissing in the woods--like Rosa or Germaine; it was unthinkable! She, with her hard-won prestige of dignity and reserve, exposed to Nina's laughing insinuations, or, worse, Nina's prim disapproval. How she had weakened her position here! How she had risked--her heart contracted with pain--severing of her association with Crownlands.

Luncheon, under its veneer of gaiety and foolishness, offered fresh terrors. For old Madame Carter had come down, and it occurred to Harriet that if Nina had seen anything in the wood, she might naturally interest her grandmother with an account of it. Nina rarely had so interesting a topic of conversation. The old lady would go instantly to her son. And Richard-- Harriet could imagine him, tired, harassed, heartsick over the recent inexplicable weakness of his wife, having to face another woman's treachery, having to listen to the demure announcement of the little secretary's engagement to his son.

Perhaps not treachery, exactly, thought Harriet, as the birds, and the asparagus, and the crisp little rolls went the rounds. She ate, hardly knowing what she tasted, and spoke with only a partial consciousness of what she said. No, not treachery exactly, especially if she went to Richard first with the news.

But break in upon his painful speculations with the blithe announcement? What must he think of such utter lack of consideration? He was experiencing the most overwhelming shock of all his life now; he must shortly be exposed to all the whirl of scandal: the silenced gossip, the averted eyes of his world, the weeklies with their muddy insinuations, the staring fact headlined above his breakfast bacon. This was her time to efface herself and the household, to help him to lift the load.

"I'm afraid I wasn't listening, Mr. Blondin?"

"Miss Nina and I want to know what day we may have our party?" Royal repeated.

"The studio party?"

"The roof-garden party. We're going to have it from half-past six to half-past seven only, because then it won't be too hot. We shall only ask the people we like! Gira Diable will come and dance for us, and Tilly will read something--"

"That's Unger Tillotson, the actor!" Nina interpolated, ecstatically.

"We're not sure that we'll let Francesca and Amy come," Blondin pursued. "Maybe we won't let them know anything about it! And everybody has to wear costumes, so that the picture won't be spoiled."

"He doesn't like Amy and Francesca," Nina confessed, with a guilty little laugh.

"Not at all. I like them very much." Blondin's languid, rich voice corrected her. Nina shrank sensitively. "I think they're very charming little schoolgirls. But I don't want them for my friends!"

At this Nina blossomed like the rose. Emotion choked her, and she looked down at her plate with a fluttering laugh. This was irrefutable; before Miss Harriet and Ward and Granny, too.

"That's what I meant!" she murmured, thickly.

"Why not have it at night, with lanterns?" Harriet said, quite involuntarily. And again a pang of self-contempt swept over her. It was hateful, it was incredible, but she was playing his game as calmly as if doubts and reluctance had never entered her heart.

"People won't go to the city, summer evenings," Royal explained, "but a great number are there in the afternoons. And then twilight, over the city, and the bridges lighting up--I assure you it's like fairyland!"

"I wonder if I am to be invited to this party?" said Madame Carter, royally. She had been watching this exchange of pleasantries with approval.

"You? You're the queen of the whole affair!" Royal assured her. "You don't have to costume unless you feel like it."

"Oh, Granny'll have the nicest there!" Nina predicted, gaily. Her grandmother bridled complacently, although shaking a magnificent head. Harriet knew that she would spend as much time upon her dress as the youngest and most beautiful woman who attended.

"Come," said Madame Carter, brightly, "you didn't think I was going to let you carry out this little plan without a chaperon!"

If there was a self-conscious second after this remark it was no more than a second. Harriet's quick colour rose, but before Nina's nervous little laugh had died away Blondin said easily:

"Ah, we'll surround the Little Duchess with chaperons; I'm not going to be a party to her losing her heart anywhere around MY diggings!"

"From what I said at luncheon, I hope you didn't imagine that I thought there was anything--well, in questionable taste, in your coming to Nina's party!" said Madame Carter to Harriet an hour later, when the men had started on their long run back to camp, and she was about to go upstairs for her daily siesta.

"Not at all; I understood perfectly!" Harriet assumed an air of abstraction, of pleasant unconcern. Her red lips were firm, and closed firmly after the brief answer. The smoky blue eyes regarded Madame Carter with innocent expectancy. The girl was amazingly handsome, thought the old lady reluctantly.

"Of course, if Mrs. Carter can spare you, and considers it suitable, you will be there!" said Madame Carter, amiably, mounting the first stair.

"Surely!" Harriet said, with a murderous impulse. She watched the erect, splendid old figure ascending. What was there about this old lady that could put her, and indeed almost any one else who chanced to be marked by her dislike, into a helpless fury of anger? "If I were once safely married to Ward," the girl said to herself, "if--"

It was a tremendous "if," of course. There were a great many things now that might turn the scales one way or another. Richard's attitude was supremely important. He might feel that his son was taking a wise, a desirable step. He might feel that to have the boy settled was to lift just one care from the many that burdened his shoulders. On the other hand, was it more probable that this untimely announcement, with its accompanying merry-making and rejoicing, would utterly exasperate and antagonize him? Harriet fancied him asking, with weary politeness, just what their plans were? Did Ward propose to finish college? Had he formed any idea of the means by which he should earn his living? He had his uncle's legacy, of course, the larger part of it. Did the young people propose to begin with that?

Harriet perfectly understood Richard's attitude to the average son of the average wealthy family. She had heard his caustic comments upon them often enough. He had earned his own education; he showed for Isabelle's spoiling of her son the patience of helplessness. To make a man of Ward, in his father's estimation, would have meant a readjustment of their entire scheme of living and thinking. It was simpler, pleasanter, to sacrifice Ward to the general comfort, especially as he, Richard, was very busy, and as there was always a possibility that the women were right, and would make a man of him anyway. Harriet's keen eyes saw, if Isabelle's did not, that Ward had been steadily gaining in his father's good graces for the last year or two. His cheerful, casual manner masked no weakness, every muscle in the young, big body was hard from tennis and baseball. If there were sins of self-indulgence, natural to youth and money and charm, Ward never brought them home with him. Lately he had begun to talk of getting out of college at Christmas time, and "getting started." His father watched him, Harriet saw, almost wistfully. Was the lad really becoming a man, in a world of men?

"The probability is that he will favour our engagement," Harriet reflected. But this was no time to risk the chance of crossing him. She must wait. She must choose the lesser risk of Nina making mischief with old Madame Carter; the contingency was there, but it was a remote contingency.

CHAPTER X

At four o'clock Richard came home, and the instant Harriet saw his face she realized, with a shock even sharper than the original moment of incredulity, that he had had no success in his search. He was alone.

She was standing in one of the doorways of the lower hall when he crossed it, but he did not see her. His face was drawn and gray, he looked hot and rumpled and utterly weary; more, he who had always been the pink of well-groomed perfection looked old. He asked Bottomley briefly if Madame Carter was in her room, and, being informed that she was, went hastily upstairs.

Harriet could only imagine, later, that he had gone in to see his mother before brushing and changing, or perhaps to avoid Nina, who with Amy catapulted down the stairway a few seconds after he went up. At all events, it was to the old lady's beautiful sitting room that Harriet was summoned a few minutes later. She knew at once that he had told his mother all he knew and feared.

Madame Carter was shockingly agitated. She had a deep sense of the dramatic, but she was not entirely acting now. Her face was pale under its rouge, and the painful tears of age stood in her eyes. She was sitting erect in a chair beside the divan where Richard sat; he did not look up as Harriet came in, but continued to stroke his mother's hand.

"Miss Field!" said Madame Carter, "we have just had a most terrible-- a most unexpected--blow!"

Harriet simulated expectancy.

"There is every reason to believe," pursued Madame Carter, majestically, "that my unfortunate daughter-in-law, Mr. Carter's wife, Isabelle, has yielded to the passion of her lover! No, let me talk, Richard," she interrupted herself, as the man raised haggard eyes to watch her impersonally, "far better to face the facts, my dear! My son tells me, Miss Field the--the well-nigh incredible statement that--forgetting the honour of womanhood, and the tender claims of maternity--"

"Miss Field," Richard did not have the manner of interruption, but his quiet voice dominated the other voice none-the-less. Madame Carter fell silent, and watched him with mournful pride. "Miss Field," he said, "we want your help. The facts are these: Williams had all the roads watched; they did not go by motor. Mrs. Carter reached New London at five o'clock yesterday; Pope's boat, the Geisha, pulled out at half-past six. From what Williams' men picked up, at the dock, Pope did not expect her, was to have sailed this morning. She arrived, and evidently he thought it wise to hurry their start. The pier had a dozen boxes for the Geisha on it, groceries and what not, that they left behind! They will probably skirt the coast for a few days, and put in somewhere for supplies. But that"--he passed his hand wearily across his forehead--"that doesn't concern us now. We got there at ten last night--hours too late, of course." His voice fell, he mused, with a knitted brow. "Well!" he said, suddenly recalling himself. "Now, Miss Field, I want you to get hold of Ward. I want the boy home at once! He must know. But there is of course a chance that Mrs. Carter is--is planning to return. There may be a woman friend with her--it's not probable, but it's possible. I don't want any one in the house, or out of it, to suspect, and if you think it is possible, I should like Nina protected!"

"I understand," Harriet said, quietly, in the silence.

"You will remember, Richard," Madame Carter said, in the accents of Lady Macbeth, "that this is exactly what I always expected! I told you so, twenty years ago. You brought it on yourself, my dear. A Morrison--who ever heard of the Morrisons?--their mother--Mrs. Banks tells me--was a school teacher! I have always felt--!"

Harriet heard the man's patient murmur as she slipped away. She crossed the hall, and for the first time in four years entered Isabelle's suite unannounced. It was in exquisite order; streams of late afternoon light were falling on the gay walls and the bright chintzes. The novels Isabelle had been skimming, the gold service of her dressing table, the great four-poster with its deeps of transparent white embroideries over white, all spoke of the beautiful woman who had spent so many hours here. On the dressing table, with its splendid length doubled in the mirror, was the great fan that her hand had idly wielded, only a few days ago, in an hour of domestic felicity and happiness. And the inanimate plumes, that Harriet picked up and idly unfurled, had played their little part in the drama that had ended that bright scene once and for all.

What to tell Nina?--Harriet wondered, going downstairs. But Nina proved pleasantly indifferent to the maternal absence when she and Amy came up from the tennis court for tea. To the guest or two who came calling Harriet, installed quite naturally now behind the cups and saucers, explained that Mrs. Carter was visiting with friends--having a beautiful time, too, apparently. To an accidentally direct remark from Amy she answered that she believed they were taking a motor trip just at the moment, but she would forward a note, if Amy liked. Madame Carter did not come out for tea; they were very quiet on the terrace. But Richard was there, and Amy and Nina were developing their youthful conversational arts upon him, when a maid came to stand respectfully beside Harriet. "If you please, Miss Field, Mr. Bottomley would like to know if you are to have your dinner downstairs to-night, please," said Pauline, incidentally feeling as if she was in a dream of bliss. Her last position had been in a well-to-do stationer's family in Newark, and consesequently she might have entered into the feelings of Miss Field far more intelligently than either imagined.

Harriet hesitated, glanced at Richard, wondering if he had heard. More rested on this decision than there was any estimating. She dared not decide.

"Miss Field will dine downstairs," Richard said, without glancing in their direction. And when the maid had gone he said with pleasant authority, "I wish you and Nina would do that regularly, Miss Field, when you have no other plan."

"Thank you," Harriet said, with her heart singing.

Perhaps Nina suspected that something about his high-handed domestic readjusting was unusual. She looked from her father to Harriet, and after a moment's silence asked abruptly:

"When is Mother coming back?"

"I don't know!" her father answered, quickly.

"Say, listen, are we going to dress?" asked Amy. Nina, instantly diverted, suggested that they go in. Nina's awkward bigness and Amy's mousy neutral tones were as well displayed in one garment as another, but both girls debated over pinks and blues, crepes and mulls, every evening, as if the world was watching them alone. Harriet lingered for only a word.

"Mr. Carter, it occurred to me that old Mrs. Singleton is going to California, in her own car, to-morrow. Would it be possible to let Nina and Amy and the household generally think--"

"Yes?" he encouraged her as she paused dubiously. He had risen to his feet, and fixed his tired eyes on her face.

"I was wondering if we might confide in Mrs. Singleton--she was always very fond of Mrs. Carter--and give out the impression that Mrs. Carter had suddenly decided to make the trip with her."

"That's an idea," Richard said, thoughtfully. "I could see Mrs. Singleton to-night--and--and talk it over."

"It might serve for only a few days," Harriet submitted.

"Yes, I see," he agreed, slowly.

"Well, I can give Nina a hint now!" Harriet said, going. The late golden sunshine struck her bright hair to an aureole, as she went up the brick steps and disappeared.

But it was too late for any soothing deception of Nina. A scene was in full progress in Nina's bedroom, and Harriet's eye had only to go from the prone form on the bed to the crushed newspaper that had drifted to the floor, to know that the secret was out. Isabelle's face, radiant and happy, looked out from the page. It was flanked by two smaller pictures, Richard's and Anthony Pope's. Harriet could see the big letters: "Young Millionaire--Wife of Richard Carter." The deluge was upon them.

"Oh--it's a lie--it's a lie! My beautiful little mother!" Nina was sobbing. "Oh, no, it's not true! It's a lie! Oh, how shall I ever hold up my head again--to be disgraced--now just when I'm so young--and ha-h-happy!"

"Nina, my child, control yourself!" Harriet, ignoring the staring and pale-faced Amy, sat down on the edge of the bed, and shook the girl slightly. "You mustn't give way! Come now, my dear, you must face this like a woman. Think how your father and Ward will look to you--"

Acting, all of it, said Harriet in her soul. But despite the youthful appetite for heroics, there were real tears in Nina's eyes, as there had been in her grandmother's a few hours ago.

"Yes, that's true!" she said, wiping a swollen face on the handkerchief Harriet supplied. "But oh--I don't believe it, and my father will sue them for libel, you see if he doesn't! My mother's the purest and sweetest and best woman ALIVE--and I'll KILL any one who says any different!"

"Oo--oo, to see it in the paper there, right on the bed," said Amy, in her reedy, colourless little voice, as Nina stopped suddenly. "Oo--oo, I thought Nina would die!" Nina began to cry again, but more quietly. "I guess I had better go--" Amy finished, plaintively.

"Oh, no!" said Nina in a choked voice, as she clung to her friend. "No, darling! you stay with me. Oh, I must go see my father, and my poor, poor grandmother! Oh, Amy, perhaps you HAD better go, for my family will need me to-night. My mother--!" said Nina, crying again.

She and Amy parted solemnly, with many kisses.

"It's a thing that might happen to me, or to any girl," said Amy, gravely. Harriet had an upsetting vision of stout, high-busted Mrs. Hawkes, panting as she discussed the details of the Red Cross drive, but she was very sympathetic with the young girls, and even agreed with Nina, when Amy was gone, that it would be much more sensible to take her bath, and put on her white organdie, and then go find her father.

They dined almost silently, and were about to disperse quietly for the night, after an hour of half-hearted conversation in the drawing room, obviously endured by Richard simply for his mother's sake, when Ward burst in. He had travelled almost four hundred miles by motor that day, his face was streaked with dirt and oil, and ghastly with fatigue. He went straight to his father.

"Say, what's all this!" he said, in a voice hardly recognizable. Harriet saw that he had been drinking. "I got your wire, and we started. I thought the Mater was sick, perhaps. My God--THAT worried me!" he broke off bitterly. "Blondin came with me; we stopped on the road for dinner, and the man had a paper there. Is that what you wanted me for--I don't believe it! It's a dirty lie, and the bounder that put that in the paper--"

"I'm glad you came home, my boy," Richard said. "I've been waiting for you--"

Harriet heard no more; she slipped from the room. There were genuine tears in her own eyes now; for the boy had flung himself face downward against a great chair, and was crying. All the household knew it; Harriet could read it in Bottomley's carefully usual manner and quiet speech. In the little music room across the hall Royal Blondin was waiting.

"This is a terrible thing!" he said, seriously.

"Oh, frightful!" Harriet agreed. A rather flat silence ensued. She seemed to have nothing to say to Royal now.

But she was not surprised when a moment later Nina came softly in, the picture of girlish distress, with her wet eyes and fresh white gown.

"I thought it best to leave Ward with Granny and Father," Nina said, in vague explanation, going straight to Blondin, who rose, dusty and weary, but with a solicitous manner that was infinitely soothing.

"I hoped you wouldn't mind just seeing me," he said in a low tone. "I'm not quite family, and yet I felt myself nearer than all the neighbours and friends, eh?"

"I shan't see any one for ages," Nina murmured, plaintively, "but you--you're different."

"And shall we talk about her sometimes?" Royal pursued, still close to her, and holding both her hands. "As she was, beautiful and sweet and good. For who are you and I, Little Girl, to judge what passion--what love will do with human hearts?"

"Yes, I know!" Nina, who never could keep pace with him, said mournfully.

Harriet could hear the undertones, and imagine what they said. She felt extremely uneasy. If this unforeseen calamity had lifted her suddenly in the family estimation, it would appear to be drawing Royal Blondin closer as well.

His manner, she had grudgingly to admit, was perfection. When Richard and Ward joined them a few moments later, he expressed himself with manly brevity to the older man. He realized, said Blondin simply, that he was absolutely de trop; he had merely imagined, as "the lad" had imagined, that the sudden summons from camp meant illness or ordinary emergency, or he would not have intruded at this time. He would not express a sympathy that must sound extremely airy to the stricken family. And now, if they would lend him Hansen, he would go over to the club---
-

"Nonsense!" Ward said. "You're all dirty and tired and hungry, and so am I. We'll clean up, and then we'll have something to eat first! Miss Harriet'll look out for us."

"And I'd like to see you for a moment in the library, Miss Field," Richard said, rather wearily. He had been obviously displeased at seeing the stranger, but Blondin's manner would have won a harder heart than his. "I want something sent to the papers," Richard explained, in an undertone.

Ah--they all wanted her, and needed her! How quick, and how efficient, and how self-effacing Harriet was, as she went about the business of making them all comfortable! She and Nina talked with the young men while they demolished the cold roast and drank cup after cup of coffee. Then Blondin selected several books, and went upstairs, and Harriet and Nina disappeared in their own rooms; but Ward came downstairs again, and he and his father settled in the library for a talk.

They talked deep into the night, Harriet knew, for she herself was sleepless, and she could see from the upper balcony that a stream of golden light was pouring across the brilliant flowers beneath the library windows.

She had wrapped herself in a warm robe, over her thin nightgown, and thrust her feet into fur-lined slippers, and after Nina was fathoms deep in youthful slumber Harriet crept out to the balcony, and sat thinking, thinking, thinking. She reviewed the incredible events of the past few days, and the actors drifted before her vision fitfully: Isabelle, white-bosomed and beautiful, in her prime; Tony Pope, passionate and wretched; Royal, low-voiced, dreamy, poetic, with his eloquent black eyes; Nina, newly awakened; Ward, weak, boyish, ardent; Madame Carter full of theatrical dignity and well-rounded phrases, and lastly--simple, strong, anxious to protect them all, even from their own follies--Richard.

"Not one word of blame, not one ugly insinuation," she mused, "yet she has shamed him, and he is so honourable; and she has made him conspicuous, when he is so modest!"

She thought of Isabelle, fresh from Germaine's careful hands, lying in her exquisite white against the cushions of a deck chair, smiling, in the rosy flattering light under the green awning, at the infatuated man beside her. Isabelle was a splendid sailor, and loved the sea. They would land at some dreamlike Italian city, rising in tiers of pink and cream and blue beside the sapphire Mediterranean, and Isabelle would unfurl her white parasol, and walk beside him through the warmth and beauty--

"Ugh!" said Harriet, with a healthy uprush of utter disgust. These few months would not be cloudless for Isabelle, by any means. And after them, what? Was it conceivable that those fatal sixteen years would fail to identify Tony and Isabelle wherever they went, even if the press was not eagerly assisting them? Supposing that Isabelle never thought of Crownlands, of her handsome son and her young daughter, of the man whose patience and cleverness had lifted her to all this luxury from an apartment in a small town, would no memory of the place she had held, and the friendships she had commanded, haunt her? Truly there was always society for the Isabelles, but to Harriet's clean sense it seemed but the society of a jail.

"I wouldn't change places with her!" Harriet decided, in the soft silence and darkness of the summer night.

From Isabelle's problem her thoughts went to her own, to Royal Blondin. She was wakeful and restless to-night simply because she could not decide just how much she need fear him. Firstly, was there any reason for antagonizing him, and secondly, would he hurt her if she did? For Royal could not punish her without punishing himself, and could not banish her from Crownlands if he ever hoped to show his own face there again.

Nina, reaching her room that night, had flung her arms about Harriet's neck.

"Oh, I'm so happy! Oh, Miss Harriet, were you ever in love?" she had demanded, with a girl's wild, exultant laugh.

This was moving very fast indeed. Harriet had managed a sympathetic yet warning smile.

"I think I have been. But, my dearest girl, you'll be in and out a dozen times before the real thing comes along!"

Nina had smiled inscrutably at this, and slightly diverted the conversation.

"Don't you think it was awfully decent of Mr. Blondin to want to go off to the club to-night? Oh, I thought he looked perfectly stunning when he looked at Father that way! He told me to telephone the club to-morrow if I felt like just a quiet walk. Of course I shan't see any one for weeks, after this. But he said some day when I'm in town with Granny he didn't see why we couldn't go over and have a cup of tea with him, even if we postponed the regular tea. Do you? He's different from any one I ever knew. He says I am different from any girl he ever knew. Do you think I am? I said I thought I was just like the others, except that I like to read poetry and have my own ideas about things, and that I couldn't flirt, or wouldn't if I could, and that the average boy just bored me. I said that those things were sacred to me--"

Sacred to her! Long after the chattering voice was still, Harriet, out on the balcony, remembered the phrase and winced. There would be small sacredness in the hour that gave Nina to Royal Blondin. And yet, if in his cleverness he won her first tenacious affection, it would be a difficult thing to prevent. Isabella, her natural protector, was gone; Richard saw nothing; the old lady was on the lovers' side, and Ward also had been captivated by Blondin. It was only Harriet, only Harriet, who saw and who understood.

Was he so bad? She tried to ask herself the question honestly, and an honest shudder answered it before it was fairly framed. Nearly twenty years Nina's senior, with an interest that could not, he confessed, have existed except for the girl's fortune, that was arraignment enough. But there was more. Harriet knew the smooth coldness, the contemptuous superiority that within a year or two would blast the youth and self-confidence of a dozen Ninas; she knew what his moral code was, a code that made desire and opportunity the only law, and that honoured passion as the crowning emotion of life. She tried to picture Nina's marriage, their early days together, the breakfast table, where the crude little girl blundered and floundered in conversation, her helpless devotion, that would annoy and exasperate him. She saw Nina's near-sighted eyes welling with hurt tears; Nina's check book eagerly surrendered to win from her lord a few delicious hours of the old flattery, the old attention. Harriet fancied Nina, poor, plain, obtuse little Nina, home again: "But you don't know how hard it is, Father. He is never there any more--he hardly ever speaks to me!"

"It would take a clever woman to hold him," Harriet thought, "and it wouldn't be worth a clever woman's while."

Nina-Ward-Royal-Richard. The wearying procession began again. Royal might treat her with honesty and honour. He was not small in everything, and she had never done him harm. But--there might come the terrible moment when she had to face Richard with the confession. Yes, she had known him before. Yes, they had entered into a tacit compact. Yes, she had kept from Nina's father a secret that, while it might be unimportant, certainly should have been told him.

Impossible to think the thing to any conclusion! Too many possibilities might alter the entire situation. If she were married safely to Ward, for example--? But then she dared not marry Ward until Royal's attitude was finally defined. For if her position were dangerous now, what would it be if she had committed herself irrevocably to deception by marriage? Ward's young, crude intolerance sitting in judgment upon his wife!--Harriet shivered.

Suddenly she fell upon her knees, and dropped her bright head against the wide balustrade. She wanted to be a dignified, honourable, helpful woman; not selfish, like Nina; not an intriguer, like Isabelle; not proud, like Madame Carter. Something was changing in her heart and soul; she did not feel angry and bitter any more. With Royal's reappearance had come the realization that the old, sad time was no longer a living wound in her life, it was merely a memory, young, and mistaken, and to be forgotten. For years she had felt that it had maimed her; now it seemed only infinitely pitiable. She could go on, to honour and happiness, despite it. And how she longed to go on, with no further handicap! If he would go away again, and leave her mistress of the field. She only wanted her chance. She wanted to win her way, here in this fascinating world; she wanted to be beloved and successful; above all she wanted to be GOOD!

For a long time Harriet had not prayed. But now, in a few words, and quite without premeditation, there burst from her the most sincere prayer of her life. She looked up at the stars.

"God!" she said, softly, aloud, "help me! Make me do what is right, however hard it is. Father, don't let me make another mistake!"

CHAPTER XI

Sudden peace and confidence flooded her spirit. She sat on, dreaming and planning, but with no more mental distress. With the prayer she had gained, in some subtle fashion, a new self-respect. She would not let him frighten her again; after all, while she commanded her own soul, Royal Blondin could not hurt her.

"And he shall not marry Nina, either!" Harriet decided, going in, stiff and cold, but full of resolution. She looked at a clock, it was almost four. Three hours' sleep was not to be despised, but Harriet was in no mood for it. Instead she took a bath, and just as the dawn was beginning to flood the world with mysterious half-lights and long wet shadows, she crept out into the dew-drenched garden, and with a triumphant sense of being alone, went into the wood. Early walks were one of her delights. She was rarely alone otherwise; her position afforded her almost every other luxury, but not often this one. Nina's plans were usually cut to fit Harriet's; even the shortest errand, or least interesting trip into town was pleasanter to Nina than her own society.

It was exquisite in the wood. The light flashed on wet leaves, the birds were awaking. A little steamer went up the satiny, dreaming surface of the river, and when Harriet walked through the village, heartening whiffs of boiling coffee and wood smoke came from the labourers' cottages. She was young; she could have danced with exultation in the hour and mood. It was almost seven o'clock when she came back, glowing, beginning to feel warm and headachy, beginning to realize that the July day would be hot, beginning to be conscious of the eight-mile tramp. In the garden at Crownlands she met Royal, leaving the house.

He studied her approvingly.

"Harriet, do you know you are extraordinarily easy to look upon? What gets you up so early?"

"I've been walking," she said, briefly and unresponsively. His social pleasantries instantly antagonized her, and he saw it.

"Well, I thought perhaps I had better get out. I'm at the club for a day or two. I believe Miss Hawkes, Rosa, the eldest sister, wants me to get up a reading, the great Indian Epic Poems, something along that line. It's for the Red Cross, of course." He yawned, and smiled at the early summer sky. "Ward tells me," he added, giving the girl a sharp glance, "that you and he--eh?"

Harriet flushed.

"I'm sorry he told you!"

"Oh, my dear child!" Blondin made a deprecatory motion of his hands. "Of course, I think you're very wise," he added.

This smote upon her new-born self-respect, and all the glory departed from the day. She had taken off her loose white coat, and pushed back the hat that pressed upon her thick, shining hair. It clung in damp ringlets to the soft duskiness of forehead and temples, her cheeks glowed rosily under their warm olive, and her clouded smoke-blue eyes were averted; he could see only the thick, upcurling black lashes that fringed them so darkly. The man saw her breast rise and fall with some quick emotion as he half-smilingly watched her.

"The lad gets a beautiful and wise and very discreet wife," he was beginning, but Harriet silenced him angrily.

"We need not indulge in compliments, Roy! If I marry Ward--"

"If--? I supposed it definite!"

"Well, when I marry him, then, it will be because I truly---" She paused, halted at the great word. "Because I truly do admire and care for him," she substituted, somewhat lamely.

"It isn't quite a pillar of smoke by day, and of fire by night?" he suggested, quietly. Harriet saw the words written, in the handwriting of a girl of seventeen, and had a moment of vertigo. She attempted no answer. "In other words, you would hardly consider him if he had his own way to make, if he had a salary of two hundred a month, like Fred Davenport!" Royal added. "There's a certain magic about a background of motorcars and Sherry's, and the opera Monday nights, and the bank account, isn't there?"

Silence. But it was only for a moment. Then Harriet raised her eyes.

"He loves me," she reminded the man, quietly. "I don't know what a boy's love is worth; he's only twenty-two, after all. But he does love me! But believe me, Royal, you couldn't hurt me--as you ARE hurting me!-if there was no truth in what you say. Ward has had three years at college--I've not been a member of the family all that time without knowing that he is not a saint! He has lived as other men do--as women permit decent men to live, I suppose. Nina's different. She's younger. She has never had an affair---"

"We were not discussing Nina!"

"No, I know it. But you reminded me that what I object to in you, with her, I myself am doing with him--or something very like it! Except that--" Harriet floundered a little, but regained her thread--"except that he does care for me," she repeated; "he loves beauty--I can say that to you without your misunderstanding!--and then, he knows me, we have been intimate for years, we are congenial!"

"He knows everything about you," Royal repeated, innocently, as if the defence she made were perfectly acceptable. But again she was stung to silence.

"I am going to tell him frankly, exactly what you have said to me," Harriet said, presently, with decision and relief in her voice. "I shall remind him that I have always been poor, and that it is utterly impossible for me to separate the thought of him from the thought of what my life as his wife would gain."

"Be careful how you play your hand alone!" the man said. "Half confidence isn't much more than none at all!"

A moment later they parted: the woman entering the house for a cup of coffee, and some conference with butler and housekeeper, and the man starting off briskly for his early walk. But Blondin was smiling, as he went upon his way, and Harriet was white with anger and impotence.

"I'll put everything else I have in this world in the balance, Roy!" she said to herself, in the sunshiny silence of the breakfast room. "But I'll hold no more stolen conversations with you! I'll break my engagement with Ward, I'll go to Richard Carter and humiliate myself, I'll go back to Linda's house without a penny in the world--but I'll be done with you! Thank God, however the story may sound, especially with your interpretations on it, you haven't my honour in your keeping, though you may seem to have!"

The house was absolutely quiet; the clock on the stairs struck a silvery seven. Harriet went noiselessly to her own room; Nina was sleeping heavily. She flung off her clothes, sank into bed. And now at last sleep came, deep, delicious, satisfying. Nina awoke, had her breakfast in bed, tubbed and dressed, and still Harriet slept on.

"Miss Harriet, it's nearly noon!" The monitory voice penetrated at last; Harriet awoke, smiling. "Father's gone to the city, and Ward with him," Nina said, "and I telephoned the club and asked Mr. Blondin to lunch-- Granny said I might. And the papers--you ought to see them! Father said to Bottomley that he was to say that the family was not answering the telephone. Granny was darling to me this morning. She thinks I could keep house for Father. I said no, thank you, not while Miss Harriet was here. She said, Oh, no, she didn't mean immediately, but if you married, or something. But of course I may move into Mother's room, after awhile, although--isn't it funny?-I keep thinking that she may come back. And

Father said I was not to leave the place to-day. I had nine letters; Amy said that she had cried all night, and Mrs. Jay wrote Father, and oh--Father had a letter from Mother written just before the boat went; he didn't show it to any one. And she said they were going to Italy, and maybe Spain, he told Granny. Isn't it TERRIBLE?"

Thus Nina, excited and pleased by the importance of being so close to the calamity.

"I'll be dressed directly," Harriet said, in a matter-of-fact voice. "Get at your Spanish, Nina, and I'll be with you in a few minutes!"

A day or two later there was a family conference in the library, and Harriet realized more clearly than ever that it was impossible to forecast the march of events. Richard announced that after consideration he had decided that it would be wiser for the family to weather the storm of talk that would follow Isabelle's disappearance, in some neighbourhood less connected with her. He had therefore leased an establishment on Long Island, where the children could have their swimming and tennis, and his mother her usual nearness to town, but where they would be comparatively inaccessible to a curious press and public, and might disappear for a grateful interval. The life at Huntington would be less formal than at Crownlands, but the house he had taken was comfortable and roomy; there would be plenty of room for Nina's girl friends and Ward's guests. Miss Field, Bottomley, and Hansen would please see to it that the move was made with all possible expedition. He would join the family there every week-end, possibly now and then during the week, and he hoped the change would do them all good, and bridge the difficult first months of-- their misfortune. "I have explained to my mother and the children," he said, quietly, to Harriet, "that Mrs. Carter has asked for a divorce, which will, of course, be immediately arranged.

"The trip," he ended, turning to his mother, "is only about the distance this is, in the car. I've not seen the place, but I'm confident that you'll like it."

"I shall of course remain there steadily, Richard," said the old lady, with graciousness. "The length of the trip makes no difference. You naturally have not had time to consider--how should you--that there is a change in your circumstances, my son. The presence of an older woman in your house is imperative."

He smiled at her patiently, and Ward laughed outright.

"You mean on Miss Field's account, Mother?"

Madame Carter was outraged at this outspokenness; she had supposed herself somewhat obscure.

"If I do, my dear, it is a feeling that any WOMAN would share with me, although possibly men--as the less delicate--"

"Oh, shucks, Granny!" Ward said, affectionately. "Where did you ever get that line of dope?"

"Never mind, Ward," his father interrupted in turn. "We needn't discuss that now. We'll be delighted for every hour you can spend with us, Mother, whether it's for Miss Field's sake or ours. She'll take care of us all, and herself into the bargain, I'm sure of that. Now, Miss Field, about your check book; I've arranged---"

"The world, my dear, is less blind than you imagine!" his mother reminded him pleasantly, gathering her draperies for departure.

"Well, about your checks," Richard said, with his indulgent smile, when she was gone. "Where were we?"

"I have never respected and admired and been so grateful to any human being as I am to you," thought Harriet. "I think you are the finest and the strongest man I ever saw in my life!" Aloud she said, "I can send Bottomley and his wife, and one or two of the girls down to-day, if you think best. Then he can telephone me how things go."

Nina interposed an objection on the score of the tennis tournament at the club, was overruled, and departed in her turn to discover, as Harriet tactfully suggested, the condition of her bathing suit. Ward had already gone to do some necessary telephoning, so that Harriet and her employer were alone.

"Now, Miss Field," Richard said, when various details of management were delegated, "you understand that you are in charge from now on. My mother will--well, you know how to handle her! She is old--enjoys her little bit of mischief sometimes! Anything unusual you can refer to me; I shall be there every week, anyway."

He paused, and ruffled the scattered papers that were on the flat-topped desk before him. Harriet watched him anxiously. She thought he looked tired and old, and her heart ached at the troubled attempt he was making to simplify the tragedy for them all. He was not handsome, she reflected, but surely there had never been keener or pleasanter gray eyes, and a mouth so strong when it was in repose, so honest when it smiled. Not like Ward's ready and incessant laughter, not like Royal Blondin's carefully calculated amusement.

Reaching this point in her thought, facing him with her whole beautiful face alive with emotion and interest, Harriet smiled herself, involuntarily and faintly. It was a smile of almost daughterly sympathy and comradeship, friendly and innocent, and wholly irresistible. As usual, her masses of hair were trimly pinned and braided, but stray little golden feathers had loosened about the soft olive forehead, and the neck of her thin white blouse was open, showing the straight column of her young throat; the effect was unstudied and youthful, almost childishly engaging and fresh.

Richard, catching the look, was perhaps unconsciously cheered by it. Even at forty-four, and under his present difficulties and harassments, he must have been dead not to be refreshed by the vision of earnest youth and beauty that was so near him in the tempered summer light of the great library.

"Thank you!" he said, as if she had spoken. "There is one more thing, Miss Field," he added, idly rumpling his papers again, and then moving his fine hand to his thick brown hair, whose shining order he rumpled, too. "About this man Blondin. Do you know anything about him?"

A more direct shot at her innermost fastnesses could hardly have been made. Robbed of breath and senses by the suddenness of it, and with dry lips, Harriet could only falter a repetition:

"Know anything about him?"

"I don't know much, and what I do know I don't like," Richard continued, noticing nothing amiss in her manner, perhaps because he was so deeply absorbed in what he was saying. "He's a handsome fellow; he knows his subject, I guess. He's the modern substitute for the mediaeval minnesinger," he added, "a sort of father confessor--and the women like to talk to him! But I don't like him. Now, I don't know how he feels to Nina, or she to him, but as you know, she will come into her uncle's fortune in a few months, unless the trustee, who is myself, decides to defer payment for another three years. I merely want to say that it might be as well to intimate to this young fellow that there are conditions under which I would see fit to defer it, and anything that brought him into that connection would--well, would constitute one!"

"I didn't know of that!" Harriet exclaimed, in such obvious relief that the man smiled involuntarily.

"Then you agree with me?" he asked, eagerly.

Here in the sombre sweetness of the library, with the man she admired and respected above all others looking to her for confidence and counsel, what could she say? Even had Royal Blondin been present, Harriet might have cast every secondary consideration to the winds as readily. As it was, she could only tell him the truth.

"Oh, yes--yes! I told Ward that I would rather see Nina dead!"

"Why do you say so?" Richard asked. "Now, I'll tell you why I do," he added, as Harriet was, not unnaturally, groping for definite phrases, "I've been watching this man. I had his record looked into. There's nothing extremely bad in it--he seems to be a gentleman adventurer. But there was an affair several years ago, his name mixed into some divorce, and it developed then that he holds rather peculiar ideas about free love, natural relationships--I needn't go into that. I don't want him mixed up with my family. I'm going to speak to Ward about it, warn him that his sister's happiness mustn't be risked by having the fellow about at all. Meanwhile, you can take it up with Nina. Just let her see that she isn't the only girl who has ever listened to him reading 'In a Gondola.' You might hint that there was a good deal of talk about him five or six years ago; there was a Swedish woman--I didn't get the details!--but I imagine trial marriage comes pretty close to it. You're tired," said Richard, abruptly.

"Indeed I'm not!" the girl protested, with white lips.

"You don't imagine the man is serious?" Richard asked, alarmed by her manner.

"I don't know!" Harriet answered at random. "They've--they've hardly known each other three weeks!"

"Ah, well! And she's only seventeen," her father said. "Distract her, amuse her--if she's inclined to mope a bit. Get riding horses!"

No time to think--no time to trim her course. Harriet must plunge blindly ahead now.

"Mr. Carter, would you--if you think wise--give your mother a hint of this? Madame Carter is romantic, you know--"

"Oh, certainly! Certainly!" he said, approvingly. "I'll speak to her. We must keep Nina a little girl this summer. And, Miss Field--"

It was said with only a slight change in the pleasant voice. But it brought a sudden change in their relationship, a tightening of the bonds that were all Harriet's world now.

"--Miss Field, I may say here and now that it is an unmixed privilege, in my estimation," Richard Carter said, simply, "that my daughter, and my son, too, for the matter of that, should have the advantage of your influence, and your example, at this time. Of course it infinitely simplifies my own problem. But I don't mean only that. I mean that with your knowledge of the world, of work and poverty--I know them, too, I know their value--you are infinitely qualified to balance their whole social vision just now. I have never been unappreciative of the value of a simple, good, unspoiled woman in my household. I have seen the effect in a thousand ways. But at the present moment, I hardly know where I could turn without you. I can only hope that in some way the Carters may be able to repay you!"

The secretary's shining head dropped, and she rested her elbow on the table, and pressed a white hand tight across her eyes for a moment of silence. When she faced him again her face was a little pale, and her magnificent eyes heavy with tears.

"I love all the Carters," she said, simply. "I only wish I were--half what you say!"

And without another word she stood up, folded into a tiny oblong the paper upon which she had been making a few notes, and went slowly to the library door. More deeply stirred than she had been since the days of her passionate girlhood, she turned on the threshold for a look of farewell. But Richard Carter had left the desk, and was kneeling on one knee before his safe; he had forgotten her. Harriet went across the hall, mounted the stairs, and found her own room. She was hardly conscious of what she was doing or thinking.

"Oh, what shall I do?" she whispered. "He trusts me to protect her! Oh, why didn't I--the moment I knew that Royal was thinking of her--why didn't I go to him then, and make a clean breast of it all! Now--now I've promised! And they trust me and love me--and what shall I do! Oh, God," whispered Harriet, sinking on her knees beside the bed, "You know that I am good--You know that I can really help them all--can really protect the girl! You know how I have chosen what was fine and good, all these years, how I have longed for an opportunity to be useful and happy! Don't let him come into my life again, and spoil it again. Don't let Richard Carter lose faith in me, and despise me! I don't know what's the matter with me," sobbed Harriet, burying her brimming eyes in the pillows; "I never cry, I haven't cried like this for years and years! I think I'm losing my mind!"

CHAPTER XII

The move to Huntington was made quickly and quietly, and lazy weeks followed, to Harriet weeks of almost cloudless content. She and Nina walked and rode, swam and practised their tennis stroke, paddled about in a canoe, motored over miles of exquisite country. Madame Carter was often with them, suggesting, disapproving, meddling, awaiting her chance to score. Ward, early in August, after a serious talk with Harriet, joined some friends for a motor run of three thousand miles, and presently was sending them post cards from Monterey and Tahoe. There was naturally no entertaining or formal social life for the family this summer, but Richard almost always brought men down for golf, over the week-ends, and seemed, if quiet and reserved, to be well content.

They had been in the new home only a few days when Harriet had reason to stop short in a busy morning of unpacking with one hand upon her heart, and a great satisfaction in her eyes. Nina, reading from a note from Royal Blondin, announced the sensational news that he had broken his ankle. He was with friends at Newport, and must remain there now for weeks, perhaps a month. Nina was please to write him, and to give his regard to Miss Field, and ask her not to forget him.

Harriet was quite willing to overlook the delicate menace of the message for the sake of the other news. For several weeks they were safe. Nina did not know the family Royal had been visiting, there was a long interval before she could possibly see him again. He would write to the girl, of course, and Harriet knew with what absorbing emotion she would look for his letters. But Nina was young and Nina wrote wretchedly, and anything might happen, thought Harriet, consoling herself with a vague argument that was in itself youthful, too.

Old Madame Carter was the only stumbling block now; there was no question of her definite hostility. It was partly the jealousy of age for youth, of departed beauty for beauty in its prime, but it was mainly actuated by the old lady's sense of pride, her firm belief that there was some mysterious merit of birth in the Carter blood, and that to friendship with the Carters a mere upstart, a secretary, a working-woman, could not with any justice aspire. In a thousand ways, many of them approaching actual mendacity, she undermined Harriet's usefulness, and annoyed and distracted the domestic force. If Harriet decided that the weather was too warm for an out-of-door luncheon, Madame Carter pleasantly overruled her, and there was much running to and fro for the change. Messages undelivered by the old lady were attributed to the secretary's carelessness, and there was more than one occasion when Harriet had no choice between silence toward Madame Carter or the flat accusation of untruthfulness.

Every hour under his roof, however, helped to convince her that Richard Carter was unaware of very little that transpired there. His reading of Nina's young secret had proved that; Harriet never remembered his ready allusion to "In a Gondola" without surprise. How he had managed to obtain that particular detail she could not imagine. But she hoped that he read the relationship between her and his mother as truly, and that time would reconcile the old lady to her presence in the house.

With September came changes. Blondin wrote that he was limping about with a stick, and wanted to limp down to them as soon as they would ask him. Ward was home again, as always irresponsible, a little older and in some vague way a little coarser, Harriet thought, but still a most enlivening element in the quiet household. Madame Carter had brought with her, for several weeks' stay, a friend of Isabelle's, a pretty, dashing little grass widow, Mrs. Tabor. The resolute brightness and sweetness with which Ida Tabor attempted to amuse Richard gave Harriet some hint of the plan which was taking shape in the back of his mother's head. But she could only make Mrs. Tabor comfortable, and fit her somehow into the youthful plans of the household.

"Miss Harriet," Nina said, without preamble, lying flat on the gently rocking float, and catching little handfuls of water as she spoke, "what'll I wear to-morrow?"

Harriet had already settled this question several times, but she was always patient with Nina.

"White is prettiest," she said; "didn't we decide for the organdie?"

"The white with the rolled hem," Nina said with unction, "and pale pink stockings, and white shoes."

"That will do nicely!" Harriet, always happiest in the water, was sitting on the edge of the float, with her feet idly splashing. A glorious September sun blazed down upon the water, there was absolute silence up and down the curving shore. Above the plumy tops of the trees, rising abruptly from the beach with its weather-burned bath houses, the gables and porches of the new home showed here and there. There were other country mansions scattered up and down beside the blue waters of the Sound, but the Carters had no sense of having neighbours.

Nina, Ward, and Harriet fairly lived in the water, and Ward had unconsciously served his father's cause by bringing home with him a tongue-tied pleasant youth named Saunders Archer, whose presence in the house had helped to keep Nina pleased and amused. She had already imparted to Harriet the valuable information that Saunders had never known his mother, and had never had a sister, "and of course I have always been such an oddity in the family," said Nina, "that I got right at his confidence in that dreadful way of mine! He said he didn't know why he talked to me so frankly."

Harriet had seen to it that a variety of delightful plans awaited the young people at every turn. The retirement natural after the recent domestic catastrophe was too dangerous to risk now. They drove to Piping Rock, to Easthampton; they yachted and swam; and the evenings were filled with riotous entertainments of their own devising, and once or twice with country club dances ten or twenty miles away. And Harriet hoped, hoped, hoped, feverishly, incessantly, wearyingly, that the danger was past.

But Amy came down, mild and colourless as ever, yet still more poised, more socially adept than Nina, and with Amy innocently diverting Saunders's bashful attentions, Nina returned to thoughts of Royal. The "to-morrow" for which the white organdie had been selected was to bring Royal for his first visit to Huntington. He was coming down with Madame Carter and Mrs. Tabor in her car. The man, the old lady had protested indignantly, had already been asked to visit them, and it was preposterous, just because Richard fancied every man who looked at Nina was in love with her, that he should be insulted! No matter, Richard said, in an aside to Harriet, accepting the situation philosophically, there was no need for suddenness. Harriet tried to be philosophical, too. Richard was bringing two men down for golf this week-end, and with Saunders and Amy, Royal and Madame Carter and Mrs. Tabor, the house would be filled. She had plenty to do with the managing, the endless details that were brought her mercilessly, hour after hour, by maids and housekeeper. And yet under her quiet busyness and her happy hours with the young people there lurked incessantly a fretted sense of danger approaching.

Something of this was in her mind as she and Nina basked on the gently heaving float, in the sunshine. Amy, with no particular desire to hide the fact that she was a better swimmer than Nina, had essayed a swim to the buoy, a hundred yards out in the channel. Nina, therefore, was naturally turned to thoughts of a male who quite frankly did not admire Amy; and she talked incessantly of Blondin. Harriet, the best swimmer among them, remained with Nina, and now fancied she saw an opening for a little talk she felt extremely timely.

"Mr. Blondin likes you, Nina, just because you aren't flirtatious and silly, like the other girls. But he isn't the sort of man to get very deeply interested in any woman, dear."

"No, I know he's not!" Nina said, quickly, turning suddenly red, and looking attentively at the print of her wet hand on the dry, hot boards.

"And I would be sorry if he were," Harriet pursued, not too seriously, "for I want you to marry a man of your own age, when you do marry, and not a man who has had--well, other affairs, who has that confidential, flattering manner with all women!"

"If you think I don't realize perfectly that you don't like Royal Blondin, you are mistaken!" Nina said, airily, even with a yawn. "I am perfectly able to manage my own affairs in THAT direction!"

"Yes, I know, dear. But we want you--" Harriet was beginning pacifically. But Nina angrily interrupted:

"Oh, I know you and Father talk about me, if THAT'S what you mean!"

"No, dear, listen. We want you to see other types of men, to see all kinds. You will be rich, Nina--"

"Why don't you say that Royal is after my money!" Nina burst out, with symptoms of tears. The ready name frightened Harriet afresh; she knew that they corresponded, that grass was not growing under Royal's feet. She and Nina were sitting close together now, their drying hair tossed backward, their faces flushed. "The first man I ever really liked," Nina said, with a heaving breast, "the first man who ever understood me--!"

"Nina," Harriet said, "you don't want to have to write your husband a check on your honeymoon?"

She felt it a cruel cut; but seventeen years of flattery and smoothness had armed Nina in impregnable complacence. She gave a sneering laugh that trembled on the brink of tears, and tried to control a mouth that was shaking with anger. One look of utter scorn she did manage, then she shrugged not so much her shoulders as her whole body, and flung herself furiously into the water. Harriet called "Nina!" first impatiently, and then coaxingly. But the younger girl swam steadily to the shore, and Harriet saw her a minute later, shaking herself outside the shower, before she disappeared into the big bath house. With a grave face, as she absentmindedly tossed and spread the glorious mass of her glittering hair, Harriet sat on, pondering. They had reached a crisis; Nina, between delicious confidences to Amy and aggrieved appeal to Royal, would commit herself now. There was no help for it; she, Harriet, must act.

Amy and Saunders swam by her, breathless and screaming as they made for shore, and fought and shrieked under the shower. Then they, too, entered the dressing rooms, and there was absolute silence in the world. Harriet had entirely forgotten Ward, until he swam under the float, and with a characteristic yell, rose streaming like a seal under her very feet.

Genuinely startled, she gratified him with a scream, and they both laughed like children as he flung himself dripping on the hot boards, and proceeded to bake luxuriously in the sun.

"It's the most gorgeous thing I ever saw, do you know that?" he asked, with one hand touching the river of sparkling gold that blazed and tumbled on her shoulders. "Listen, Harriet, do you remember the little talk we had some weeks ago?"

"Perfectly," she said, a little unwillingly.

"Before I went to California, I mean," he further elucidated.

"Yes, I know what you mean, Ward!"

"Well, how about it?" the boy said, after a pause. Harriet, her beautiful flushed face framed in curtains of shining hair, was regarding him steadily, and almost sorrowfully.

"Do you mean to ask if I have changed?"

"Well--" he looked up. "I thought you might! They do--the ladies!"

"It wouldn't be fair to you. Ward," the girl said, slowly, after a pause. "I love you, but I don't love you the way your wife will!"

"Why do you talk like that--it's all bunk!" he said, impatiently. "If you try it and don't like it, why, you can get out, can't you?"

"Ward, don't say those things!" the girl said, distressedly.

"I want you!" he said, sullenly. "I'm crazy about you! My God--"

"Ward, please don't touch me!" she said, sharply, getting to her feet with a spring, as he put his arm about her. "Don't--! I shall tell your father if you do!"

"You didn't talk that way at Crownlands last June," the man said, sulkily. "I don't see what has made such a difference now!"

"I think perhaps I'm different, Ward. The summer--" Harriet's voice died into silence. Her eyes were fixed upon the figure of a man who came down the little pier, and dove into the shining water. Two minutes later, with a great gasp of satisfaction, Richard Carter drew himself up beside them.

"Ha! That is something like! My Lord, the water is beautiful to-day! How about the buoy? Who swims with me to the buoy?"

"Come on, Harriet!" Ward said, poising.

The girl hesitated, glanced toward the shore. Saunders, with a white-clad girl on each side of him, was walking up to the house.

"Did your friends come down with you, Mr. Carter?" she asked, before quite abandoning all responsibilities.

"Briggs and Gardiner--yes. They're getting into golf clothes. We're going to play nine holes anyway, at the club. What time is dinner?"

"Eight o'clock. Unless you prefer--"

"No, no! Eight is fine. We'll be back at seven. My mother and Mrs. Tabor and Blondin will be down from town at about six."

Harriet rose, too, and bundled the glory of her hair into a blue rubber cap that made her look like a beautiful rosy French peasant. With no further speech she made a splendid dive, and the men followed her.

It was one of life's beautiful hours, she thought, as in a great splash of salt water she reached the buoy, and hung laughing and panting to its restless bulk. Ward had preceded her by a full minute, Richard was half a minute behind her. With much vainglorious boasting from the men, they all rested there before the homeward swim. Harriet hardly spoke, her cup was full to the brim with a mysterious felicity born of the summer hour, the heaving waters, and the joyous mood of father and son. When Richard praised her swimming she flushed in the severe blue cap, and the blue eyes met his with the shy pleasure of a child. It was while she was hastily dressing, in the hot bath house a little later, that a sudden thought came to her, and flushed the lovely face again, and brought her to a sudden pause.

A tremendous thought, that made her breast rise suddenly, and her eyes fix themselves vaguely on space for a long, long minute. Her palms were damp, and she put them over her hot cheeks. But that--she whispered in the deeps of her soul, that was nonsense!

When Blondin arrived she did not see him, for Mrs. Tabor and Madame Carter, elaborately entering at five, reported him "perfectly wonderful" on the trip down, and that he had shown such transports at the sight of the woods and the water that they had put him down perhaps a mile away, to walk alone for the rest of the way, and commune with his own exquisite soul. The expectantly waiting Nina, at this, followed Amy upstairs in the direction of the white organdie, and Harriet felt a little premonitory chill.

"Oh, Miss Field!" said Madame Carter's voice, an hour later, as Harriet passed her door. The old lady had been talking with her grandson, while she was resting, magnificent in a pale blue negligee, but her maid was now extremely busy at the toilet table, and an elaborate dinner costume was laid out upon the bed. Harriet entered.

"Well, how has the little household been running?" asked Madame Carter, who had been away for almost a week. "Miss Nina looks sweet." And without waiting for a reply, which indeed would have been of no interest to her, she added, blandly, "Ward tells me that you are a beautiful swimmer!"

"Ward did not find that out to-day," Harriet said, mildly, thus informed that her radiant hour with both the Carters was known to the mother and grandmother.

"My son is a brilliant man," said Madame Carter, with apparent irrelevance, "but the most brilliant men in the world are the stupidest in domestic life, isn't that so?"

Harriet, ready for the knife, said pleasantly that perhaps it was sometimes so.

"Now my son," Madame Carter said, confidentially, "is a man of scrupulous honour. But he is capable of placing a young woman, and"-- she bowed graciously--"a beautiful young woman, in a very false position! I confess that if I were in that young woman's place, I should resent it. I should feel--"

"If you mean me," Harriet said, interrupting the smooth, innocent old voice, "I assure you that I do not feel my position here at all false--" ["She always gets me wild, and gets me talking," Harriet added to herself, with anger at her own weakness, "but I can't help it!"] And aloud she finished, "I am Nina's companion, and in a sense, housekeeper--"

"Pilgrim is housekeeper," Mrs. Carter corrected, Miss Pilgrim, a one-time maid, was really Mrs. Bottomley, and had been manager below stairs for a long time.

"There are things Pilgrim cannot do," Harriet suggested.

"I feel myself the difficulty of explaining your position here!" said the old lady, raising both hands and arms in an elaborate gesture of deprecation, and smiling kindly. "You put me in a false position, too!"

But Harriet had now reached the point she always did reach, sooner or later, in these talks with Madame Carter, the point of mentally pitying the old lady, and recollection that after all her mischievous tongue could do no real harm.

"You will have to discuss that with Mr. Carter, of course!" It was always ace of trumps, and Harriet only blamed herself for ever beginning a conversation with anything else. Now she retired from the field with all honours, forcing herself to dismiss the unpleasant memory the instant she was out of reach of Madame Carter's voice. But the old lady fumed for an hour, and took up the subject with her son when he came dutifully in to take her down to dinner.

"Ida feels as I do," she said, when Mrs. Tabor, charming in blue, joined them on the way downstairs. Richard felt a sensation of anger. It was poor taste to involve a casual stranger like Ida Tabor in this rather delicate family discussion. But he thought that the little widow showed excellent sense in her rather slangy fashion.

"Well, of course, she's filled the bill this summer, Dick, ab-so-loo-tely! But, let me tell you, that Nina of yours is beginning to take notice, and she won't need a governess forever! With you to keep an eye on things generally, Nina will soon be able to manage Dad's affairs. I know just how you feel--never'll forget how utterly blank I felt when Jack Tabor just quietly packed his trunks and walked out! Why, I couldn't get hold of myself for months!"

"Where is Miss Field?" Richard was looking for the demure blue gown and the bright head as they joined the young group downstairs.

"She is not coming down, Richard," his mother explained.

"Why not?" he asked, abruptly. His mother gave him a magnificent look, warning, silencing, appealing.

"I'll explain it to you later, dear!" she said, half-annoyed and half-pleading. "You may announce dinner, Bottomley!"

Bottomley duly announced dinner. But he might have added something to the conversation, had he been permitted. He had had some simple and direct conversation with Madame Carter, not an hour before, and had in consequence sent up a dinner tray to Miss Field. Rosa, taking the tray, had been instructed to say simply that Madame Carter had told Mr. Bottomley that Miss Field wished her dinner upstairs. But Rosa was perfectly in touch with the situation, too, and carried the news below stairs that Miss Field had got as red as fire, and had stood looking from Rosa to the tray, and from the tray to Rosa, for--well, full five minutes, before she had said, "Thank you, Rosa, you may put it there on the table!"

Madame Carter sparkled her best that evening. Mrs. Tabor, too, carried along the conversation noisily if not brilliantly, until the young people got well under way. Richard was rather silent, but then he was always silent. And after awhile the rich, significant tones of Royal Blondin were heard. It was well after nine when they all drifted out into the cool dimness of the porch for coffee; Ward started music, Saunders and Amy danced. The men attempted a little pool, but were too weary, and by half-past ten Mrs. Tabor had tripped upstairs after the young girls, with a buoyant good-night for her host, and the old lady, lingering for a minute, had a chance to explain.

"About Miss Field, dear. I gave her just a kindly hint as to the propriety of her being ALWAYS present at dinner, and she was sensible enough to take it! Now and then, of COURSE--"

He jerked impatiently.

"I wish you would be a trifle more careful with your kindly hints, Mother! Miss Field is a most exceptional girl--"

"My DEAR boy," said the old lady, fanning rapidly, "I could get you a dozen women infinitely more capable--"

"--and I don't want her feelings hurt!" Richard finished, with a return to his usual gentleness.

"You won't hurt her feelings!" his mother predicted, roundly. "Not while the entire household is taking her orders, and the bank honouring her checks--oh, no, my dear! don't worry about that!"

"To-morrow night," Richard said, half to himself, "I shall make it a point to ask her to come down to dinner. If she prefers her room--"

"Richard," his mother said, in a low, furious tone, "if you do that, you may be kind enough to excuse me! While poor Isabelle was here, while Nina was a child, it was all well enough! But nothing could be more unfortunate for your daughter, for your young son, than to have any fresh gossip--the sort of thing people are only too ready to say, and are beginning to say now!"

"Why, how you do cook up things from whole cloth, Mother!" the man said with his indulgent smile. "You see the thing too closely, you are right in the middle of it!"

"I see that Harriet Field is an extremely pretty woman," his mother said, hotly.

Richard looked from the tip of his unlighted cigar into his mother's eyes, looked back again.

"Why, yes, I suppose she is!" he said, thoughtfully. "Gardiner said something about it just now. Said she'd make her fortune in the movies."

"I don't know about that," Madame Carter said, indifferently.

"Why can't you consider that we are fortunate to have her, Mother?"

"Because I don't want to see you in a false position before the world, my son. You must consider---"

The man kissed her hand lightly, with a laugh that closed the conversation.

"Consider nothing! It's all nonsense!" he said, and as she began her leisurely and dignified ascent he turned toward the porch and the solace of his cigar. While he and the other men smoked and mused, he decided to see Harriet and have a long talk with her the next day, to tell her that no matter what his mother said or did her word in the house was law, to assure her that in his eyes at least her position was secure beyond any question. Even with the varied group at the table to-night, he had missed her; there was an influence even in her silences, and a certain power in her very glances.

"Why the boy isn't heels over head in love with her I don't know!" he thought of Ward. And when Gardiner, who had had merely a chance encounter with her in the hall spoke again of the gold hair and dark blue eyes, Richard fell into a benevolent dream of the little secretary married to Gardiner, who was rich and a bachelor, and a very decent fellow, too. He fancied young Mrs. Gardiner coming to visit the Carters, and himself toasting her at a formal dinner, and wondered if he had ever seen Harriet in evening dress. He would tell her to-morrow that she must get an evening gown. Richard, always the man of business, selected the hour on Sunday that would be most suitable for his talk with her. He and the other men would get up at seven, and go to the country club, where they would manage eighteen holes before breakfast was served on the club porch, the famous chicken Maryland and waffles of which the golfers dreamed for six days. After that they might get into a game of bridge, pleasantly tired, well fed; there were less agreeable things to do than sit on the shady club porch, ordering mild drinks, and quarrelling over two or three hard-fought rubbers. Nina and her crowd were to lunch at the club; last Sunday Harriet Field had come out with Nina and looked on for a hand or two, other people were drifting about, and it was extremely social and agreeable.

But he would be home to dress for dinner, at six, and then he would get hold of Miss Field, and somewhat clear up the situation. Richard slept upon the resolution, and arose in the sweet summer morning to a satisfied recollection of it. He looked from his window into the green, warm garden, and saw Miss Field herself emerging from the wood, and Nina's friend, Blondin, beside her. Harriet had evidently been to church; she carried a prayer-book; a broad-brimmed hat made the slender figure, from this distance anyway, extremely picturesque. The man and she were in earnest conversation.

"Now THAT" thought Richard, still paternally busy with matrimonial plans for her, "that wouldn't do at all. I hope she isn't wasting any time on that fellow. He's clever, he has a good manner, but by George, that girl could marry any man, and make him a magnificent wife, too! I rather thought we'd disposed of this Blondin, anyway! But they seem friendly enough--"

For they had parted with a nod unmistakably familiar.

CHAPTER XIII

Blondin had been waiting for her at the church door. Harriet, coming out, had indicated without a word that he might walk beside her. The service had been ill-attended, and the few women who drifted away from it did not walk in their direction, so they found themselves alone. Harriet had been realizing ever since his arrival that Blondin had lost none of his unique and baffling charm. His handsome person, his unusual voice, his fashion of dreamily contributing to the conversation some viewpoint entirely unexpected and fresh, his utter indifference to general opinion--these made him a distinct entity in any group, and would account for Nina's immediately renewed alliance, and for the general disposition on the part of the household to accept him on his own terms.

Harriet opened the conversation this morning with a frank yet reluctant confession.

"I'm so sorry, Roy! But it is only fair to you to say that I've changed. You will have to do what you think fit about it, of course. But I can't pretend that I'm--I'm playing your game any longer."

"What game?" Blondin, falling into graceful step beside her, asked pleasantly.

"I mean any possible--idea you might have of Nina!" Harriet said, bravely.

"Oh, Nina!" he shrugged his shoulders lightly. "Don't take me too seriously, my dear Harriet," he said. "Why, whenever we are alone together, should you promptly begin to cross-question me about that little person? Look about you--isn't this a divine morning? I always rather fancy September, somehow. It's dry, panting, finished--and yet there's something about the mornings and the evenings--"

Harriet made a faint, impatient ejaculation.

"Well, anyway, you know where I stand!" she said.

"And you know where I do," he answered, after a pause. "I can see Carter has no particular enthusiasm for me--I suppose that's your work."

"I've said nothing definite," she answered, in a troubled voice.

"Then I shall!" Royal said, with sudden feeling. "I'm sick of this shilly-shallying, and weighing words! If he will accept me as I am, well and good--if not, I'm done! But he has a high opinion of you, Harriet; what you say really counts!"

"You know where I stand," she could only repeat. They had reached the garden now, and were at the foot of the steps.

"I don't quite see how you can take that tone," Blondin hinted. "Do you expect to marry the boy?"

Harriet did not answer, except by a faint shrug. Her heart was sick with fright, but there was no reason why he should be informed that she had definitely broken with Ward. But he had never come so near a threat before.

"Of course I am entirely at your mercy," she said, simply. Blondin watched her for a full moment of silence before he said suddenly:

"All I ask you to do is assume, for the time being, that you and I met as strangers a few weeks ago!"

"Oh, Roy," the girl exclaimed, "as if I were likely to do anything else!"

She despised herself for the sense of relief that flooded her heart.

"Look here then," he said, after a moment of thought. "I'll make a bargain with you. If you will consent not to make any allusion to--well, to ten years ago, I'll do the same. I'll give you my solemn promise on it. Say what you please about me now. You're under no bond to protect me. I can hold my own. But the past is dead. Neither you nor I will speak of it without agreeing to do so. How about it?"

She hesitated, the black lashes dropped, her restless hands twisting and torturing her handkerchief. It protected her, she thought, while leaving her free to oppose him.

"I'll agree," she said, finally.

"Promise?"

"Oh, I promise!" She bit her lip, and frowned, as if she would add something more. But no words came, only her troubled eyes met his fully and splendidly for a second.

Then with the brief, familiar nod which Richard Carter saw from his upstairs window, she turned, and without another word went into the house.

The morning dragged. It was dry and hot, with promise of a storm later. The men piled into the car, and went off for their golf. It was ten o'clock before Nina and Amy came chattering downstairs; Royal was in the music room then, evoking a tangle of dim chords from the piano, smoking endless cigarettes. Presently Ward and his friend thundered down to join the girls at breakfast; a maid circled the table with toast and covered dishes.

Madame Carter's breakfast had been sent upstairs, and Mrs. Tabor had joined her, for when the old lady sent a message to Harriet, the two women were together, in elaborate negligee, and a litter of Sunday papers was scattered about the beautiful bedroom. Upon Harriet's entrance Mrs. Tabor gracefully rose to go, but she paused for a pleasant good-morning.

Alone with her determined old enemy, Harriet assumed her usual air of respectful readiness. Madame Carter had sent for her?

"Yes," said the old lady, looking aimlessly about her before gathering her garments together, and sinking into a chair. "I wanted you to know that the young people propose to drive to Easthampton, at about two o'clock-- my granddaughter has been here, teasing Granny for the plan, and I have consented. They will dine there and be back at about--well, after dinner."

"But won't that tire you?" Harriet asked.

"I? Oh, I shall not go. Ward will chaperon his sister, and Nina, Amy. Mr. Blondin will see that they get home in time. It's quite all right, Miss Field; I am entirely satisfied. They--"

"But, Madame Carter!" Harriet interrupted her as she had expected to be interrupted. "Surely it would be better--"

"We won't discuss it, please, Miss Field!"

Harriet's cheeks reddened; she was silent.

"Your devotion to my son and his family is extremely praiseworthy," said Madame Carter, coldly. "But, as Mrs. Tabor, who is of course a woman of the world, and comes of a very fine family--she was a Kingdon, the Charleston family--as Mrs. Tabor was saying, Richard is just the sort of chivalrous, splendid man who is perfectly helpless in his own house!"

Harriet smiled, with a touch of scorn.

"When Mr. Carter is dissatisfied with me, Madame Carter, I shall of course consider myself--dismissed. But until that time I am very glad to make his own house comfortable for him."

The hard, angry colour of old age had been rising in Madame Carter's face during this speech, and now she was quite obviously enraged.

"You are hardly in a position to dictate to me in this matter!" she said, shaking. Harriet watched her gravely as she rose from her chair, made a few restless turns about the room, opened and shut bureau drawers, dropped and plucked up handkerchiefs and newspapers. In a dead silence the girl asked:

"Was that all?"

A sort of sniff was the answer, and, leaving the room, Harriet saw the door of Mrs. Tabor's room, adjoining, open cautiously. The ally was creeping back for news of the fray, thought the girl, with a little grin at the thought of the two women's discomfiture. But she sighed again as she entered her own suite to find Nina and Amy complacently dressing themselves for the afternoon's run.

"We're going to Easthampton, Miss Harriet; Granny said it was all right," Nina said, in great spirits. "I know you won't feel hurt, because the car simply won't accommodate more than five, and it's too long a run to sit on laps--"

"But, dearie child," Harriet said, in her friendliest manner, "I don't believe you had better do that! You're all pretty young, in case anything occurred--"

A mutinous line marked Nina's babyish mouth. She would not yield to any nursery control before Amy!

"Granny said it was all right, Miss Harriet, so just don't bother your head about us!" she said, airily.

"Yes, I know, dear. But Granny's ideas are old-fashioned--"

"Old-fashioned people are apt to be even more rigid than we are, aren't they?" Amy submitted lightly and sweetly.

Harriet, a trifle nonplussed by this determined resistance, stood looking from one to the other, pondering.

"Anyway, I'm going!" Nina muttered, lacing high white buckskin shoes, with some shortening of breath. "Granny says a girl's brother--"

Harriet paid no further attention to them, and the two developed a splendid case for themselves. But she went down to find Ward, and took him partially into her confidence. Would he please be a darling, and see that there was no nonsense? She could not well cross his grandmother and Nina without his father to back her. She disliked to call his father at the club and make too much of the whole thing. Would he promise her that they would be home by ten o'clock, at latest?

Somewhat comforted by Ward's affectionate loyalty, Harriet went up to dress for the one o'clock luncheon, and while she was dressing a new idea came to her. For a few minutes she shook her head, stood thinking, with a face of distaste.

"I COULD do that!" she said, aloud. And she picked up the gingham dress that she had laid on the bed.

But there was a prettier dress in Harriet's wardrobe, a gift from Isabelle, that she had never worn. It was a flowered silk mull, of a soft deep blue that was exactly the colour of Harriet's eyes, and at the throat and wrists it had frills of transparent lace. The soft ruffles that made the skirt were cunningly edged with black, and there was a great open pink rose at the belt.

Harriet put on this enchanting garment, and as she did so she felt some half-forgotten power rise strong within her. There was one trump in her hand that she had never thought to play in a game with Nina Carter, but she was glad to find it now.

She went downstairs, and found Royal Blondin lounging in the billiard room, and idly knocking balls about. The second thing he said to her was of the gown, the third of her eyes. Harriet stood beside him, raising the eyes in question, and smiling. When she turned and went slowly away, Blondin went after her.

At half-past two o'clock the car was at the side door, and Nina and Amy came downstairs with their wraps, and Saunders and Ward ran about laughing and confusing things. Blondin watched the performance lazily from a basket chair on the porch, but when Nina called him a half-laughing, half-daring, "We're ready, Mr. Blondin!" he sauntered down to the car with his pleasantest expression, but with the regretful statement that he was not going: a vicious headache had developed since luncheon.

Whatever the effect on Amy and the young men, to Nina this was a staggering blow. Harriet felt sorry for her as she saw the girl try to meet it gallantly; she knew that the heart died from Nina's day there and then. Nina had triumphed all through luncheon, had laughed and chattered, had made Ward telephone a dinner reservation for five, and had assumed a hundred coquettish airs. Now all this crumpled, faded away, and Harriet knew, as she stood beside the car looking down at the folded light rug on her arm, that she was ready to cry.

"No, you'll have a far nicer time without me," said Royal, throwing away his cigarette, and resting one arm on the car. "I wouldn't interfere, because I knew you'd all give it up! You just all have a perfectly wonderful time, and I'll be down next week-end and hear about it!"

Nina stood irresolute; too choked with sudden disappointment to risk her voice. It was all hateful, maddening, horrible! Those two boys and Amy--ah, there would be no "fun" now! She loathed Amy, getting in so briskly, and saying, "Come on, Nina!" She hated Ward, she wished that they were all dead, and herself, too. It was impossible that she should be carried farther and farther away from him--after last night and to-day!

The storm came at Good Ground, and they all had to scramble with curtains, "smelly" curtains, Nina called them. And the dinner was eaten in warm, sticky half-darkness on a hotel porch, with horrible music making a horrible racket, according to the same authority. Saunders and Amy held hands all the way home, too, and Nina thought it was disgusting; everyone was too tired to talk, they bounced along silently and crossly.

And upon getting home, Miss Harriet came out of the shadows on the porch, looking perfectly exquisite in her new gown, sweetly interested and cheerful. She said that she was so sorry the dinner was poor, they had had such a nice dinner at home, and that she had had a talk with their father, and they were to go back to Crownlands next week. Nina did not see Blondin; she heard his voice from the smoking room, but her arrival caused no cessation of the men's laughter and voices in there, and the only news she had from him that night was from her grandmother, who was in a bad temper, and reported that he and Miss Field had been walking half the afternoon. Nina, for the first time in her life, cried herself to sleep.

"Never mind, my dear," said the old lady with terrible insight, "if I ask my son to choose between me and any other woman, I have no doubt of the outcome!"

Harriet had assuredly triumphed, but it was on terms that for more than one reason did not entirely please her. To affect a confidential intimacy with Royal Blondin was utterly distasteful, and to have poor little Nina sulky and silent far from pleasant. But most disquieting of all was the immediate result of old Madame Carter's meddling.

For Richard, finding the pretty secretary prettier than ever in her blue gown, and warmed by a relaxed day at the club and a mood of friendliness, had specifically instructed her that she was to dine with the family on all occasions, and to dress as the others did, and to regard herself as "a member of the family." And this, Harriet was quick to realize, really did place her in a peculiar position, made difficult by Richard's kindly championing no less than his mother's hostility, by the adoring sympathy of the servants, and the affectionate familiarities of the Carter children. Richard's friends took their cue from him, as was natural, and in the first early winter dinner parties at Crownlands Harriet could not but sparkle and lead; she had reached her own level at last.

Perhaps the master of the house but dimly saw the truth of this, but he did see a most charming and pretty woman at the head of his establishment, his daughter and son protected, his affairs capably managed, and such hospitality and entertainment as he felt suitable well handled. She and Nina shared Isabelle's old rooms, and Harriet balanced Nina's first evening gowns with discreet but dignified black.

A sense of well-being and happiness began to envelop Richard Carter for the first time in many years. He was conscious of a desire to express his appreciation to Miss Field. It was natural that this should take the form of money; a little present, in the form of a check. She had a sister who was not rich; she would like to go home with laden hands. But the question was, how much?

He was musing over this very point and other matters of deeper moment one morning when Harriet herself came in. She returned his smile with her usual bright nod, but he thought she looked pale and troubled.

"Mr. Carter," she said, bravely going to the point, "do you think Nina is able, with your mother's help, to manage your house?"

Richard looked at her silently for perhaps two minutes. Then he said, quietly:

"Mr. Blondin, eh?"

The girl looked bewildered.

"My mother has given me a hint, indeed I've seen, that he would want to take you away from us!" Richard said.

Harriet, without any show of emotion, looked down, and was silent in her turn. But it was not, he saw with surprise, the silence of confusion. On the contrary, she seemed simply a little thoughtful and puzzled.

"Mr. Carter," she said, presently, "I have reason to believe that Mr. Blondin would be a very bad husband for Nina. I had no scruple in--in diverting his thoughts. But if he was the only man in the world"--and to his surprise, she slowly got to her feet, and spoke as if to herself, her eyes fixed far away--"I would sooner kill him than marry him!" she said.

Richard sat genuinely dumfounded. Her beauty, her assurance, and the cleverness with which she had managed that Blondin's allegiance should be temporarily shifted from his own daughter, held him mute. It was with the charm of watching perfect acting that he followed this extremely amusing and unexpected woman.

"I confess that I am glad to hear it!" he said, drily.

"Nina is very angry at me," Harriet said. "Well, I have to stand that!"

And she gave Nina's father a whimsical and friendly look.

"But what then?" Richard asked. Harriet immediately became serious again.

"But this," she said, "you know your mother is right. You're all too kind to me; I am really a member of the family. I love it. I love to dress for dinner, and order the car, and charge things to your accounts! But--it's not possible. You see that?"

Richard was quietly looking down. Now he made several parallel lines with a pencil before he looked up.

"No. I don't see that!"

"Mary--Mrs. Putnam, for instance, who is very fond of me, and Mrs. Jay. They want to ask me to dinner--to Christmas parties--and they're not quite comfortable about it. I am not a member of your family even though you are kind enough to treat me as one. I am a paid employee, and Madame Carter naturally resents their treating me as anything else. But most of all," said Harriet, seeing that she was not making headway, "it's myself. Nina, and your mother, and Mrs. Tabor--it's just a hint here and there--nothing at all! But it undermines my position--even with Bottomley. I dress, I entertain your friends, I join you in town; it makes talk. And I can't--I can't--"

She stood up, and turned her back on him proudly, and he knew that she was crying.

"Just a minute," Richard said, finding himself more shaken than he would have believed. "It is--you're sure it isn't Blondin?"

"Royal Blondin!" There was in her tone a pleasant, childish scorn and indignation that again he thought amusing. She sat down facing him again, and quite openly dried her eyes, and smiled. "No, it's more serious," Harriet said. "It means constant irritation for your mother. It means that she is always in a state of exasperation. I think--I don't know, but I have reason to think--that she made it a choice, for Mary Putnam, between us!"

"She has no right to do that," said Richard, soberly.

"I'm not--you know that!--criticizing," Harriet said. The man sighed, and tossed a few papers on his desk.

"Sometimes I have hoped," he began, on a fresh tack, "that you and the boy might fancy each other. I'm not satisfied with Ward. He needs an anchor. That would be a solution for us all!" It was a random shot, but to his surprise she flushed brightly.

"Ward knows that there is no chance of that," she said, quickly, "dearly as I love him!"

Richard's eyes widened with whimsical amusement again.

"So you've refused Ward, have you?"

"Long ago," she answered, simply. The man laughed; but a moment later his face grew dark and troubled again as he said:

"I hardly know what to do! The girl is the first consideration, of course, and she needs you. I feel that she is not only safe, but happy, when you are here. My mother needs you, too; she would pay, like the rest of us, for worrying you out of the house. She couldn't manage it--bringing Nina into town, ordering her clothes, entertaining the boy's friends, answering letters--I know what it is! I've unfortunately reached a place where I've got to feel free. You've heard us all talk of this new asbestos merger--my dear girl, that will keep me going like a slave for months, perhaps years! I won't know when I am to be home, or what I shall have to cancel. I wish I could convince you that a woman of seventy-five and a girl of seventeen are not exactly a jury--"

"This is the jury!" Harriet said, touching her own breast lightly. He looked at her sombrely.

"I suppose so! I suppose I can't convince you how badly we need you. My mother--well, she has always taken life that way; she can't change now. I shall have Ida Tabor as a fixture here, I suppose, Nina running wild, Ward never home! You--you give me exactly what I want here! Good dinners, fires, hospitality, a good report from Nina and Ward; I can bring men home, I can--" He mused, with a smile touching his fine, tired face. "In short, I wish there was some fortunate young man somewhere to make you Mrs. Smith or Jones, Miss Field, and let you come back to the Carters immediately again!"

Harriet laughed, sighed sharply immediately upon the laugh.

"Unfortunately, there isn't such a man," she said. And she added, "Even a widow, sometimes, is vulnerable!"

Richard smiled, but some sudden thought made the smile but an absent one, and he sat quite obviously plunged in meditation for a long minute. The clock and the fire ticked sleepily, and outside the high windows the first tentative flutter of snow was melting on bare boughs and brick walls.

"Here's another suggestion, Miss Field," he said, suddenly, looking up, "I don't know how this will strike you; it has occurred to me before. Gardiner hinted it--or I thought he did, and the more I think of it, the more possible it seems. You are a business woman, and I am a business man. You know exactly what I am, exactly what occurred in my married life, after twenty-two years. That--that sort of thing is over, of course. But there is that way of settling it, if you care to consider it--"

He paused, with a questioning look of encouragement, embarrassment, and affectionate interest. Harriet had grown pale, and had fixed her eyes upon his as if under a spell.

"You mean--" Her voice failed her.

"I mean marriage. I mean that you and I shall quietly get married in a few weeks, when I am free," he answered. "I have just indicated to you what it would mean to me. I hope," he added, watching her closely, as she sat stunned and silent, "I hope that it would also have its advantages to you.

Your position then would be unquestionable, my mother--Nina--the world, would have nothing to say. I think you know how thoroughly we all like you, and that my share of our--our business partnership would be to make you as happy as was in my power. Your influence on Ward is the one thing that may save the boy. Of Nina we've already spoken. My mother--I know her!--would immediately become the champion of her son's wife. There would be a three days' buzzing--that would end it!"

The swift uprushing of joy in Harriet's heart was accompanied with the first agonies of renunciation, was perhaps all the more poignantly sweet because of them. She had not come to this hour without knowing what he meant to her, this quiet man with the splendid mouth and the keen gray eyes, and she trembled now with an exquisite emotion that seemed to drown out all the past and all the future--everything except that she loved him, and he needed her! But when she spoke it was as coolly as he:

"Mr. Carter--what of your wife?"

His eyes met hers wearily.

"Divorce proceedings were instituted immediately it was definitely established she had gone with young Pope. The decree will be absolute."

"But that will not--cannot alter the situation--" Harriet faltered.

"You mean--" the man hesitated "--you mean you--that you regard me as married still?"

Harriet, mute with emotions absolutely overpowering, nodded without speaking.

"Will you--will you let me think about it?" she faltered. A sudden brightness came into his face. "You know how I was brought up to think of divorce," she went on, pleadingly. "I've made plenty of mistakes in my life, but I've never deliberately done what I felt was wrong."

"And this would be?" Richard asked, slowly.

"Well--I haven't thought about it!" she answered, slowly. "My people--my sister and her husband--would say so! I--I would have said so of some other woman!"

"This would not be an ordinary marriage; you would be entirely your own mistress," Richard said, with quiet significance. "It would be a marriage only in the eyes of the world. You--have a higher tribunal!"

"My own, you mean?" she asked, thoughtfully.

"Your own. You would know exactly why this marriage was not in violation of any code of yours! The world might not acquit you, but you would know in your own heart."

"I see," she said. "I--I must have time to think about it!"

"As long as you like!" She had risen, and now he rose, too, and went with her to the library door, and opened it for her. "When you decide, come and tell me," he said, bowing.

She turned to give him a parting smile, with a desperate wish to tell him half the honour and joy she would feel in taking his name, in sharing his responsibilities, but the pleasantly impersonal nod he gave her chilled the words unspoken. Harriet fled to her room, and to the porch beyond it, and flinging herself into a basket chair, covered her face with her two hands, and for half an hour rocked to and fro audibly gasping, half-laughing, half-crying, almost beside herself with amazement and excitement.

To be Mrs. Richard Carter--to be Mrs. Richard Carter--to be mistress of Crownlands, to command the cars and the maids, to enter the opera box and the big shops--recognized, envied, triumphant--ah, it was a prospect brilliant enough to dazzle a far more fortunate woman than Harriet Field! To sign "Harriet Carter," to enter his office with assurance, to say at the telephone, "Mrs. Carter, if you please--!"

"My chance," whispered Harriet, pressing her cold finger tips to her hot cheeks again, "my chance at last--and I can't take it! No, I can't take it--I don't care what his world does or thinks--my world doesn't permit it! My father would never have spoken to me again--Linda wouldn't! No--I can't. Not a divorced man, not a man with a living wife! I've been a fool--I've been wrong, plenty of times, but I've never committed myself to folly and wrong!"

She stared blindly ahead of her. After awhile she spoke again, half-aloud:

"Oh, but why does it have to be this way! If I could go to him, tell him what he means to me, if we were poor--if we could take a little place next to Linda--never see Nina or his mother or Ward or Roy again--Oh, what Heaven! How I should love it, planning for things together, as Linda and Fred did, having him come home to me every night!

"But it isn't that way," Harriet suddenly recalled herself sensibly, "and it is folly even to think about it! He is a rich man, and a married man, and that ends it. That ends it."

A great desolation swept her spirit. She fell from bitter musing to weakening. The law permitted it, after all. Plenty of good women had shown her the way. The family needed her; she might do good here. And above all, she loved him. Again the dream triumphed, and she was Mrs. Carter, young, beautiful, and radiant, taking her place beside him. How she would watch him, how she would guard him, what a life she would build for him!

"But no, I mustn't think of that," Harriet said, sternly. "It would be even different if he loved me. But he made that very clear! He made that extremely clear! And the fact is this: that I marry a divorced man the week he is free, a man who does not love me, but who can give me an establishment! No--no--no--everything I've tried for all my life counts for very little if I can do that!"

She heard a stirring in the bedroom.

"What time is it, Rosa?" she called, suddenly aware of weakness and fatigue.

"My goodness, how you frightened me, Miss Field! It's just noon."

"Do you happen to know if Mr. Carter is still downstairs?"

"Yes'm, he is; he's expecting Mr. Fox to come!"

Harriet smoothed her tumbled hair, and went slowly downstairs.

"But I love him!" she said, suddenly standing still on the landing, to look out at the softly falling snow with brimming eyes. "I love him with all my soul!"

A moment later she knocked at the library door, opened it in answer to his call, and went in, closing it behind her.

CHAPTER XIV

There was trouble at Linda's house; trouble so terrible that Harriet's unexpected arrival caused no comment, caused no more than a weary flicker of Linda's heavy eyes. Pip, the adored first-born son, lay dangerously ill, and the whole household moved on tiptoe, heartsick with dread. Fred, a white and unshaven Fred, was home in the cold gray midday; the telephone was muted, the hall door stood ajar, the maid was red-eyed. Harriet, entering with a cheerful call hushed suddenly on her lips, kissed her brother-in-law while her eyes anxiously questioned him, and put a heartening arm about Josephine, who came out in a kitchen apron, and wept pitifully on her aunt's shoulder.

It was diphtheria, very bad, Fred stated lifelessly. Linda hardly left the room; they were afraid for her, too, "if anything happened." "If anything happened!" Harriet thought she had heard the phrase a hundred times before the dreadful night came. The sympathetic neighbours whispered it, the doctor said it gravely, the nurse muttered it in the kitchen, and the little sisters, clinging together, faltered it with trembling lips. The invalid was isolated on the upper floor; Harriet only waited to get into a thin gown before noiselessly mounting to the sick room. Linda, sitting beside the haggard little feverish boy, looked at her sister apathetically, the nurse was glad to whisper directions and slip away.

A bitter winter afternoon was waning, but the air in Pip's room was warm, and there was the order and silence of recognized crisis. The swollen little mouth moved, the heavy eyes; Linda bent above the child.

"What is it, my darling? Mother is right here--"

There was a new note in the passionate, tender voice. Linda was all alive for the few seconds he needed her, then she sank into her voiceless apathy again, and the short winter afternoon wore away, and there was no change. The doctor came, the nurse returned, Fred appeared at the door. After awhile it was dark, and a shaded lamp was lighted, and Harriet went downstairs, to the world of subdued voices, and smothered sobs, and fearful glances. And always horror brooded over the little house, and over the simple, normal family living that had been so taken for granted a few days before.

Harriet talked to the little girls, and while they were going to bed amused Nammy, whose lighter attack of the disease, a week ago, had begun the siege. Fred, tenderly attempting to reassure his daughters, buttoned his small son into woollen sleeping-wear, brought the inevitable drink, heard the garbled prayers, glancing now and then toward the door, as if fearing a summons, and looking, Harriet thought, stooped and gray and suddenly old.

She took Linda's place for an hour, but before it was up the mother came back, and they kept their vigil together. Fred answered the strange, untimely ringing of the door-bell, brought in packages, conferred in the halls with the doctors. Midnight came, two o'clock, four o'clock.

Suddenly there was panic. Harriet, by chance in the hall, saw Linda and Fred and the doctors together, heard Linda's quick, anguished "Yes!" and Fred's hoarse "Anything!" Her heart pounded; the nurse ran upstairs. Harriet fell upon her knees with a sobbing whisper, "No--no--no!" and Linda clung to her husband with a cry torn, from the deeps of her heart, "Oh, Pip--my own boy!"

They were all needed; they were back in the sick room, there was hurry, quick whispers, breathless replies. No time to think now, though Harriet cast more than one agonized glance at Linda's drawn face, and nodded more than once to Fred that she should not be here. The child protested with a choked cry; and Linda's voice, that new, deep, terrible voice, answered him, "Never mind, my dearest--just a minute, that's all! Mother is taking care of you!" And Harriet heard her sister say, in a breath almost inaudible: "Thy will be done--Thy will be done!"

Dawn came slowly and reluctantly at seven; the village lay bleak and closed under a sky of unbroken gray. Here and there smoke streamed upward from a chimney, or a window-pane showed an oblong of pale light. The dirty snow, frozen in thick lumps about the yard, was trodden by a furtive black cat, that mounted a fence and meowed desolately.

Harriet saw this from Linda's kitchen, when she put out the light that was becoming unnecessary. But her heart was singing for joy, and the house was brimful of an inner light and cheer that no winter bleakness could touch. The girl had been crying until she was almost blind, but it was a crying mixed with laughter and prayers of utter thankfulness. She and Fred had built up a roaring fire, had given the nurse a royal breakfast, had had their own coffee, and now Harriet was waiting for Linda, in that mood when the commonplaces of life take on an exquisite flavour, and just to be free to eat and sleep and live is luxury.

She met Linda at the door, a weary Linda, ghastly as to face, grayer as to straggling hair, but with such radiance in her eyes that Harriet, clasped in her arms, began to cry again.

"What YOU need is coffee!" she faltered, trying to laugh, as Linda sat down and rested her head in her hands.

"Oh, Harriet--if I can ever thank God enough!" Pip's mother said, beginning on her breakfast with one long sigh. "Oh, my dear--! He's sleeping like a baby, God bless him, and dear old Fred is sleeping, too. Oh, Harriet, to go about the house, as I just have, covering Nammy and the girls, and feeling that we're all going to be together again, in a few days-- my dear, I don't know what I've done to be so blessed! My boy, who has never given any one one moment's care or trouble since he was born--my darling, who looked up at me yesterday with his beautiful eyes--"

The floodgates were loosed, and Linda laughed and cried, while she enjoyed her breakfast with the appetite of a normal woman released from cruel strain, whose whole brood lies safely sleeping under her roof. Nammy's light illness, Pip's wet feet, Linda's unwillingness to believe that it was anything but a cold, every hour of the four awful days of danger, she reviewed them all. And oh, the goodness of people, the solicitude of nurse and doctor, the generosity of God!

"Fred has been a miracle," said Linda, with her third cup of coffee, "this will cost him five hundred dollars, but Harriet, I'll never forget the way his voice rang out yesterday, 'I don't want you to think of anything but giving me back my boy!' And Harriet, only ten days ago--it seems ten years--I felt so terribly, I ACTED so terribly, about that old house that I've been wanting so long! They sold it at auction, and the Paysons got it for forty-three hundred, and I was perfectly sick that Fred wouldn't bid! But now," said Linda, reverently, putting her arm about Josephine, who came yawning into the kitchen, in her blue wrapper, "now, if the Father spares me my girls and boys, and their daddy, I shall never ask anything happier than this! Pip's better, Jo," she said to the child, who was kissing her dreamily, over and over, "they put a tube in his throat last night, and saved him for us! And now Mother must get a bath, and change, and perhaps some sleep, and then go back and stay with him when he wakes up!" It was the afternoon of the next day when Harriet could first speak of her own affairs. Pip, recuperating with the amazing speed of childhood, was asleep, the other children walking, the nurse gone. She could lay the whole matter before Linda, who listened, over her mending, nodded, pursed her lips, or raised her eyebrows.

If Linda might ever have been worldly minded, she had had her lesson now, and the viewpoint she gave Harriet was the lofty one of a woman who has faced a supreme sacrifice without shrinking and with unwavering faith.

"You did right, dear," she assured her sister. "You could not stay there, under the circumstances. Whatever their code is, yours is different, yours has not been vitiated by luxury and idleness. As for Mr. Carter's talk of marriage, that, of course, is simply an insult!"

"No, I don't think it was that," Harriet said, feeling herself revolt inwardly at this plain speaking. She listened to Linda; she knew Linda was right, but she fought an almost overwhelming impulse to say rudely, "Oh, shut up, you don't know what you're talking about."

"I don't see what else it could be," Linda pursued, serenely. "A married man--you would be no better than his--well, it's not a nice word--but his mistress!"

"Not at all," Harriet said, trying hard to hide the irritation that rose rebellious within her, "he is legally free, or will be soon, and so am I!"

"I am speaking of God's law, not man's," Linda said, gently but awfully, and Harriet was silent. "Fred says that such men regard these matters far too lightly," Linda finished. Fred's name, thus introduced, always had the effect of angering Harriet. She was suffering cruelly, in these days, and moral reflections held small consolation for her. She was homesick with an aching, gnawing homesickness that arose with her in the morning, and went to bed with her at night; under everything she said and did was the longing for Crownlands, for just one more word or look from Richard Carter.

She had shared the family exaltation over Pip's recovery, and had thought more than once in that fearful night of his illness that even poverty, gray hairs, and the agony of parenthood, shared with the man she loved, would have been ecstasy to her. But in the slow days and weeks that followed, her spirit became exhausted with the struggle that never ended within her. Her bridges were burned behind her; it was all over. Whatever her emotions had been in leaving Crownlands, the Carters' feelings had been quite obvious and simple. Old Madame Carter had wished her well; Ward had written from college that he thought it was "rotten," and that she had been a corker to get Dad to raise his allowance for him; Nina had felt her own wings the stronger for the change; and Richard had interrupted his little speech of regret twice to answer the telephone, and had given her a check that placed, it seemed to Harriet, the obligation permanently with her. The utter desolation of spirit with which she had left them was evidently unshared; the only word she had had from that old life had been from Mary Putnam, and even this cordial note jarred Harriet with its frank revelation of the change in her position. Mary wrote:

I telephoned Mr. Carter for your address, and he reports them all well. I wanted to tell you that I am giving you a tremendous reputation with Kane Bassett, who wants someone to be with his little girls. You know their mother died, and the grandmother lives in England. It would be a beautiful thing for you if I could manage it. The Putnams are all full of happy plans for a month at Nassau, as usual running away from January in New York.

Harriet looked at the two words that stood for Richard Carter, and her heart beat thickly.

"I can't keep this up!" she told herself, playing games with little convalescent Pip, walking over frozen roads with the girls, reading under the evening lamp. "I can't keep this up! Twenty-seven, and a governess, and in love with a married man who does not know I am alive!" summarized Harriet, bitterly. "I will simply have to forget it, and begin again, that's all."

And she meditated upon David, the excellent, steady, devoted David, who was Fred's brother and a dentist in Brooklyn, and who gave the children wonderful holidays at Asbury Park. It would make Linda and Fred very happy to have her change toward him: they were a little hurt and silent about David. He always went with them to the crowded beach where they spent July and August, had had a car this year, Linda told her sister, and had been "so popular."

Harriet would look off from her book; David's nearness did not hold the thrill, the shaking, the happy suffusion of colour that the most casual remembered glance of Richard Carter still possessed. No, she was richer in her memory of Richard--

"I think you're a wonder! Don't you think Fred is a wonder!" Linda would say. Fred's precious bank-account had been almost wiped out now; he made evening calculations with a sharp pencil. But what was a bank-account to a Pip coming downstairs on Christmas Day, shaky but gay, in his wrapper, and glad to be with the family again?

David was there, Christmas Day, and there was a fire and a tree, happy children everywhere, rosy little neighbours coming in to see the toys, snowy wet garments spread on the porch after church. David took Harriet walking in the fresh cold air, a Harriet so beautiful in her furry hat and long coat, with her brilliant cheeks and her blue eyes shining under a blown film of golden hair, that Linda, as she basted the turkey in the hot kitchen, couldn't help a little prayer that that would all come out "right."

"But, Davy dear!" Harriet and David had stopped short in the exquisite, silent woods. "There is a feeling--a something that makes marriage RIGHT! And I haven't it, that's all!"

"How do you know you haven't?" he said, smiling.

"Well---" She looked up bravely; David knew her whole story. "I've had it!"

"You don't mean that old feeling ten years ago? My dear girl, that wasn't love! That was just a little girl's first feeling. But look at Fred and Linda after seventeen years. Why, it's sacred--it's holy. Harriet, if once you said you would, it would COME. Why, that's the very proof that you're as fine--as sensitive as you are--that you don't feel it now. But, Harriet," his arm was about her now, his voice close to her ear "don't let those years with rich people spoil you for the real thing, dear! Think of our hunting for an apartment--Fred and I haven't Mother to care for now; I've some of her good old mahogany, we could pick out cretonnes and things--think of next summer, all together, down at the beach! Linda's children---"

She looked up at him, with something wistful in her blue eyes.

"Sounds nice, Davy!" she said, childishly. Instantly she saw leap to his face the look he had hidden so many years; she heard a new ring in his voice.

"Ah--you darling! You will? You'll let me tell them---?"

"No, no, no!" Half-angry, half-sorry, she put away his embrace. "I'll--Davy, I hate to spoil your Christmas Day--I don't know what to say! I'll think about it!"

"And tell me--it's noon now---" He took out his watch.

"Oh, David, you make me feel as if I were catching a train!"

"And so you are, the Matrimonial Limited!" He would have his kiss, but only caught it where the bright hair mingled with the dark fur of her cap. Then she turned to go home, forbidding the topic imperatively, meeting every buoyant hint with a suddenly serious warning. Her heart was lead within her.

"I suppose there's no help for it," she thought, in a panic. "Linda'll see--it'll all be out in five seconds!"

But Linda met them at the door, full of an announcement.

"Harriet, Mr. Carter is here!"

"Mr.--WHO?"

Back came the tide with a great rush, nothing else mattered. For a moment Harriet was turned to stone. Then in a dream of radiance and delight she went into the little parlour, and Richard Carter stood up to greet her, and there was nobody else in the world. Linda had introduced herself; David was introduced. Harriet glanced about helplessly; he had not come here to say "Merry Christmas," surely.

"I suggested that Hansen take the little people for a five-minutes' drive," he explained, "and then I shall have to hurry back. I wanted to speak to you on a matter of business, Miss Field. I wonder--since you're well wrapped--if we might walk to the corner and meet them; I'll only steal you from your family for five minutes."

"Certainly!" Harriet's heart was singing. The voice, the pleasantly certain manner, the firm, kind mouth--she drank in a fresh impression as if she had been starving! She was hardly conscious of what he said; it was enough that he had sought her out, that she was to have one more word with him.

"I came here to discuss my own plans, Miss Field," he said at the gate, "but a hint from your sister has made me fear that perhaps I am too late. She tells me that you may be making plans of your own."

"David?" Harriet said, resentfully. "I have no plans with David!" she said, simply.

"I didn't know," Richard answered. "I came to ask you to come back. Things are in an absolute mess with us. We have not had a serene moment since you left us--three weeks ago."

To go back--back to Crownlands! Harriet's spirit soared. She had been strong enough to leave, to leave Nina's young impertinence, and Madame Carter's coldness, but she knew she must go back! She had only despaired of their ever needing her again. Every fibre of her being strained toward the old life.

"Linda, my sister, thinks it would be unwise," she began. The man interrupted her.

"There has been a new turn of events, Miss Field. I had some information last night which may make a difference," he said, gravely. "I received a wire from Pope, in France. My wife--Isabelle--died on an operating table yesterday afternoon, in Paris."

Harriet, stupefied, could only look at him fixedly for a long minute. Her lips parted, but she did not speak.

"DIED?" she whispered, sharply. The man nodded without speaking. "But--but what was it?" Harriet said.

For answer he gave her the crumpled cable, with the bare statement of fact. She read it dazedly, looked at his sombre face, and read it again.

"I need not tell you that it is a shock," Richard said, looking off toward the bare village in its mantle of trampled snow. "It--it is--a shock." And he folded the cable and returned it to his pocket. "We were married twenty-three years," he said, simply. "She was an extremely pretty girl, vivacious and happy--I imagine hers was a happy life!"

"I can't believe it!" Harriet said.

"Well, now," Richard began presently in a different tone, "we are, as I said, Miss Field, in a mess. I haven't told the children this; they have a lot of young people there over Christmas. Bottomley tells me that he is leaving on the first. My mother and Nina are planning some entertainment for New Year's night, and I suppose this will end all that; I should suppose that Nina and her brother must have a period of mourning. I am deeply involved in a big project in Brazil, committee meetings all through January--I can't swing it, that's all.

"Now, when we last talked of the subject together," Richard pursued in a businesslike way, "you objected to the suggestion of a marriage, because my wife was then still alive. Am I correct?"

"Yes, that's correct!" Harriet said, voicelessly. She felt herself beginning to tremble.

"My purpose in coming to-day was to suggest that, if that was your sole objection," the man continued, painstakingly, "you might feel the situation changed now. I need you. We all do. If it is my mother who makes it impossible, or some other thing that I cannot change--why, I must get along as best I can. But my proposition is that you and I are quietly married to-morrow; you come back to-morrow night, and announce it whenever you see fit. Of course, it might be wiser not to have the two announcements come together; there will be the usual talk; Nina and my mother prostrated; and so on, and perhaps--but you must use your own judgment there. I may seem a little matter-of-fact about this, Miss Field, but I am hoping you understand. You have impressed me as a woman of unusual intelligence and sagacity; I am making you an unsentimental business offer. I need you in my life and I offer you certain advantages which it would be silly and school-boyish for me to deny I possess. I have a certain standing in the community which even Mrs. Carter's madness has not seemed to impair seriously. The boy and the girl both love you, and you have my warmest friendship. As for the financial end there will be the usual provision made for you in case of my death and I will make the same monthly arrangement with you that I had with Isabelle. I mention these matters so that you may understand that your position in my household will be as free and independent as was Isabella's. I do not know whether you will consider this a fair return for what I ask, for after all you are giving your services for life to the Carter household--

"Now, this is of course entirely subject to what pleases you in the matter," he broke off to say emphatically. "I merely throw it out as a suggestion. It would please me very much. I would draw a long breath of relief to have it settled. Mrs. Tabor is there--stays there; takes the head of my table. I spent last night at the club; I had cabled Pope--and expected an answer, but my mother telephoned me at three o'clock this morning to say that Ward and some of his friends had gone out ice-skating. Ward's been dropped from his university. I can't have that sort of thing, you know!"

"When--did you want me?" Harriet brought her beautiful eyes back from some far vista.

"To-morrow?" he said, with sudden hope in his voice.

"To-morrow!" the girl echoed, in a dream.

"I thought that if you could meet me at my office to-morrow, I would have all the arrangements made. Nina is to be at the Hawkes'; I send the car for her at three. I thought that you and she could go home together to Crownlands. I'll have to be in town that night."

"Home--to Crownlands!" Suddenly Harriet's lip quivered, and her eyes brimmed with tears. "I'll be very glad to go back," she said, in a low voice.

"Good!" he said. "I needn't tell you how I feel about it, it helps me out tremendously. Now, about to-morrow, how would you like that to be?"

"Well," she laughed desperately through her tears. "We're Church of England!" She laughed again when he took out his notebook and wrote the words down.

"Once it's done," he said, reassuringly, "you'll see my mother and all the rest of them come into line! It puts you in a definite position, and although I may seem to be rushing and confusing you now, there is a more peaceful time to come--we'll HOPE!" he added, grimly. "Here's Hansen now. Lovely children," he added, of the young Davenports and some intimates who were tumbling out of the car, "lovely mother."

"You'll not speak of this yet?" Harriet said, suddenly thinking of David and Linda. "My sister might think it lacked deliberation--so close upon Mrs. Carter's death. I'd rather have a little time, get things straightened out---"

"Oh, certainly--certainly!" She could see he was relieved, was indeed in cheerful spirits, as he gave his furred hand to the children's mittened ones. They thanked him shrilly and Hansen smiled warmly upon Harriet as he touched his cap. Then they were gone. Linda, watching from the window, thought that the chauffeur's obvious respect for Harriet was rather impressive. She came to the porch, and Richard waved his farewell to them en masse.

"He's very nice," said Linda. "Poor fellow, he probably would have had an entirely different moral code, if his life had been different!" Harriet inwardly writhed, but she did not stir in the sisterly embrace of Linda's arm. "Now if he would marry this Mrs. Tabor, whoever she is," Linda resumed, comfortably, "that would be quite suitable! Then you could go back with perfect propriety--"

"Oh, HUSH, for Heaven's sake!" Harriet said, in the deeps of her being. But she said nothing aloud as they turned back into the warm house.

Fred's face was radiant; for no apparent purpose he caught his sister-in-law in his arms as she passed him, and kissed the top of her hair.

"Here--here--here--what's all this!" Linda laughed.

"Nothing at all!" Fred said, evidently in boisterous spirits. Harriet looked sharply at David, but he was innocently laying train tracks for little Nammy. But she suspected at once that the elder brother had had a hint that matters were at least under consideration, and the rather aimless laugh with which Linda presently embraced her, and the air of suppressed excitement that marked the Christmas dinner, all confirmed the suspicion. She felt a prickling sensation of the skin; a flush of helpless annoyance.

CHAPTER XV

At three o'clock the next afternoon, Nina Carter, leaving the Hawkes' mansion in New York City, with a great many laughing farewells, descended to her father's waiting car, and discovered, sitting therein, an extremely handsome young woman, furred and trimly veiled, and deep in pleasant conversation with Hansen.

"Miss Harriet!" Nina ejaculated, in a tone that betrayed a vague resentment as well as a definite surprise.

"Nina, dear!" Harriet accepted Nina's kiss warmly. "Are you glad to see me?" And as Nina stumbled in, and established herself, Harriet continued easily, "Your father and I had a talk, my dear, and he suggested that I come back for awhile. So Hansen picked me up at the office, and here I am! He tried to telephone you, I know, but you were out. And now," said Harriet, glancing at her wrist watch, "I think we will go right home, please, Hansen!"

Nina had been her own mistress for several delicious weeks, and to have any sort of restriction again was very unpalatable to her. Harriet could almost have laughed at her discomfiture, although she was sorry for her, too. Nina smiled and listened with notable effort; Harriet knew she was chagrined.

She sulked all the way home, and Madame Carter, meeting them at Crownlands, gazed rather stonily at the newcomer, granting her only the briefest greeting. But oh, how homelike and welcoming the beautiful place, mantled in snow, looked to Harriet's eyes. The snapping fires, the warmth and fragrance of the big rooms, and the very obvious welcome of the maids, all were enchanting to her. Her first duty was to make a brief tour below stairs, after which she went up to her own room.

When they returned from Huntington in the fall, she and Nina at Richard's suggestion had taken Isabelle's handsome rooms, turning both into bedrooms, and sharing the dressing rooms and bath that joined them. It was here that Harriet found Nina awaiting her, still with her hat on, and loitering with obvious discomfiture. There had been no actual changes in her room except that the personal touch was gone. Bottomley had put her bags here, and Nina spoke first of them.

"You've got a new suitcase?"

"Yes, I got that this morning; isn't it stunning?" Harriet eyed its shiny blackness with satisfaction. "I had to get a gown or two," she added, "and some little things! We've been so quiet at Mrs. Davenport's that I hadn't any new clothes. Pip was ill, you know."

"Miss Harriet!" Nina said with a rush. "You're so sweet about things like this, I wonder if you will mind taking the yellow guest room--it's really much larger--and leaving this room? You see when I have friends--"

Harriet, at the dressing table, had raised her hands to remove her hat. Like any general, she realized the crisis of the apparently unimportant moment, and met it by instinct.

"But you have an extra bed, besides the couch, in your room, Nina!"

Nina cleared her throat, threw back her head, regarded Harriet between half-closed eyelids in a manner Harriet realized was new, and drawled:

"I know. But if you would be so very kind---?"

"Do you know, I'm afraid I shan't be so very kind!" Harriet said, briskly. "You're one of my duties here, you know, little girl, and I think Daddy would prefer to have me near you! Now, if you like to ask him, perhaps he'll not agree with me; in which case I shall move immediately! But meanwhile--" She picked up a thick book from the table, read the title idly: "'Secret Memoirs of the Favourites of the French Courts!' Where on earth did you get this?" she asked, surprised. "'Five Dollars Net,'" she mused, glancing through it. "How well I know this sort of rubbish! There are thousands of them on the market, exquisitely printed, beautifully bound, and just so much--rot! Secret memoirs of the favourites of the French Courts indeed! Most of them hadn't the brains to write a decent note!" scoffed Harriet, cheerfully.

Nina's face was scarlet; she left the room abruptly. A moment or two later Harriet sauntered into the adjoining room, and found her again. The younger girl was assuming a ruffled and beribboned negligee, and tossing her wraps and street dress about carelessly. Harriet noted this with disapproving eyes, but said nothing. There was an immense picture of Mrs. Tabor on the dressing table, and she found in that a sudden solution of the strange change in Nina.

"'With Ladybird's unending devotion, to Ninette,'" read Harriet, from the inky scrawl across the picture. "Do you call her Ladybird, Nina? You and she have formed a pretty strong friendship, haven't you?"

"Oh, something more than that!" Nina drawled in her new manner. But, being Nina, she could not resist the desire to display the new possession. She jerked open a desk drawer, and Harriet saw thick letters, still in their envelopes, and tied in bundles. "We write each other almost every day!"

said Nina, yawning, as she flung herself down upon a couch, and reached for a book.

"I should fancy she would make a loyal friend," Harriet observed, generously. Nina softened a little, although her voice was still carefully bored and arrogant when she spoke:

"Oh, she's the best sort!"

It was one of Mrs. Tabor's phrases, Harriet recognized. She moved easily about the room, picking up other handsome, superbly illustrated volumes: "An American Woman in the Sultan's Harem," "A Favourite of Kings."

"Does she have my room when she is here?" Harriet presently suggested, sympathetically. "Now, my dear," she added, as Nina's quick self-conscious and hostile look gave consent, "Mrs. Tabor is too thoroughly acquainted with convention to blame you if your father keeps you under a governess's eye for a little while longer. You're the most precious thing your father has, Nina, and as I used to remind you years ago, you don't begin to have the restrictions that the European princesses have to bear!"

This view of the case was always pleasing to Nina's vanity; she was quite clever enough to see that a friend protected and confined, watched and valued, would lose no prestige with the charming "Ladybird." She pouted; and Harriet saw that for the moment the battle was hers.

"Darling gown!" said Harriet of the picture.

"Oh, she has the most wonderful clothes!" It was the old Nina's voice. "She doesn't spend much, but she goes to the BEST places, and they know her there, and the women at Hatson's will say, 'I've got a gown for you, Mrs. Tabor!' She picked out this negligee, and she picked out another gown for me that you haven't seen. That was one thing that made trouble between her and her husband," Nina said, eagerly. "She can't help looking smart, and he used to get so jealous, and she told me that she told the judge exactly what she spent for clothes the last year, and he said that that was less than his wife spent, mind you, and he said he didn't know how she did it! And that was the judge, that had never laid eyes on her before! She used to cry and cry, after she got her divorce, because she said that she thought there was a sort of disgrace about it. But this judge in Nevada said that a man like Jack Tabor ought to be horsewhipped!"

"Has she--been here very much?" Harriet said, after a moment.

"Oh, lots! She loves to be here, and I can't think why," Nina said, "because people are all crazy to get her, and she could go to the most wonderful dinners and things. But she really is just like a girl, herself; sometimes we burst right out laughing, because we think exactly the same about things! And she just loves picnics, and to let her hair down--and she's so funny! You'll just love her when you know her--"

Nina, Harriet reflected, had had a thorough dose of poison. It would take, like many diseases, more poison to cure her, a counter dose. Going to her room to change to one of the new gowns, Harriet had a moment of contempt for the new-found intimate, who could so unscrupulously play upon the girl's hungry soul. But with this situation it was possible to cope; there was definite comfort in the fact that Nina had not mentioned Royal Blondin.

Brave in the new gown, whose lustreless black velvet made even more brilliant her matchless skin, Harriet went to find Ward. She met instead one of his house-guests, Corey Eaton, a man some years older than Ward, a big, rawboned, unscrupulous youth, with a wild and indiscriminate laugh. Mr. Eaton, greeting her enthusiastically, admitted frankly that he was just up from bed, and that he had been "lit up like a battleship" last night, and that he still felt the effects of it.

"Mr. Eaton," Harriet said, in an undertone, making another strategic decision, "come in here to the library, will you? I want to speak to you."

"When you speak to me thus," said Corey Eaton, passionately, "I can refuse you naught!"

But he sobered instantly into tremendous gravity at Harriet's first confidence. She told him simply of Isabelle's death.

"Well, that surely is rotten--the poor old boy!" said Corey, affectionately. "Ward's mad about his mother, too! Well, say, what do you know about that? We'll beat it, Miss Field, Nixon and I. We came in my car and we'll go to the Jays' for dinner. Say, that is tough, though, isn't it?"

It was not eloquent, but it was sincere, and Harriet made her thanks so personal and so flattering that the young man could only fervently push his plans for departure, swearing secrecy, and evidently touched by being taken into her confidence. The fastnesses were yielding one after another; Harriet could have laughed as she left him at the foot of the stairs. Bottomley respectfully addressed her as she turned back into the hall:

"Miss Field, I wonder if you'd be so good--?"

She nodded, and accompanied him instantly into the pantry where they could be alone.

"It's Madame," said Bottomley, bitterly, "she's just 'ad me up there agine, it's really tryin'--that's what it is. It's tryin'! Now she'ad to'ave her say about you bein' at table, Miss Field. I says that you 'ad stipulited that you WAS to be there. Now, I says, and I says it arbitrarily like, and yet I says it respectful, too---"

"Now, just wait one moment, Bottomley," Harriet said, soothingly. "I want to talk to you and Pilgrim. Is she in her room? Suppose we go there?"

Pleased with the consideration in her manner, the outraged Bottomley led the way. Mrs. Bottomley was enjoying a solitary cup of tea; she bustled hospitably for more cups.

"I want to tell you that your comin' has taken a load off my soul," said Pilgrim, a gray, round-visaged woman who had a sentimental heart, "and so I said to Mr. Carter not three days since! I know that Bottomley," said Pilgrim with an Englishwoman's admiring look for her lord, "would never have spoke so harsh if he had but known you might come back. It's been very bad, indeed, Miss, since you went, as we was tellin' you a bit back. Impudence, orders this way and that, confusion and what not, and Mr. Ward very wild, really very wild, and so at last Bottomley said he couldn't stand it."

"I'm hoping he will reconsider that," Harriet said, pleasantly, with a glance at the face Bottomley tried to make inflexible. "For I'm going to tell you two old friends some news. We have always been friends, haven't we?" said Harriet.

"It would be 'ard to be anything else, and I've said it before this! It's a different 'ouse with you in it!" Bottomley said. Pilgrim, rocking to and fro, clasped Harriet's hand to her breast, and beamed. With no further preamble Harriet announced Isabelle's death.

The servants were naturally shocked. There were a few moments of ejaculatory and sorrowful surprise. Her that was so young and so 'andsome, and went off so bold and high! It didn't seem possible, so far away from 'ome and all.

When this had died away, Harriet had more news.

"I'm going to tell you two something," she began. "You are the very first to know, and I know you'll be glad. Before I left the house last October, Mr. Carter did me the--the great honour to ask me to--to marry him."

It gave her inward delight even to voice it; it made the miracle seem more real. Bottomley and Pilgrim exchanged stupefied glances in a dead silence.

"I met him at eleven o'clock to-day," Harriet finished, simply, "and we drove to Greenwich in Connecticut, and we were married at one o'clock."

Bottomley and Pilgrim glanced again at each other, glanced at Harriet, opened their mouths slowly.

Then Pilgrim dropped the hand she was familiarly caressing, and Bottomley rose slowly to his feet.

"Oh, no!" Harriet said, flushing in utter confusion and with a nervous laugh. "Oh, please! Please sit down, Bottomley, and please don't either of you think that it has made any difference. Although I am Mrs. Carter now, I'm still Miss Nina's companion!"

"To think of you bein' Mrs. Carter!" Pilgrim marvelled in a whisper.

"Oh, sh--sh--sh! You mustn't say it even!" Harriet caught both their hands. "No one must know. I only told you so that you would help me, so that you would understand! There will be no change, anywhere--"

Bottomley shook a dazed head; but Pilgrim looked at the other woman with kindly eyes, and presently said:

"Well, now, it's hard on you, so young and pretty and all, and goin' right on as if you wasn't married a bit!"

Harriet only smiled, but she blinked black lashes that the little touch of sympathy had suddenly made wet. And presently when Bottomley was gone, and she about to follow him, she laid one hand on Pilgrim's broad black alpaca shoulder, and said:

"I had my own reasons, Pilgrim, you know. Reasons that make it all seem--right, to me!"

"Well, why wouldn't you?" Pilgrim said, approvingly. "You'd have been a very silly girl not to take him, and--as I always tell the girls--love'll come fast enough afterwards!"

The words came back to Harriet, hours later, when the house was quiet, and when, comfortably wrapped in a loose silk robe, she was musing beside her fire. Nina was asleep; to Ward, who was headachy and feverish, she had paid a late visit. He had been sick enough, after the revel of Christmas Eve, to summon a doctor to-day; and was dozing restlessly now, under the effect of a sedative. Madame Carter had not come down to dinner, and when Harriet had sent in a message, had asked to be excused from any calls, even from Nina and Miss Field, this evening.

Nina had chattered constantly during the meal. Granny had had a terrible time with them all. And Ward and Nina and "Royal"--the name suddenly leaped between them again--had been arrested for speeding. And Daddy had threatened Nina with a boarding-school, and Granny had cried.

"Where is Mr. Blondin now, Nina?" Harriet had asked.

"Oh, he's round!" Nina had said, airily. "I suppose you put Daddy up to saying that I wasn't to see so much of him!" she had added, with her worldly wise drawl.

"Not at all," Harriet had said.

"Ladybird and I are planning a trip," Nina had further confided. "I shall be eighteen in February, you know, and we want to go round the world. Would'nt it be wonderful to go with her, for she's been about fifty times!"

"Wonderful!" Harriet had been obliged to concede.

"You know"-and Nina, in good spirits, had put her arm about Harriet as they left the table--"you know, some day I'd love to do it with you!" she had said, soothingly. "And some day we will, for I mean to travel a great deal. But just now--she spoke of it, you know. And it would be such an unusual opportunity. We're going to Algiers--and Athens--Mr. Blondin is making out the list for us, and wouldn't it be fun if he could go, too? He's afraid he can't, but if he could--!"

"But, dearest child, what does your father think?"

"Father--" Nina had shrugged regretfully. "But I shall be of age!" she had reminded her companion.

"Yes, I know, dear, but Father's ward for another three years, you know!"

"Why, Ladybird says"--the girl had been ready, and had spoken with flushed cheeks--"Ladybird says that in that case we'll go anyway, and she'll pay all expenses! That's the kind of friend SHE is!"

And Nina had flounced to a telephone, and had telephoned her friend in New York, laughing, coquetting, and murmuring for a blissful half hour.

"Love'll come fast enough afterward!" Pilgrim had said, and Harriet thought Pilgrim was rather a wise woman, in her homely way. The girl stirred the fire and settled herself to watch it again.

After what? Well, certainly not after anything so short, simple, and unconvincing as that three minutes with the clergyman to-day. The utter unreality of that had seemed to blend with the silent, snowy day, and with the dulled and dreamy condition of her own brain. Snow was falling softly when she had met Richard Carter at the office, at half-past ten, and snow lisped against the windows of the limousine as they two, with Irving Fox, Richard's kindly, middle-aged, confidential clerk, were whirled out of the city, and on and on through the bare little wintry towns. They had all talked together, sometimes of herself and her sister, sometimes of Nina and Ward, of Fox's amazing grandchildren, and of business. Fox had had some papers to which they occasionally referred; the old clerk was the only person to congratulate Harriet warmly when the brief and bewildering business was over and she had her wedding ring. It was alone with Fox that she made the return trip. Richard came back by train, saving an hour, and was at the office when they got there. Harriet did not see him again; he was in conference; and presently she quietly got back into the motor-car, and on her way to meet Nina she slipped the plain circle of gold into her hand bag.

She had it out to-night, and put it on her bare, pretty hand, and held it to the fire, and slowly the events of the bewildering and tiring day wheeled before her, and only the reality of the ring assured her that it was not all a confused dream. Married! And all alone before the glowing coals, weary from hostile encounters, on her marriage night! Ward, to be sure, was always her champion, but Ward was drinking heavily just now, and her influence was none the stronger because he admired her while she held him at arm's-length. Nina was all ready to flame into defiance, and the old lady's message had not been reassuring.

"But Bottomley and Pilgrim will stand by me!" Harriet said, with a shaky laugh. She looked about the beautiful familiar room, the room that had been Isabelle's for so many years, and wondered to think of Isabelle, lying dead so far away, and a usurper already holding her name and place.

She had intended to write to Linda to-night; Linda was vexed with her, and small wonder! For Harriet had left the little New Jersey house almost without farewells, had come down to an earlier breakfast even than Fred's, and had said briefly that she was returning to the Carters, and would see them all soon.

Why hadn't she told Linda? Well, for one reason, she had hardly believed her own memory of the talk on Christmas Day with Richard. Then she had feared opposition, feared Linda's shocked references to decent intervals of mourning; Linda's frank unbelief that there was no strong personal feeling involved on Richard's part; Linda's advice to a bride.

Harriet's face burned at the mere thought of it. No, she couldn't tell Linda yet; she was too tired to write to-night, anyway. Linda and Fred had not been at all approving, Christmas night. David had reproached her, had disappeared earlier than was expected or necessary; they had not failed of their suspicions.

"Well! I must go to bed," she said aloud, suddenly. She stood, one elbow on the mantel, her beautiful eyes fixed on the dying fire. It was midnight, the room and the house very still. Outside the snow was still falling--falling. Her loose gown slipped back from the round young arm, fell in folds about the slender figure; her rich hair was braided, and hung in a rope of gold over one shoulder. Her smoke-blue eyes, heavy-lidded in a rather white face, met their own gaze in the mirror. "It isn't exactly what I expected marriage to be," mused Harriet, smiling at the exquisite vision upon which no other eyes would fall. "But after all," she said to herself, beginning to move about with last preparations for bed, "I'm married to the man I love--nothing can change that. And if he doesn't love me, he likes me. I've done nothing wrong, and if my life is just a little different from most women's, why, I shall have to make the best of it! And I did tell him--I did tell him--"

And her thoughts went back to the first few minutes she had spent in Richard's office that day. They had been alone, discussing the last details of their astonishing plan, when she had suddenly taken the plunge.

"Mr. Carter, there is just one thing! Of course," Harriet's cheeks had flamed, "of course, this marriage of ours is not the usual marriage, and yet, there is just one thing of which I would like to speak to you before we--we go up to Greenwich." And finding his gray eyes pleasantly fixed upon her she had gone on, confused but determined: "I'm twenty-seven now-and perhaps I might have married some other man before this--except that-when I was seventeen-I did fall in love with a man! And we were to be married--!" She had stopped short; it was incredibly hard. "He had--or I thought he had, brought something tremendously big and wonderful into my life," Harriet had continued, "and I was a stupid little girl, just taking care of my sister's babies and reading my father's books--"

"You are under no obligation to tell me anything of this," Richard had said, kindly, far more concerned for her distress than interested in what she was saying. "I must have known that there were admirers! I assure you that--"

"No, but just a moment!" Harriet had interrupted him. "I was infatuated--I knew that at once, God knows I've known it ever since! I went away with him, little fool that I was!"

A gleam of genuine surprise had come into Richard Carter's eyes, and he looked at her without speaking.

"I was taken ill the day I left with him. While I was getting well I had time to think it over. I knew then I was too young and too ignorant to be any man's wife. I was frightened and I--well, I ran away; I went back to my sister. Both she and her husband regarded me after that as in some way marked, unprincipled, unworthy--"

"Poor child!" Richard had said. "They naturally would. You were no more than Nina's age!"

"So that's my history," Harriet had finished, simply. "I thought I had done with men. And there have been men, men like Ward, for instance, to whom I could have been married without feeling that I need make any mention of that old time. But I wanted to tell you."

"Thank you very much," Richard had said, gravely. "If the protection of my name and my house seems welcome to you, after some battling with the world, it will be an additional satisfaction to me."

And then before another word was spoken Fox had come in, announcing the car, and they had begun the long, strange drive. And now, deep in the quiet winter night, she was back at Crownlands, alone beside her fire, able at last to rest, and to remember. It seemed to her that ever since Richard's call on Linda's Christmas household yesterday she had walked strangely detached and isolated, with odd booming noises in her ears, and a panicky thumping at her heart. Now she felt suddenly safe and secure again; none of the oppositions she had vaguely feared, from David, from Linda, from the family at Crownlands, had interrupted the mad plan; she was in a stronger position now than ever, and if the path before her was dangerous and difficult, she was not too weary to-night to feel confident of following it to the end.

She got into the luxurious bed, put out the bedside light, and lay with her hands clasped behind her head, thinking. The clock struck one; snow was still falling steadily outside, but in here the last pink glow of firelight flickered and sank--flickered and sank lazily. It touched the flowered basket chairs, the roses that filled a bowl on the bookshelf, the table with its shaded lamp and its magazines.

Some sudden thought made Harriet smile ruefully. She indicated that it was unwelcome by turning over to bury her bright head in the pillow, and resolutely composing herself for sleep.

CHAPTER XVI

Morning found them half-buried in a bright dazzle of snow, the midwinter miracle that sets the most jaded heart singing and the weariest blood to moving more quickly. The bare trees glittered in a glassy casing, and every twig carried its burden of soft fur. Half-a-dozen shovels were scraping and clinking about Crownlands when Nina and Harriet came downstairs, and Harriet saw the men laughing and talking as they worked. The telephone announced Francesca Jay, with an eager luncheon invitation for Nina and Ward; they were bob-sledding, and it was perfectly glorious!

"I wish I liked people as much as they like me," Nina remarked over her breakfast. "Now I like the Jays--but this being invited everywhere--all the time!" Harriet, who suspected that Miss Jay's hospitality was really directed at the engaging Ward, good-naturedly persuaded him to go with his sister, thus assuring a real welcome from Francesca. He looked pale, complained of a headache, and breakfasted on black coffee, but agreed with her that fresh air and exercise would be the one sure cure for him, and tramped off beside Nina at eleven o'clock willingly enough.

Harriet was through with her housekeeping and her luncheon, and meditating a letter to Linda, when Ida Tabor fluttered in. Harriet heard the gay voice at the foot of the stairs: "Oh, sweetheart! Where's my little girl?"

Mrs. Tabor looked a trifle dashed when only Harriet responded, although she immediately assured Miss Field cordially with bright insincerity that she had known of her return, and was "so glad!"

"I've been a sort of big sister here," she said, laughingly, "and, my Lord, these kids have managed things wonderfully! But I suppose sooner or later the machinery would have stalled without your fine Italian hand!"

"Mr. Carter asked me to come back," Harriet stated, simply. She thought the truth her best weapon, but Mrs. Tabor was ready for her.

"Mary Putnam told us that you were just resting and looking about," she said, innocently, "and Dick--generous that he is!--couldn't feel comfortably about it, I suppose! Well, I wanted to see Nina--?"

Harriet explained Nina's absence, and Mrs. Tabor pouted.

"I'd have stopped there," she said. "I'm on my way to the Fordyces'; they have a regular New Year's party, you know--"

This was deliberate, Harriet knew. Ida Tabor had not always been admitted to the Fordyces' sacred portals.

"Blondin and I are getting it up," she further elucidated, "I want Nina in it, and Ward, too. Blondin is lending us the most gorgeous tapestries and things you ever saw!"

Harriet was not concerned for Nina's plans after today; for Richard had telephoned her at three o'clock that the morning papers would have "the news," and that he was coming home to tell his children of their mother's death, to-night. But she must get rid of this woman now, somehow. It would be fatal to have Ida Tabor here when Richard Carter returned. Her time was short, Harriet thought anxiously, for at any minute now the young people might stream back for tea.

"I might run up now and see the old lady!" said Mrs. Tabor who had flung off her furs, and beautified herself at her hand-bag mirror. "I don't really have to get to the Fordyces' until just before dinner--really not then, if Nina wanted me!" She pressed her lips together for the red colouring. "Mr. Carter be here to-night?" she asked, casually.

Bottomley caused an interruption. Harriet turned to him with relief. But unfortunately he answered the very question she was trying to evade.

"Mr. Carter had just telephoned, 'm, and says that he'll be 'ere at about six, 'm!"

"Oh, thank you, Bottomley!" Harriet turned back to Ida, to see her complacently loosening outer wraps.

"I came in the Warrens' car," said she, "they were to run over and say Merry Christmas to the Bellamys, and then pick me up. But--if I won't be in the way!--perhaps I might stay and see Nina; we've become great chums. I suppose I'd better go to the room I always have? Then I'll run up and get the latest news of the Battle of Shiloh from Madame Carter!"

It was now or never; Harriet's heart began to beat.

"Madame Carter has gone driving," she said. "She may be in at any moment, but before she comes, I want to speak to you. We've had terrible news here, Mrs. Tabor. Mr. Carter is coming home to tell the children and his mother to-night. Mr. Pope cabled from Paris on Christmas Eve that Mrs. Carter suddenly died that day!"

Ida Tabor never felt anything very deeply, but her emotions were accessible enough, and violent while they lasted. She grew white, gasped, somehow reached a chair, and burst into honest tears. Isabelle--! Why, they had been friends for years! Why, she had been so wonderfully well and strong!

"My God, isn't that the limit!" said Mrs. Tabor, drying her eyes. "I don't know why I'm such a fool," she added, with perhaps a faint resentment of

Harriet's calm, "but I declare it's just about taken my breath away! And they don't know it! Isn't that simply terrible!"

"Nobody knows it," Harriet said. And not quite innocently she added: "The Fordyces, the Bellamys--everyone who knew her--are in total ignorance of it! If you do tell them, Mrs. Tabor--and there is no reason why you shouldn't--"

"Oh, I shall stay here with Nina to-night, anyway!" the visitor said, decidedly. "She'll need me, of course! Poor little thing!"

"It seems too bad to spoil your New Year's plans," Harriet said, smiling, "but you know Nina! She will put those long arms of hers about you--and she won't hear of your leaving her for days! With Nina," Harriet pursued, thoughtfully, "it isn't so much that one can't find a good excuse, as that she won't hear of excuses at all! I remember when Mrs. Carter first went away, there were days of it--weeks of it!--just talk, tears, tears, and talk--my arm used to ache from the weight of Nina's arm! Mr. Carter intends to leave for Chicago to-morrow, Ward will probably go up to the Eatons'---" Harriet rambled on, not unconscious that she was making an impression. "Anyway," she finished, "we shall be fearfully quiet and alone here, and your being here would simply save the day for Nina!"

"Oh, I really couldn't stay over New Year's," Mrs. Tabor, looking slightly discomfited, said slowly. "You see, the Fordyces--"

"Nina may keep you," Harriet said, lightly. Perhaps the other woman had a sudden vision of the overwhelming Nina, a Nina so convinced of her friend's real desire to stay that with a certain sportive heaviness she would do the necessary telephoning and explaining herself, to keep her. Perhaps she saw the alternate vision of herself at the Fordyces' inaccessible, and it must be confessed dull, dinner table, electrifying them all with the news of Isabelle Carter, coming as one admitted to the family confidence and councils. She looked undecided, and bit her under-lip.

"One wonders--?" she said, musingly. "Of course, I shouldn't want to intrude to-night--it would be merely to have them feel that I was HERE--"

"Mr. Carter has asked me to see that the family is alone to-night," Harriet said, courageously, "but of course he may feel that you are an exception," she added, with the impersonal air of a mere employee. "I only want to be able to tell him that I repeated his request, and told you the reason for it. That's"--and she smiled pleasantly--"that is as far as my authority goes, of course. I shall say simply that you know of his wishes, and if you remain, I know I can say that it was to please Nina!"

And now the two women exchanged an open glance that needed no pretence and no concealment, and it was a glance of enmity.

"When I visit this house it is not at your invitation, Miss Field!" said Mrs. Tabor, frankly. "I am aware of that," Harriet said, simply.

"Will you be so kind as to tell Nina and Madame Carter," the visitor was resuming her wraps, and arranging her handsome hat and veil, "that I will be here to-morrow, and that anything I can do I will be so glad to do!--Is that Mrs. Warren's car, Bottomley? Thank you. Good afternoon, Miss Field!"

"Good afternoon, Mrs. Tabor!" Harriet followed her to the hall door, and heard a Parthian shot, ad-dressed in a cheerfully high voice to kindly old Mrs. Warren, Mrs. Fordyce's mother, who was in the limousine.

"Nobody home! All my trouble for nothing!"

Old Mrs. Warren leaned against the frosted glass; waved from the holly-dressed interior at Harriet, and the girl saw her lips frame "Merry Christmas!" The door slammed; Bottomley came with stately footsteps up to the hall again. Harriet gave a little laugh of triumph. Now the coast was clear!

Thus it was that Richard Carter found only his mother and his children at the dinner table that night, and no guests under his roof. Miss Field, to be sure, was at the head of the table, but then Miss Field was a member of the family. He interrogated her briefly as they went in.

"Ward's gang? That Eaton ass?"

"Oh, they went yesterday!"

"Speak to Bottomley?"

"Yes. He and Pilgrim are quite reconciled to remaining." Harriet buttoned a cuff, to hide a dimple that would come to the corner of her mouth. "And Mrs. Tabor came, and would have stayed," she could not resist the temptation to add, "but I persuaded her that some other time would be better!"

"Scene with Nina about it?" Richard had asked, curiously.

"Nina was not here," Harriet answered. And there was a faint smile in the deep blue eyes that she raised suddenly to his.

"Ah, well, I knew of course that you would manage it!" he said, contentedly. "It seems black art to me. I had enough of it!"

She smiled again, and went quietly to her place. But when he summoned Ward and Nina to his mother's room, after dinner, she had disappeared, and the family was quite alone when he broke the news to them.

Harriet, presently needed again, was astonished at the emotion of the old lady, who had been genuinely fond of her daughter-in-law, and had always been loyal to Isabelle, as one of the Carters. Madame Carter was greatly shaken, Nina hysterical, Ward aggrieved, irritated at his own feeling. He had not seen his mother for seven months, she had brought nothing but a certain unpleasant notoriety to her children, yet her death struck both the young creatures forcibly, and they felt shocked and shaken.

"We can't be in the Fordyce tableaux," said Nina in an interval between floods of sobs. "Not that I would want to, now! But I don't know; it seems to me that I am the most unfortunate girl in the world!"

"I think both you and Ward should wear black for a certain period," Richard said to her. He had been walking the floor nervously, stopping now and then beside the great chair where his mother sat silent and stricken, to put his arm about her shoulders, and murmur to her consolingly.

"When my mother died," Madame Carter quavered, with her handkerchief pressed to the tip of her nose, "my sisters and I wore black, and refused all social engagements for one year. We then, I remember distinctly, began to wear white and lavender--"

Harriet smiled inwardly at the picture of Victorian mourning and compared it to the mourning of to-day, as different indeed as was the conception of motherhood to-day.

"I remember that a cousin of my mother, Cousin Mallie we used to call her, got in a sewing woman, and all our black things were made right there in the house--" the old lady was pursuing, mournfully, when Nina broke in pettishly:

"I don't see why I have to wear black!"

"Why should you?" Ward said with bitter scorn. "It's only your mother!" Nina began to cry.

"You and I will go down to Landmann's early to-morrow, Nina," Harriet suggested, "and we'll have someone show us what is simple and nice--not crape, you know," Harriet said with a glance at Richard Carter, "but black, for a few months anyway."

"I think that would be the least, Richard," his mother approved. "I believe I will go with you," she condescended to Harriet, "after all, Isabelle was my daughter-in-law, and the mother of my grandchildren!"

"And I won't go to California or Bermuda or any-where else unless Ladybird comes!" Nina burst out, with a broken sob.

"Nonsense!" her father began harshly. Harriet said:

"Bermuda? Is there a plan for Bermuda?"

"I suggested it for a few weeks," Richard said, frowning, "but I don't propose to have Nina invite a group of friends. That isn't exactly the idea."

"We could ask Mrs. Tabor," Harriet said, soothingly; "it is right in the middle of the season, and perhaps she will feel she can hardly spare the time. But I'm sure that if she can--"

"If I ask her, she'll go," Nina said, in a sulky, confident undertone.

Harriet had her doubts, but she did not express them. A month at Nassau, in the undiluted company of Nina and her grandmother, was enough to appall even Harriet's stout heart.

The event proved her right, for while Ida Tabor flew at once to her disconsolate little friend, and assured Richard with tears in her eyes that she would do anything in the world to help him, she weakened when the actual test arrived.

"If just you and I and your dear grandmother were going, dearest girl," she said to Nina, "then it would be perfect. But as long as Miss Field, who is perfectly charming and conscientious and all that, feels that she must accompany us, why--you and I would never be a moment alone, sweetheart, you know that! I DON'T like to think that it's jealousy--"

"Of course it's jealousy," Nina was pleased to decide, gloomily. "Granny says that we don't need her, but Father just sticks to it that she must manage everything!"

"I am going to run in every few days and amuse your father, and get the news of you," said Ida Tabor. "You don't think that your father perhaps trusts Miss Field too far, do you?" she added, carelessly. She was standing behind Nina at the dressing table, experimenting with the girl's thick, straight hair. "You look like one of the little Russian princesses with it that way!" said she.

Nina was instantly diverted.

"I had to laugh at Christine yesterday," she said. "She said, 'Oh, Ma'm'selle, you've got enough for two people here!' 'Oh,' I said, 'then I ought to pay you double'!" Nina laughed. "And I did, too!" she finished. For Nina, without ever being unselfish, was often extremely generous. Ida Tabor smiled automatically.

"I don't suppose your father sees anything in Miss Field," she submitted again, lightly.

"Oh, Heavens, no!" Nina said, studying herself in a handglass. "Christine says that I ought to have my eyebrows pulled," she added, thoughtfully. There was a rather steely look in the eyes of her friend

Ladybird, but she did not see it. Her smile of pleasure gradually gave place to a pout. "I'm going to ask Father if we need Miss Harriet!" she said.

And that evening she did indeed attack Richard on the subject, although not as decidedly as she had planned. He listened to her interestedly enough, with his evening paper held ready for his next glance.

"Let you roam about the country with Mrs. Tabor," he said, as the girl's faltering accents stopped. "No, my dear, it's out of the question! In the first place, she is not the sort of companion I would choose for any girl, and in the second place I would never know where you and your grandmother were, or what was happening to you! While Miss Field is in charge I shall feel entirely safe. Of course, if Mrs. Tabor chooses to invite herself, that's her affair!"

"Then I don't want to go!" Nina stormed. But in the end she did go. The alternative of moping about Crownlands, and seeing her idol only at intervals, was not alluring, and Mrs. Tabor herself urged her to go. Madame Carter, Nina, and Harriet duly sailed, in the second week of January, and Ward joined them almost a month later, in Nassau. And here Harriet had the brother and sister at their best, free to show the genuine childishness that was in them, to swim and picnic and tramp, and here she indulged Nina in long talks, and encouraged her to associate with the young people she met. Madame Carter found the island air a help to her rheumatic knee, and consequently made no protest against a lengthened stay. She slept, ate, and felt better than in the cold northern winter, and at seventy-five these considerations were important.

Harriet wrote once a week to Richard, making a general report, and enclosing receipted hotel and miscellaneous bills. His communications usually took the form of cables, although once or twice she received typewritten letters.

In mid-April they all came home again, and Crownlands, in the year's first shy filming of green, looked wonderful to Harriet's homesick eyes. With joyous noises and confusion Ward and Nina scattered their possessions about, and the old lady bustled, chattered, and commented. Bottomley and Pilgrim were apparently enchanted to welcome home their one-time tormentors, and in the fresh, orderly rooms, and the scent of early flowers, and the burgeoning winds that shook the blossoms, there was a wholesome order and familiarity delicious to the wanderers.

Richard was to join them at dinner; it had been impossible for him to meet them when the boat arrived, but Fox had been there and attended to the formalities. It had pleased them all to make the occasion formal and to dress accordingly. Nina looked her prettiest in a white silk, and the old lady was magnificent in diamonds and brocade. Harriet deliberately selected her handsomest gown, a severe black satin that wrapped her slender body with one superb and shining sweep, and left her white arms and firm, flawless shoulders bare. The weeks of sunshine and fresh air had been good for her, as for the others, and when she was dressed, and stood in the full blaze of the lights, looking at herself, she would not have been human not to be pleased. Her bright hair was dressed high, and shone in rich waves and curves against the soft, dusky forehead, and above the black-fringed, smoke-blue eyes. The firm young lines of chin and throat, the swelling white breast that met the encasing satin, the slippers with their twinkling buckles--she could not but find every detail pleasing, and her scarlet mouth, firmly shut, was twitched by a sudden dimple.

She glanced at the clock, went slowly to the door, and slowly down the big square stairway. Richard and his children were in the lower hall, and they all glanced up.

Down in the soft glow of light came Harriet, smiling as she slipped her left arm about Nina, and gave the free hand to Nina's father. She was apparently cool and unself-conscious; inwardly she felt feverish, frightened and excited and happy, all at once. Richard was in evening dress, too; he looked his best; his dark hair brushed to a shining crest, and his gray eyes full of pleasure.

"Well, Miss Field--!" he said, a little breathlessly. "Well! Your vacation hasn't done you any harm!"

"We had to make an occasion of our coming home!" Harriet said, with a nervous laugh, trying not to see the admiration in his eyes.

"I must say I like the gown," Richard said, simply. It was impossible not to speak of it, and of her; they were all staring at her.

"You look wonderful!" Nina said.

"Why, you saw this gown at Nassau," Harriet protested.

"Louise--or whoever she was of Prussia, or whatever you call it, turned in the family vault when you walked down those stairs!" Ward said. "Oo-oo--caught you under the mistletoe--oo-oo, you would!" he added, with an effort to envelop her in his embrace.

"Ward, behave yourself!" Harriet said, evading him, and walking toward the dining room with his grandmother, who came downstairs in her turn, and joined them. "No pain in the knee?" Richard heard her say, solicitously.

"Not a bit!" the old lady said, eagerly. "Why, my dear," she added, grandly, "there's no rheumatism in our family! Not a bit! It was just that fall I had, ten years ago, that settled there, that was all! Immediately after that fall---"

Harriet had heard of the fall before. She had heard of it one hundred times. But she listened attentively. She had an aside for Bottomley, she drew Nina into the conversation, she was most at ease with Ward, teasing him, drawing him out.

Richard Carter watched her, the incarnation of young and beautiful womanhood. Clever he knew her to be, capable and conscientious, but to-night she was in a new role. He liked to see her there at the other end of the table; he realized that she was the centre of things, here in his house, and that he had missed her.

After dinner it chanced that Bottomley called her to the telephone, and that a moment later she passed the call on to Richard.

"It's Mr. Gardiner, Mr. Carter. He didn't know that you were here, but he would rather speak to you," Harriet said. Richard went to the telephone, and as she moved to make room for him, and gave him the receiver, he had a sudden breath of the sweetness and freshness of her, of hair and young firm skin, of the rustling satin gown, and the little handkerchief that she dropped, and that he picked up for her. He smiled as he gave it, and flushed inexplicably, and his first few words to the bewildered Gardiner were a little shaken and breathless. But Richard was quite himself again an hour or two later, when he sent for Miss Field, and she came into the library.

"I needn't say that I'm entirely pleased with the way matters have gone, Harriet," said Richard, when she had seated herself on the opposite side of his big, flat desk, and locking her white hands on the shining surface, had fixed her magnificent eyes on him. "Nina seems in fine shape, and I have never seen my mother better. You seem to have a genius for managing the Carters. Ward, of course, is the real problem now--I wish the boy might have made his degree; but it wasn't to be expected perhaps. He's clever, but his heart wasn't in it; he never made the slightest effort to get through. I'm seriously considering this offer from Gardiner; he's got to take his boy out to Nevada for his health. Ward wants to go, and would very probably like it when he got there. Gardiner's brother is a magnificent fellow, 'P. J.,' they call him; he and his cattle are known all over that part of the country. He's got two or three pretty girls--I hope Ward will try it, anyhow! So that leaves Nina, who is safe enough with you, and my mother, who seems perfectly well and happy. Meanwhile, while you've been gone, we've gotten the

Brazilian company well started, so that I shall have a little more freedom than I've had for years."

"You look as if you needed it," Harriet observed.

"YOU look wonderful," Richard returned, simply. "Wonderful! Is that a new gown?"

"Well, I had it made last November just before I went away. Mrs. Carter gave me the material a year ago." Harriet glanced down at herself and smiled.

"You might wear pearls--or something--with it," Richard said. "Do you like pearls?"

It was astonishing to see the colour come up in her dusky skin; her eyes met his almost pleadingly.

"Why--I never thought!" she said, in some confusion.

"I suppose a man may ask his wife if she likes pearls?" Richard said, impelled by some feeling he did not define. He had leaned back in his chair, and half-closed his eyes, as he studied her.

"Oh--please!" Harriet said in an agony. She gave a horrified glance about, but the library was closed and silent. "Someone might hear you!" she whispered. And a moment later she rose to her feet, and eyed him quietly. "Was that all, Mr. Carter?" she asked. It was Richard's turn to look a trifle confused.

"That's all--my dear!" he said, obediently. The term made her flush again. He was still smiling when she closed the door.

CHAPTER XVII

It was the gayest spring that Harriet had ever known at Crownlands, for even at her best, Isabelle had been socially an individualist, devoting herself to one man at a time, and to nobody else, and the whole family had necessarily accepted Isabelle's attitude. Richard had been too busy to notice or protest, the old lady helpless, and Nina a child.

But now there was a beautiful and gracious woman in Isabelle's place, and long before the world knew that Harriet Field was really Harriet Carter, there was a very decided change in the social atmosphere. Nina would be eighteen in June, and affairs for Nina and her friends began to assume a more formal air. Ward, who seemed anxious to placate his father, and convince him of his genuine reform, was almost always at home, and Madame Carter was willing to accept the comfort and amusement that Harriet's return brought to the house, and rarely raised an issue with the triumphant secretary. And, more strange than all, Richard began to bring his friends to the house; he was proud of his smoothly running establishment, and proud of the charming woman who neither flirted with nor ignored the men he brought home. They were plain men sometimes, business associates who might have been ill at ease at Crownlands, and voiceless at the dinner table. But Harriet drew them out, and seemed to have some conversational divining rod by which she touched with unfailing instinct upon the topic of each in turn.

Always beautiful and always busy, constantly in demand on all sides, she went about his house like a smiling worker of miracles, and Richard watched her. When she went home to her sister for a day or two he missed her strangely, and wandered about the empty rooms with a desolate sense of loss.

She was presently back, and amused the young people at the dinner table with a spirited account of her sister's move into a new house--"really an old house," that she and her family had been watching for years. It had been auctioned, forfeited by the purchaser, it had figured in a lawsuit, and now at last it was in the possession of the delighted Davenports. And the move--with the baby carrying his puppy, and Pip the goldfish, and the girls wheeling the old baby-carriage full of their treasures, and Linda whitening her hands with a cut lemon, as she walked the seven short blocks--! Harriet made them see it all, and Richard laughed with the children. His mother, always reminiscent, recalled a move in his own third year, when he had tasted furniture polish, and made himself ill.

Nina and Amy and Ward had rushed from the dinner table to an early dance at the club, and Richard, after a talk with his mother on the terrace, had wandered about with a vague hope of finding Harriet somewhere with her book. But she was not downstairs.

He went back, and presently accompanied his mother to her door. The old lady stopped outside of Nina's open door, from which a subdued light streamed.

"Oh, Miss Field--" said Madame Carter.

"Yes, Madame Carter!" The rich, ready voice responded instantly. Richard hoped she would come to the door, but his mother's message was delivered too quickly to make it necessary.

"You're waiting up for Nina?"

"Oh, yes, Madame Carter!" Harriet answered. The two exchanged good-nights; Richard loitered into his mother's room, left her in her maid's hands, and went back into the dimly lighted, spacious upper hall. He felt oddly stirred; there were letters downstairs, his usual books and amusements, but he felt curiously impelled to try for one more word with Miss Field.

He opened the door of Nina's room, and went in, and knocked on the half-open door within that connected it with Harriet's room.

"Come in. Is it you, Pilgrim?" the pleasant, quiet voice said. Richard stepped to the doorway.

Harriet, seated in a square basket chair, under the soft flood of light from a basket-shaded lamp, rose precipitately, and stood looking at him with widened eyes and parted lips, without speaking. She was plainly frightened, though she made herself smile. She wore a scant, long-sleeved garment of a deep, oriental blue, that covered her from her white throat to her feet, and yet that was obviously only for bedroom wear, and to which she gave a quick, apologetic glance, as the man came in. He noticed that in this mellow light her blue eyes seemed to communicate a blue shadow to their neighbourhood, brows and lids, and the clean arch in which they were set, all wore the same shadowy blueness. The beautiful room was full of shadows; at the wide-open windows thin curtains stirred in the cool night air.

"Frighten you?" Richard said.

"Is there something--?" Her eyes were those of a deer that is afraid to turn.

"Why, I wanted to suggest that we tell our little piece of news to the family," Richard suggested, after a momentary search for a suitable subject. "I came very close to telling my mother, just now. Is there any good reason for further delay?"

"Why, no, I don't--I don't suppose there is!" Harriet stammered.

"You see, my mother had left me in no doubt of her intentions with Mrs. Tabor," Richard said, smiling. "I'll give Mrs. Tabor credit for being as innocent as I am in the matter," he added, simply. "But there's a plan for a Montreal trip--I believe Ida arrives for a week to-morrow, and so on. I should be very glad to let the world know that--my arrangements--in the line, are already made. It will be fairer to you, too, I think. Gardiner asked me last night if the coast was clear--Ward asked me if I thought there was any use in his trying again--"

"There will be talk," said Harriet with distaste, as he paused.

"I suppose so," he answered, simply. "But what we do is our own affair, after all. I shall explain to my mother that for us both it seemed a practical and a--well, not unpleasant solution. There need be no change here, but you will simply have a more assured position--"

She had been watching him, with all June in her face. But as he went on the colour slowly drained away, and about her beautiful eyes a look of strain and even of something like shame gradually deepened. When she spoke, it was as if the muscles of her throat were constricted.

"Yes, I see. Certainly, I see. We will have to let them talk. This is-- simply the best arrangement possible under the circumstances!"

"It is an arrangement that a man perhaps has no right to ask of a woman," Richard said. "Love means a great deal in a girl's life, and I suppose there is nothing else that makes up for the lack of it. But you are not an ordinary woman, and I assure you that in every way that I can I mean to prove to you how deeply I appreciate what you are doing for us all."

"Thank you!" Harriet said, almost inaudibly.

"Simply change your name on your checks," Richard said, thoughtfully. "I shall have Fox step into the bank with the authenticated signature. And if there is anything else, use your own judgment. Perhaps, if I tell my mother, you would like to write to certain friends--? You can continue to draw on the Corn Exchange, that's simplest, and I hope you'll remember that you have a large personal credit there," he added, with a smile. "It occurred to me to-night that you--you mustn't let your sister worry about that new house. If you want your own car--"

"Oh, good heavens, Mr. Carter!" Harriet said, suffocating.

"Ask me anything that puzzles you," the man said. And with a brief good-night he was gone. Harriet, who had dropped back into her chair, sat absolutely motionless for a long, long time. Her eyes were fixed on space; she hardly breathed; it almost seemed as if her heart was stopped.

Richard went downstairs, surprised to feel still vaguely unsatisfied. He had had his word with Harriet, had said indeed much that he had not expected to say. However, it was much better to let the world know their relationship; he was perfectly satisfied to have it so. But still, as he settled himself to an hour's reading, the plaguing little impulse persisted. He would like to go upstairs again; he missed her companionship.

There was something very appealing about this woman, thought Richard, suddenly closing his book. Her beauty, her silences, her complete subjugation of her own interests to his, he found strangely fascinating. She had looked extremely beautiful in that long, dark blue bedroom gown, reading Shakespeare. He wondered why she read Shakespeare.

"By George, she has made a most interesting woman of herself!" Richard decided, opening his book again. "She ought to be right in the middle of things, that girl!"

He was still reading when Nina and Amy came in, and yawned him good-nights from the library doorway. He heard them go upstairs, heard a burst of laughter and nonsense, and then Harriet's rich voice, and then the closing door. Then there was silence. Richard discovered that he was sleepy, and went upstairs, too.

A day or two later Madame Carter came out to the terrace at eleven o'clock, beautifully groomed and gowned, and with an imperative hand arrested Harriet, who was tumbled and sunburned from the tennis court and was going toward the house.

"Just a moment, Miss Field," said she, magnificently. Harriet obediently stood still, and watched Madame Carter's magnificence settle itself slowly in a basket chair. The old lady freed an eyeglass ribbon deliberately, straightened a ruffle, laid her magazine beside her on a table. "There was a little matter of which I wished to speak to you," she said, suavely, bringing her distant glance to rest dispassionately for a moment upon Harriet's face.

Harriet waited, amused, annoyed, impatient.

"I understand," Madame Carter said, "that you and my son--for some reason best known to yourselves--have entered into a secret marriage?"

"Your first object, my dear, is not to antagonize his mother!" Harriet reminded herself. Aloud she said mildly: "You have no reason to disbelieve it, have you?"

"No reason to disbelieve my son!" his mother echoed, scandalized. "Why should I have! Mr. Carter is the soul of honour--absolutely the soul. Upon my word, I don't understand you!"

"I said you have no reason to disbelieve him," Harriet repeated. "You said that you UNDERSTOOD that we had been married. It is true!"

And she looked off toward the river with an expression as composed as that of Madame Carter herself.

"I suppose you know that old saying: 'A secret bride has a secret to hide!'" the older woman pursued, pleasantly.

"I never heard it. I did not play much with the children of the neighbourhood when I was a child," Harriet answered. "My father was very anxious to protect us from picking up expressions of that sort!"

There was a silence. Harriet, beginning to be ashamed of herself, did not look at her companion.

"A girl of your age has a great deal of confidence when she marries into a family like mine," the old lady said, presently, in a tone that trembled a little. "My son is a rich man--he is a prominent man. He has used his own judgment, of course. But I confess that in your place I should not carry myself with quite so much an air of--triumph! It seems to me--"

Harriet had had time to reflect that such an opening would certainly lead to tears and hysteria now, and might easily begin an estrangement that would sadden and disappoint Richard. A few more such exchanges, and his mother would retire worsted to her room, might possibly leave his house, and punish Harriet cruelly through him. She determinedly regained her calm, and taking the chair next to the enraged old lady, quietly interrupted the flow of her angry words.

"I hope I have shown no air of triumph, Madame Carter," Harriet said. "You yourself--and most wisely!--pointed out to us a few months ago that the arrangement here was unconventional--"

"Everyone was talking, if you mind that!" the old lady snapped. But she was slightly mollified, none-the-less. "But upon my word, you'd think marrying into the family was something to be done every day--!" she was beginning again, when Harriet interrupted again.

"No--no," she said, soothingly, conceding the last words an amused smile that itself rather helped to placate her companion. "It is, of course, the most serious step of my life! But the secrecy--as of course you will appreciate--was because there has been so much terrible notoriety this year! Why, Mr. Carter tells me that never in the history of all the Carters--"

This fortunate lead was enough. Madame Carter launched forth superbly upon a description of the usual Carter weddings, the ceremony, the state. In perhaps twenty minutes she was blandly patronizing Harriet, giving her encouraging little taps with her eyeglasses, warning her of mistakes that Isabelle had made with Richard. Harriet knew that before three days were over her terrible mother-in-law would be telling the world just how wise, under the trying circumstances, the whole thing was, and just how clearly she had foreseen it. She was still listening respectfully, if a trifle confusedly, when Ward bounded from the house, and gave her an effusive embrace.

"Hello, Mamma!" Ward said. Harriet laughed, as she pushed away the filial arm. Hardly knowing what she said or did she made her way to the house, and up to her own room.

But here, in Nina's room, were Nina and Mrs. Tabor, and from their eyes, as she came in, she knew that they knew. Nina got up, and came forward with a sort of sulky graciousness.

"I hope you'll be very happy, Miss Harriet--I suppose I oughtn't to call you Miss Harriet any more," Nina said, with an effort to smile that Harriet thought quite ghastly. She gave Harriet one of her big hands, and hesitated over a kiss. But they did not kiss each other. Ida Tabor watched them with the half-closed eyes of a cat.

"Confess you took my breath away," she said, frankly, "because it doesn't seem the sort of thing that Dick Carter does! Always knew he idolized Isabelle, poor girl, and never dreamed he'd put any one in her place! Of course, Dick's a rich man, and he's the dearest fellow in the world, at that, but knowing, as I do know--for I've known him since we were kiddies--exactly what a firebrand Dick always has been-mad as a hatter when he was in love, and consequently this talk of a sensible arrangement--"

She had a quick, vivacious way of speaking, this pretty little angry and disappointed woman, that often carried an offensive very successfully. As she spoke, in an innocent voice, she glanced in and out of the magazine she had caught up, and was apparently unconscious of Harriet's blazing cheeks and darkening eyes. But now Harriet interrupted her.

"I don't quite see the point, Mrs. Tabor," Harriet said, bravely and deliberately, "you speak of Mr. Carter's being a rich man, and of his love for his wife, and his having been a fiery young man. What has that to do with me? I was here in his house as his daughter's companion--

"As far as being a companion to ME was concerned," Nina interpolated, rapidly, in an airy undertone, and with a toss of her head. But Harriet suppressed her with a glance.

"--that position I could not keep," she pursued, "but for Ward's sake and Nina's there had to be some social life. My birth," said Harriet, steadily, "is quite the equal of theirs; I was well able to fill that place. Mr. Carter took the step that made it possible. That's all!"

There was a silence when she finished speaking. Ida Tabor was outfaced, and she knew it. Her cheeks burned scarlet, and she was able to gasp only the feeblest response.

"Thank you for your kind explanation!" she said, somewhat breathless, and with a bow. Nina, giving Harriet a resentful glance, went over to put her arm about her friend, who had risen, and was facing Harriet.

"It need make no difference with us, Ladybird!" Nina said in passionate loyalty.

"Why, of course not," Harriet hastened to assure them. "Why should it? It has been just as true since December, only you didn't know it!"

"THANK you!" Mrs. Tabor said again, with another twitch of countenance intended for a smile.

"Will you want both these rooms now?" Nina said, insolently. "I don't want to be in your way!"

"Be careful, Nina!" Harriet said with ominous calmness. And going into her own room she added, in her usual quiet manner, "There will be no changes, dear!" She realized that her heart was beating fast with anger, but it died down rapidly, and she consoled herself with some prophecies that the next few days were to justify to the fullest extent. Nina's inseparable Ladybird would find little to interest her in Crownlands now, Harriet suspected, and they would not long be troubled by her company. She smiled as she heard Nina and Ida in the next room.

"Put on your yellow gown, sweetheart," Ida said. "We're going to the Bellamys' after lunch."

"Oh, I don't feel like going anywhere!" Nina said, pathetically. "Would you just as soon stay here--and just read and talk, and fool around as we did yester-day?"

"Just as soon do anything!" But there was a tiny edge to Ladybird's tone that had not been there yesterday. "Only, dearest girl," she added, lightly, "we're expected!"

For answer Nina only gave her rich, mischievous laugh, and Harriet knew that she was embracing her friend.

"But a lot you and I care for that, don't we? We'll get into wrappers and be comfortable. I'll have Bottomley simply telephone after lunch, and say that we are unexpectedly detained. I can't get over it," Nina said, luxuriating in surprise. Her voice sank to speculation, and the two murmured awhile. Then Harriet heard Ida return the attack. "But about the Bellamys, dear," and smiled a little sadly, to think of the swiftness with which, to calculating Mrs. Tabor, the Carter stock was declining, and the Bellamy market looking up.

"That crazy man who--you said--admired me last night," Nina was presently saying, "tell me again what he said. I don't see how he could have said I was picturesque, for there's nothing picturesque about that old blue rag. I don't know, though, it's always been awfully smart. But I'll tell you honestly, Ladybird, I'd rather be picturesque than almost anything else."

"You're certainly that!" said Ida's bored voice.

"Well, if you say so, I'll believe you!" Nina said. Harriet knew that they had been aware of her nearness, but now she very deliberately closed the door.

At luncheon everything was exactly as usual; Richard had gone to the city, not to return for a night or two, and several social engagements distracted the young people from the contemplation of their father's affairs.

Harriet had not dared to hope that they would accept the situation so quietly, or that the world would. There were callers on the terrace every afternoon, there were pleasant congratulations and good wishes, there were a few paragraphs in the social weeklies. Richard had for years been too busy for mere entertaining, and the dinner parties and luncheons to the new Mrs. Carter, it was generally felt, must wait until next season.

Meanwhile, the speculating world saw her going quietly about the house, advising Nina, conferring with the domestic staff, laughing with Ward. She immediately formed a habit of going into the old lady's room every morning: Madame Carter had quite accepted her as a member of the great house of Carter now, and came to depend upon the half-hour of morning gossip. The world saw her in a box at the theatre, with the young Carters, saw that Richard presently joined them, and laughed, in the shadowy back of the box, at something his beautiful new wife said to him over her shoulder. The world was obliged to decide that the little secretary took her promotion very coolly, that there was something queer about it.

But inwardly the little secretary was thrilled to her heart's core. Even to glance at the gold ring on her finger made Harriet feel as if a happiness almost shameful was bared to view. Her new position, modestly as she filled it, was yet a high position. She saw Richard's growing affection and trust, if he did not. She could afford to wait.

She visited Linda, almost afraid to show new gowns and new generosity, almost afraid of the constant "Mrs. Carter."

"They'll be ruined!" Linda laughed, of the children's summer gowns and the camera and wrist watch that transported Julia and Josephine to Paradise. This rustling and perfumed Harriet, with the flowered little French hat, and the filmy little odd gowns, was almost bewildering.

Decorously having tea on the terrace in the June afternoons, knowing herself the centre of interest, Harriet's heart sang with a wild inward delight. She smiled; she could afford the friendliest interest for everyone's affairs. When her own were touched, there was a youthful flushing, a deprecatory smile. But she took no one into her confidence.

"But when are you and Dick Carter going to dine with us?" Mary Putnam said, one afternoon, at tea. Madame Carter, whose Victorian ideal of romance was not at all dissatisfied with the idea of the employer marrying his daughter's beautiful governess, smiled significantly.

"They're very odd lovers, my dear," she said to Mary with an eloquent glance. Mary laughed, and looked at Harriet, whose face was suddenly crimson, though she tried to laugh, too. The visitor, with instant kindness, covered the little break.

"Whenever they're ready, they're going to dine with me!" she said, patting Harriet's hand with real affection and understanding. The arrival of a group from the tennis court, Nina, Ida, Ward, Francesca Jay, and their friends, changed the subject immediately, the old lady was distracted, and Harriet busy. But Mary was free to reflect. She had the eyes of a contented woman, freed from her own problem for those of others. "And Harriet is certainly mad about Richard," Mary mused.

But with the rest of the world she had to decide that there was something in the affair that she did not understand.

When everyone else had gone from the terrace, and the late afternoon light was throwing clear shadows across the warm red bricks, Nina and Ida Tabor remained, talking. Nina had seated herself on the arm of her friend's chair, and was chattering away in happy ignorance of the fact that the older woman was seething within. Nina saw no reason for jealousy because Harriet had just had an hour's petting from everyone, had dominated the scene in her striped blue muslin, had finally sauntered to the house between no more important persons than Granny and Ward.

But to Ida it was insufferable, and she could only revenge herself upon her innocent admirer.

"And now we positively must go in, Nina!" she said. "We've wasted this whole afternoon!" And she added, of the embracing arm: "Don't! It's too hot."

"Is playing tennis and talking with me WASTING an afternoon, Ladybird?" Nina asked, archly.

"You know I don't mean that!" Mrs. Tabor said, impatiently, if fondly, freeing herself. "But I have to get packed if I'm going to the Jays'!"

"But you're not going to the Jays'!" Nina said in soft, sweet, confident reminder.

"But I must, darling!"

"Not if I ask you not to!" Nina persisted.

"Truly I must," Mrs. Tabor said, wearily.

"No, you mustn't!"

"But, dearest, I truly have to---"

"But, Ladybird," Nina laughed, happily, "I sent them a message this afternoon that you were staying with me! So now," she finished, triumphantly, "that's settled! And we'll go to bed early, with books, and talk, and maybe creep down for something to eat about eleven, as we did that other night--"

"Nina," Mrs. Tabor said, in a new voice, interrupting her, "you didn't telephone Mrs. Jay, did you?"

"Indeed I did!" Nina was still smiling over the thought of her midnight raid on the pantry with a flattering and laughing and girlish Ladybird, a Ladybird who had simply "never gotten over" that chance encounter with Father in the upper hall, and who had talked of it, and of their slippered feet and kimonos, through hours of delicious giggling and embarrassment.

"Well, then, you were extremely impertinent and officious," said a new voice, that Nina hardly recognized.

Poor Nina! Harriet found her sobbing on her bed, half an hour later, and took it for a sign that the wound would cure, that Nina did not resent her sympathy and comfort. Nina was still heaving with deep sobs, albeit taking steps toward a hot bath and a becoming gown, when Ida went away. Her farewells were made only to the composed interloper, who went with her pleasantly to the hall door, and turned back with some remark for Bottomley that was in the perfect tone of the mistress. Ida's heart was hot within her as she looked her last at Crownlands, in the mellow light of the summer twilight.

CHAPTER XVIII

Royal Blondin presently came to pay his respects to Harriet in her changed position. Nina had told her that he had been forbidden the house, in December; they had seen him only two or three times since their return from Bermuda, and then accidentally. Harriet was thankful to believe the affair between him and Nina well over. The girl was growing up now, there were other men in her world, and for the list for her eighteenth birthday party she had merely mentioned his name among others.

"You'll see that Royal gets a card, Harriet?" she had said.

"Well--yes, if you want him, but somehow one doesn't see the mysterious and artistic Royal in so juvenile a party," Harriet had answered. Nina might have disquieted her with her serene: "Oh, he'll come!" But Harriet knew Nina was often over-sure of her own powers.

Three days before the garden party that was to mark the girl's anniversary Royal drifted in with the assurance that was quite characteristic of him. He rarely accepted an invitation, or waited for one. Perhaps he was clever enough to know that half his acquaintances detested him theoretically, but were glad to have him about. Nina and Harriet came in from an afternoon at the club to find him playing with languid hands at the piano, and he lazily rose to greet them. While Nina was there, his attitude toward both was pleasantly impersonal, but his suggestion, which was more like a command, that she run upstairs and dress early, so that they might have a talk before dinner, sent the girl flying, and he and Harriet could speak more freely.

"Well, Harriet, I congratulate you! How does it feel to be a married woman? I was with Lenox, in his camp--we went up there to look it over," Royal went on, in his musical voice. "It's a beautiful place, in the Adirondacks. I saw your name in an evening paper; of course I was delighted for you."

"Money and position don't really mean much to me," Harriet said, unencouragingly.

"They don't?" he asked, with an upward glance.

"Not lately. Not as much as they always seemed to!" the girl added, uncertainly.

"Perhaps because your dream is captured," Blondin suggested. "It's no longer a myth! I wonder if it isn't always so?"

"I remember his taking that dreamy, silly tone years ago," Harriet thought.

"My first sensation," Blondin said, "was one of satisfaction. I thought to myself that my own cause, with Nina, was safe now. That you trusted me, and I had every reason to trust you."

Harriet looked away for a brief silence, brought her eyes to his face. She felt suddenly sick.

"Roy, you're not still serious about Nina?"

"I have never been anything else," he said, delicately.

"But--but why?" Harriet asked.

"I like the girl," he reminded her pleasantly. "I hope she is not entirely indifferent to me--"

"Indifferent! She's at the age that marries anybody!" Harriet said, indignantly.

"You give me hope," Royal said with a bow.

"Her father very violently opposes it," Harriet said, after a troubled silence.

"I am well aware of that, my dear. Her father forbade me the house last December. I submitted; the girl submitted. But we made our plans. I fancy we will not have any difficulty now."

"You mean that you are engaged?"

"An understanding. We have corresponded, seen each other now and then through Ida Tabor. It's," he smiled, dreamily, "extremely romantic, of course," he said.

Harriet felt that she could have killed him.

"You understand that she won't have one penny, Roy. I know her father. He won't yield. He'll forbid it; he'll not hesitate. If she does it against his will, she will have to wait three years for her money. Three years--! Roy, she wouldn't be happy three weeks! Mr. Carter spoke to me about it the only time we've spoken of you. He said that he was glad the affair had ended naturally; that you were not the man to make Nina happy, and that he would rather have her suffer anything, and find out her mistake at once, than have her heart broken, and her money wasted, through several wretched years!"

Blondin had listened to this quietly, his eyes moving from her lips to her own earnest eyes, and wandering over her animated face.

"I count on you to be my advocate, my dear Harriet," he said, after a moment's silence. "Richard Carter believes in you; he has great faith in your judgment. If you represent to him that you believe this to be a wise step all round, we shall have no further trouble--'

"I can't honestly tell him so, Roy!" the girl interrupted.

"Can't you?" Blondin said. He looked across the open hallway to Nina, descending in fresh ruffles and ribbons, and raised his voice. "Here she is--looking like the very rose of girls! Come on now, Nina, you aren't going to belong to anybody else but me for a while!" he said. But as he turned to leave Harriet, he added again: "Can't you? Think it over."

The girl thought it over with a maddening and feverish persistence that presently caused her a sensation of actual sickness. How serious her countenancing of Nina's love-affair might prove to be--how unimportant it might prove to be--what Nina might do or might not do, these vague speculations churned and seethed in the weary brain that could find no beginning and no end to them. To have made a clean breast of the whole matter months ago would have meant a delicious sense of freedom from responsibility now, but then under those circumstances would she, Harriet, have been here now? Certainly, even in the present purely technical sense, she would not have been the second Mrs. Richard Carter, nor would she have held her present position of trust and responsibility.

While Nina and her lover murmured on the terrace Harriet brooded on these things, and after dinner that evening she gave Richard so sharp a warning that he sent at once for Nina, and with a clouded brow and angry eyes briefly requested Harriet to be present while he spoke to her.

Nina came at once, with an innocent expression on her rather heavy young face. She seated herself near Harriet, and her father went to the point at once.

"Nina," he said, seriously, "you saw Royal Blondin this afternoon, didn't you?" And as Nina answered only with an ugly glance at Harriet, the betrayer, he added, "Didn't I ask you not to see him any more, several months ago?"

"Yes, you did," Nina said, in a low tone, and with a heaving breast. She was sure of herself, but she felt a little frightened.

"I hope, and we all hope, that you will marry some day," Richard said. "But you are too young now to make a wise choice. And until you are a little older, you will have to take my word for it that such an affair would only lead you to misery and regret."

Nina mumbled something bravely.

"I didn't hear you," her father said.

"I said, I didn't see what you could do about it!" the girl repeated, desperately.

For a few moments of silence Richard merely looked gravely at his daughter. Then he clasped his fine hands on the desk before him, and cleared his throat.

"I cannot do as much as I should like, Nina," he conceded, "but I shall do what I can. But first let me ask you: have you promised to marry Mr. Blondin?"

Silence. Nina looked at the floor. Richard repeated his question.

"Yes, I have-and you can't kill me for it!" Nina said, and burst into tears.

"Well," the father resumed, when Harriet had supplied a consolatory murmur and a handkerchief, "I'm sorry, of course. Mrs. Tabor carried letters between you, did she? You met him occasionally?"

"Two or three times," Nina said, sniffing and drying her eyes busily.

"You know my reasons for disliking him, Nina," her father said. "He is a man more than twice your age; he has a certain sort of unsavory reputation in his affairs with women. He has no income, no profession, no home; all those things tell against him. But the most serious of all, to me, is his mental attitude. The man has no wholesome, decent code. He dabbles in the occult, in Oriental morality--or immorality. With an older woman, that mightn't matter. She could guide him, perhaps influence him. But you're only a child--"

"I shall be of age Tuesday!" Nina burst forth, resentfully.

"You will be of age Tuesday. True. But you will be my ward, as far as your Uncle Edward's legacy is concerned, for another three years. Now, Nina, if you persist in this folly, against my most earnest advice, I can only forbid the man the house, and lock you in your room in the good old-fashioned way. That I shall do. I shall then give out to the world--that has already had a rare treat at the expense of the Carter family!--the news of my utter disapproval of the match. If you manage the marriage in spite of me, I shall forbid you and Blondin my house, and as a matter of course use my right to withhold the payment of your legacy for three years, and stop your present allowance, and your credit with the shops. That's all I can do! And I do it, Nina," said Richard in a softer tone, "I do it to hasten the inevitable, my dear! I do it to bring you back to your father sooner instead of later; to give you only one year of disillusionment and suffering, instead of seven or eight!"

It must be a brave girl, thought Harriet, who could persist in any course, after that. But Nina had the impregnable armour of ignorance and pride, and she only sniffed pathetically again, and shrugged her shoulders.

"You do everything in the world to MAKE my marriage a failure!" she said with the irrepressible tears. "And I suppose you'll be delighted if it is! Uncle Edward's money belongs to me; Ward has got his; and I don't see why you just want to shame me before the world for your own satisfaction! Royal is a perfect child about money; he says that I will have to manage our business affairs, anyway. And I don't see--if a woman can marry a rich man, why a man shouldn't sometimes be glad if a girl has money! I'm PROUD to help him out, if he'll let me. He says he won't--why, we had planned going--well, just everywhere, Honolulu and southern California and just everywhere, only now he won't go! He says he is going to stay right here, and take a position with an art magazine that he just hates, and work it all off--before we go, if it takes years--"

"Work what all off?" Harriet asked, simply and quietly.

"This money that a friend of his really lost, but he has taken it upon himself," Nina answered, a little mollified. "It was eleven thousand dollars, and he has PAID OFF about four, and anyway, I hate so much talk about money!" she finished, angrily.

"My dear," Harriet said, as Richard, with a troubled face, remained silent. "It isn't the money that we are worrying about. Why, ask your father, Nina! Ask him if he wouldn't write Royal Blondin a check for any sum to-day, ANY sum, if you and he would promise solemnly to wait three years more. You will only be twenty-one then, Nina, still such a child!"

Harriet paused, glancing at Richard for encouragement; he nodded eagerly, and she went on:

"Marriage is a tremendous thing, Nina, and the only thing that makes it right---"

"If you're going to say love," Nina broke in, scornfully, "you didn't marry Father for love!"

"I was going to say mutual understanding and respect," Harriet said, quietly, but the splendid colour flooded her face as she spoke, "and you do not understand life, Nina, or men, or marriage. Royal Blondin is a charming man, and a gifted man, but he is an adventurer, dear; he is a man who has lived in all sorts of places, known all sorts of persons, accepted all sorts of queer codes. There are coarse elements in him, Nina, things that would utterly sicken and frighten you! Your father is right; you would be back with us in a few months or years, perhaps with a child, perhaps shattered in body as well as soul--not free to take up your life again with Ward and Amy, but scarred and embittered and changed--!"

"My God, how that woman loves the child!" Richard said to himself, watching her. To him she seemed inspired. Her eyes were blurred with tears, her voice shaking, and she had leaned over to clasp Nina's hands, and so hold the girl's unwilling attention.

"Nina, can't you trust your father that far?" Harriet finished. "Can't you realize that a man like Royal, embarrassed for money--no matter if he truly admires you, and truly means to make you happy--can't think of you without thinking also of what your generous checks are going to mean to him? Write him a check for eleven thousand, Nina, as a consolation for delaying the marriage a year. Try it!"

Nina rose to her feet. Her trembling mouth was desperately scornful, and her eyes brimming, although she fought tears.

"I don't know why my own family is the first to think that nobody could possibly love me for myself!" she said, in a breaking voice. "First Harriet ruins my friendship with Ladybird--and then--then--!"

"Listen, Nina," her father said. He and Harriet had come around to stand beside her, and he had encircled the shaking and protesting shoulders with his arm. "I have just telephoned Fox to make reservations for me on the next Brazilian steamer. I shall have to be a month or six weeks in Rio de Janeiro every year now. Now I've just been wondering why you and Harriet don't come with me this first trip? We stop at the Barbadoes and Bahia; it's a magnificent steamer--swimming tanks and gymnasium; you'll love it, and you'll love a touch of the South American countries, too, a chance to try your Spanish. Why not put off this marriage idea for a year, come along with me, you'll make steamer acquaintances, you'll broaden out a little bit--"

"I won't go anywhere!" sobbed Nina, wildly, turning for flight, "because I'm going to kill myself!"

Harriet only waited long enough after her dramatic exit to give Richard a reassuring nod. Then she hurried after Nina.

The girl was sobbing on her bed, and for awhile she answered Harriet's soothing touch of voice and hand only with angry jerks. Then they fell to talking, and Nina confided for the first time fully in the older woman. Royal's letters, his exquisite cards, sent with flowers, the poems he had written her; here they all were. Harriet sympathized, sighed, and consoled her affectionately. Presently she was able to suggest a new thought to Nina, one that could not but be palatable to the girl's hurt spirit.

"You see, you're only seventeen, Nina," Harriet said. "The age when most girls are still in the schoolroom, long before they have affairs! Well, you're not interested in college, so that ought to give you three or four clear years of girlhood. You're bound to have other affairs, you've proved that! You go to South America--perhaps there is some interesting man on the steamer; you go to Canada--to California, the world is yours. Now, Royal is different. He is an experienced man of affairs; he will always have an attraction for women, and they for him. You aren't his match, now, Nina. In a few years you may be--"

"I'm not jealous!" Nina said, proudly. But Harriet smiled.

"Yes, you are jealous. You wouldn't be a real true woman if you weren't!" she accused. A reluctant dimple tugged at Nina's pouting mouth. She did not dislike the idea of potential despotism, of the travelled, experienced woman of the world, confident of her charm.

"If I offered a check to Royal, do you suppose he'd accept it!" she remarked, after dark musing. She was sitting on the edge of her bed now, and Harriet was brushing her hair.

"If you really are worried about his business affairs, Nina, why not try it?" Harriet suggested, sensibly. To this Nina returned a pouting:

"I'm perfectly willing to try it!" And as a great concession she added with a sigh, "And I'll tell him what Father thinks!"

"Now you're talking like a woman who has herself well in hand!" Harriet said, approvingly. "When are you to see him?"

"He's coming over especially to see Father to-morrow," Nina said. "I suppose I might as well go down," she added, eyeing herself gloomily in her mirror, "for Ward and that boy seem absolutely at a loss for amusement!"

"And I'll be down presently," Harriet said. But when Nina was gone she walked slowly to her own dressing table, and sat down, and regarded herself steadily, and with heavy eyes. Unexpectedly, here between the family dinner and the early going to bed, on a June evening, a crisis in her life was confronting her, and she knew that she must meet it.

Ward's guest was only the young Saunders boy, who had been with them constantly last summer, and who was of absolutely no significance in their lives. And yet Harriet had been introduced to him all over again as "Mrs. Carter"--there was no halfway, in the eyes of the world at least, in this relationship of hers with Richard, and she must begin to take her place in the family.

"Mrs. Carter!" Bottomley and Pilgrim were beginning to call her so; she must sign checks as "Harriet Carter" now, she must say "by Mrs.

Carter" in the shops, in a thousand little ways she must claim the dignity of being his wife.

And Harriet loved that distinction as if the title, the signature, and the dignity had never been vouchsafed to womankind before. She had marvelled at her old self, that had taken "Miss" and "Mrs." with cheerful indifference--why, there was a worldwide chasm between the two! Just to have this silly Saunders boy call her Mrs. Carter, as a matter of course, was to receive the accolade that gave her all her longed-for dreams in one. It was the name of the man she loved, and, even though in a shadowy and unloved way, she liked the title that made her his.

But this dignity had its sting, too, and its responsibility. Harriet's soul had been growing during this past year. She had thrown off the old shell of bitterness and discouragement, she had become ambitious again, even if only in the shallow, mercenary way that the life about her encouraged. And then that had changed, too, and it had seemed to Harriet only good to serve and to be busy, to work out the difficult problem that was presented her with all the accumulated years of study and dreams, philosophy and courage, to help her. Then love had come, sweeping all her old life away before it--the flotsam and jetsam of discouraged years; what was ignoble and sordid and outgrown had still lined the river banks, it was true, but that was carried away now, the man she loved needed her, and by some instinct deeper than any dull male reasoning of his, had drawn her to him.

And now she owed him the truth, the whole, painful, humiliating story. If she had told him months ago, so much the better and braver woman she! She had not done so; she had been fighting Nina and his mother then; she had been afraid. But she was not afraid now; he could forgive that long-ago girl of seventeen because her advocate was the woman of twenty-eight, the finished, cultivated, capable woman who had served him and his house, who must win his respect back because she loved him with every fibre of her being.

The words in which she would tell him came to her in a rush. Why--it was nothing! It was less than nothing. In half an hour she would be back here in her room again, with all the past clean and straight at last, with the cloud gone, and with her whole soul singing with hope of the glorious future. For a moment she knelt by her bed, her face in her hands.

She rose to her feet. There was a tap at the door.

It was Bottomley. "If you please, 'm--Mr. Carter would be so much obliged if she would step down to the library, 'm." Harriet gave herself a parting glance, and followed the man downstairs.

"Courage!" she said to herself, with her hand on the library door. "I've exaggerated and enlarged upon this thing too long! I've imagined it into an importance that it really hasn't at all!"

Richard was back at his desk; he smiled and rose as she came in. There was another man in the library, who rose and faced her, too.

And when Harriet saw him she knew that she was too late. It was Royal Blondin.

A dizziness and sickness came over her as she went slowly to the chair opposite Richard. She touched the desk for support as she sat down, and felt that her fingers were cold and wet.

"Mr. Blondin has come to talk to me about Nina," Richard said. Harriet somehow moved her dizzy eyes toward Blondin, and she smiled mechanically. But she had to moisten her lips before she could speak.

"I see!" Her voice sounded horribly choked to her; she could find nothing to add to the meaningless words.

"Mr. Blondin asks my consent to an immediate marriage," Richard said. "You know my objections to that, Harriet, of course! We have just been discussing them, as I explained to him. This is a painful matter to me, and I regret it. But Mr. Blondin has given me no choice but to tell him frankly why I think him an unsuitable husband for my daughter. I have told him exactly what my procedure will be in such a case, and I think we understand each other!"

Royal was smiling the serene, dreamy smile that was characteristic of him.

"Nina," he said, tenderly, "is warm hearted. And a chance allusion to my financial position, which I thought I owed her, has distressed her unnecessarily. It will, truly, be out of the question for me to travel, as we had planned. The unfortunate speculations of my friend--"

"Whose name you withhold," Richard interrupted the musical voice to say, drily.

"Because of a promise!" Royal flashed promptly. "But," he resumed, turning to Harriet, "I shall be able to negotiate this business, as I assure Mr. Carter, without any assistance from him or his daughter," his lip curled scornfully, "and I do not propose to give her up for any three years--or three weeks!"

Harriet could only look at him fixedly, with an ashen face.

"God help me," she breathed in her soul. "God help me!"

"Well," said Richard, with weary impatience, "we did not call you down to bore you with this! I asked to see you, Harriet, because Mr.

Blondin has made the statement to me, just now, that you were heartily in accord with his plans for Nina, and that you approved of the affair!"

The prayer in Harriet's heart did not stop as she moved her wretched eyes to Blondin.

"I believed that you and she had not seen each other since December," she reminded him. "I lost no chance to advise her against the engagement! I thought it was all over!"

"Well!" Richard said, with a breath of relief. He had been watching her closely, now he settled back in his chair, and moved his contemptuous scrutiny to Blondin.

"One moment!" Royal Blondin said, gently. But he was also pale. "You believe that I would make Nina a good husband, don't you?" he asked Harriet directly and quietly.

She was not looking at him. Her eyes were on Richard Carter.

"I believe you would ruin her life!" she said, deliberately.

"Thank you," Richard said. "I think that is all, Mr. Blondin. I was aware that you had--misunderstood Mrs. Carter when you made that statement!"

"Not quite all," Blondin persisted. "You believe that Nina would be wiser not to marry me?" he asked Harriet.

"You--" She cleared her throat. "You know that I think so!" she said.

Blondin laughed.

"And now, Mr. Blondin, you will kindly leave my house!" said Richard.

The other man was watching Harriet, with a menace in his narrowed eyes. White lines had drawn themselves about his tightly closed lips, yet he was smiling. He had lost the game, truly, but she knew he would play his last card, just the same. The suavity, the calm of years fell from him, and his voice deepened into a sort of cold and quiet fury as he said:

"One moment, Mr. Carter. Why don't you ask your wife what makes her think I won't make Nina a good husband? Why don't you ask her if she has been hiding something from you all this time? Why don't you ask her if she herself wasn't madly in love--and with me!--when she was Nina's age, and whether she was married in my studio, to me, ten years ago--!"

He had shot the phrases at her with a distinctness almost violent. Now his dry voice stopped, but his swift, venomous look went from the silent man at the desk to the silent woman who stood before him. Before either moved or spoke he spoke again.

"Ask her--she'll tell you! Ask her!'

"Be quiet!" Richard said. "I don't believe one word of it!" And then as the girl neither raised her eyes nor attempted to speak, he asked her, encouragingly and quickly: "Harriet, will you tell him that not one word of that is true?"

Harriet had risen, and was standing at the back of the carved black chair with both her hands resting upon it. She had looked quietly at Blondin, when he began to speak, and the beautiful white breast that her black evening gown left bare had risen once or twice on a swift impulse to interrupt him. But now she was looking down at her laced fingers, with something despairing and helpless in the droop of her bright head and lowered lashes.

It had had its times of seeming frightful to her, this secret, in the troubled musings of the past year. But it had never loomed so horrible and so momentous as now, in the silent library, with the eyes of the man she loved fixed anxiously upon her. He had trusted, he was beginning to admire her, and like his wife and his daughter and his mother, she had failed him.

"Harriet?" he said in quick uneasiness. She raised her head now, and looked at him with weary eyes devoid of any expression except bewilderment and pain.

"Yes," she said, simply. "That is all--quite true. It sounds--" she hesitated, and groped for words--"it sounds--as if--" she began, and stopped again. "But it is all quite true!" she finished, in the troubled tone of a child who is misunderstood.

Then for a long time there was silence in the library.

CHAPTER XIX

The curtains at the French windows in the library at Crownlands stirred in the breeze of the warm summer night, the pendulum of the big clock behind Richard Carter moved to and fro, but for a long time there was no other sound in the library. Richard had dropped his eyes, was idly staring at the blank sheet of paper before him. Royal Blondin, who had folded his arms, for a moment studied Harriet between half-closed lids, but presently his eyes fell, too, and with a rather troubled expression he studied the pattern of the great Oriental rug.

Harriet stood motionless, turned to stone. If there was anything to be said in her behalf, she could not say it now. For the first time the full measure of her responsibility and the full measure of her deceit smote her, and in utter sickness of spirit she could advance no excuse. It was not that she had failed Blondin, or that she had failed Richard, but the extent of her failure toward herself appalled her. She was not the good, brave, cultivated woman she had liked to think herself; she was one more egotist, with Nina, and Isabelle, and Ida, unscrupulously playing her own game for her own ends.

"I'm extremely sorry," Richard said, presently, in a somewhat lifeless tone. "I imagine that if my daughter had known this, she might have been spared some suffering and some humiliation. But we needn't consider that now." He was silent, frowning faintly. He put up a fine hand and adjusted his eyeglasses with a little impatient muscular twitching of his whole face that Harriet knew to be characteristic of his worried moods. "Mr. Blondin," he said, wearily and politely, "I have had a great deal on my mind, lately, and have perhaps been hasty in my condemnation of you. However, this does not particularly help your cause with my daughter. There are a great many aspects to the matter, and I--I must take time to consider them. Nina must be my first consideration, poor child! Her mother failed her--we have all failed her! She has a right to know of this conversation--"

Harriet stirred, and his eyes moved to her. Without a word, and with a stricken look in her beautiful, ashen face, she turned, and went slowly toward the door. When she reached it, she steadied herself a second by pressing one fine hand against the dark wood, then she opened it and was gone.

"I'm very sorry--" Blondin said, hesitatingly, when the men were alone.

"Mrs. Carter," Richard said, getting to his feet, and very definitely indicating an end to the conversation, "before she consented to the--

arrangement into which we entered, of course took me into her confidence in this matter!"

"She--she did?" Royal stammered.

"Certainly she did," Richard said, harshly. And looking at him the other man saw that his face looked haggard and colourless. "She did not mention your name, I presume out of a sense of generosity to you. I could have wished," he added, "that you had been similarly generous, and had seen fit to leave her, and leave my daughter alone. I think I must ask you to excuse me," said Richard at the door. His tone was one of absolute suffocation. "I can see no object in your frankness to-night, unless to distress and humiliate Mrs. Carter. My daughter, and not myself, is the one entitled to your confidence, and you are well aware of my feeling where she is concerned! I would to God," said Richard, with bitterness, "that I had never seen your face! Mrs. Carter has been a useful--and indispensable!-- member of this family for many years; if there was in her past some unpleasant and painful event, that is her own affair--!"

"Not when she marries a man who is unaware of it," Blondin suggested, in his pleasant, soft tones.

"That is mine!" Richard said, sternly. And he opened the library door. "Good evening!" he said.

"Good evening!" Blondin, with his light, loitering step, crossed the threshold, and Richard closed the door. He took his chair again, and reached toward the bell that would have brought Bottomley to summon Nina in turn. But halfway to the bell his resolution wavered, disappeared. Instead, he rested his elbows on the table, and his head in his hands, and there sounded from his chest a great sigh that was almost a groan.

Oh, he was tired--he was tired--he was tired! It was all a mess--the boy, the girl, their mother, his own arrangements for their protection and safety. All a mess.

She had been beautiful, that girl, with her golden hair in the lamplight, and her white arms a little raised to rest her locked hands on the chair. Like some superb actress of tragedy, some splendid and sullen prisoner at the bar. The slender figure in the dull wrapping of satin, and the white bosom, had looked so young, so virginal, the blue eyes were so honestly frightened and ashamed. And she had been that bounder's wife--in his arms! Divorced! Harriet Field? Poor girl, cornered by this unscrupulous scoundrel, this bully, with all the ugly past dragged up like the muddy bottom of a river, staining and clouding the clear waters. And what a look she had given him, there under the lamp!

"It's a funny code," he mused. "Barbarians, that's what we are, when it comes to women. Nina, Ida, Isabelle, Harriet--all of them pay for the man-made rule! I shouldn't have forced her hand in this business marriage; it was taking an advantage of her. No woman wants to marry for anything but love, and if she had married for love, she would have made a clean breast of this old affair, of course. I didn't exact that. We've made a nice mess of it, all around!

"I mustn't let her work herself into a fever over all this!" he found himself thinking.

But Nina must be the first consideration. He must plan for Nina. He brought his thoughts back resolutely--his daughter must break her engagement now, there was that much gained. And for the journey to Rio--

"But why didn't she tell me!" he interrupted himself, suddenly. The reference was not to Nina. Again he saw the superb white shoulders in the soft flood of lamp-light, and the flash of the blue eyes that turned toward Blondin.

"She could have killed him!" Richard said. "My God! how she will love when she does love!"

Meanwhile, to Harriet had come the bitterest hour of her life. She had reached a crossroads, and with steady fingers and an anguished heart she prepared for the only step that to her whirling brain and shamed soul seemed possible. She must disappear. There was no alternative.

She had harmed them all, they could only think of her now as an unscrupulous and mischievous woman who had by chance entered their lives when they were all in desperate need of wisdom and guidance, who had played her own contemptible game, and added one more hurt to the hurt reputation of the house of Carter.

Harriet got out of her evening gown and into a loose wrapper. She went about somewhat aimlessly, yet the suitcases, spread open on the bed, were gradually filled, and her personal possessions gradually disappeared from tables and walls. Now and then she stopped short, heartsick and trembling; once her lips quivered and her eyes filled, but for the most part she did not pause.

Nina, at about eleven, had come to the door between their rooms, and opened it. The girl was undressed, and for a few moments she watched Harriet scowlingly, with narrowed eyes.

"Are you going away?" she said, presently. Harriet brought heavy eyes to meet hers, and stood considering a minute, as if bringing her thoughts back a long distance.

"I--going away? Yes," she said, slowly. "Yes, I may."

Nina still stood watching, which seemed vaguely to trouble Harriet, who gave her a restless glance now and then as she went to and fro. Presently she spoke to Nina again.

"Good-night, Nina!"

"Good-night!" snapped Nina, and the door slammed.

Harriet continued to move about for perhaps half an hour before Nina's odd manner recurred to her, on a wave of memory, and she seemed to hear again Nina's ungracious tone.

"He told her!" she said, suddenly. "She saw Royal, and he told her! Poor child--"

And she went to Nina's room, with a vague idea that she would sit beside the weeping girl for awhile, one heavy heart close to the other, even if no words could pass between them.

But Nina lay sleeping peacefully, and Harriet, after watching her for a few minutes, went back to her own room. She went to the open window, and stood staring absently out at the dark summer night, the great branches of the trees moving in the restless wind, and the oblong of dull light that still fell from the library window.

She could not see the horror as Richard saw it: she could not see herself as only a mistaken woman, a woman with youth, beauty, and intelligence pleading for her, one problem more in his life it is true, but only one among many, and not the greatest. She did not see him as he saw himself, his family as the somewhat troublesome, and yet quite understandable, group of selfish human beings in whose perplexities he had always played the part of arbiter.

To Harriet the thing loomed momentous, unforgivable, incalculable. It assumed to her the proportions of a murder. Bigamy, perjury, deceit--what hadn't she done! Richard, in her estimation, was not what he thought himself, a somewhat ordinary man in the forties whose life had already held poverty and disillusionment and wholesome disappointment, whose nature had been tempered to humour and generosity and philosophy; to Harriet, he was the richest, the finest, the most deserving of men, and she the adventuress who had brought his name down to shame and dishonour.

Until two o'clock she was wretchedly busy in soul and body. When the last of her personal possessions was packed, and when she was aching from head to foot, she took a hot bath, and crept into bed.

But not to sleep. The feverish agonies of shame and reproach held her. She was pleading with Richard, she was talking to Nina--she was making little of it--making much of it--she was saying a reluctant "yes--yes--yes!" to their questioning.

At four o'clock she dressed herself again, half-mad with headache and fatigue, and went out into a world that was just beginning to brighten into faint shapes and colours. The fresh cold air of morning struck her jaded senses with a delicious chill; she went noiselessly across the terrace and down toward the water, her big soft coat brushing spider-webs from the dim rosebushes as she went. The world lay silent, fragrant, saturated with dew. Yet under its chill Harriet felt the pervading warmth of the day that had gone, and the day that was to come.

She drew in great breaths of it; it was her world for another three hours. Then men would begin to stir themselves, down at the river docks, and at the stables and garages, and smoke would go up from the chimneys of Crownlands, and rakes clink on the gravel walks. She went down to the little pier, and sat on a weather-worn bench, and watched the day breaking softly over the river.

Little wrinkles crossed the satiny surface of the Hudson, which looked dark and metallic in the twilight. But presently there was a general glimmering and widening, and across the river trees and houses were touched with light, and window-panes flashed. Harriet, huddled into her coat, did not stir; she might have been, for an hour, a part of the motionless scene.

A steamer moved majestically up the river, the smoothly widening wake spread from shore to shore; pink light showed at one cabin window; and into Harriet's sombre thoughts came unbidden the picture of a yawning cook, stumbling about amid his soot-blackened pots and pans.

With the morning, the peace of a conquered spirit fell upon her. She had thought it all to an ending at last. It seemed to Harriet that never in her life had she thought so clearly, so truly, so bravely. Her duty to Richard, to his children, to Linda; she had faced them without fear and without deception, tasting the humiliating truth to its bitter dregs, planning the few short interviews that must precede her leaving them all forever.

For Harriet emerged from the furnace the mistress of her own soul. She had been wrong; she had been weak; she had been contemptible; but not so wrong or weak or contemptible as they would think her. She would go on her way now, the braver for the lesson and the shame. And what they thought of her must never shake again her own knowledge of her own innocence.

Go on her way to what? She did not know. But she neither feared what the future might hold nor doubted, it. She could make her own way from a new beginning.

"But before I go," said Harriet, resolutely, "I must tell him that I'm sorry. And I must ask Nina to forgive me."

She turned, and buried her face in the thick, soft sleeve of her coat. But she did not cry long, and when Jensen, the boatman, came out on the dock at seven, the lady he knew to be his new mistress was sitting composedly enough on her bench, studying the now glittering and sparkling river with quiet eyes.

Harriet nodded to him, and rose somewhat stiffly, to go up to the house. She mounted the brick steps with a thoughtfully dropped head--the straight shafts of the sunlight were making it impossible to face the house, in any case--and so was within three feet of Richard Carter before she saw him.

He looked fresh, hard, even young, in his white flannels. They stood looking at each other for a moment without speaking.

"Where have you been?" said Richard, sharply, then. "You look ill!"

Tears, despite her desperate resolution, suddenly stung Harriet's eyes. And yet her heart leaped with hope.

"I wanted to see you, Mr. Carter," she faltered. "I couldn't sleep very well. I've been down at the shore. But later--any time will do!"

"You couldn't sleep!" he exclaimed with quick sympathy. He looked from her about him, as if for a shelter for her emotion. "Here," he said, "come down the steps a bit. I was just going down to the court for a little tennis; Ward may follow me, but he won't be dressed for half an hour yet. Sit down here; we can talk."

They had come to the marble bench on the terrace, where Isabelle and Anthony Pope, sheltered by these same towering trees and low brick walls, had had their talk a year ago. Harriet, to her own consternation, felt that she was in danger of tears.

"I--I hardly know how to say it," she began. "But--but you know how ashamed I am!"

"I know--I know how you feel!" Richard said with a sort of brief sympathy. "I'm sorry! But you know you mustn't take this all too hard. I didn't--I was thinking of this last night; I didn't ask you for--well, any more than you gave me, in this marriage of ours. Your divorce was your own affair--"

The girl's tired eyes flashed.

"There was no divorce!" she said, quickly.

"No divorce?" he echoed with a puzzled frown.

"I want to tell you about it!" she said. But the tears would come again. "I'm tired!" Harriet said, childishly, trying to smile. "I've been up--walking. I couldn't sleep!"

The consciousness that he had been able to forget the whole tangle, and sleep soundly, gave Richard's voice a little compunction as he said:

"You don't have to tell me now. We'll find a way out of it that is easy for everyone--"

"No, but let me talk!" Harriet, in her eagerness, laid her fingers on his wrist, and he was shocked to feel that they were icy cold. "I want to tell you the whole thing--I want you to understand!" she said, eagerly. Richard looked at her in some anxiety; there was no acting here. The rich hair was pushed carelessly from the troubled forehead. She was huddled in the enveloping coat, a different figure indeed from his memory of the superb and angry girl of last night in the library lamplight.

"Mr. Carter, I never knew my mother--" she began. But he interrupted her.

"My dear," he said, in a tone he might have used to Nina. He laid his warm, fine hand on hers, and patted it soothingly. "My dear girl, if you feel that you would like to go to that motherly sister of yours--if you feel that it would be wiser--"

"Oh, I am going to Linda at once!" Harriet said, feverishly, hurt to the soul. "I had planned that! But--but won't you let me tell you?" she pleaded. She had framed the sentences a hundred times in the long night; they failed her utterly now, and she groped for words. "I was only three years old when my mother died," she said. "Of course I don't remember her--I only remember Linda. I was shy, my father was a professor, we were too poor to have very much social life. I lived in books, lived in my father's shabby little study really; I never had an intimate girl friend! Linda was always good--angelically good--talking of the Armenian sufferers, and of the outrages in the Congo, and of the poor in New York's lower east side--she never cared that we were poor, and that we hadn't clothes!"

"I know--I know!" Richard's eyes were smiling, as if he knew the picture, and liked it.

"Well, Linda married when I was ten, and Josephine came, and then Julia came. I still lived for books and babies. But, unlike Linda, I cared." Harriet's whole face glowed; she looked off into space, and her voice had a longing note. "I cared for clothes and good times!" she said. "I adored the children, but I dreamed of carriages--maids--glory--achievements! I knew that other women did it--"

"I remember feeling that way!" Richard commented, mildly, as she paused.

"Well," Harriet said, "I met Royal Blondin one night. He lived in our town--Watertown. He had a dreadful, artificial sort of mother. My sister didn't approve of her at all. A friend of his named Street was an artist, and he had a nice little wife, and a baby, and they lived in a big, barnlike sort of studio. It seemed wonderful to me. They loved each other, and their baby, but they were so free! They would have the whole crowd to dinner, twenty of us, bread and red wine and macaroni and music and talk, it was wonderful--or I thought so! It was so different from Linda's ideas, of frosted layer-cake, and chopped nuts, and Five Hundred. I loved the studio, and they--they all loved me, and he--Royal--loved me especially. He used to talk about Yogi philosophy and Oriental religions and poetry, and after awhile it was understood among them all that he loved me, and I him. And we were engaged. Of course Linda suspected, and there was opposition at home, but in the studio, helping the Streets get their suppers, it seemed so right--so simple! Royal said he did not believe in the orthodox ceremony of marriage. He argued that no one could live up to its promises, and I believed him. Miriam Street, the artist's wife, was a poet, and she wrote the ceremony by which we were married. We had a big supper, and they were all there, and this poem--this marriage poem--was beautiful. It was published in a magazine, afterward, and called 'A Marriage for True Lovers'. It had a part for the woman to say, and a part for the man, and Royal and I said those, and then it had a part for the woman's friend, and the man's friend, and for all their friends. And then there was a promise that when love failed on either side, the two were free, to keep the memory of the perfect love unstained by the ugly years."

She paused; Richard did not speak. She had told him this much in a simple, childish voice, a voice that was an echo of that old time, he knew. Presently she went on:

"There was music, and then they all kissed me, and we had supper, and they drank our health. I went back that night to my sister's; Royal stayed with his mother. We planned to go away on our honeymoon the next day.

I did not tell Linda and Fred that I considered myself married. I knew they would not understand and would try to interfere.

"The next morning I slipped away from the house, with my suitcase, and I met Royal Blondin downtown. We motored to Syracuse, and took a train there for New York. I had felt sick when I awakened--it was partly excitement, and partly the supper the night before, when we had all eaten and drunk too much. But I was very sick in the train, I thought I was going to die. Royal persuaded me to eat my lunch in the dining car, and that only made me worse. There was a nice woman in the train, with two little girls, and she took care of me. And when she got to New York--I had told her that I was on my wedding journey, and perhaps that made her kind--she took us to her boarding-house, in West Forty-sixth Street. The landlady was a dear, good woman, a Mrs. Harrington, and--I was very sick by this time!--she put me into her own room, because the house was full, and sent for her own doctor.

"It was a time of horror," Harriet said, smiling a little, after a moment of thought. "The strange women and the strange room, and Royal coming in with flowers, and sitting beside me. The doctor said it was a touch of poisoning, and I was ill only a few days. But the home-sickness, and the strangeness! Somehow, I didn't feel married, I felt like a lost little girl. I wanted to be back in Linda's kitchen again, safe, and scolding because nothing interesting ever happened.

"Well, I was sick for three or four days. It was the fourth day when I was well enough to go out. Royal thanked them, and paid Mrs. Harrington and the doctor and we went to lunch downtown--it was at Martin's, I remember, and Royal was so excited and interested in everything. But I still felt limp and dull. We shopped and went about seeing things after lunch, and then we went to the hotel where he was staying. We were registered there as Mr. and Mrs. Blondin; it was all quite taken for granted."

Harriet stopped; her face was drawn and white, her words coming with difficulty, the phrases brief and dry. Richard was paying her absolute attention, his eyes fixed upon her face.

"We had dinner upstairs," she said. She paused, her lips tight pressed.

"I can't tell you," she began again, suddenly, "I can't tell you how it was that I came suddenly to know that I was too young for marriage! In Miriam Street's little studio, where they were laughing about the baby and the supper, it had seemed different. But here, in a hotel, I suddenly wanted my sister, I wanted to be home again.

"We were talking and planning naturally enough. Royal was coming and going in the two rooms; I had plenty of chance to--to escape. Every time I let one go by my heart beat harder."

He could tell from her voice that her heart was beating hard now with the memory of that old time.

"If I had let them all go by," she recommenced, "my life would have been different. In a few weeks we would have come back to Watertown, as man and wife, and perhaps had a studio near the Streets', and perhaps found a solution. But I couldn't!

"I caught up my coat; left my hat and bag. I went down the stairs, not daring to wait for the elevator. And I went to Mrs. Harrington's. She was very kind and took me in; she said that perhaps it would be better to wait--until I was older. I cried all night, and the next day Mrs. Harrington lent me the money and I went back to Linda.

"Of course, it was terrible, at first. But they were kind to me, in their way. And I was--cured. I went into hysterics at the first mention of the whole hideous thing. They saw Roy, and they told me that I need never see him again. The papers--for it got to the papers!--said that a divorce had been arranged, but there was no need for a divorce. It was all hushed up-- Linda and Fred never spoke of it. I--ah, well, I couldn't!

"But when Fred's brother, David, who was in dental college then, began to like me, then they began to make light of it," Harriet remembered. "There had been no marriage, of course, either in law or in fact. They all knew that. And I suppose if I had married David it might have been happier for me. But as it was, I angered them. I didn't want to marry David. And so it was what folly girls got themselves into--what the world thought of a girl who had been 'talked about'--what the least breath of scandal meant!"

"And you went back to Blondin?" Richard suggested.

"I? No, I never saw him again until a year ago in this garden!" Harriet said.

"You never saw him again!" the man ejaculated.

"Not for nine years!"

"But--my God, my dear girl, he spoke of you as his wife!" Richard said.

"He said I had been. Not that I was now!"

The man looked at her, looked away at the river, and shrugged his shoulders as if he were mystified by the ways of women.

"But--you were never his wife?" he said, flatly.

"Oh, no! You didn't think," Harriet said, hurt, "that I would have married you, or any one else, if I had been!"

"You let him blackmail you for that," Richard further marvelled.

"I knew--in my own mind, of course, that I was not to blame," the girl said, anxiously. "But it sounded--horrible."

Richard bit his lower lip, looked critically at his racket, slowly shook his head.

"I didn't mind what any one thought," Harriet said, reading his thought. "But they did!"

"They?" Richard repeated, patiently.

"Everyone," she supplied, promptly. "Your wife, your mother, Mary Putnam! Even Mrs. Tabor."

"I suppose so!" he conceded, after a pause. And beneath his breath he added, "Isabelle--Ida Tabor!"

His tone was all she asked of exquisite reassurance.

"I hoped you wouldn't!" she said, standing up with clasped hands and a sudden brightening of her tired and colourless face. "That's what I tried to make myself believe you would feel! I wanted so to leave it all behind. I thought he had gone, that it was all over, that what it was mattered more than what it sounded like! I thought I could save Nina better, with what I knew, than any one else! But last night," Harriet added, "proved to me that I had been all wrong. I've been so worried," she added, with utter faith in his decision. "I don't know what you think we had better do."

For a full minute Richard watched her in silence. Then he said, mildly: "About Nina, you mean?"

"About everything!" Harriet suddenly laughed gaily, like a child. Life seemed once more straight and pleasant in this exquisite June morning; she felt puzzled, but somehow no longer afraid. The menacing horrors of all the years, the vague uneasiness that she had never quite dared to face, were fluttering about her awakening spirit like Alice's pack of cards.

"Nina will come into line," her father said, thoughtfully, "she doesn't know what she wants. I wish--I wish he loved her!" he added, with a faint frown. "I'll see him about it again. We'll take her to Rio. She'll get over it."

"And--" Harriet stopped, and began again: "And do you want things to go on just as they are?" she asked.

For answer Richard smiled at her in silence.

"No," he said, finally. "I can't say that I do. I want you to worry less, and to buy yourself some new gowns, and to begin to enjoy life! Shakespeare had you down fine when he talked about conscience making cowards of us all. What did you do it for? A young, capable, good-looking girl scared by a lot of old women! Now, we'll take up this Nina question, later on. You'd better go up and get yourself some coffee, and go to bed for awhile. Better plan to be in town for a day or two, for you'll both need clothes for the steamer--"

"You're very kind," the girl said, eyes averted, voice almost inaudible. They were both standing now, Harriet's head turned aside, so that he could not see her face, but her soft fingers resting in his.

"I'm not kind at all!" Richard said, with a rather confused laugh. He patted her hand encouragingly. "The sea trip will shake both you and Nina up, and do you a world of good!" he said.

"You think--" Harriet raised the soft, dark lashes, and her splendid, weary eyes met his, "You really aren't worried about Nina?"

And she tried by a very faint stirring of her fingers to free them, and finding them held, dropped her eyes again.

"I think I have Blondin's number," Richard said, with more force than eloquence. Then with a little laugh that was partly amused and partly embarrassed, he let her go.

He watched the young, slender figure and the shining, bare head until they disappeared among the great trees about the house.

CHAPTER XX

The summer Sunday ran its usual course. Ward and his sister went to luncheon at the club; Madame Carter drove majestically to a late service in the pretty, vine-covered village church. Harriet, at last able to relax in soul and body, slept hour after glorious hour. Richard, returning from golf for a late luncheon, asked for her. Mrs. Carter was still asleep, Bottomley assured him, and received orders not to disturb her. But when Mr. Blondin called, Richard told the butler he was to be shown to the terrace at once.

At three o'clock, therefore, Royal Blondin followed his guide out to the basket chairs that were set under the trees, and here he found Richard, comfortably smoking, and alone. The host rose to greet him, but they did not shake hands, and measured each other like wrestlers as they sat down.

"I had your message," Royal said, as an opening.

"You've not seen Nina to-day?" Nina's father asked.

"I broke an engagement with her at the club," the other man assured him. "We will probably meet at the Bellamys', at dinner this evening."

"Ah, it was about that I wished to speak." Richard paused, and Blondin watched him with polite interest. "You have held your knowledge of Mrs. Carter as a sort of weapon for some months," Richard said, presently, "to use it when you saw fit. I have always been in my wife's confidence--"

He paused, but for no reason that Blondin could divine. As a matter of fact, it gave Richard a sudden and unexpected pleasure to speak of her so, to realize that he really might give the most wonderful title in the world to this beautiful and spirited woman.

"And I have also talked with Nina this morning," he went on. "I regret to say that her intentions have not altered."

"A loyal little heart!" Blondin said, gravely and contentedly. "I knew I could depend upon her!"

Richard looked at him steadily for a moment, and felt carefully for his next words.

"You know how I feel about her marrying you--" he began.

Royal nodded, regretfully, broke the ash from his cigarette with a delicately poised little finger, and regarded Richard questioningly. "That is my misfortune," he said, resignedly; pleasantly aware that Nina's father would never be his match in phrases and self-control.

"I needn't go over all that," Richard said. "I love my daughter; I believe she will make a fine woman. But she isn't anything but a child now!"

"Perhaps you fail to do her justice in that respect," Royal Blondin said. Richard flushed with anger, but felt helpless under the other man's quiet insolence.

"I said I wanted to see you on business, Mr. Blondin," Richard continued, trying to keep impatience and contempt out of his voice, "and we'll keep to business. I don't know what your circumstances are, of course--"

He hesitated, and Blondin looked at him with a faint interest.

"I live simply," he said. "Nina's money will be all her own."

"Nina will have no money, not one five-cent piece, for exactly three years!" Richard said.

Blondin shrugged.

"She is quite willing to try it!" he reminded her father.

"I know she is! But how about you?" Richard asked. "You are not a boy, you have some idea of what marriage means. For three years you must take care of her, dress her, amuse her, satisfy her that she has not made a mistake. Then she does come into her money--yes. But three years is a long time in which to keep her certain that the wisest thing she can do is turn it over to you."

He paused; Blondin smoked imperturbably.

"The marriage must be a notorious one, in any case," Richard pursued. "For I intend to make my stand too clear ever to permit of a retraction. I shall forbid it--let the world know that I forbid it. I shall forbid my daughter the house, and her wedding gift will be simply the clothes she happens to have. From Tuesday--her eighteenth birthday--she will turn to you for her actual pocket money, for her theatre tickets and cab fares."

"I understand that perfectly!" Royal said, serenely. But underneath, while not moved from his intention, he felt his customary assurance shaken.

"She is extravagant, naturally," her father said. "She will want new gowns, want to display her new importance a little. Those bills will come to you, Mr. Blondin. All the world will know as well as you do that I have washed my hands of the whole affair."

Royal nodded again. He began to be conscious of a growing disquietude. He had naturally given much thought to this exact question during the past few weeks, and had solved it only by dismissing it. He had assured himself that with his only daughter no man as generous as Carter could be really harsh, and had always held his knowledge of Harriet comfortably in the back of his mind, as an irresistible lever. Now both these considerations were losing their force, and the empty satisfaction of defying Richard seemed to be losing its flavour, too.

Blondin had no money, and lived with an extravagance that kept him perpetually worried for money. The rent of his studio had been raised; he was conscious of the necessity of returning hospitalities, of buying clothes. His credit would receive an immediate assistance from a marriage with Richard Carter's daughter, to be sure, but to sustain a credit for three years upon that shadowy footing would be extremely trying.

He liked Nina; despite his contempt for the girl, there was a certain pitying affection for her stubborn loyalty and simplicity. But he knew exactly what hideous scenes must follow upon his marriage with her. What could he do with her, even suppose him to have borrowed money enough to make their honeymoon a success? He imagined her dawdling about his studio, imagined his social standing as necessarily affected, imagined Mr. and Mrs. Royal Blondin attempting to reach an agreement as to which invitations would be accepted and which rejected. Railway fares, luncheons downtown, all these cost money--lots of money. Nina would want to entertain "the girls." And Royal had at present several serious debts. He had lost money on three morning lectures, delightful lectures and well-attended, but still a financial loss. He had been foolish enough to lose money at bridge, at the Bellamys' a week ago, and young Bellamy was carrying his check for three hundred and twelve dollars, drawn upon a bank where Royal was already overdrawn. Then there was an unpleasantness about three rugs, rugs he had taken four years ago, in a moment of unbelievable prosperity, but for which seven hundred and twenty dollars had been promised, and never paid. Royal had indeed offered Hagopian the rugs and a bonus, back again; he was sick of the studio, and the endless reminders from his landlord's agent that the monthly one hundred and seventy-five dollars was overdue; he was sick of the whole business.

But Hagopian had refused to take back the rugs, and the rent had reached the four-figure mark, and until he had settled for the last lectures, he did not feel encouraged to begin more.

This was not a cheerful outlook with which to begin three years of penniless matrimony. Royal, suavely smiling, and smoking on the terrace, wondered suddenly if old Madame Carter, who had always been his champion, would help out.

But Richard seemed to read his thought.

"Nina has appealed to her grandmother," he said, "and I know my mother sympathizes, and would be glad to help you. But her affairs are in my hands. She preferred it so, when I offered her some securities years ago, and it has always been so. Her bank account receives a monthly check; she sends all her household bills to my secretary, Fox. He O. K's and pays them. Consequently, she is not able to act in this matter, and I think she is glad of it! I believe she would regret the--the inevitable estrangement as much as I."

Blondin elevated his eyebrows politely, as one interested but not concerned. But he knew, with a sort of rage, that he was beaten. His only recourse now would be to plead to Nina an all-important wire from the Pacific coast, a dying friend, a temporary absence. He could sub-let his studio for twice the rent, and live on the margin until kindly Fate, as always, turned up a new card. Nina would protest, would weep that her beloved studio, where her first exciting housekeeping was to begin, was occupied by strangers, but that was unavoidable. However, he would annoy this gray-eyed, firm-lipped business man first.

But Richard had taken a small slip of tan paper from his pocket, and was studying it thoughtfully. Royal saw it, and his eyes narrowed.

"Now, Mr. Blondin," Nina's father said, simply, "I'm a business man. I can't beat about the bush, and call things by pretty names. I want a favour of you, and I'm willing to pay for it. I telephoned you this morning that I wanted to see you on a matter of business. This is my proposition."

He leaned forward, and Royal saw the paper. He boasted to women of his indifference to money, it was true, but as with all adventurers, it held first place in his thoughts. No man who was in debt could look upon that check unmoved. Royal might win at cards to-night, to be sure; Carter might weaken to-morrow, it was true. But this check bore his name, and it was sure.

To enter the bank, with Richard Carter's check for so substantial an amount, to deposit it, exchange a careless word with the cashier, to write his check for the overdue rent, with a casual apology; to play bridge again, this evening, with young Bellamy, and this time win back that accursed check of his own, as he knew he would win it. ...

It all fluttered before his eyes, despite his attempt to look indifferent. It weighed down the little tarnished thing he called his pride, already half-forfeited in this group. His last attempt at bravado was obviously that, and he knew it.

"Just one moment, Mr. Carter. You say that you and I know what marriage is. How do you reconcile it with your knowledge of Nina, your knowledge of her upbringing, to plan deliberately what would make our marriage--or any marriage--foredoomed to failure from the start? I didn't spoil Nina, I didn't form her tastes. She has thought of herself as an heiress, she has spent money, lived luxuriously. I only ask a fair chance. Make it an allowance, if you like. Keep the matter in the family; don't blaze to the world that you disapprove! Many a less-promising marriage has turned out a brilliant success. She loves me. I--I am devoted to her. I see tremendous possibilities in her!"

"She loves you as a child does, and because she doesn't know you," Richard said, inflexibly. "But you haven't heard what I propose, Blondin. Hear me out. I give you this now, to-day, on condition that before to-night you talk to Nina. Represent anything you wish to her. Tell her what you please. But convince her that she must wait for two years--with no letters, no meetings, no engagement--that's all.

"On my part, I promise that nobody in the world, not Mrs. Carter, not anybody, will hear of this for two years from to-day, at least. Meanwhile, we'll amuse Nina. Her grandmother wants to take her to Santa Barbara next fall--Gardiner wants both the youngsters on his ranch this summer, or she may go with me to Brazil. She'll have enough to think about. We'll not hurt you with her, you may take my word for it. And I tell you frankly that I shall be deeply grateful. I'm not paying you for giving her up. I'm paying you for two years' delay. Young Hopper will be at the Gardiners' this summer--she likes him, and he likes her! Well, that's speculation." Richard dismissed it with a movement of his fine hands. "But we'll distract her!" he promised. "Hopper may buy a ranch out there--that sort of thing might suit Nina down to the ground!"

"Buy it with Nina's money," Royal could not help sneering.

Richard eyed him in surprise.

"When Joe Hopper died he left that boy's mother something in the millions," he said. "There's an immense estate." And then, with a reversion to business: "Come, now, Mr. Blondin. We understand each other. Nina's dining at the Bellamys' to-night; you're staying there. Will you see her?"

The check fluttered to the table between them. There was a long silence. Then Blondin ground out his cigarette in a stone saucer, rose, in all the easy beauty of his white summer clothes, his flowing scarf, his dark, romantic locks. He lifted his straw hat, put it on, picked up his stick, and laid it on the table. Then he took the check and read it thoughtfully.

"Thank you!" he said. Yet the shameful thing struck him, an adept now in evading and lying, as surprisingly easy, and as he sauntered away in the

June warmth and silence, it was not of Nina, or her father, or even of himself that he was thinking.

He had met the widow of Joe Hopper a few nights ago: a faded little pleasant woman of fifty, pathetically grateful for his casual politeness in her strangeness and shyness. He had chanced, quite idly and accidentally, to make an impression on her. She had promised to come to the studio and look at his rugs.

Royal wondered why she dressed so badly; she needed simple materials and flowing lines. He heard himself telling her so.

Richard sat on, on the terrace, thinking, and presently his mother came out and joined him. Wasn't he, the old lady asked elaborately, going to the club? It was almost five o'clock, her son reminded her. Two or three of his business associates were coming to dinner; Hansen was to drive them all into the city later. Now, he just felt lazy.

"No tea to-day?" he asked, presently. People usually went to the club on Sunday, said his mother. She added, irrelevantly, that Harriet was asleep. Richard said that she had looked tired this morning; sleep was the best thing for her.

But suddenly life became significant and thrilling again; he heard her voice, her laugh. She came swiftly and quietly out to them, smiling at him, settling herself in the chair beside his mother. She wore white, transparent, simple; there were coral beads about her firm young throat. The dew of her deep sleep made her blue eyes wonderful; her cheeks were as pink as a baby's.

"Aren't the June days delicious?" she said. Richard studied her, smilingly, without answering. What would she say next, where would she move her eyes, or lay her white hand, he wondered. When she murmured to his mother in an undertone, he tried to catch the words.

"We're to have tea," Harriet announced. When it came, she poured it; for awhile the three were alone. Richard found himself talking to make her talk, but she was apparently interested only to draw out his mother and himself. "I'm starving," she presently said, apologetically, "this is luncheon and breakfast, too, for me!"

"Did you have a good sleep?" Richard asked. She flashed him an eloquent look.

"Oh--the most delightful of my whole life! Eight hours without stirring!"

The Hoyts arrived: a handsome mother and two equally handsome daughters. Harriet went to them gracefully; Richard saw that she was accepting good wishes. She took the callers to his mother, and filled their cups herself.

"She certainly is wonderful!" Richard said. He perfectly realized his own suddenly deepening feeling for her, but he dared not analyze it yet. When Mrs. Hoyt hinted at a dinner, he took part in the conversation. "Thursday? Why not, Harriet? We have no engagement for Thursday?"

She flushed brightly, signalling to him that she had already indicated an excuse. They had never dined together away from home. He need not think, said Harriet's anxious manner, that he need carry the appearance of marriage so far.

"But--but aren't Nina and I to be in town Thursday?" she ventured,

"Shopping. You can make that next week!" Richard said. He loved her confusion.

"Then we surely will! Thank you," she said to Mrs. Hoyt.

"Thursday, then, at eight!" the caller said, departing. Richard sauntered with them to their car, and returned to find Harriet half-scandalized, half-laughing.

"But do you want to dine with them?" she asked.

"Why not?" His smile challenged her, and she laughed hardily.

"I suppose there is no reason why not, Mr. Carter!"

"You can wear"--he gestured--"the black and goldy thing. They'll all be watching you!"

"Oh," she said, considering earnestly, "I have a much handsomer one than that. Blue and silver. You've not seen it."

"Blue and silver, then." Richard felt a distinct regret when the men he expected appeared. There was but one figure of any interest to him on the shady, flower-scented terrace, and that was a woman's figure in a white gown.

For two or three days he was conscious of a constant interest in her appearances and disappearances, a constant desire to please her. He found himself liking a certain young man, in his city club, for no other reason than that he had asked admiringly for Mrs. Carter. He found Harriet deeply interested in a book, and took the time to go into a bookstore and ask the clerk for something "on the same line as the Poulteney Letters." In Nina's old Kodak album, idly opened, he was suddenly held by pictures of Nina's governess, beautiful even in a bathing-suit, with dripping hair; lovely in the gipsy hats and short skirts of camp life.

Richard Carter was conscious of one mastering curiosity: he wanted to know just how Harriet regarded him. It seemed suddenly of supreme importance. He thought of it in his office, and smiled to himself during important business conferences, wondering about it. It seemed incredible to him, now, that his experiences of the past year had been so largely concerned with Harriet. His wife's companion, his daughter's governess, his own capable and dignified housekeeper, the woman he had so hastily married, all seemed a different person, a quite visionary person, with whom just such businesslike arrangements had been possible.

But Harriet was beginning to seem to him a stranger who possessed at once the most mysterious and childlike, the most beautiful and the most baffling personality that he had ever known. He made excuses to go home early, just to catch glimpses of this wife who was not his wife. That he had ever taken a fatherly, advisory tone with this woman was unbelievable; her mere approach made him catch his breath and lose his coherency. He had walked into her room--he had patronized her--he had asked her as casually to marry him as if she had been fifty, and as plain as she was lovely!

Richard shuddered as he thought of it. He made constant efforts to engage her in personalities, but she evaded him. There was a real thrill for him in the quiet dinner at the Hoyts'. Mrs. Carter, said slow old bewhiskered John Hoyt, was an extremely pretty woman. My wife--Richard in answering called her that--looks particularly well in an evening gown. Indeed she looked exquisite in the blue and silver dress, laughing--still with that adorable mist of strangeness and shyness about her--with her neighbours at the table, and afterward in the drawing room, waving her silver fan slowly while Freda Hoyt, who quite obviously adored her, whispered her long confidences.

Coming home in the limousine they had neighbours with them, old Doctor and Mrs. Carmichael, so he might not have the word alone with her for which he had been longing all evening. But he stopped her in the wide, dim hallway when they reached Crownlands.

"Tired?" he said, at the foot of the stairs.

"Not a bit!" There was an enchanting vitality about her. She had slipped the thin wrap from her shoulders, and she turned to him her lovely, happy face. "Did you want me?"

"I wanted to say something to you," Richard said, feeling awkward as a boy.

"In there?" She nodded, suddenly alert, toward the library.

"Why in there?" he asked, with a little husky laugh. His one impulse was to put his arms about her.

"I thought--bills, perhaps?" Harriet said, innocently. It was the third day of the month; he had often consulted her as to expenses before this.

"No," Richard said, with another unsteady little laugh. "It wasn't bills. I was just wondering--if I had been very stupid," he said, taking one of her hands, and looking up from the fingers that lay in his to the face that now wore an expression a little frightened despite the smile.

"Never with me!" Harriet said, in a low tone.

"Never so blind," Richard said, "never so matter-of-fact that I hurt your feelings? Nothing of--that sort?"

"Always the kindest friend I ever had!" the girl answered, unsteadily, and with suddenly wet eyes. "The--the most generous!"

He looked at her hand again, looked up at her as if he would speak. But instead she felt her fingers pressed, and felt her heart thump with a delicious terror.

"Do--do you like the blue and silver dress?" she asked with an excited laugh.

"I like it better than any dress I have ever seen!" Richard answered, seriously. Her hand free now, Harriet, standing on the lowest step, made him a little bow that displayed the frail silver fan, the silver slippers, the stockings with their silver lace.

"And wait until you see our frocks for the boat!" she warned him. "Nina has a yellow coat--and I have a black lace and a white embroidery! Really--REALLY I have never seen anything like the white one. SHEER, you know--"

Bottomley came noiselessly, discreetly, across the hall. Instantly the woman in blue and silver was all the mistress.

"Is Mr. Ward in, Bottomley?"

"He dined at 'ome, Mrs. Carter."

"Oh, thank you! You may lock up, then. Good-night, Mr. Carter! Good-night, Bottomley!"

She was gone. The blue and silver gown and the bunched folds of the furred coat vanished on the stairway landing. The tall clock that she passed struck eleven. And Richard, going into his library, realized that he was deeply and passionately in love. He could think of nothing else--he did not wish to think of anything else. Her face came between him and his book, her voice loitered in his ears, her precise, pretty phrasing, the laughter that sometimes lurked beneath her tones.

He went upstairs, and to his own suite. There was a door between his own sitting room and the room that had been Isabelle's. From the other side of his door, to-night, came the murmur of voices: Harriet and Nina were talking. Their conversation seemed full of fascination to Richard, although he could not hear a word, and would not have made an effort to do so. But he liked the thought of this lovely woman near his little girl, of their conferences and confidences.

Next day Harriet told him that Nina had been talking of young Hopper.

"It seems that this awkward, tongue-tied youth is desperately enamoured of Rosa Artures, of the Metropolitan Opera Company," Harriet said in rich amusement. "Of course the Artures is forty-five, and has a domestic life that is the delight of the women's magazines. But poor little Hopper haunts her performances, and sends her orchids, just the same. He had never met her until a week or two ago, then some friends had her and her husband on their yacht, and he was there. And she ate, it seems, and laughed, and even drank a little too much--he's entirely disillusioned! Isn't it too bad? And somebody told me about it, so I encouraged Nina to get him to talk last night. They talked only too well! They exchanged tragedies."

"Well, that won't hurt her!" Richard said, thoughtfully.

"Hurt her!" Harriet answered, eagerly. "It will be the best thing in the world for her!"

They were at the country club; Harriet chaperoning Nina, who was down at the tennis court with a group of young persons; Richard breathless and happy from a hard game of eighteen holes. He had encountered her on the porch, on his way to the showers, experiencing, as he did so, the thrill that belongs only to the unexpected encounter. Now they loitered at the railing, in the shade of the green awnings, as entirely oblivious of watching eyes as if the clubhouse were the library at home.

"Nina is charming as a confidante," Harriet said, "and she would make a boy of that type a delightful wife. She is the sort that marries early, or not at all, and I'm going deliberately to encourage this affair in a quiet way. He's a dear fellow, domestic and shy; they'd love their home and their children and Nina would develop into the ideal wife and mother. She's discriminating, she makes nice friends, she has splendid French and Spanish. She looks lovely to-day; I persuaded her to leave her glasses at home, even if she did miss them a little, and she has on one of the gowns we bought for the Brazilian trip."

"I made the reservations to-day. We sail the third of August," Richard said. "We've got to have your pictures taken for the passports."

"South America!" Harriet gave a great sigh of joy. "You don't know how excited I am!" she said. "Three weeks on a big liner--and we have to have bathing-suits, somebody said for the canvas tank, and they have all sorts of things on board. I've always wanted to go to Rio!"

"There are eight big staterooms with baths on this liner," Richard said. "I've taken two adjoining ones, so we ought to be very comfortable. Yes," he conceded, enjoying her enthusiasm, "it ought to be a great trip! Will you and Nina want a maid?"

"A maid?" She widened her blue eyes. "Oh, no! Why should we?"

Richard laughed at her surprise.

"You might take Pilgrim," he suggested. And with an amused glance he added: "You forget that you are a rich man's wife."

"Indeed I don't!" Harriet said, quickly. "I spend simply scandalous sums! When I saw my sister last week," she confided, gaily, "she explained that the payment on the new house would prevent the usual six weeks at the beach this year, and I simply made them go! I paid the rent on their cottage and bought the tickets, and--oh, all sorts of things, little dresses and sandals and shade hats, and off they went! You never saw such joy!"

Richard blinked his eyes, and managed a smile.

"What did you pay it out of?" he wondered,

"My bank account! Linda and I shopped a whole morning, and had lunch downtown--it was more fun!" Harriet said, youthfully. "The rent," she explained, "was eighty dollars--"

"What? For six weeks!" Richard interrupted.

"Do you think that's a lot?" she asked, anxiously.

"Go on!" he said. "They all went off, did they? Eighty dollars gives them a cottage until the middle of August, does it?"

"Until school opens," she nodded. "All the other things--well, it came to about two hundred."

"That's happiness, isn't it?" Richard said. "A cottage on a swarming beach. Sons and daughters in bathing-suits, no real housekeeping for the mother, nothing but sleep and swimming and plain meals!"

"They love it!" But Harriet's eyes drank in the awninged shade of the country club porches, the flowered cretonne on the wicker chairs, the women in their exquisite gowns, the smooth curves of the green links, where brightly clad figures went to and fro. Riders were disappearing into the green shade of the bridle paths; girls in white, demanding tea, came up the shallow steps. A group of four women, at a card table, broke up with laughter. "Yes, it's honester than this," she said, bringing her eyes back to his. "I'll have Linda and the girls here some day," she added, "and they'll think it is wonderful. But after all, they get more taste out of life!"

"You know they do!" Richard said.

"Mrs. Carter," said a woman in bright yellow, coming up to them suddenly, "will you be a darling and come and talk to my French officer? The girls have all been practising their Berlitz on him, and he's almost losing his mind! Dick," added this matron, who had linked her arm about Harriet's waist, "for heaven's sake go clean up! Can't you find time to talk to your wife at home? I've been watching you for five minutes, getting my arms burned simply black--will you come, Mrs. Carter? That's the poor soul, over there with Sarah. I don't know why I've had a French governess for that girl for seven years!"

"To save the life of a fellow creature--" Harriet said in her liquid French. She went off, laughingly, in the other woman's custody; Richard looked after them a moment.

He saw them join the group of smiling girls and the harassed Frenchman; saw the alien's face brighten as Harriet was introduced. A moment later a boy with a tennis racket dashed up to them, and there was a scattering in the direction of the courts. The girls surrounded the boy, and streamed away chattering. The matron in yellow came back to her card table. And Harriet, unfurling her parasol, deep in conversation with the captured soldier, sauntered slowly after the tennis players. The afternoon sunshine sent clean shadows across the clipped grass; the stretched blue silk of Harriet's parasol threw a mellow orange light upon her tawny hair and saffron-coloured gown.

Richard had a child's desperate wish that he was dressed, and might run after them.

"They are playing the semi-finals," he said to himself, hurrying through his change of garments. "I wish to the Lord I had gotten through in time to get down there!"

But it was not at the tennis that he looked, twenty minutes later, when he reached the courts; although a brilliant play was being made, and there was a spattering of applause. His eyes instantly found Harriet's figure; she was still talking to the Frenchman, whose olive face was glowing with interest and admiration, and not more than eight inches, Richard thought, from her own. Harriet's own face wore the shadow of a smile, her lashes were dropped, and she was gently pushing the point of her closed parasol into the green turf. The chairs in which they sat had been slightly turned from the court.

Richard engaged himself in conversation with two or three men and women who were watching the youngsters' game, and presently found himself applauding his son for a brilliant ace. But after perhaps five minutes he walked quite without volition, straight to Harriet's neighbourhood, and she rose at once, introduced her new friend, and with a glance at her wrist, announced that she must go.

"Ward said he would drive me home the instant it was over," said Harriet, clapping heartily for the triumphant finish of the set.

"I'll drive you home!" Richard said, instantly. "I've the small car."

"Friday night!" Harriet smiled. For Friday night was the night for a men's dinner and poker game at the country club, and Richard usually liked to be there.

"I can come back!" he persisted, suddenly caring more for this concession than anything else in the world. Without another word she agreed, bade her Frenchman what seemed to Richard a voluble good-bye, and when the bowing officer disappeared turned with a reminiscent smile.

"And now what?"

"Where did you learn to chatter French that way?" Richard said, leading the way to the line of parked motors.

"Oh, we lived in Paris--old Mrs. Rogers and I," Harriet reminded him carelessly. And reaching the little rise of ground that lay between the clubhouse and the parking field, she stood still, looking off across the exquisite spread of fields and valleys, banded by great strips of woods, and flooded now by the streaming shadows and golden lights of the late afternoon. "What a day!" she said, filling her lungs with great breaths of the sweet air. "What an hour!"

"What I meant to say to you up there on the porch," Richard said, "when that--that woman interrupted--"

Harriet herself interrupted with a laugh.

"You say 'that woman' as if it was a bitter, deadly curse!" she said.

"Well--" They had reached the car now, and Richard was investigating the oil gauge and spark plugs under the hood. "Well, a woman like that breaks in--nothing to her!" he said with scorn, straightening up.

"Yes, but at a country club?" Harriet offered, placatingly, as she got into the front seat, and tucked the pongee robe snugly about the saffron-coloured gown.

"I suppose so!" He got in beside her; there was a moment of backing and wrenching before they glided out smoothly on the white driveway. "What I meant to say was this," he added, suddenly, with a sidewise glance from his wheel. "I--I want you to realize that I appreciate the injustice--the crudeness of my rushing to you in New Jersey that Christmas Day. I realize that we all have imposed on you--we've taken you too much for granted! I was in trouble, and I couldn't think of any other way out of it. But for any man to put a proposition like that to any woman--"

They were driving very slowly. He looked at her again, and met a wondering look in her beautiful eyes that still further confused him. He had been uncomfortably conscious of an odd confusion in touching upon this subject at all. Yet his mind had been full of it all day.

"I never felt it so, I assure you!" Harriet said with her lucid, friendly look. Richard felt that there was more to say, but realized that he had selected an unfortunate time for these confidences.

"I'm afraid I've been extremely stupid in the matter," he said, feeling for his words. "I've gone about it clumsily. To tell you the truth--What does that boy want?"

It was Ward who was coming toward them across the green, with great springs and leaps, like some mountain animal.

"Give us a lift!" shrieked Ward, flinging himself upon the car as its speed decreased. "Something is the matter with my engine--engina pectoris is what I call it! Father, Mr. Tom Grant expects you to dine at his table to-night, he said to remind you. And, Harriet, angel of angels, we will be about six or seven about the groaning board; is that all right?"

"I told Bottomley six or seven," Harriet said, serenely. "Ward, get in or get out," she added, maternally, "don't hang over the door in that blood-curdling way!"

She had put her arm about the boy to steady him; they began to discuss tennis scores with enthusiasm. Richard drove the rest of the way home almost without speaking.

He planned to see Harriet again that evening, and left the club at eleven o'clock, after an incredibly dull game, with the definite hope that the youngsters would dance, or in some other way prolong the summer evening at least until midnight. His heart sank when he reached Crownlands; the lower floor showed only the tempered lights that burned until the latest member of the family came in, and Bottomley reported that the young persons had gone upstairs at about half-past ten, sir. It was now half-past eleven.

Richard debated sending Harriet a message to the effect that he would like to see her for a moment. The flaw in this plan was that he could think of nothing about which there was the slightest necessity of seeing her. He felt restless and anything but sleepy, and glanced irresolutely at the library door, and at the stairway.

Suddenly uproar broke out upstairs: there were thumping feet, shrieks, wild laughter, and slamming doors. With a suddenly lightened heart Richard ran up the wide, square flight to the landing. His son, in pajamas that were more or less visible beneath his streaming robe of Oriental silk, was pirouetting about the upper hall with a siphon of soda water. Subdued giggles and smothered gasps indicated that the young ladies were somewhere near, in hiding. Young Hopper, under Ward's direction, was investigating doors and alcoves.

"Amy Hawkes--Amy Hawkes--Amy Hawkes--come into court!" Ward intoned. "Drunk and disorderly!"

"Here, here, here!" Richard said. "What's all this?" Amy and Nina, with hysteric shrieks, immediately forsook cover, and dashed down to him, clinging to him wildly.

"Oh, Father! Make them stop! Oh, Mr. Carter, save us!" screamed the girls in delicious terror. "Oh, they got poor Francesca--she's locked up in your room! They climbed up our porch, after they swore to Harriet that they wouldn't make another SOUND--"

Harriet now appeared in the hallway, her hair falling in a braid over her shoulder, and the long lines of the black robe she wore giving her figure an unusual effect of height. She did not see Richard immediately, for she had eyes only for Ward, as she caught his shoulder, and took away the siphon.

"Now, Ward--look here," she said, sternly. "What sort of honour do you call this! Half an hour ago I thought all this nonsense was STOPPED. Shame on you! Those girls promised me--"

She saw Richard, and laughed, the colour flooding her face.

"Aren't they simply shameless!" she said. "I had them all settled down, once! Nina, where's Francesca? You see," Harriet said, in rapid explanation to Richard, "I gave the girls my room to-night, so that they could all be together, and this is my reward!"

The girls, entirely unalarmed by her severity, had deserted Richard now, and were clinging to her with weak laughter and feeble explanations.

"Francesca unlocked that door, and rushed into Mr. Carter's room!" Amy explained, wiping her eyes. "And then the boys locked her in there!"

The composed reappearance of Francesca at this point, however, added to the general hilarity.

"You DID NOT lock me in, Smarties!" Francesca drawled, childishly. "They climbed to the balcony, and we were--well, we were undressing," she said to Richard, "and here they were hammering and yelling like--like Siwashes! We grabbed our wrappers, we wanted to---"

"We wanted to lock them out there!" Amy explained, laughing uncontrollably. "But--"

"And I snapped off the light--" Nina interposed, with deep satisfaction.

"And, mind you--"

"And, Father--"

"And the wonder was that we didn't die of fright--"

"Now, look here," Harriet said, in the babel, "I'll give you all exactly two minutes to QUIET DOWN. Never in the course of my life--"

Richard thought her maternal indulgence delightful; he thought the young people who clung about her charming in their apologetic and laughing promises. Ward and Bruce Hopper mounted to their own region; Richard went with the girls and Harriet to the rooms that had been attacked. Pilgrim, the tireless, was already there, replacing pillows, straightening beds, untwisting curtains. The girls, with reminiscent bubbles of laughter, began to help her.

After the last good-nights, Richard and Harriet had no choice but to cross the hall again, and they stood there for a moment, laughing at the recent excitement.

"After twelve," Harriet said, with a smiling shake of her head. "Aren't they young demons! However," she added in an undertone, "it's the best thing in the world for Nina! This sort of nonsense will blow cobwebs away!"

Richard was only conscious of a desire to prolong this intimate little moment of parental consultation.

"She doesn't speak of Blondin?" he asked.

"Not at all. The birthday came and went placidly enough," Harriet answered, suddenly intent after her laughing. And as he did not speak for a second, she looked up at him, innocently. "You don't think she's hiding anything?" she asked, anxiously.

"I--no, I hardly think so," Richard answered, confusedly. Their eyes met, and he smiled vaguely. Then Harriet slowly crossed the hall to the door of the guest room where she was spending the night, and gave him an only half-audible good-night. Richard stood watching the door for a moment or two after it had closed upon the slender, dimly seen figure. Then he went to his own rooms, and began briskly enough to move about between the mirrors and dressing room, windows and bed. But two or three times he stopped short, and found himself staring vacantly into space, all movement arrested, even thought arrested for whole long minutes at a time.

Harriet, entering her room, closed the door noiselessly, and remained for a long time standing with her hands resting against it behind her, her eyes alert, her breath coming as if she had been running. There was only a night light in the bedroom; the covers were still tumbled back from her sudden flight toward the rioting youngsters in the hall. She got back into her bed, and opened her book. But for a long time she neither slept nor read; her eyes widened at the faintest sound of the summer night; her heart thumped madly when the curtains whispered at the window, or the wicker chairs gave the faintest creak. It had not been only for Richard that the midnight hour of responsibility and informality shared had had its thrill.

One o'clock. Harriet closed her book and snapped off her light. But first she went to the window, and leaned out into the sweet darkness. There was shadow unbroken everywhere; no light in all the big house was burning as late as her own.

214

CHAPTER XXI

After that life took on a mysterious fragrance and beauty that made every hour of it an intoxication to the master and mistress of Crownlands. The fact that their secret was all their own was all the more enchanting. To the domestic staff, to the children, to the outside world, life went upon its usual smooth way. Mr. Carter would be in town to-night, Mr. Carter was detained at the office, Mrs. Carter was chaperoning the young people, there were flowers for Mrs. Carter. That was all Bottomley and Pilgrim and Ward and Nina saw.

But to Harriet and Richard the delicious, secret game of hide-and-go-seek made everything else in the world insignificant. Harriet opened the boxes of flowers he sent her with a heart suffocating with joy. Richard consented to be absent from the dinner table over which she presided with an agony of renunciation that almost made him feel ill. When he chanced one day to meet her with Nina, in a breezy, awninged summer restaurant, the sight of the slender figure thrilled him as he had never been thrilled by any woman he had ever known. He was to speak to her, to hear her voice! One day he bought her shoes; in the shop she looked at him for approval. He thought the shoes, low shoes with buckles, that showed the silk-clad ankle, very suitable and pretty. He was thrown into sudden confusion when the shoe clerk turned to him with a murmured mention of the price.

Ten dollars? Richard fumbled for his purse. He had met her walking alone in the Avenue; she had said that she must get shoes. Hundreds of other men were presumably buying their wives shoes, up and down the brilliant street. But Richard found the adventure shaking to the soul.

"They're lovely shoes," Harriet said, as they walked out into the sunshine. She told him that she was to meet Nina at his mother's at five. Richard, with sudden eagerness, wondered if she would spend the interval in having tea somewhere, but instead they went into a bookshop, and she carried a new book triumphantly away. "It's a frightful day in town," Harriet said, "and if we're a little early we may all get away to the country that much sooner!"

She established herself contentedly beside him when they did finally start for Crownlands. Ward, beside Hansen, did most of the talking; Nina was silent, and Harriet noticed that she was very pale. Richard was repeating to himself one phrase all the way; a phrase that he found so thrilling and absorbing that it was enough to keep him from speaking aloud, or listening to what the others said.

"I love her--I love her--I love her!" thought Richard. And sometimes he glanced sidewise at her, her beautiful hair rippling in thick waves under the thin veil, her face a little pale from the heat of the day, her glorious eyes faintly shadowed. When the swift movement of the car brought her shoulder against his, their eyes met for a smiling second, and it seemed to Richard that his heart brimmed with the most delicious emotion that he had ever known.

Nina complained of a headache when they reached home, and went early to bed. Harriet, when she had tubbed and changed to an evening gown, glanced in at Nina, and thought the girl asleep. There were men guests for dinner, and afterward there was bridge. Harriet sat with Madame Carter for awhile, for the old lady had also dined upstairs, went about the house upon her usual errands, and, going to her own room, found Nina reading, at about ten o'clock. Nina did not look up or speak as Harriet came in.

The door that led to Richard's room was not only unlocked, but actually ajar. Harriet gave it a surprised glance, and spoke to Nina, in the next room.

"Nina, did you unlock this door?"

"What door?" Nina called. "Oh, yes!" she added. "I did."

"Oh," Harriet murmured. And she stepped to the door, and looked into Richard's room.

It was a sort of upstairs sitting room, furnished simply, in man fashion, with deep leather chairs on each side of the fireplace, broad tables carrying only the essential lamps and ashtrays, a shabby desk where Richard kept personal papers, and bookshelves crammed with novels. Harriet, making a timid round, saw Balzac and Dickens, Dumas and Fielding, several Shakespeares and a complete Meredith, jostling elbows with modern novels in bright jackets, and yellow French romances losing their paper covers.

With a great sense of adventure she looked down from the unfamiliar windows at a new perspective of driveway and garden, peeped into the big square bedroom beyond. Two large photographs of Nina and Ward and an oil painting of his mother were here; there had been several pictures of Isabelle once, Harriet knew, but these had long ago disappeared.

Suddenly her heart turned to water; some tiny sound in the silence warning her that someone had entered. She turned, discovered here in the very centre of his own private apartment. He was standing not three feet away from her. For a second they stared at each other with a sort of mutual trepidation.

"Hello!" he said; then matter-of-factly, "I brought home a paper to-night; I wanted Unger to see it! I left it in the suit I wore."

He stepped to the dressing room, and groped in a pocket, without moving his pleasant look from her.

"Giving my room the once over?" he said.

"Nina left the door open. I've never been in here before," Harriet said, trying to make her voice as natural as his own. Confused and ashamed, she was hardly conscious of what she said.

"Here we are!" Richard glanced at the paper he had found. "See here," he said, presently, going to a window, "come here a minute, I want to show you this! You see," they were both looking out into the moonlight now, "you see, this is where I propose to build on that big room downstairs, throw the library into the blue room, and have a big sleeping porch upstairs here," he explained. "Perfectly feasible, and yet it will make a different house of it!"

Harriet commented interestedly enough. But she heard his voice rather than his words, and saw only the well-groomed, black-clad figure, the shining patent-leather shoes, the fine hand that indicated the changes.

Perhaps he was conscious of confusion, too, for his words stopped, and presently they were looking at each other in a strange silence, Richard still smiling, Harriet wide eyed.

Then suddenly his strong arms held her close, and her blue, frightened eyes were close to his, and she felt everything else in the world slip away from her except the exquisite knowledge that she loved this man with all her heart and soul.

"I want to tell you something," Richard said, quickly and incoherently. "I want you to know that I love you--I think I've always loved you! This wasn't in our bond, I know, but I think I couldn't have wanted you so without loving you! If--if the time comes, Harriet, when you can care for me, you'll tell me, won't you? That's all I want, just to know that you will tell me. You're going to tell me, yourself! I'm going to make you love me! I'll be patient--I'll not hurry you--but some day you'll have to tell me that I've--I've won you!"

He had spoken swiftly, almost sternly, with a sort of desperate determination. Now he freed her arms as suddenly as he had grasped them, and added, in a lower tone:

"Until that time I'll not--not even--kiss the top of your hair, Harriet," he said.

In the mad rushing of her senses she could not find the right word, but she detained him with an entreating hand. Her eyes, shining with a look that he had never seen there before, were fixed on his. But Richard did not look at her eyes, he looked down at the hand she had laid on his own.

"I don't think," Harriet said, breathlessly, "that I can ever like you any more than I do!"

She had meant it for surrender; her heart was beating wildly with the glorious shame of a proud woman who gives herself. But Richard was not looking at the betraying eyes. In the great new love that had swept him from all his old moorings there was a deep humility. He only heard her say that she could never learn to love him. He bent his head over her finger tips, and kissed them, as he said quietly:

"But I'm going to try to make you, just the same!"

Then he was gone, and Harriet was standing alone in the softly lighted room. For a few moments she remained perfectly still, with her white hands pressed to her burning cheeks. Then, shaken with joy and surprise, with a delicious terror and something of a child's innocent chagrin, she went noiselessly back to her own room, closed the communicating door, and undressed with pauses for the dreams that would come creeping over body and soul, and hold her in their exquisite stillness for long minutes together.

She was brushing her hair when Nina suddenly appeared, and came lifelessly in to sit on the edge of Harriet's bed. "I want to ask you something!" Nina said, in an odd voice. "And, Harriet, I want you to tell me the truth!"

Harriet, turning, faced her between two curtains of rippling gold. She saw a new Nina, a subdued, thoughtful, serious woman in the old confident Nina's place.

"But first I ought to tell you that I wasn't with Amy to-day!" Nina said.

"Oh, Nina! Must we begin that sort of thing?" Harriet reproached her. But she was puzzled by Nina's manner. "Back to school-girl tricks!" she said.

"Never back to a school-girl," Nina said, with trembling lips. "No," she added, passionately, "I'll never be that again. Harriet," she went on, "I've written Royal three times, since my birthday, and I've seen him twice."

"You saw him to-day?" Harriet ventured.

"I went there this afternoon," Nina admitted, heavily. Then suddenly, "Harriet, did my father pay him--did he take money--to break our engagement?"

"Nina, what a horrible thought! Of course not!" Harriet could fortunately answer in perfect honesty.

"Oh, Harriet," the girl caught her hands, turning sick and imploring eyes toward her, "are you sure?"

"Nina, dear, your father would have told me!"

"He might not--he might not!" Nina said, feverishly. "But if he did----!" she whispered, half to herself. "That's Pilgrim, I rang for her," she said, of a knock on her own door. "Ask my father to come up, will you?" she said to the maid, when Pilgrim appeared. "We'll settle it now!"

"Mr. Carter is just coming up," Pilgrim said. And a moment later Richard, with an interested face, came through Nina's room, and joined them. Harriet had had time only to knot her hair back carelessly, and slip into the most formal of her big Chinese coats.

"Father," Nina said, when they three were alone together, "did Royal Blondin take a check from you ten days ago?"

Richard, taken unaware, glanced sharply at Harriet, who shook her head, with an anxious look. He sat down beside Nina on the bed, and put a fatherly arm about her.

"Ah, Father, DON'T put me off!" the girl begged. "I wrote him, after my birthday," she said, "and told him that money made no difference to me. He didn't answer. Then I got Bruce Hopper to ask his mother to have Blondin meet her at the club for tea, and I saw him then. Bruce," Nina cast in, still in the new, self-contained tone, "has been wonderful about it! I know he only seems a silent sort of boy, but I'll never forget what he's done for me! Royal," she resumed, "didn't want to see me, and said he had promised Father that it was OVER. He--but I needn't tell you all he said. It sounded----" Nina clung to her father's hands, and shut her eyes. "It sounded so--so false!" she whispered, bitterly. "So I went to his studio to-day!" she presently continued. "And--there were two or three women there, but it wasn't that. They were--well, perhaps they were just having fun. But----" And Nina looked pitifully from Harriet's sympathetic face to her father's troubled eyes. "But I've not been having much fun!" she faltered, with a suddenly trembling mouth. "I've been planning--PRAYING!--that somehow it would come out right. He told me to-day that he had promised not to see or speak to me for two years," she said, slowly. "I--Father, I KNEW that he had a reason! He was changed. I never saw him so! And two hours ago," she pointed to the door that led into her father's room, "two hours ago I went in there," she said, "and I looked over your own check book. Father, did you write him a check? Was that the stub that had 'R.B.' on it?"

Richard looked at her sorrowfully.

"I'm sorry, Nina," he said, simply. "I told him you should not know, from me! I would have spared you that."

For a few minutes there was silence in the room. Then Nina said bravely, through tears:

"I don't know why you should be sorry for what will save me months of slow worry, all at one blow! You and Harriet needn't worry any more. I'm cured. I've been a fool, I let him flatter me and lie to me," said this new Nina, with bitter courage, "but I'm over it now. I'm sorry I gave you so much trouble, Father----"

"My darling girl," her father said, tenderly. "I only wish I could spare you all this!"

"Better now than two or three years after we were married," Nina said. "Plenty of girls find it out then! Father, I want you to get that check, through the clearing-house, for me," she said, heroically, "and I want to keep it. If ever I'm a fool about a man again, I'll take it out and look at it!"

"I have it, I told Fox to get it to-day," Richard said. "You shall have it!"

Nina had turned suddenly white; it was as if a last little hope had been killed.

"You have it!" she whispered. "He cashed it, then!"

"He cashed it the next morning," Richard said. Nina was silent for a moment.

"How you must laugh at me, Harriet!" she said then.

"I? Laugh at you!" Harriet said, stricken. "My darling girl, I am the last woman in the world who could do that! I was only your age, Nina, when I met him--you know that story. Why, Nina, you're but eighteen, after all, you'll have many and many an affair before the right man comes along," Harriet said. "You'll look back on this some day, and say, 'It was an experience, and I learned from it! It is only going to make me happier and more sure when the man whom I really love comes to me!' Aren't you much richer now, in actual knowledge of men, than Amy and Francesca, who haven't had anything but school flirtations?"

Nina, sitting between Richard and Harriet on the bed, looked wistfully from one face to another.

"I'll try to make it so, Harriet!" she said. And somewhat timidly she added, "Father--and Harriet--shall you feel dreadfully if I say that I don't want to go to Brazil? I'll tell you why. Ward is going out to the Gardiner ranch, and Bruce is going, too, and it seems to me that riding and camping and living in the open air will be--well, will seem better to me than just being on the steamer! I dread seeing strange places and meeting people," said Nina. "The Gardiner girls were simply darling to me the term they were in school, and--don't you remember, Harriet?--we were the only people who took them out for Christmas and Easter holidays, and they like me! And--if you wouldn't be too disappointed, Harriet, I believe I would like it better!"

"My darling girl," Harriet said, warmly, "you must do what seems right to you. But you won't need me?" she added, tactfully.

"Well, you see Mrs. Gardiner and Mrs. Hopper are sisters," Nina explained, readily, "and they'll be with us. But if you'd LIKE to come--we are going camping in the most glorious canon that you ever saw!" Nina interrupted herself with sudden enthusiasm. "And I am so glad I really can ride! I'd feel so horribly if I couldn't!"

"I think you'll have a wonderful two months of it," Harriet said, "and then Granny'll be coming West, to spend the winter in Santa Barbara, and that will be delightful, too! And now, Nina love, it's after eleven o'clock," she ended with a change of tone, "and you have had a terrible day! We will have to do some more shopping to-morrow afternoon, and try on the riding habits, and do a thousand things. And, Nina," Richard heard her add tenderly, when his daughter had given him a rather sober good-night kiss at the door of her room, "whenever you feel sad and depressed about it, just remember to say to yourself, 'This won't last! In a few months the sting will all be gone!'"

"Nina is in safe hands!" Richard said to himself, thankfully, as he closed the door. He carried a memory of Harriet's earnest eyes, her low, eager voice, her encouraging arm about Nina's shoulders.

They were all at breakfast when he came down the next morning.
His mother, in one of the lacy, flowing robes she always wore before noon, laid down a letter half-read, to smile at him. Ward, his dark head very sleek above his informal summer costume, was deep in talk with Bruce Hopper, who had evidently ridden over from the country club, and was in a well-fitting, shabby jersey that became his somewhat lanky frame. Nina, somewhat silent, but interested in everything, wore an expression of quiet self-possession that her father found touching. Nina was growing up, he thought.

Completing the group, and officiating at the foot of the table, was the radiant Harriet. She looked as fresh as one of the creamy rosebuds that were massed in the dull blue bowl before her, her shining hair framing the dusky forehead like dull gold wings, the frail sleeves of her blue gown falling back from her rounded arm.

"You're late, my son," said Madame Carter, as he kissed her temple.

"Never mind," Harriet said, serenely, "I've just this instant come, and he saves my face! Do turn that toast, Ward!" she added. And to the maid, "Mr. Carter's fruit, Mollie, please."

Breakfast was the least formal of all the informal meals at Crownlands. Bottomley was never in evidence until the late luncheon; mail and newspapers, and the morning gaiety of the young people all made for cheerful disorder.

"If you're going into town at ten, Father, we'll go, too," Nina suggested. "But I can't," she was heard to murmur in an undertone to the disappointed Bruce. "I have to get CLOTHES, don't I?"

"Oh, Brazil--Brazil--Brazil!" the youth said, disgustedly. "I hate the sound of it!"

"THESE clothes are for the ranch," Nina said, smiling. Both her father and Harriet augured well from the youth's instantly transformed face.

"Say--honestly?" he asked, ineloquently, with an irrepressible grin.

"I think so," Nina murmured. The rest of their conversation was inaudible; they presently wandered forth to finish it on the tennis court. Ward followed his grandmother upstairs, and Harriet and Richard were left to finish their breakfast alone.

"You look tired," Harriet said, rising, when his omelette came in, and pausing beside the head of the table for an instant on her way to the pantry.

"I had a bad night," Richard admitted. "But that's not all you're going to have for breakfast?" he protested.

"I never have more!" Harriet smiled. "I'm sorry about the bad night," said she.

"I couldn't help thinking----" Richard began.

"What is it, Mollie?" he added, harshly, to the hovering maid.

"Nothing--no matter--sir," Mollie stammered, retreating. "It was just that the man about the sheep came, sir----" she faltered.

"The sheep!" Richard echoed, frowning. Harriet laughed gaily.

"Oh, yes!" she said. "I told you I had ordered two or three young sheep," she explained, "to keep our lawns cropped. They look so adorable, and they do it so nicely! Has he got them, Mollie?" she added, eagerly. "Oh, I must see them! I'll be back in exactly five minutes, Mr. Carter," she said.

"What are we supposed to do with them in winter?" Richard asked, smiling.

"Oh, they will have a little--a little byre!" she answered, readily. "You'll--you'll like them!" And he heard her joyous voice following Mollie away.

Richard pushed back his plate, and looked irresolutely after her. Then suddenly he rose, and walked through the pantry, asking two startled maids for Mrs. Carter. Etelka had been several years in the house without ever seeing "him" in this neighbourhood before.

Richard crossed a sunshiny brick-walled yard, where linen was drying, and went through a brick gateway that gave on a neglected little lane. The lane had once been the driveway for a carriage and a prancing pair, but there were only riding horses at Crownlands now, and three of these were looking over the wall at the grass-grown road. And Richard found Harriet here.

She was on her knees, in the pleasant green shadow of the old sycamores and maples, her back was toward him, she was looking up into the face of the old stableman, Trotter, who stood before her, his crooked, dwarfed old figure still further bent, as he held two strong young ewes by their thick, woolly shoulders.

As Trotter gave him a respectful good morning, Harriet sprang to her feet, and whirled about, and Richard saw the woodeny stiff legs of a very young lamb dangling from her arms, and the lamb's meek little black-rubber face close to the beautiful face he loved.

"Oh, Richard!" she said, carried away by her own delight. "Look at it! Isn't it the sweetest darling baby that ever was! Oh, you sweet!" she said, putting her lips to the little woolly head.

"You are!" Richard said quite without premeditation.

Harriet laughed, surrendered the little lamb to Trotter, and followed the old man's departure to the stables with an anxious warning.

"They're to have this little enclosure all to themselves," she explained to Richard, when they were alone. "He's going to build them a little shed." And as Richard, his back leaning against the low brick wall, made no immediate attempt to move, she looked at him expectantly. "Shall we go back?" she suggested.

"That sounded very pleasant to me," Richard said, with deliberate irrelevance.

Harriet looked at him in puzzled silence.

"I mean your calling me Richard," he said.

She flushed brightly, and laughed.

"Did I? I always think of you as Richard!" she explained.

"So you abandon me on the Brazil trip?" he asked, watching her seriously.

"Well----?" Harriet shrugged. "I thought you had to go," she added. "I'm--I'll confess I'm disappointed. But to have Nina want to do anything is such a relief to me that I'm only going to think of that!"

"Yes, I have to go," Richard said, slowly. "I must be there for a month at least. But I'm disappointed, too. I got thinking of it, in the night--I couldn't sleep! I'm disappointed, too." He fell silent. "I wish," he said, hesitatingly, "that you had not told me that you--you don't feel that you-- are going to love me!" he said. "I love you with all my heart and soul. It-- well, it's all I think of, now. I want----" He turned, and picking an ivy leaf from the wall, looked at it intently for a moment, and tore it apart before he let it fall. "However," he said, philosophically, smiling at her, "we'll let that wait!"

Harriet, close to him, laid one hand upon his shoulder.

"You misunderstood me," she said, steadily. "What I said was that I could not love you more than I do! Aren't you--ever--going to understand?"

For a long minute they looked straight into each other's eyes.

"Harriet, do you mean it?" Richard said then, simply.

"Yes," she answered, "I mean it! I've always meant it. I've always loved you, I think. No man could want any woman to love him more!"

The blue eyes so near his own were misty with sudden tears. In the deserted little lane, in the blue summer morning and the green shade of the sycamores, they were alone. Richard put his arms about her.

And for a moment he held all the beauty and fragrance and laughter and tears that was Harriet close to his heart; the soft hair tumbled, the brown, firm young hand resting on his shoulder, the warm cheek against his own.

A breeze rustled through the branches high above them; the blue river, beyond the brick wall, flowed on in an even sheet of satin; two birds looped the enclosure in a sudden twittering flight; and from the stable region came the plaintive bleating of a mother sheep. But to Harriet and Richard the world was all their own.

"My wife!" said Richard Carter.

THE END